I0588754

FRAGILE
PUBLISHING

NEIL J HART

HARPER HALE

AND THE CRYSTAL OF SHADOWS

First published worldwide in 2025 by Fragile Publishing

Copyright © 2025 Neil J Hart
Edited by Manda Waller | www.mandawaller.co.uk
Cover illustration by Shane Melisse | www.shanefaced.com
Cover design and layout by Neil J Hart

A CIP catalogue record of this book is
available from the British Library.

ISBN: 978-0-9554832-5-7
Also available as an ebook

www.neiljhart.com

For those who look up and wonder.

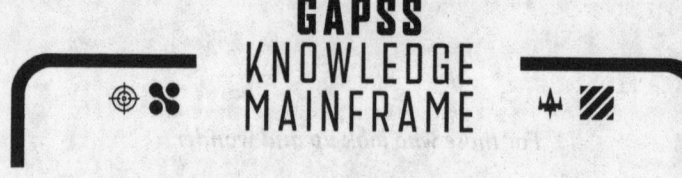

GAPSS
KNOWLEDGE
MAINFRAME

SPIRALVERSE, THE
[GALAXY]

Known to Earthlings as the Milky Way, the SpiralVerse is 13.8 billion years old. It spans over one hundred thousand lightcycles in diameter, consisting of more than one hundred million stars, and thirty-five civilised worlds.

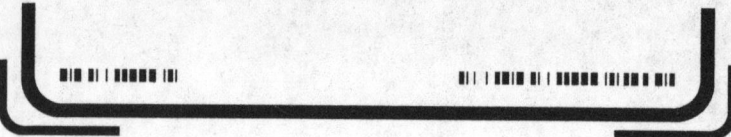

THE GIRL WHO DYED

Chalk swished a lock of vivid pink hair from her eyes and scanned the mesmerising night sky. With John Williams' *Star Wars* theme blasting in her earbuds, she wondered if every distant star had its own exhilarating saga of empires and rebellions, heroes and villains, darkness and light.

At any other moment in history this would have seemed a fanciful notion.

But six months ago, the world had changed.

Forever.

Above the Tri-Shard Buildings—casting the timeless landmarks of St. Paul's Cathedral, Tower Bridge, and Big Ben into shadow—hovered the GAPSS mothership.

Chalk had streamed and read hundreds of alien encounter stories. They rarely ended in civility, or profitable trade routes, or the betterment of humanity. The Martian Army? Harvesters? Cylons? Deceivers and destroyers, one and all.

It seemed inevitable that a devastating laser blast would spike the skyscrapers and tourist attractions of London, reducing them to all ash.

Every morning she checked.

Every morning London stood.

And every morning Chalk's skin rippled with excitement and wonder, for the GAPSS mothership meant more than a potential extinction-level event. It had become the embodiment of her wildest, most elaborate dreams.

Life beyond Earth.

Beyond the solar system.

From outer space.

Aliens.

She'd spent countless hours wondering and wishing that such things were possible. She discussed them with her grandpa—the world's biggest sci-fi nut—hoping that one day, she might know.

And here it was.

The GAPSS mothership.

Truth.

Hope.

Fear.

Chalk's iPhone Firebird vibrated, pulling her from an elaborate space-battle daydream. She tapped the new message icon.

KIT: Decision???

She swiped the message away with a dramatic flourish, sank into an office chair, and spun to face a huge sash window that framed the mothership like the cover of a near-future sci-fi paperback. Advertising blimps for the latest Harriet Starlight movie floated through the accumulating skeins of gas and vapour beneath the starship.

Chalk plonked her lime-green Converse high-tops on her mother's desk—monogrammed stationery front and centre—and let the aroma of polish and earl grey consume her. "The handwritten letter is an endangered talent," her mother had said, boring Chalk on numerous occasions. "Something private and personal. Something the cloud cannot store and dissect and monetise."

Framed photographs peppered the wall. Each featured her mother with famous faces: the King of England, the Pope, two different US Presidents, and handfuls of actors and influential businesswomen.

And one other.

A picture quite unlike the rest.

Chalk shunted forward and studied the photo of her mother

and the GAPSS welcome committee stood atop the Tri-Shard Buildings. Above, a million lights reflected off the mothership like an inverted twilight lake.

Chalk yanked out her earbuds, drummed her lip, and opened the message again.

KIT: Decision???

She punched the reply button.

CHALK: Still in a holding pattern.

KIT: We'd love to see you!!!

CHALK: I know.

KIT: It's gonna be insane!!!

CHALK: I can't.

Kit's response took forever.

KIT: We love you!!!

Her end-of-year school party promised to be the highlight of the academic calendar. An all-you-can-eat buffet by international chef Zamora Ramsey, anti-grav effect dance floor, electro-pop holographic set from the late great NSYNC, brand-new *Star Wars* VR campaigns—designed by Georgina Lucas herself—and how could she forget the legendary party bags?

It was happening right now.

At the infamous Titanium nightclub in New Leicester Square.

But Chalk was stuck at home.

In 10 Downing Street.

With her books and toys and games.

Not celebrating this rite of passage with Kit, and Bloue, and Zara.

She swiped a pen from the desk and let it roll on her palm. She took a long, slow breath, narrowed her eyes and focused. Moonlight glinted off the slim silver cylinder. The distant buzz of epic space anthems strained to reach her ears.

"Ugh," she groaned impatiently, scrunching her fingers around the pen and firing an accusatory glare at the GAPSS mothership. "Still no Jedi powers!"

In her bedroom at the front of 10 Downing Street, Chalk could just make out the hubbub and lilting waltzes of *another* party. The most important party of her mother's premiership. Outside, electric motorcades and limousines delivered continent leaders, ministers, lords, celebrities, and the GAPSS welcome committee to the famous black door.

Camera flashes peppered her window.

Muffled, excited screams swirled into the night.

She slipped her battle-damaged VR helmet on. A customised three-billion-pixel readout surrounded her. A calm breath whistled through her teeth.

Playing as Wario, Chalk tore round various retro *Mario Kart* tracks, purposefully annihilating Princess Peach and Yoshi every chance she had. Switching to a completed download of *Resident Evil: Incubus*, she wasted thirty minutes blasting zombie hordes with laser pistols and plasma grenades. But, in the midst of blood clouds and flying limbs, she couldn't shake the allure of the GAPSS mothership and the important, historic party unfolding downstairs.

She quit the game. Exited to the main menu. Trophies and updates scrolled across the display. Kit's, Bloue's, and Zara's latest scores appeared. Chalk laughed. Even on their best day her friends stood zero chance of toppling her hi-scores. Swishing game titles aside, she landed on *Green Death*, a favourite from last year.

First-person shooter.

Global alien invasion.

Although similar to dozens of other games, it was the customisable playing options that really oiled Chalk's gears. She could play as the military in 'Open Warfare' mode; city-based civilian resistance in 'Guerrilla Warfare' mode; a terrified family in 'Survival' mode; or as the aliens themselves in 'Operation: Death To Humanity'.

Chalk always played as the aliens.

She'd even created her own Greenie—a tooled-up, maxed-out, cigar-smoking human-killing machine—called Double Aitch, the initials of her real name.

Harper Hale.

Before *Green Death* could load, the whiff of Chanel No.23 stole into the room.

Chalk tore the helmet off. "Mother?"

Prime Minister Sakura Hale wore a dark suit, her hair cut sharply to her shoulders. A slim hand coiled her hip.

"Chalk."

"What is it?" she grumbled, easing herself out of a life-size Hagrid beanbag. "I'm here. Alone. Satisfied? Not putting my life in danger at Titanium with all my friends."

They stared at one another.

"It'll be safe," Chalk insisted. "I have cast-iron promises."

"I'm sorry," Sakura said, crossing the room.

"You say that so often. It's almost lost its meaning."

"I—"

"The war ended two summers ago, Mum."

"But—"

"I know what you are going to say. And you're right. The world is a dangerous place. It will always be a dangerous place. You and I appreciate that more than most."

Memories of the Hundred Hours War bobbed in her mind's eye like putrid apples.

"Still nothing on Dad?"

Sakura took a quick breath. "No. Nothing."

"I just thought … maybe … what with it being this big intergalactical event that—"

"Chalk," the Prime Minister said, "no matter how much you want life to mirror your favourite movies—"

"Don't patronise me. I know what's real and what's not. I just—"

"I want that happy ending too, Chalk," she said in soft tones and pulled her daughter close. "As I promised two years ago, if I hear anything—*anything*—you will be the first to know."

Chalk moved away. "How are things going with the *Declaration of Intergalactical Wossnames*?"

"*Interplanetary Inclusivity*." Prime Minister Hale levelled her shoulders. "Fine, fine. Champagne reception is in full flow. I have meet-and-greets with film and sports stars, YouTubers and bloggers, continent leaders, General Waxler and Professor Snider, and a young girl with the Make-A-Wish Foundation. Then, the speeches and the signing of the Declaration itself."

"Sounds a lot."

"No more than usual."

"Who are General Waxler and Professor—?"

"—Snider. Faculty members. Part of GAPSS. They are here to select the first human for enrolment this autumn."

Chalk tightened. "Enrolment?"

"Yes."

"Into GAPSS?"

"No," Sakura said. "A … school."

"In … space?"

"It is a complicated selection process. Last-minute thing."

Chalk glared at her mother, unblinking. "Tell me *everything*."

The Prime Minister fished a TekTonik Touch10 tablet from inside her jacket. "So, yes, they have a school." The tablet lit up, casting pale green light on their faces. "On a space station somewhere in the Milky Way." Sakura's fingers moved cautiously over the smooth surface. "Only they do not call it the Milky Way." She pressed several info pads and half a dozen layer screens rose from the tablet like a stack of holographic pancakes. "They call our galaxy the SpiralVerse."

"I know," Chalk said witheringly. "I have seen the news."

Sakura spread her fingers, neatly positioning the layer screens in a wide arc.

"This," her mother said, "is the Galactic Institute."

Inside each floating layer screen were images of vast halls

and corridors, gleaming white walls striped with orange and blue and chrome. One image revealed an enormous disc, mounted with hundreds of circular towers, inside a moon-sized semi-transparent orb.

"They have a Death Star!"

"It is *not* a Death Star." The Prime Minister tutted. "It is a school. On a space station."

Chalk's heart hammered against her ribs. Adrenaline shot to her fingertips. She felt compelled to skip and jump and scream. "It's Spacewarts!"

Sakura sighed, clearly resisting the urge to roll her eyes. "That is your grandpa talking."

Chalk could barely breathe. "Do people travel there on magical rocket-trains accessible through secret flight decks beneath Gatwick Airport?"

"Highly unlikely," Sakura replied.

Chalk's skin rippled. Her insides churned. "And you're telling me this because—?"

Sakura straightened. "Ten of Earth's best and brightest have been shortlisted by GAPSS. They are here tonight for the Declaration. General Waxler and Professor Snider will make their decision by morning."

Chalk's dizzying high crash-landed. Nose first. She turned away from the alluring images of the prestigious school, overwhelmed and hollow. She imagined this was how it felt to arrive at Disneyland only to discover you were too short for all the best rides.

"You seem ... disappointed?"

Chalk picked at the decals on her VR helmet. "It's fine, Mum. Just another amazing place—in the long line of amazing places—that I'll never visit."

"Do not talk like that, Harper Hale."

Chalk curled her lip, snorting at the use of her full name.

"Would you even *want* to go?" her mother asked.

Chalk flicked her eyes across an obsessively curated

bedroom of science fiction and fantasy books, toys, posters, and merchandise. A sarcastic eyebrow twitched. "To Spacewarts? *Spacewarts!* To the Starfleet Academy?" she said, arms outstretched, spinning in circles. "Me? In space? Whatever gave you that idea?" Chalk's attention switched back to the layer screens. Her heart quickened. "It looks utterly amazing."

"Yes," Sakura admitted, biting her lip. "I suppose it does."

"So, who are these lucky ten?"

"The top one per cent of the top one per cent."

"Standard nerds and boffins."

Slipping the tablet away, Sakura smoothed her palms over Chalk's hair and planted a kiss on her forehead. "I will send Clive up with your dinner at eight o'clock. Do your homework and try to rest. See you in the morning. Wish me luck."

But Chalk had already turned, dumped the VR helmet over her head, and was flying at Mach-10, hell-bent on eradicating half the civilised world.

Chalk played *Green Death* for over an hour, routinely checked her iPhone, and even practised defensive stances with her custom double-ended replica lightsaber. Yet all she could think about was the sleek lines, dazzling technology, colossal scale, and intergalactic adventure that enrolment at the Galactic Institute promised.

"Why did she have to go and tell me?" she muttered to herself. "I could have gone my whole life without knowing about a school in space and I'd have been just fine."

She dropped to her haunches in front of a display cabinet.

"Best and brightest they are!" she said to her Yoda Funko Pop. "There's more to Earthlings than just pure academia." She directed this statement at a seven-inch action figure of Captain Picard before turning to her much-loved hand-painted Dumbledore statue. "I mean, Harry was never the smartest, yet he won the Triwizard Tournament and survived Voldemort." She scooped a plush of Captain Marvel from the bottom shelf. "Fear is not a choice, huh?"

Captain Marvel's fabric expression remained distant, yet powerful.

Late summer rain broke against the window.

Chalk spun and stared at a Harriet Starlight fly-poster that dominated the opposite wall. The androgynous bi-curious space wizard—from the epic book series by D K Gramplin—seemed to stare back.

In *a universe of infinite black*, rattled Harriet's distinctive voice, *there will always be stars to guide you.*

"I know," Chalk grumbled at the poster. "It's okay for you. You had Mads Maddeson, and Rikochet, and Cosmo Mackensie. An elite band of space misfits and unlikely companions to help you overcome it all."

Chalk checked her iPhone again.

Nothing.

She glanced at her warm inviting bed, her VR helmet, and the rain-streaked window that stood between her and the dangerous world beyond.

"Am I really doing this?" she asked Harriet Starlight.

The poster had no cliched greeting-card wisdom for her this time.

"Mum's going to lose her mind."

Chalk yanked the wardrobe open and plunged her nervous hands inside.

GAPSS
KNOWLEDGE
MAINFRAME

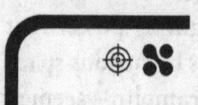 

GALACTIC ALLIANCE OF PLANETS AND SOLAR SYSTEMS, THE
[GAPSS] [ORGANISATION]

Founded by the ten original civilisations of the
SpiralVerse—following the devastating Thousand Moons
War—the Galactic Alliance of Planets and Solar Systems
[GAPSS] was designed to maintain intergalactic peace
and sovereignty. Since then, the reach of GAPSS has
grown. Branches now spread throughout the galaxy,
handling trade, finance, research, pharmaceuticals,
technology, weapons, and education.

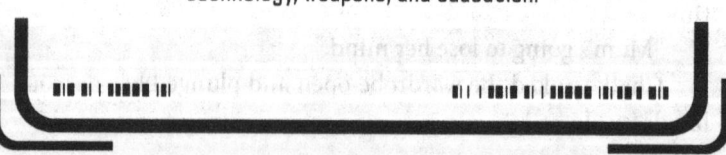

THE DECLARATION OF INTERPLANETARY INCLUSIVITY

Chalk edged into the Cabinet Room. Another gentle waltz mingled with the chime of champagne glasses and burble of excited chatter. She tried to blend in, leaning casually against a pillar, her feet crossed. But with pink hair slicked to one side, the other shaved close, and her ears decorated with silver skulls and lightning bolts, she stuck out like a compound fracture.

Chalk had no posh dresses or expensive shoes. Well, none she would wear. Instead, she'd opted for dark flares with neon stitching, a mauve and black striped T-shirt, and fitted leather jacket. She couldn't have looked more Harriet Starlight if she'd tried.

Failing to snatch a flute of champagne from a passing waiter, she spied her mother and the other continent leaders congregated beside the fireplace. They talked animatedly while cradling tumblers of amber liquor. Chalk shuffled close but a lofty figure obscured her view.

"Greetings," came a voice from above, fierce yet feminine.

"Hey," Chalk replied, looking up, dazzled by a chandelier.

"You must be Harper Hale."

"Everyone calls me Chalk."

"Why is that?"

"Family secret," she replied plainly. "Are you … part of the government?"

"No," the woman said. "I am with GAPSS."

Chalk's skin turned to ice.

A white cape flowed from the woman's shoulders over a grey bodysuit that clung to her lean physique. High boots rooted her to the ground. Wavy blonde hair, shot through with silver, had been parted on one side.

"You look … human," Chalk said. Faint scars cobwebbed the woman's face. "Are you human?"

"I am what you would consider *humanoid* in appearance," she said, adjusting a single white glove. "But to be human is an Earthbound term. I am a Genk. From Gaia 23. It is much like Earth, but fundamentally different … if that makes sense."

"What happened to your other glove?" Chalk asked, scanning the geometric patterned carpet. "Did you lose it?"

"Lost my whole arm," the Genk said and pulled her glove down an inch to reveal metallic springs and tendons whirring beneath.

"Grisly." Chalk whistled approvingly. "Are you a soldier?"

"I have seen my share of battles."

"Space battles? Cool."

"Not really. War has no redeemable features."

"Yeah, sorry," Chalk replied, her palms moist. "So, are you—?"

"I currently serve as headmistress at the Galactic Institute." Time slowed.

"My name is General Waxler."

"Of course it is. Stupid Chalk. What a bonehead. Should've known."

"You were expecting a man," the general said. "Dominant female leaders appear to be in the minority here. Your mother being an excellent exception."

"I understand you're here for the—" Chalk tried.

"The Declaration of Interplanetary Inclusivity?"

"Oh, no. I'm mean … sure. The signing is going to be really exciting … I suppose," Chalk bumbled, cheeks flushed, head pounding. "I meant the application process to Spacewarts."

"Spacewarts?"

"Sorry … the Galactic … Academy?"

"Institute."

"Yep. Again, sorry."

General Waxler sipped her champagne.

"Professor Snider and I have been all over your homeworld meeting potential candidates. We have invited the best here tonight," she said, considering Chalk like a science experiment. "The decision to enrol an Earthling at the Galactic Institute so soon was a surprise, but not unexpected."

"Mum showed me the digital brochure," Chalk said. A slew of trepidation roiled in her gut. "Looks utterly brilliant. You must be incredibly proud."

"The Galactic Institute has a long history, Miss Hale. Headmasters and headmistresses from all thirty-five civilised worlds have held my seat. Others will succeed me." General Waxler's eyes shone. "Who knows, perhaps an Earthling will follow in my footsteps."

"Wow! Really?"

"The future is mostly unknown, Miss Hale."

"Yet filled with infinite possibilities."

General Waxler smiled curiously. "You are not like the others."

Chalk shrugged. "Others?"

"Earth's best and brightest."

"Yeah, I'm more … normal, I guess? Not a weapons-grade nerd!"

"A nerd?"

"A socially awkward academic. I'm more your classic dork. Cosplayer too. Just came out of an all-consuming Sith phase, but moving into a Knights of the Old Republic aesthetic right now."

The general smiled politely. "It was lovely meeting you."

"Um—"

"Have a lovely evening."

"But I haven't … I wanted to—"

The headmistress spun away. Her long cape swirled across Chalk's vision like the curtain coming down on a particularly awkward performance.

Frustration and relief ricocheted through her like burning shrapnel. It reminded her of the time Harriet Starlight destroyed the Chalice of Everlasting Night in *Harriet Starlight and the Forsaken Particle*. But Chalk was no Harriet Starlight. She'd never be a hero. And certainly not one of Earth's best and brightest.

She flexed her fingers and wondered what it would be like to be part machine. Like Luke Skywalker or the Terminator.

She bent her head to one side. Her neck cracked.

Kit is right, she thought. *I'm never getting out of here.*

She settled into an all-too-familiar emotional free fall.

And braced for a hard landing.

The continent leaders congregated on a raised platform, beneath the furthest chandelier. Chalk swiped a handful of cheese vol-au-vents from the buffet table and did her best to blend into the crowd.

Prime Minister Hale approached the microphone.

TV cameras swivelled.

"Welcome," she said. "Welcome to you all: my friends and esteemed colleagues, continent leaders, people of Earth. And, of course, a warm greeting to the GAPSS welcome committee."

Three strange figures breezed into the room.

A swarm of reporters and photographers snapped and scribbled furiously.

Her mother continued. "Please welcome High-King Cillian Van Wyrm of the Veroselli. Kydra of the Garrangulars. And Lord Milton Barclay XVI of the Sagaroaches. Welcome, one and all."

Veroselli, Garrangulars, Sagaroaches.

Chalk's mind exploded with dreams she'd had of the faraway worlds these creatures hailed from, what majestic starships they flew, and what shadowy business they might conduct in villainous outposts and cantinas.

Cillian, the Veroselli, stepped forward, towered over the audience, and surveyed the room with large, dark eyes. He had long, elegant ears, a sharp nose, and vibrant skin, the colour of Lara's original tomb-raiding vest. Flowing grey robes whispered against the floor.

Cillian's voice sounded familiar, yet his language was distinctly alien. Chalk glanced at a monitor where a translation appeared.

"Thank you, Prime Minister Hale and continent leaders for the warm welcome. I hope the Declaration of Interplanetary Inclusivity will be mutually beneficial to everyone present, and to every living thing across the Galactic Alliance of Planets and Solar Systems, for aeons to come."

Live long and prosper. Got it.

Kydra lumbered on all fours. The Garrangular heavily muscled torso sat atop powerful hind legs, coated in matted, coarse fur. Thick metal bands, etched with glowing patterns and glyphs, encased her neck, wrists, and ankles. Large, yellowing teeth crowded her mouth. Suspicious eyes took in the room.

The translation screen converted her savage bark. "I echo my planetary counterpart. Our two species, Veroselli and Garrangulars, have a ferocious, bloody history. But, through dedication and diplomacy, have achieved a symbiotically-enhanced existence on Zorik Minor, a world without war. One we hope to share with you and trillions of others throughout the SpiralVerse."

Mysterious, violent backstory. Intriguing.

The hard-skinned Sagaroach took his turn. Looping antenna flicked wildly above his pincered face. He stood upright on robust hind legs wearing a light-blue uniform and a dark robe. "As the sixteenth lord of my name—Milton Barclay—I extend a humble welcome from the Xenothropod colonies: a civilisation of invertebrates and insects in its hundreds of trillions. It is my understanding that creatures of a similar nature—spiders and scorpions and cockroaches—inhabit Earth. I hear these creatures terrify and repulse. Clearly they have not developed into the artistic, cultured, sage thinkers like those you will find on the colonies. At least, not yet anyway!"

Nervous laughter eased through the room.

The only good bug is a dead bug! Hoo-ha!

Sakura Hale returned to the microphone. "And now, the signing of the Declaration of Interplanetary Inclusivity."

The Prime Minister held her TekTonik Touch10 for a retinal scan, authorised with thumb identification, and etched her signature onto one of eight layer screens. She moved to a table beneath a sash window and scribbled her name at the bottom of a long sheet of manuscript with an antique emerald fountain pen.

The continent leaders mirrored the Prime Minister. When all opticals were scanned, thumbs, digits, and pincers authorised, layer screens and parchment signed, Cillian Van Wyrm returned to the microphone.

"Congratulations," the High-King said. "Welcome to you all: my friends and esteemed colleagues, continent leaders, people of Earth. Welcome to the Galactic Alliance of Planets and Solar Systems. Welcome to GAPSS!"

Chalk weaved through the room, desperate for a second encounter with General Waxler, but a gaggle of teens surrounded the headmistress, ensconced in a frenetic Q&A. The general motioned for Chalk to join them.

Her courage wavered. Another shadow blocked her path.

"Mum," Chalk said despondently, without looking up. "I'm sorry. I know I shouldn't be here, but I wanted to meet the Waxler woman. I wanted to see the students who might be going into space. And guess what? I made a complete bonehead of myself. Probably best if I go upstairs and—"

A thick, obnoxious sniffle emanated above.

She looked up. "Um ... who are you?"

"Snider," the man said drearily, dabbing his nose with a

napkin. "Professor Calignious Snider. I serve at the Galactic Institute alongside … *the Waxler woman.*"

"Of course you do," Chalk said, shuddering sheepishly. Despite being several inches shorter than the general, he was no less imposing, with horribly pale skin, and large watery eyes. His clothes were black: boots, jumpsuit, high-collared jacket. And over his shoulders hung a padded cape made of strange materials that were definitely sending Chalk's allergies into overdrive. He had a strange aura about him. Something cold and empty. And a peculiar, unrelenting stench.

"So, what are you?" she asked. "The general's assistant?"

"Do not test my patience, child!" Professor Snider spat. "I—not that it'll mean anything to you—am Head of Casting."

"Right. Cool."

Snider tipped his head to one side.

"So, what is—?"

"Casting is the ancient art of Aether. A scarce and dangerous anomaly that fuels the three great powers."

A fire sparked. "Powers?" Chalk whispered. "Are you for real?"

Professor Snider studied her.

"What are you doing?" she said, self-conscious of his roving eyes. "Are you using your powers on me now?"

The professor sniffed. "It is not important. Not to *you* anyway. As a species you are barely out of the mud. And this *planet* is bereft of Aether. I do not know what GAPSS or the general see in it. I registered my objections of course, but, as usual, I was overruled."

"Are you a Genk too?" she asked.

"I most certainly am not," Snider bit. "I am a Pyramist, from the dark hostile wastes of Pyramax. A notable system—held in high regard by GAPSS—nestled deep in what you would call the Perseus Arm of the Milky Way."

Chalk was relieved to see General Waxler breezing towards them, a trail of nerds and boffins in her wake.

"Calignious," the general said brightly. "I hope you are not bothering Miss Hale."

"Bothering?" he grumbled, picking at a dark fingernail. "At your request, I am conducting interplanetary relations."

"He was about to tell me the secrets of Casting," Chalk added hopefully.

"Was he?"

"I most certainly was *not*."

Waxler smiled at Chalk then turned and quietened the eager applicants. "Thank you for making Professor Snider and I welcome on your homeworld. I have studied your grades, your extra-curricular activities, charity work, hobbies, internet search histories, and the individuals you have chosen as friends. The Galactic Institute can only offer one place in the first cycle, but we hope to enrol more Earthlings in the future."

Chalk hung her head. These words weren't for her. She didn't want to hear them. She didn't want to be teased, tempted, tortured by everything the Galactic Institute had to offer. But she remained. Frozen to the Cabinet Room carpet.

"For now, we shall retire to consider our decision. By morning, one of you will receive a contract of acceptance. The rest will no doubt be disappointed. It is extremely close, but there can be only one."

General Waxler flashed her smile again. Her eyes twinkled.

Snider grunted.

Together, they merged into the crowd.

Earth's best and brightest gossiped among themselves. Unfrozen, Chalk slalomed between footballers and actors, scientists, chefs, and reality stars, before retreating to her games and books and toys. The party faded with every footfall, leaving nothing but the sway of another infernal waltz reverberating in her mind.

And disappointment clawing at her heart.

GAPSS
KNOWLEDGE
MAINFRAME

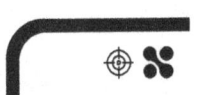 

GALACTIC INSTITUTE, THE
[GI, THE COIN] [EDUCATION]

Following the instigation of GAPSS, Centurion H—a
decommissioned battle-class space station—was
reassigned as an institute for educational excellence.
Each cycle, the galaxy's top young minds are invited to
study everything from language to science, technology
to law, history to art. Six cycles, each consisting of four
class shifts [chronotypes or sleeping patterns] inhabit the
Coin, currently totalling over seven hundred students, and
fifty-two permanent faculty members.

CLEVER GIRL

Chalk woke to a torrent of badly constructed messages and light-trail photos from Kit, Bloue, and Zara. She smiled for her friends, yet her stomach turned at all she had missed.

She kicked the duvet aside and balled her fists into the pillows. Frustration rode her bones. It wasn't her mother's fault, but she had to blame someone. After all, Sakura *had* kept her here, inside Number 10, away from the world, away from her life. Chalk knew why—by Q she knew—but it stank.

Big time.

She wrestled her feet into a pair of ravaged hobbit slippers, threw on her Gryffindor dressing gown, and trudged downstairs. Breakfast was served in the Green Room at Number 11. Members of the Cabinet had assembled, boring each other's socks off with talk of education budgets, social housing, and prison reform. Instead of joining them, Chalk swiped two croissants and a banana from a serving trolley and scurried into the hall.

Her iPhone buzzed.

KIT: Genks??? Pyramists??? What the hell???
ZARA: Legs R ded. 2 much dancing.
KIT: Need the info!!! Chalk. Come on. Spill!!!
BLOUE: Broken. Haha.
ZARA: Luv ya. Miss ya.
KIT: Chalk???
KIT: Chalk?!?!?!?
KIT: CHALK!!!

Not looking where she was going, she turned a corner and bumped into the Prime Minister.

"Here you are," Sakura said solemnly.

"Okay, okay. Caught me red-handed. Dead to rights." She grinned, then asked, "What is it? Why are you frowning?"

"I think you had better come with me."

Chalk followed Sakura through twisty, portrait-lined corridors and up several flights of stairs. "Seriously. You're wigging me out," Chalk moaned. "What's happening?"

"We have guests," Sakura replied, opening her study door to reveal the GAPSS mothership framed in the window. Chalk peered into the stuffy office and there, to her astonishment, stood General Waxler and Professor Snider.

Sakura entered and promptly greeted them.

Chalk loitered in the doorway, unsure.

"Good morning, Miss Hale," said General Waxler, her hair glistening. "It is lovely to see you again."

"Is it?" Chalk said anxiously. "I mean, yes. Good to see you … both … too."

Professor Snider seemed monumentally disinterested.

"Come in and close the door," issued her mother.

Chalk obliged, suddenly aware of her attire and the crumbling pastry in her hands. "What did I do?"

"This," Sakura said, lifting a pristine white envelope from her desk and handing it to Chalk, "is a letter from the Galactic Institute."

"Um … okay."

"It is addressed to you," General Waxler added.

"What do you want with me?" Chalk said. "Did I offend you? Either of you? Is this an intergalactic court summons? Is there a death penalty in space? Do you fire people out of airlocks or encase them in carbonite—?"

"Chalk. Breathe."

"You should open it," Snider rattled.

Pastry clung to Chalk's buttery fingers.

Sighing, her mother slipped a fingernail into the envelope, tore the seam, and removed the paperwork. Once scanned, she held the document under Chalk's nose.

"What does it say?" Chalk asked. "It's too long. I don't have my contacts in. I can't even—"

"Miss Harper Hale." The headmistress beamed. "It is my utmost pleasure to request your presence at the Galactic Institute."

"Wh-at?" Chalk spat. "For a day visit? A whirlwind tour of the sights, then back home for tea and cake?"

General Waxler shook her head.

"You want ... *me*"—Chalk felt like dancing and vomiting all at once—"to join the Galactic Academy?"

"Institute."

Croissant forced its way down her throat.

"Yes, Professor Snider and I, along with other members of the faculty, would like you to enrol at the Galactic Institute."

"Don't talk rubbish."

"Harper Hale!"

"But Mum," Chalk bleated, "I'm not in the top one per cent of the top one per cent."

She snatched the acceptance letter from her mother and dropped onto a high-back chair. Each sheet of manuscript was thin yet impossibly brittle. At the top, the emblem of the Galactic Institute shimmered in orange, blue, and chrome.

Squinting, she struggled to read the inscription.

To Miss Harper Hale ... The Galactic Alliance of Planets and Solar Systems ... a long-standing commitment to the advancement and education ... the SpiralVerse and beyond ... the Galactic Institute, built on the foundations ... exploration and study and excellence ... would cordially invite you to begin your studies with us immediately ... Yours expectantly, General Gertrude Prodigious Waxler, Headmistress.

Chalk scanned the words again. Excitement and confusion bubbled like a witch's cauldron. "I'm actually ... properly ...

certifiably—you're not joking and this is not a dream—officially ... *in*?"

General Waxler smiled.

Snider shuffled his feet.

"But that's not possible. I wasn't up for consideration. Don't get me wrong, it's literally every dream I've ever dreamt and every wish I've ever whispered to the night, so I'd be a fool if—" Chalk's gaze switched between each face in the room. "This is impossible. It cannot be real."

"I can assure you it is," the general said. "Do you accept?"

"Why?" Chalk blurted. "I'm not especially smart, or athletic, or charismatic, or ... anything."

"I told you last night ... the future is *mostly* unknown."

"Yet filled with infinite possibilities."

"Exactly."

Chalk wrinkled her nose.

"I've enrolled thousands of students," the general told her. "Students from every civilised world in the SpiralVerse. And yes, grades and conduct and ability all factor into the decision-making process." She moved closer. "But I cannot dismiss my instinct, my intuition, my seventh sense."

"You have *seven* senses?"

Waxler knitted her fingers. "And I *sense* something in *you*."

"Something? What something?"

The general's eyes glazed over, as if daydreaming. "It's a feeling. A knowing. Faint, yet determined. Something as old as time. Akin to fate, destiny, the principles of determining, and universal truth."

"I don't understand."

Waxler blinked the daydream away. "Our decision has been made, Miss Hale."

"Please call me Chalk."

The general nodded.

"Mum?"

Sakura frowned. "How did this happen? I can only presume

you attended the Declaration last night against my instructions. You were supposed to stay in your room. You were supposed to stay safe." The Prime Minister rolled her shoulders. "Chalk and I have been through a lot," she told General Waxler. "We're *still* going through a lot."

"I have read many accounts of the Hundred Hours War and the horrific events Chalk and her father endured," Waxler told them. "But rest assured, the Galactic Institute is far more secure than any building or institution here on Earth. With students from thirty-five civilisations, we have sensors configured to detect and eradicate adverse, violent conduct."

"Blimey."

General Waxler's face softened. "What safer place for your daughter than a sanctuary thousands of lightcycles from harm?"

Tears formed in Chalk's eyes. "Mum—?"

Sakura tightened. Her nostrils flared. "You … should go."

"But, Mum—"

"But nothing."

"I can't."

"You can."

"I want to."

"I know."

"What about—?"

"It is okay. It will be okay."

"No," Chalk said. "I cannot leave you here all alone."

"Yes, you can. And I am not alone. I have … people."

"Politicians aren't people."

"Chalk, this is the opportunity of a lifetime … of a generation! You *have* to go."

"What about Dad?"

"He would want you to go too."

"That's *not* what I meant."

Sakura and Chalk held each other's gaze.

"A prompt decision would be preferable," Snider snapped, clearly unmoved by the emotional tableau developing before him. "Tomorrow at the latest."

"Tomorrow?"

"I am afraid so," Waxler confirmed. "The first cycle begins in eight rotations and there is much to organise."

Chalk stared out the window. She could feel the gentle rumble of the GAPSS mothership against her skin. Her fingers curled around the acceptance letter. A letter inviting her to attend an interplanetary school, on a state-of-the-art space station, on the other side of the SpiralVerse.

Chalk bit her lip. "I'll need additional council."

Sakura nodded. "I'll get him on the phone."

"No," Chalk replied. "This *has* to be face to face!"

A clear monorail car, occupied by a handful of weary-looking souls and three members of her mother's security detail, zipped along beside the River Thames. The London Monorail Network had recently succeeded the Underground as the city's primary transport system, allowing developers to convert the labyrinth of tunnels into a subterranean city of two and three bedroom apartments for the vitamin D deprived.

They whizzed past Tower Bridge, the Tri-Shard Buildings, and St Katherine Docks. Rising high over the city, the lozenge-shaped carriages rolled from side to side as they zoomed towards the Ed Sheeran International Airport, before splitting right and dropping down to the Cutty Sark. Chalk alighted and took an EcoElectroBus to Lewisham High Street and fired a message to her mother.

CHALK: *Arriving now. Not dead.*

Scrolling through desperate messages from Kit, and pointless nonsense from Bloue and Zara, she switched to the group chat.

CHALK: *Got accepted to the Galactic Institute.*

CHALK: *Would leave next week.*

CHALK: Undecided.

Knowing this info grenade would cause a retaliation of unimaginable magnitude, she stopped by an industrial door, adjacent to an abandoned Boris-Bike repair shop, and buried her phone at the bottom of her rucksack. Punching the door buzzer, a figure appeared on the security monitor wearing a stormtrooper helmet.

"Let me see your identification," a man said, old and playful.

Chalk waggled her fingers mystically in front of the camera. "You don't need to see my identification."

"I don't need to see your identification."

"These aren't the droids you're looking for," she said, thumbing towards the security officers. "I can go about my business."

The man chuckled. "Move along. Move along."

Chalk shouldered the door open and pounded up the stairs.

At the top, the man removed his helmet and placed it on a sewing mannequin. "Hope you left your droids outside. We don't serve their kind here."

"Grandpa!" she shrieked, launching herself into his arms.

"Dearest Chalk," he said, spinning the girl in his frail arms. "What are you doing here?"

"Oh, come on. Mother definitely called ahead."

"Yes, yes, alright," he said, straightening his cardigan. "I can't believe you're here. It's been almost two years!"

"It's so good to see you." Chalk smiled. "It's so good to be here!"

Framed posters of sci-fi and fantasy movies clung to the walls of Grandpa Milo's boxy flat. Hordes of superhero comics and graphic novels towered on shelves and windowsills, guarded by an army of action figures, vehicles, and dioramas.

While her grandfather made snacks, Chalk told him about the signing of the Declaration of Interplanetary Inclusivity, the Veroselli, the Garrangular, the Sagaroach, and her awkward conversations with General Waxler and Professor Snider. "I mean, had I known who they were, I'd have probably used long words and fancy talk, like mother does in her press conferences."

"People write those for her." Grandpa Milo sniffed.

"And then, this morning, Mum takes me into her office and I get this letter." Chalk fished the envelope from her bag. "I got in. To the Galactic Institute. A school in space. They have Aether and Casting. Sounds like space magic to me."

Grandpa Milo took the letter. "Amazing." Tears collected in his eyes. "Truly amazing."

Chalk threw her arms around him. "Don't be sad."

"I'm not sad," he confessed. "I'm unbelievably happy. And, I must admit, riotously jealous. When do you leave?"

"They need a decision by tomorrow?"

"Are you considering … *not* going?"

"Don't look at me like that. I … need more time."

"Time is the fire in which we all burn."

"I know, I know."

The old man scratched his chin.

"Can we watch movies?" she asked.

"Which ones?"

"All of them."

With curtains drawn and blankets pulled to their chins, they devoured the original *Star Wars* trilogy, *E.T. the Extra-Terrestrial*, and *WALL·E*.

"I guess you're staying over," he said. "It's eight o'clock already."

"Do you mind?"

"Of course not."

"*Deathly Hallows* double-bill before bed?"

"My poor eyes," Grandpa Milo joked. "But, as this could be one of your last nights on Earth for some time, you should do exactly as you please."

Chalk raided her grandfather's cupboards for crackers and cheese as he dozed through the Harry Potter finale. Chalk took it all in. Every struggle, every battle, every spell, and every devastating heartbreak, wondering if life at the Galactic Institute would be anything like studying at Hogwarts and battling the Dark Lord.

She risked a glance at her iPhone. Hundreds of messages filled the group chat. She switched to a private chat with Kit.

CHALK: What do you think?

He answered immediately.

KIT: How is that a question???

CHALK: You know why.

KIT: The old Chalk wouldn't hesitate!!!

CHALK: The old Chalk is gone.

KIT: I doubt that. She's in there. Somewhere!!!

Grandpa Milo shifted in his sleep, muttering, "Expecto patronum!"

CHALK: Maybe. I dunno.

KIT: You'll find her. I miss her!!!

CHALK: I miss her too.

Perhaps she *should* embark on an extraordinary adventure, make excellent friends, fight the Big Bad, fall in love, and save the galaxy. Or maybe she'd struggle to pass her exams and graduate with a modicum of dignity. What was the alternative? Stay home with her mother, where things were clear and normal and safe, study classes online, and grow up to be—? What *did* she want to be?

CHALK: No fate but what we make.

KIT: May the odds be ever in your favour!!!

Morning sun pulled Chalk from anxiety-laced dreams.

Grandpa Milo presented her with a cream cheese bagel and a cup of green tea.

"It's seven o'clock. You should probably head home."

"I suppose," she said, straightening her clothes.

"Oh, that reminds me!"

Chalk munched down her breakfast while he wandered off and returned with a cardboard box, the sides plastered with stickers and doodles. "I bought these for your father when he was your age but, as you know, he wasn't keen."

"Is this the moment you pass on his lightsaber?"

"Not exactly." Grandpa Milo looked disappointed. "Although, I do have something arguably better than any lightsaber, blaster, or protocol droid. Retro T-shirts!"

There were a dozen T-shirts representing all her favourite fandoms, but two instantly caught her eye. The first, a dark grey tee with a velociraptor and *Clever Girl* detail below. The other was sky-blue. Surrounded by stars, a determined-looking Harriet Starlight floated above the words *The Future Lies Within Us*.

"These are amazing!"

"I know."

"And they're 100% cotton!"

"Eczema *is* hereditary."

"I can't believe they're *all* mine?"

"Start believing."

"Mother will hate them."

"Of course she will. She's Hufflepuff."

Plastic wrap crinkled beneath her fingers.

"What's the sit-rep?" Grandpa Milo asked, removing the cardboard box.

Chalk sighed. "I've spent most of my life reading books and watching films and playing games about adventures among the stars. And now I've got the chance to go into the unknown and perhaps live those dreams for real."

"But—?"

"You know the *but*. The whole world knows. I'm—"

Grandpa Milo sighed. "Chalk, my dear, sweet child. You could be the first human, the first young woman, to travel beyond the boundaries of our solar system. Your name will adorn the pages of every history book, remembered for all time. You'll be to space education what Neil Armstrong is to the moon and Diza McNaught is to Mars."

Chalk finished her bagel and bundled the T-shirts into her rucksack. "Would you go, Grandpa? If you were me?"

"Like a shot!"

"Really?"

"Truly."

"I guess I'm just … afraid."

Grandpa Milo pulled her close. "I've not been through an ordeal like you and your father. I can only imagine what effect that had. Perhaps this is the change you need, the chance to find your smile again." He dabbed his eyes. "And don't worry about me and your mother and your friends. We'll all be here when you return."

Chalk zipped her leather jacket. "I think I know what to do."

He smiled. "You've always known."

"All wings report in."

"Red Leader, standing by."

"Red Five, standing by."

"The Force will be with you," he whispered. "Always."

GAPSS
KNOWLEDGE
MAINFRAME

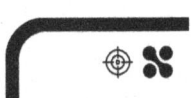

SPIRAL WARS, THE
[HISTORY]

A twelve cycle battle against the rise of the Dark Trinity—Graven, Oddrax, and Miasma, three entities of unknown origin—who used dark cerebral Casting to control, manipulate, and devastate the civilisations of the SpiralVerse. GAPSS declared the Spiral Wars officially over when the Dark Trinity were banished through experimental worldgates. However, suspicion and distrust surround these events and many fear the Dark Trinity's return.

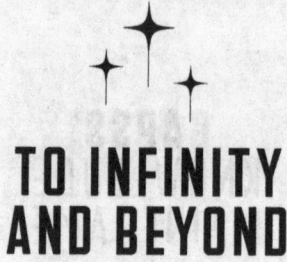

TO INFINITY AND BEYOND

On any normal morning, Sakura Hale would take time out from running the country to remove Chalk's lazy backside from her bed. But not this morning. With all that had happened over the last seven days, Chalk had barely slept a wink.

Media teams outside Number 10 quadrupled every day. Press conferences with Chalk played on every news cycle the world over. *Vogue* and *Cosmopolitan* and *Time* magazine were in constant contact, pushing for lucrative cover shoots. T-shirts and mugs and flags emblazoned with Chalk's face sprung up in every corner of the planet, while endorsement contracts from all the top brands replaced the monogrammed stationery on her mother's desk.

When Sakura Hale arrived, leaving the Chancellor and the Secretary of State to kick their heels in the hallway, she found Chalk staring at the GAPSS mothership.

"Today's the day," she said, not turning to look at her mother.

The Prime Minister placed her hands on Chalk's shoulders. "I am truly excited for you. And for all the girls and boys around the world inspired by your adventures."

"Way to add the pressure!"

A wrinkle of concern found its way to her forehead.

"You are not worried, are you?"

"Worried? Me? About leaving home or about the eyes of the entire world watching my every move? About being rocketed onto that enormous spaceship and blasted off into an endless vacuum? Nope. Not a flicker."

"Chalk—"

"I'm terrified, Mum. But, also, uncontrollably excited. It's an … odd feeling."

One of the Prime Minister's colleagues rapped on the door.

"I have much to do before our transport arrives."

"Is everything as I requested?" Chalk asked, facing her mother.

Sakura's nose twitched. "You could have chosen somewhere … more serious."

Somebody coughed outside the door.

"Eat some breakfast and meet me in the entrance hall. Twenty minutes."

"Affirmative," Chalk replied, saluting with two fingers.

The kitchen staff had provided her with more than croissants and bananas for her last meal on Earth. Recently, she'd been wondering what sort of food they'd serve in space. Would it be those horrible-looking hi-fibre nutrient-rich bars that floated about on the Walmart International Space Station? Perhaps processed smoothies in foil bags? Or would it be outrageous banquets like they have at Hogwarts?

And what do aliens eat? Other aliens probably.

In the Green Room at Number 11, Chalk sat at the top of a grand table. Laying a sharply folded napkin before her, a platter of galia melon, pineapple, and mango slices appeared. She scooped up her cutlery and polished them off in no time. Next came a huge plate brimming with scrambled eggs, hash browns, veggie sausages, baked beans, mushrooms, and two rounds of toast. To finish the meal, a bowl of ice cream landed before her. Cookie dough, chocolate fudge brownie, and salted caramel. Smearing the napkin across her face, Chalk slumped in her chair and let out a satisfying burp.

"I hope everything was to your liking?" asked the server.

"Perfect," she told him. "Exactly as I ordered!"

He bowed slightly, holding out a brown paper bag. "Pecan plaits and pain au chocolats for the journey, Miss Hale."

Chalk stood and winked. "Thanks, Clive."

"You're welcome, Chalk," he whispered. "Have a wondrous time."

The Prime Minister blustered into the entrance hall, talking on her phone, pursued by a gamut of office clerks holding out iPad Paperthins for her to thumb-sign. Quickly appeasing them, she ushered Chalk through the front door and onto Downing Street.

Cameras erupted.

Questions flew.

Fans squealed.

Chalk stumbled from the sensory overload and made her way to a sleek electro-limousine. A member of her mother's security team loaded her suitcase into the boot. Sakura Hale waltzed around the vehicle, acknowledging the boisterous crowds and eager reporters with a courteous wave.

Once inside, Sakura finished her call and signalled to the driver. The car eased silently over the reconditioned cobbles, turning left onto Whitehall and on towards Trafalgar Square.

Thousands of people had taken to the streets, waving Union Jacks and raising placards that read: *Go, Harper, Go! … Blast Off! … Do, or do not. There is no try! … Harper Hale is a Space Cadet! … All Hail, Harper Hale! … To Infinity and Beyond!*

"I have something for you," Sakura said.

"For me?" Chalk replied. "Is it Valium?"

Her mother frowned. "It is this," she said, taking a slim emerald fountain pen from her pocket and handing it to Chalk.

"A pen? Gee! Thanks, Mum."

"Now, I know it is considered redundant, perhaps corny, to give someone a pen in a world where the written word has become obsolete, but I have carried this pen with me for over thirty years. I wrote *my* university notes with it, signed the deeds to our first house, my marriage vows, and countless political and ministerial documents, not least of which being the Declaration of Interplanetary Inclusivity."

"It's seen a lot of action," Chalk said, turning the pen in her hands.

"I hope it gets to see plenty more."

"Thanks, Mum." Chalk smiled. "It's a little piece of home."

Sakura returned to her phone.

The limousine swept through London's crowded streets. Chalk slipped her earbuds in and fired up her *Space Vibes* playlist. She made it through Bowie's 'Space Oddity', 'Cosmic Strangers' by Hatestreak, and the first chorus of Katy Perry and Taylor Swift's epic duet 'Star-Crossed' before they pulled into a designated slot on the zebra hatchings outside King's Cross Station. Enormous crowds swarmed the pedestrianised zone. Barriers and tape and teams of police officers formed a protective wall.

Chalk waved tentatively.

Girls screamed. Boys whooped. Hands reached out, desperate to touch her.

Chalk's skin prickled.

Her eyes darted in all directions.

Shadows formed dangerous shapes, creeping closer.

The Prime Minister's security detail flanked Chalk and ushered her into the station. She walked down a man-made aisle, ecstatic fans going bananas on either side. A circular zone of smooth granite opened before her.

Here, General Waxler and Professor Snider waited, heads high, arms locked behind their backs. The GAPSS welcome committee stood to the general's left; Kit, Bloue, and Zara to the right.

Cameras flashed in their hundreds, their thousands.

Chalk's legs wobbled, suddenly weak and overcome by the frenetic buzz and chaos. The huge breakfast sloshed about in her stomach.

She nodded politely at the GAPSS delegates, smiled at her friends—who were having an impossible time controlling their emotions—before stopping in front of General Waxler and Professor Snider.

"Hey."

Her mother took a sharp breath, adding, "Hello, General. Professor. And welcome to King's Cross Station. One of our nation's leading transport hubs."

"Greetings," replied the general. Tilting her head at Chalk, she scanned the T-shirt that Grandpa Milo had given her. "Clever Girl. I do hope so."

She coiled away from Chalk, stepped onto a podium, and scanned the crowd. General Waxler spread her arms and the noise suddenly quelled. TV cameras spun, zoomed, transmitting the images to hundreds of networks and channels across the globe, including the Qwork News Network—the official station of GAPSS.

"Ladies and gentlemen, boys and girls, Londoners, people of Earth, human beings, citizens of the SpiralVerse! Today marks a historic moment in history. Global history. Galactic history. Today, the first Earthborn student will enter the Galactic Institute. She will walk upon the Coin and the Flipside, among hundreds of students from all over the SpiralVerse, led by professors and advisors and historians in a faculty that is simply out of this world. Miss Harper Hale"—screams and cheers bloomed through the station—"is about to embark on an adventure like no one from Earth has ever known. I wish her the best of luck. She is certainly going to need it."

Chalk swallowed hard.

Anxiety and trepidation moistened her skin.

General Waxler stepped down. Prime Minister Hale took her place.

"People of Earth, delegates of GAPSS, General Waxler and Professor Snider. The past six months have been nothing short of world-changing. The existence of life beyond our own planet has been established. The Declaration of Interplanetary Inclusivity has been signed. New and exciting relationships—dare I say friendships—have been forged. And now, Harper Hale, my daughter, Chalk, is about to take one small step for a woman, the next giant leap for humankind!"

The crowd went berserk.

Streamers and popping fireworks cracked and whizzed through the air, falling in harmless, colourful rivulets across the plaza.

Chalk dashed to Kit, Bloue, and Zara. She threw her arms around them all as if this was the last time they would ever meet. The Prime Minister led her to High-King Cillian Van Wyrm, Kydra, and Lord Milton Barclay XVI—nodding, fist-bowing, and wriggling her fingers as was customary for each species—before passing the podium and approaching General Waxler.

The headmistress had repositioned herself beside a brick wall, a luggage trolley buried halfway in. Above, the sign read *Platform Nine and Three-Quarters*.

Chalk grinned so hard it almost hurt.

Next to the trolley and world-famous sign stood a large metal ring dotted with pulsating amber diodes. The ring was housed in two blocks of chunky, rectangular tech, surrounded by a weave of chaotic vents, pipes, and coloured tubing. To the right sat a complex tablet displaying mysterious symbols and glyphs.

The device hummed gently, like a contented cat.

Chalk hugged her mother one last time. "Thank you."

"For what?"

"For everything. For being as much of a regular parent as possible."

"I wish your father was here to see this."

"Grandpa too."

Sakura smiled.

"I'm sure they're watching," Chalk said.

"*Everyone* is watching."

"I know. It's scary. How do you do this every day?"

"Practice."

Professor Snider approached, flipped open a box, reached in and prised out a small device, matt-black and lined with silver.

"For me?" Chalk asked.

"Of course," he said, laboriously. "It's your GI-VR."

"My what?"

"Galactic Institute Vital Recorder. You wear it on your body. A wrist or an ankle is usual for bipedals. It monitors your physical statistics, location, and is primarily used for learning and language. It has a multitude of other functions. I suppose you'll work it out. *Eventually*."

"Sounds fairly intrusive."

"Rules are rules." Snider grinned. "Wrist or ankle?"

Chalk held out her left arm.

Snider snapped the GI-VR onto Chalk's skin amidst a horde of colourful charity wristbands and fastened the buckle. The screen flashed pale green and something shot out the back, burrowing itself in Chalk's skin.

"Ouch!" she said, grabbing the device.

"Sorry. Should have said." He grinned. "Might pinch a bit."

"That kills!" Chalk moaned. "And it won't come off."

"Good," Professor Snider replied. "Can't have GI-VR-less students running about the place."

GALACTIC INSTITUTE . . .

VITAL RECORDER . . .

VERSION 23.5 . . .

The words appeared in the corner of Chalk's eye.

HOST DETECTED . . .

She tried to blink the words away.

ACTIVATING . . .

Then prodded at them with her index finger.

SYSTEM INITIALISED . . .

"Nobody told me about this!"

"Do not worry, Miss Hale," Waxler said. "You will become used to it in no time. It will become part of you."

"Resistance is futile." Chalk snorted. "Any more surprises?"

"Yes," the general said, inspecting her own GI-VR. Ice white. Trimmed with copper. "She will be here imminently."

Chalk's chin angled back. "Who?"

"The first of your Galactic Institute relay partners."

"My what now?"

The general's mouth quirked.

Across the plaza, a strange sound gathered. Gasps of astonishment rippled towards Chalk. Security teams marched between the barriers, flanking the figure of a girl who rose no more than three feet from the ground. Half her violet-skinned face was hidden by a sleek wrap-around visor. Below, her nose was as cute as a button, her mouth slim and sincere. She wore white robes that skimmed the ground and a complex algorithm of plaited jet-black hair shimmered against her scalp.

Her voice crackled as if arriving through an ancient radio. Chalk gazed at the GI-VR. It burbled with audio frequencies.

TRANSLATION SOFTWARE ENABLED . . .

"What fresh hell is this?"

TATTORIAN DIALECT ACTIVATED . . .

"My name is Aidriendretta Kromm-Nargulantis. However, I will accept the abbreviation Aida," she said, her voice suddenly clear and crisp. "I am here to give you this."

"Give me what?" Chalk said, and Aida's GI-VR translated in return.

A violet-skinned claw shot out from beneath her white robes. In its grip, she held a round object. Black, edged with gold.

"It is a data drive," Aida told her. "It will tell you what to do next."

"Next?"

"Any questions?"

"Um—"

"Then I must go. See you on the Coin. And good luck."

Aida approached General Waxler. The headmistress's mechanical fingers worked their way over the keypad. The metal rings began to spin. A dark film etched across the space, hiding the bricks beyond. It rippled and flexed like an oil slick. The lights around the device turned from pulsing amber to a solid blue.

"Congratulations, Miss Kromm-Nargulantis," said General Waxler. "You may proceed."

Without looking back, Aida sank slowly into the black film. The device slowed. Lights faded to amber and the black film dematerialised.

"Miss Hale. It is your turn."

"Is this a … portal?"

"Of course."

"To the GAPSS mothership?"

The general didn't answer.

"And this?" Chalk said, holding the circular object Aida had given her.

"A data drive. It goes into the aperture on the side of your GI-VR."

The device still stung but the initial pain had begun to ebb. Turning her palm up, she found the port and slipped the data drive inside.

"It will activate when you arrive."

"Okay. Sure. On the mothership, right? Or am I going straight there?"

"Everything you need to know is on the drive," the general said. "And up here." She tapped her temple and smiled. "Ready when you are."

Chalk spun and looked at her friends, at the swarming crowds, the GAPSS welcome committee, the security teams, and her mother's proud, beaming face.

"I love you."

"I know."

Chalk faced the glimmering black of the portal, drew a long, calming breath, and stepped through.

GAPSS
KNOWLEDGE
MAINFRAME

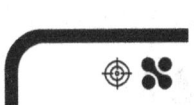 

LAYER SCREENS
[TECHNOLOGY]

Holographic digital pages. Designed to function as additional workspace, they materialise and hover above compatible devices. They can be spread flat, stacked, or displayed in any number of arrangements. Layer screens are predominantly rectangular or spherical, although any conceivable shape, or colour, is permissible.

DATA DRIVE RELAY

The moment Chalk's skin broke the black film, she braced for the exhilarating hyperspace jolt of the Millennium Falcon or the chaotic, stomach-churning horror of a portkey. Instead, the experience equated to little more than stepping through rubbery batwing doors.

Disappointment and bewilderment consumed her, for Chalk didn't find herself standing on an impressive transportation deck or inside one of the magnificent white halls from the Galactic Institute digital brochure. There were no circular towers, mind-boggling technology, unfamiliar clusters of stars, or clamour of excited students.

Instead, it was quiet.

And impossibly hot.

Before her, the world swayed in a thousand shades of green. Interrupting the lush jungle canopy were a collection of egg-shaped buildings. Each had been sculpted from rough stone, circled with yellow bands, and punctuated by numerous round windows.

Chalk's tongue stuck to the roof of her mouth. Sweat glistened on her forehead. Rivulets crept down her back. She spun to face the portal—consumed by the urge to return home—but the black film slipped away and the spinning blue lights were amber once more. "No, no, no," she muttered. "This must be a mistake. Where am I? Costa del Endor?"

Her GI-VR buzzed. The sensation was unexpected, but not unpleasant.

NEW LOCATION DISCOVERED...

REVUS X...

Instinctively tapping the GI-VR, a layer screen materialised above her wrist. It showed a wireframe detail of the surrounding terrain. A white ring flashed at the centre.

"I guess you're me."

DATA DRIVE DETECTED...

LOCATE RIPLEY FLINCH...

"Huh?"

DELIVER THE DATA DRIVE...

"Ah, okay. Relay partner. Got it." Chalk nodded. "Aida had to find me and now I have to find this Ripley girl."

TIME IS A FACTOR...

"Fastest wins or time limited?"

The GI-VR gave no indication.

"Fat lot of good you are!"

Chalk studied the map and fanned her hand to expand the environment. It showed a city to the north where most of the egg buildings were huddled. Hundreds of pulsating blue dots swarmed about the terrain at various speeds.

"Alien life forms detected."

She zoomed in.

Street names, landmarks, and places of interest were designated in blocky type.

With the portal deactivated, Chalk followed a muddy track that ran towards the city. She brushed heavy, water-laden leaves, fronds and ferns aside, soaking her porous high-tops in thick, pungent slop.

At the end of the track rose a bustling metropolis. Here, the ground had hardened into sandy roads that snaked between egg buildings of all sizes. Armour-plated vehicles rattled by. Locals wandered along, chatting, gesticulating provocatively. Others sat in cafes, sipping from large steaming bowls, and tapping away on layer screens.

They seemed human.

Two arms. Two legs.

Torso and a head.

Eyes, nose, mouth.

LOCATE RIPLEY FLINCH . . .

"Alright. Calm down. Give me a minute."

But before Chalk could go anywhere, ask for assistance, or form the loosest of plans, two large hands reached out of the jungle and grabbed her.

Chalk's world went dark. Full blackout. A helmet slammed over her head. Her hands swiftly fastened. Muttered words found their way to her ears. The scuff of hurried feet on arid ground. A minute passed, two, then Chalk found herself being hoisted into a vehicle.

"What is this?" she yelled as the engine fired. "What's going on? General Waxler? Professor Snider?"

She struggled to breathe. Panic took control.

The vehicle juddered over uneven ground before making half a dozen violent turns and skidding to a halt. The infernal heat vanished as calloused hands dragged her through several doors and dumped her onto a cool stone floor.

She rolled helplessly like a snared fish.

"General Waxler? Snider?" Chalk's voice became small. "Mum?"

Silence.

A vile sickness sloshed in her belly. Sorrowful memories ghosted her mind. She slipped back in time, to the despair and horror of the Hundred Hours War. Dust coated the floor. The thick smell of bleach filled her nostrils.

"Dad?" she whispered. "Are you there?"

Silence.

She took long, steady breaths and recounted her father's advice.

Remain calm, be polite, co-operate with our captors.

Was this really happening again? Perhaps this was part of the Data Drive Relay? Chalk cursed, realising she should have quizzed Aida about her experience in London and how she'd found her way to Platform Nine and Three-Quarters.

LOCATE RIPLEY FLINCH . . .

A door yawned.

Feet shuffled in.

Chalk became airborne, then dumped into a chair. Around her ears the helmet hissed and lifted to reveal a large man in military overalls. He sat on a stool, kneading his huge hands. A single stuttering bulb swung from a frayed cable. The door behind had been left ajar.

"Harper Hale," he rumbled, as a thin figure in a grotesque mask removed her hand restraints. "What an honour."

Chalk fussed her hair, fixing the man with a sideways look. Behind him, a stocky woman in fatigues and smudged warpaint leant nonchalantly against a stone pillar.

"What is this?" Chalk asked.

"What does it look like?" the man said, slamming his fists together.

Chalk jolted back.

Remain calm, be polite, co-operate with your captors.

"What do you want?"

"We already have what we want."

"M-me?"

"They said you'd be smart." He laughed, interlacing his fingers.

"They?" she managed. "The Hundred Hours mercenaries?"

A flicker of confusion bloomed in his eyes.

"What do you want with me?"

"Money. Information. The usual."

"I have little of either."

"Where are you headed?" he asked. "Who are you meeting? What's on that drive?"

Chalk glanced at her GI-VR. "I don't know," she said honestly. "I have to find someone."

"Who?"

"Ripley ... um ... Flinch."

"Where?"

"I don't know."

"How?"

"I've no clue." Tears smoothed the hard grey room into soft watercolour. "I just—" she tried and failed. Fear paralysed her tongue.

"Galactic Institute business?"

"Yes," she managed. "It's my first time and—"

"Quit the theatrics," the man barked, grabbing the side of her head. Sweat and smoke lingered on his fingers. "I just want the data drive."

Chalk met his eyes. "The drive—?"

"Are you going to give it to me or am I going to have to take it?"

"Who are you?"

"Who I am, and what I want, are no concern of yours ... *Earthling!*"

He spat the last word as though it were poison.

Sweat dripped from Chalk's nose. Her chin trembled.

"Thumb-sign your GI-VR, deactivate the drive, and give it to me, Miss Hale," he ordered, their faces inches apart.

Remain calm, be polite, co-operate with your captors.

Chalk wanted to take the last seven days back, reject General Waxler's invitation to enrol at the Galactic Institute, and bury herself in duvets and pillows and pain au chocolats and endless online *Green Death* all-you-can-kill-mega-tournaments.

"Give it to me!"

It was happening again. Capture, imprisonment, the senseless terror that haunted her every day. Chalk studied the GI-VR. The data drive hummed happily in its slot. Fire burned through her. An anxious, determined fire. She pushed his hand away, shaking visibly in the dim light.

"No," she whispered.

"What?"

"I said NO!"

Chalk exploded out of the chair. Her right heel connected with the man's toes, sending a wail of dismay around the room. She grabbed the lightbulb, smashed it into his face, and drowned the room in shadows. Skidding between his legs, she bolted for the door. The accomplices lurched. Chalk twisted, batting away their outstretched fingers, and launched herself through the door.

"Don't just stand there," the man roared. "GET HER!"

Chalk's heart pounded. Her vision speckled with tiny white lights. Adrenaline spiked, arrowing through her legs, forcing her onward. She darted down a corridor where spears of sunlight burst from high windows. Shouldering a door aside, she staggered into the heat.

Three pairs of feet approached with haste. Voices cried out in alarm. Chalk orbited a battered transport stacked with teal-skinned livestock then slipped into a shady alley between two buildings. Bursting out the other end, she snaked through a tight marketplace that buzzed with excitement, colour, and a cavalcade of unfamiliar aromas.

Chalk ran. Desperate and wild. Her limbs whirred like pistons.

Her feet took her in directions her brain had no time to rationalise. Each alley became narrower and narrower until they were nothing more than high stone walls striped with shadow and sun. She inched through an open gate, tore across a paved courtyard, vaulted a low stone wall, and emerged on a wide, chaotic street.

Merging into the masses, she hid in a busy shop. Long red tentacles and severed green arms hung from the walls. Pools of purple and blue liquid collected at her feet.

Her stomach performed painful backflips.

LOCATE RIPLEY FLINCH . . .

Chalk crossed her arms, hugged her shoulders, and tried to focus. Who was Ripley Flinch? And where would she be? Was she the daughter of the Prime Minister of Revus X? Or simply the best student on the planet? Would she be at home, in some government egg building, or waiting in the city's most extravagant location for the start of her Data Drive Relay?

I've always found problem-solving to be equal parts critical thinking, experience, and luck, came the voice of Harriet Starlight.

"That's incredibly helpful," Chalk muttered sarcastically. "You had limitless space magic to rely on too! I, on the contrary, am waiting for mine to kick in."

She opened her GI-VR and scanned the wireframe map. Street names translated before her eyes. She scanned the north side of the city. Converted prisons and pleasure gardens. Then the south. Commercial districts and communal housing.

Blue dots appeared everywhere. There were no considerable congregations of any kind like there had been for her at King's Cross Station.

Well, that's just weird.

Chalk scanned the map again, hoping something would jump out. Her gaze arrived at the western most point of District 23. The Temple of Thoden, the Tar Pits museum, and, tucked away at the edge of the jungle, Revus X city high school.

A school! Could X really mark the spot?

She left the horrific sights and smells of the alien butchers. She ran and ran until every muscle in her body ached and her mouth turned to dust. People watched as she tore by. Perhaps the sight of someone—*anyone*—running in this heat would be enough to make the front layer screen of the local news. But a terrified girl with vivid pink hair wearing a *Jurassic Park* T-shirt was undoubtedly a first in this corner of the SpiralVerse.

Up ahead, a huge collection of egg buildings were set back from a tapestry of lush green lawns. Zigzagging paths connected one building to the next. Looking like she'd showered with her clothes on, Chalk glanced at a sign lodged between two pillars. The symbols and letters made no sense.

Her GI-VR lit up. Symbols and glyphs tumbled like a codex. *REVUS X CITY HIGH SCHOOL . . .*

Chalk barrelled between the pillars. Noticeboards amplified social warnings and school events, while signs indicated locations around the campus. Chalk's GI-VR worked overtime converting each to English. She found the main reception inside a library, positioned at the furthest point from the street.

Who in Unicron's name designed this place?

Chalk staggered, her energy reserves at critical. She swept through automated glass doors and into an atmosphere-controlled environment. Stumbling to the front desk, she landed on her forearms. Damp hair stuck to a sign-in tablet.

"Can I ... help you?" said a woman, peering over the top of thick glasses, crescent moons dangling from her ears.

"Ripley Flinch," Chalk managed. "Is she here? Please tell me she's here."

The woman accessed a large, mounted tablet. "Master Flinch is not here at present."

"Oh ... *Master* Flinch?"

The woman smiled.

"So, he *does* attend this school?"

"Yes."

Chalk punched the air. "And he's going to the Galactic Institute?"

The woman checked her listing again. "I believe so."

"Do you know where I can find him?"

"My domain extends to the library. And that alone."

Glass walkways pirouetted up the sides of the library. Chalk could see through each level to the pinnacle of the building where a circular window allowed columns of light to burn against the wall like a sundial.

She ground her teeth.

Sweat found her eyes.

"You're doing well, Miss Hale," the receptionist said. "Good luck."

"Thank you," she replied, beginning to turn, then, "Hey—"

"YOU!"

Chalk whipped about. Her back pressed to the desk. The bulky man and his two associates stood before her. The tip of a large knife shone in the light from multiple suns.

"Don't let her escape!"

Instinct told her to flee up the stairs, but her legs carried her deep into the library stacks. She shot down one corridor, then another, randomly turning left and right until she had become utterly disorientated. The kidnappers tried to follow, but the woman's ragged breath and the huge man's putrid stink were easy to detect.

The masked figure proved a more challenging assailant. Whoever or whatever it was moved silently, like a ghost, a wraith. Books toppled onto the floor, as pale hands reached for her, fingers outstretched, clawing, blocking her path. She ducked and rolled, ran at full pelt until she collided with the transparent outer wall of the library.

She spread her fingers.

Breath misted the glass.

Beyond, lay a huge sports field.

Two people waited in the middle.

And a familiar metal ring.

Chalk's ordeal in the library stacks felt like it was never going to end. An infernal game of cat and mouse. Eventually, she worked her way back to reception and sprinted into the open. The masked assailant came flying from her left, arms outstretched, dark fingernails slicing the air. The receptionist squealed as Chalk dropped and slid beneath one table, vaulted the next, and desperately nipped through the automatic doors as they hissed apart.

Back in the heat, she raced round the building and crossed the playing field.

Beside the portal stood General Waxler. "You made it," the headmistress said, smiling. "Finally."

"I have so many questions—" Chalk began but could barely speak. Instead, she turned her attention to a slender, good-looking boy, his skin dark, hair unruly. "Ripley Flinch?" she gasped, slowing to a breathless walk.

"Yeah. That's me," he replied, eyes directed at his GI-VR.

"I'm Harper ... but everyone calls me Chalk."

"Okay."

She thumb-signed her GI-VR and deactivated the data drive. "I'm here to give you this."

Ripley Flinch looked up for the first time. Chalk almost stumbled as the boy's hypnotic purple eyes met her sweaty, anxious face. "Oh my—"

"The data drive. Perfect," he said, snatching it from her. "Thanks."

"You're ... welcome. I guess."

Ripley wore dark trousers and a leather belt mounted with buckle-locked pouches. An unpressed yellow T-shirt sat beneath a three-quarter-length brown and cream jacket littered with repaired patches, dirt, scuffs, and zippered pockets.

"Where is everyone?" Chalk asked.

"Everyone?"

"Thousands of people came to see me off," she explained, looking across the field. The three kidnappers strolled towards her. "It was a huge moment. Historic, probably. Televised across the galaxy. This seems—"

"Ah," Ripley said. "You're the Earthling, aren't you?"

"Yes. So?"

"First of your kind to go to the Galactic Institute? Big deal, huh?" He scanned the playing field. "Here, not so much. Students from Revus X have been going for aeons."

"Aeons?"

"Sure."

"How long is an aeon?"

"People are kind of over it."

"I guess ... we're done then?"

The boy shrugged. "Looks that way."

"Any questions?" Chalk said, echoing the one Aida had posed.

Ripley frowned.

The kidnappers stopped beside them.

Chalk eased away.

General Waxler smiled. "Relax. It is okay."

"You need to arrest these people—"

"That will not be necessary."

"They abducted me. They forced me into—"

The headmistress raised a finger. "Miss Hale. The Data Drive Relay is an exercise to see how you perform under pressure."

"Perform? Under pressure? I was scared to death."

"You were never in any real danger."

"Didn't feel that way."

"Exactly. That's what makes it an effective exercise."

"Seriously? Couldn't you have given me a written test or something?"

"I could, but you and I both know written examinations are not your forte."

Chalk's heart stepped down from red alert.

A humid breeze ruffled the general's hair. "How do you think you got on?"

"Pretty good," Chalk lied. "Considering. Gave these fools the run around."

General Waxler turned to the kidnappers. "Professor Snider, is this true?"

"Snider?"

The thin figure, the wraith, removed his mask. "She did adequately," he rasped. "She displayed fear, resolve, and ... *courage*. A little slow on the problem-solving, but she's quick on her feet—like a Horned Sagamoth."

"Excellent, excellent."

Chalk's mouth hung open.

"And now, Miss Hale," General Waxler said, beaming brightly. "It is time for you to enrol at the Galactic Institute."

"Really?"

"Really."

"No more tricks?"

"None."

"Promise?"

"I swear it."

"By the Old Gods and the New?"

"If it pleases you."

Chalk looked at Ripley. "See you there, relay buddy," she said, but the boy was too busy stuffing the data drive into his GI-VR and rearranging his hair in a layer screen mirror.

Still shaken, Chalk slicked her hair behind her ears, wiped the sweat from her lip, and approached the rippling black film.

GAPSS
KNOWLEDGE
MAINFRAME

EDUHELPERS
[TECHNOLOGY]

Every student at the Galactic Institute is issued with an eduhelper to assist with their integration, studies, and well-being. Eduhelpers are chosen, not designated, and range from state-of-the-art battle and research droids to reconditioned classics, TekTonik Touches, mystery balls, buddy droids, and many more. Binary and AI students hailing from Raznor R76 are provided with a domesticated Qwork.

ONBOARDING

This time things were better. For one, Chalk found herself in a temperature-controlled room, not marooned on a tropical jungle planet with Professor Snider recreating the most traumatic moments of her life. A semicircle of peculiar faces stared at her. Some looked humanoid, some avian, one vulpine, others reptilian, and some ... well, she wasn't sure if they had faces at all.

A strange smell hung in the air. A mix of damp and rot, fungal foot powder, and overcooked school dinners. On the walls, which were mostly constructed of scuffed sheet metal and coated in a worrying orange-green patina, were lopsided monitors. Data scrolled across some, bizarre creatures and important-looking historical figures on others. Both feeds were interspersed with adverts for mid-cycle vacations, *Orbit Strike!* matches and merchandise, Gamma Ray's Diner Deals, and eduhelper upgrades.

Flashes of static interrupted each display.

One monitor fizzed. Gold sparks rained onto a mismatched treadplate floor.

Where am I now? Chalk thought. *Is this the Galactic Institute? Looks nothing like the digital brochure. Perhaps this is a holding cell for Data Drive Relay failures, waiting to be unceremoniously launched home.*

A round, six-limbed creature tottered towards her. He wore a fitted jacket—similar to Waxler and Snider—but impossibly creased, threadbare at the elbows, and had probably been white at some point. A high collar withered onto his shoulders concealing most of the green edging. His frail, blanched skin looked as though all the colour had been sucked out of him. Busying himself with a TekTonik Touch10 in two of his four hands, he stopped inches from her, stared through square spectacles, and scratched a greying moustache.

"Miss Harper Hale," he decided after a moment. "Hmm?"

"Ten out of ten."

Grabbing Chalk's wrist, he scanned her GI-VR with his tablet. A tower of amber layer screens appeared with a cheerful *ping!*

"Triple D?"

"I beg your pardon?" Chalk replied, folding her arms.

"Digital Digit Declaration," he muttered, spreading the layer screens like the petals of a flower. "Your thumb, Miss Hale, hmm? Here and here and here and here and here and here and here."

"Oh."

Chalk pressed her thumb against the screens, turning each from amber to blue. Confirming the final screen, they all retreated into his Touch10.

"Thank you. All correct and above board," he said. "My name is Professor Asimov. I specialise in History of the Galaxy."

"Great."

"My duties extend, but are not limited to, a mountain of clerical work, administration, and filing."

"Right."

"I'm Lord of the Treasury, Bursar, Lead Secretary, and Examination Accreditor too."

Chalk nodded.

"Uniform designer—although uniform is not compulsory at the Galactic Institute—Marketing and Promotions Officer, Motivational Speaker, and part-time Chef."

"When do you sleep?" Chalk asked, smiling.

"In Earth terms, I sleep for six point five hours, every two point eight days."

"Good to know." She tried to unravel the mathematical problem but gave up in record time.

Professor Asimov tapped the device again. Pulsating mauve layer screens appeared. He quickly rifled through the contents. "So, as I alluded to, and confirmed by my detailed notes, you are our first Earthling? Harper Hale. Informally referred to as Chalk. No reason given. Fifteen Earth years and eight months. Five foot five. Ninety-eight pounds. Black hair"—he looked up, frowned—"currently painted pink, green eyes, of Anglo-Asian descent. Imperfect vision. Broken arm, age six. Pollen allergy. Seasonal eczema condition. Herbivore." He looked at Chalk. "Hmm?"

"Sure," she said. "Although, herbivore makes me sound like a dinosaur and my hair isn't pink, it's Bubblegum Pop!"

"I have no timetable for you, Miss Hale," he continued, unfazed.

"Please call me Chalk."

"Nicknames are a touch over-familiar," he said without looking up. "A list of all first cycle classes will be sent soon. Familiarise yourself, attend as many as interest you, and complete your preliminary timetable for approval and class shift denomination by the end of phase one."

"Rotations? Phases? Class shifts?"

Sighing, Asimov enlarged a layer screen and rotated it to face her. "Says here you've read and digi-signed the *Introduction to Life, Conduct, and Discipline at the Galactic Institute* document provided seven rotations ago."

"I tried. It was over two thousand pages."

He stared at her, unblinking. "Rotations are like your Earth days, but longer. Phases consist of ten study rotations and two leisure rotations. Students are organised in class shifts depending on their sleep patterns, known as chronotypes: Aktari—that's your class shift— Osmotrino, Zalazor, and Qantoculus. You'll pick it up." Taking a deep breath, he turned to face the other students and announced, "Miss Harper Hale. Earth. Specialisms: unknown. Primaries: undecided."

The other students seemed confused.

Specialisms? Primaries? Hard pass.

Asimov gave her a gentle shove towards her classmates.

From what Chalk could tell, there were three Veroselli. Three Garrangulars, too. No sign of any Sagaroaches, thank goodness. Gathered away from the rest were four figures of varying shapes in flowing red robes. To one side sat a hulking mass of black scales and pink flesh. A long, dark tongue flicked between rows of silver, pointed teeth as its reptilian eyes stared curiously at her *Clever Girl* T-shirt. She clocked a creature with two heads; a nine-foot robot; and a gloomy-looking girl with the same watery eyes as Professor Snider. Hiding towards the rear was an utterly hairless girl, like a sphynx rat, who wore a diamond-shaped mask over her nose and mouth. Next to her floated a student with iridescent scaly skin and golden hair at the centre of a liquid orb. A plume of grey smoke hung behind them all. Chalk couldn't tell if it was an incredibly peculiar student or a vapour leak. There were half a dozen others that could easily pass as human but she assumed were Revans or Genks.

"Hey," Chalk said, clocking Aida's huge visor.

Aida angled her head. "Chalk. Hello. Thought I could smell you."

She hooked the neck of her T-shirt and took a sniff.

"I am blind," Aida explained. "Not stupid. And before you ask … I do *have* eyes." Aida lifted the visor to reveal two white orbs. "But, like everyone from Tattoraan, we are born without sight. The visor works as a humidifier, keeping our eyes from cracking, dying, and falling out."

"I don't remember asking."

"I can tell. You are staring."

"Oh, right. Sorry. I can be a real bonehead sometimes."

Aida nodded.

"This place smells terrible."

"Corrosion," Aida replied. "Iron oxide. Rust. Kraken-weevil and kritten effluence. Oh, and dinner. Hard to be exact. Dozens of dietary requirements are being prepared."

"How many species are there?"

"You will find students from all thirty-five civilised worlds on the Coin."

"Thirty-six," Chalk added, pointing both thumbs at herself.

"Very astute."

"I've met a Genk and a Revan and a Pyramist," Chalk said. "And you're a—?"

"Tattorian," Aida said. "From Tattoraan."

Lights flickered. The portal swelled with black. Excited, nervous chatter trickled from each student as they wondered who would come through next. Amber lights became blue. Ripley Flinch burst from the portal, skidded on his knees and fell face first at Professor Asimov's feet.

The boy stood, brushing red sand and—what Chalk prayed weren't real—giant cobwebs from his clothes as Professor Asimov accosted him for his DDD.

The process seemed to last forever. Ripley pressed his thumb to amber layer screens that turned red instead of blue. Eventually, after Asimov rebooted his device, and the two engaged in some animated discussion, the process was complete. Asimov opened the Revan's personal details and announced, "Master Ripley Flinch. Revus X. Specialisms: Domestic and Interspecies Languages. Primaries: Astro Anthropology."

Ripley nodded, rolled his shoulders, and went to stand with the others.

Chalk and Aida snaked through the crowd.

"Hey again," she said to Ripley.

"Ah, it's you."

"Yeah, Chalk … from Earth. And this is Aida … from, um, Tongerania."

"Tattoraan."

"She's my other relay buddy."

Ripley's eyes found Chalk, then Aida, but his attention was snatched by a pretty girl with shimmering red hair dressed in a green bodysuit.

"How was your relay?" the girl asked. Her eyes twinkled as she latched onto Ripley's arm. "Quite the dramatic entrance. Were you being chased? Were you scared? Who was after you?"

"Xenothropod colonies," he replied. "Dust and devils. Best to keep moving."

"Wow. Really?" she said, sounding impressed. "I'm Spirit. Gaia 15. Oneric by birth. Raised by Genks. You?"

"Oh, standard Revan," Ripley told her. "Descendant of the Damned and all that."

Spirit fired an accusatory look at Chalk and Aida. "*Friends* of yours?"

"Erm, Haley and, erm, Agnes?" he tried, looking awkward.

"I'm Chalk and this is Aida. Earthling. Tat—ter—"

"Tattorian."

"Listen," Spirit said, her eyes back on Ripley. "A few of us are going to the *Orbit Strike!* arena later if you want to tag along."

"Oh, sure," Ripley said. "Maybe."

"That sounds fun," Chalk said. "What's an *Orbit Strike!*?"

Spirit ignored her. "Maybe I'll see you there," she added, running a finger down the Revan's arm, and twirled away.

Ripley returned to his GI-VR.

"Xenothropod colonies, eh?" Chalk said. "Sounds … exciting."

"I'll tell you about it later. Okay? Sorry. I'm just … busy."

"Sure, sure. Sorry. I wasn't … I didn't—"

"It's okay. I'm not a complete snagger. Just … erm … later, okay?"

Chalk turned to Aida. "What's a snagger?"

"A rude, obnoxious Revan."

"What happened on your relay?' Chalk asked. 'Did you enjoy London?"

"It was odd," Aida began. "Lots of cryptic messages to do with magic and *Horcruxes* and finding the *Hogwarts Express*. What are these things?"

Chalk gave her an elevator pitch for Harry Potter while they waited for the next student to arrive. They chatted for half an hour and introduced themselves to a gaggle of Revans. Aida informed Chalk that the enigmatic, red-robed students followed a religion known as the Vyshan Order and the huge scaly reptile was a Zillamoth called Necrotta.

Eventually, Professor Asimov pulled them together. "Quiet please. Hush. Come on, come on. Opticals on me, hmm? It would appear our final cohort is having difficulty finishing his relay. We still have much to do and time—in this dimension, at least— is finite." Flicking a switch on the side of his TekTonik Touch10, the device opened like a book, revealing a second interface. The professor slid a finger across the screen and entered a passcode. Then, groaning like a dying whale, the wall behind shuddered, shifted.

An enormous space loomed beyond.

Chalk's skin-ripples hit a new hi-score.

Asimov stood dead centre as the broadening light cast him in sharp silhouette.

"Welcome," he said, "to the Galactic Institute!"

GAPSS
KNOWLEDGE
MAINFRAME

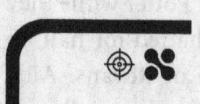 

FIRST CYCLE AKTARI
[RELAY START ORDER]

No.	Name	Species	Homeworld	Language
1	Krieg	Garrangular	Zorik Minor	Garrangulese
2	Sadler Arklan	Elmori	Marstok	Dark Wistorian
3	Clementine Von Wax	Veroselli	Zorik Minor	High Zorikian
4	Spirit	Oneric	Gaia 15	Galaxian
5	Volgar Krishnam	Dumsi	Marstok	Galaxian
6	Kroket	Garrangular	Zorik Minor	Garrangulese
7	Ironlung 8-47	Cylesian	Kraznor R76	Freeform Binary
8	Nivin Traxa	Xylesse	Seniter	Xylon
9	Jinx Traxa	Xylesse	Seniter	Xylon
10	Claridge Von Whump	Veroselli	Zorik Minor	High Zorikian
11	Necrotta	Zillamoth	Tyros	Krackeragnian
12	Renix	Karmethian	Gaia 15	Galaxian
13	Oksana Gyr	Genk	Gaia 23	Genkanese
14	Tayla Sawn	Montizoan	Centromere	Galaxian

GAPSS
KNOWLEDGE
MAINFRAME

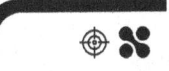 

No.	Name	Species	Homeworld	Language
15	Kiln	Garrangular	Zorik Minor	Garrangulese
16	Pristina	Moxi	Cyanol	Galaxian
17	Vitarus	Omnian	Marstok	Hydraglyphics
18	Rani Romesh	Revan	Revus X	Galaxian
19	Saul Oze	Revan	Revus X	Galaxian
20	Olivia Hondrax	Havokian	Marstok	Winter Song
21	Saffron Été	Genk	Gaia 23	Genkanese
22	Lachrymosa	Pyramist	Pyramax	Ichorian
23	Ox	Zillamoth	Tyros	Krackeragnian
24	Dana Dune	Revan	Revus X	Galaxian
25	Marcy-Kate Scythe	Revan	Revus X	Galaxian
26	Cressida Van Wyrm	Veroselli	Zorik Minor	High Zorikian
27	Aidriendretta Kromm-Nargulantis	Tattorian	Tattoraan	Moon Whisper
28	Harper Hale	Human	Earth	English
29	Ripley Flinch	Revan	Revus X	Galaxian
30	Milton Barclay XVII	Sagaroach	Xenothropod colonies	Gnix

HARPER'S CHOICE

Chalk found herself traversing a cavernous, domed hall. Like the portal chamber, nuts and bolts protruded from an uneven patchwork floor. Orange lines ran in decreasing circles. Black chevrons pointed towards an elevator at the centre of the room. Five sets of double doors hung evenly around the curved walls and rising between each loomed a mighty arch, corroded and flaked with rust, that supported a concave bio-glass ceiling.

"This is the observation hall," Asimov enthused. "And behold, the Waterfall Nebula, one of the nine phenomenological wonders of the SpiralVerse!"

Swirls of dust and ionised gas in every conceivable colour bloomed from a central point. Star trails shimmered, cascading in rivulets to the nebula's edge. Pinching the skin above her GI-VR, Chalk whispered to herself, "Well, Toto. I don't think we're in Kansas anymore."

She whipped her iPhone Firebird from her pocket and tapped the camera app.

"Miss Hale," Asimov called, doubling back. "What are you doing with that?"

"It's my iPhone."

Asimov stared incredulously. "Only Institute-issued devices are permitted on the Coin. I will have to confiscate this for a full diagnostic."

"But why?"

"It could be a threat to the SpiralVerse!"

"It's just an iPhone."

"You have a GI-VR," he said. "A device far superior to this"—Asimov inspected the Harriet Starlight decals on her phone—"technology."

"But it's my—"

"If you'd bothered to read *Introduction to Life, Conduct, and Discipline at the Galactic Institute* then you'd know this by heart!"

He slipped the phone into his jacket, a look of forced compassion on his face.

"But I have everything on my phone! Photos, videos, music. Voice messages from Mum, Grandpa Milo, and my friends on Earth. How am I supposed to contact them without it?"

"Firstly," Asimov began wearily, "personal communication devices will not work at the Galactic Institute. All communication should be conducted using your GI-VR. And—"

"I feel a kicker coming."

"—all homeworld communication in the first cycle is embargoed."

"Embargoed?"

"Yes, embargoed. Banned, restricted, forbidden, hmm?"

"What the actual—?"

"You cannot phone home."

"Why?"

"Again, *Introduction to Life, Conduct, and Discipline at the Galactic Institute* holds the answers to all your questions!"

"That's—"

"Unfair?"

"I was going to say cruel."

"Miss Hale, we've been doing this for thousands of cycles. Students that cling tightly to their homeworlds struggle to engage at the Galactic Institute. They never spread their wings, never truly soar. Trust me, hmm? It's for your own good."

Chalk stared, aghast.

"And don't panic," he assured her, patting his pocket. "I'll take good care of it."

Ahead, green smoke billowed from the breathing apparatus of the hairless girl, while the creature in the watery orb deposited a slug-like trail.

"That is Pristina and Vitarus," Aida said as Asimov spun away. "She breathes poisonous gas and he breathes underwater. Quite the pair. The enormous mech is Ironlung 8-47. I understand he is the first artificial intelligence to successfully enrol at the Galactic Institute."

"Oh snap," said Chalk, pointing at herself. "First human."

"I suppose friendship can be built from even the slimmest commonality."

"I don't usually go for chrome domes." Chalk laughed, but Aida failed to find any humour in her words. "So, what's the deal with Spirit? She seems … intense."

"She is Oneric," Aida said matter-of-factly. "Lives in a metaphysical dreamworld. Onerics have a history of confusing what is real and what is not. Gives them a peculiar confidence. As though the galaxy is theirs for the taking."

"Only-child complex."

"What is that?"

"Doesn't matter."

The ground shook, pulling Chalk and Aida from their conversation. A square of panels rose from the floor. Lights flashed. Horns honked. A vehicle emerged made of battered yellow iron. Three chipped and dented mass-haulage robots stomped over and began unloading the vehicle. Each object appeared to be some sort of tech except for a large rat-like creature that sat quivering inside a clear orb. It reminded Chalk of being in a second-hand console shop or watching re-runs of *The Generation Game* with Grandpa Milo.

"First Cycle Aktari," Asimov began, ticking his layer screens as the robots finished their work. "Before we progress, you must select your eduhelper—a synthetic droid, consciousness, or device—that will accompany you throughout your time at the Galactic Institute."

Chalk's eyes widened.

"Now, as you can see, we have one brand-new AstroTech C1000." Asimov approached an impressive seven-foot humanoid robot, constructed of metallic blue panels with silver trim. A curious amber light glowed within. "State-of-the-art. Shiny and new. Spared no expense."

He moved along the line.

"AstroTech B300s and A420s. Older, but still highly competitive. Now, let me see, what else, hmm? Yes, an Equinox P60, a Chronos Abstract80, a NebulumTek 92Pro-R, a Zenith mystery ball—owner beware—and a selection of TekTonik Touch8s, 9s and 10s for those who want to keep things simple."

Students muttered among themselves, pointing at droids and devices, trying to determine which would be most beneficial to their studies.

Asimov's head snapped towards the portal chamber. Lights inside faded from amber to blue. "Hold everything," he ordered, more forcefully than anything he'd said all day. "Stay right where you are. No touching! I said *no touching*, Master Krieg!"

The professor scuttled away.

"Which eduhelper are you after?" Chalk asked.

Aida twisted the dials on her visor. "There is a lot of interference. I have little to go on other than the smell of manufactured fibres, electricity, oil, resin, and paint. Although …" She paused for a moment. "But I do detect something … foul. Highly obnoxious. I will not be accepting that one."

"Could it be that large rat with huge ears and … a trunk?"

"Sounds like a Qwork. I do not think it is that. The smell is emanating from behind us."

"Oh, yes," Chalk said, suddenly reeling. "I've just got it. That … is … repulsive."

Ripley sidled over. "What is that incredible smell?"

"Honks like vomit."

Ripley pinched his nose and nodded to the eduhelpers. "So much choice. What have you got your eye on?"

"Oh, you're talking to us now?"

"Well, we are relay partners," he explained. "Look, sorry. I didn't mean to be—"

"A snagger?"

"—rude. It's just, you know, a lot."

"Um, yeah, sure," Chalk said, easing a little. "But we're all in the same boat."

"What's a boat?"

"Really?" Chalk said, and Ripley frowned. "It's a sea-faring vessel. Travels on water."

"Water is for drinking," Ripley said. "Earthlings travel on it? Why?"

"Ignore him," Aida said. "The Revus planets have no lakes or oceans and Revans themselves are untrustworthy, selfish creatures."

"You should judge us on a case-by-case basis."

"The C1000 will lead desirability," Aida went on, ignoring him. "The other AstroTech models would be advantageous too. Your own private security."

Chalk found this immediately appealing.

"What does the Zenith mystery ball look like?" Aida asked.

"Just a shiny black ball."

"Zenith mystery balls are a lottery," Ripley added. "Hence the name. Could be the best thing out there, could be the worst. You want to risk your entire education on a gamble?"

"So, we're all going for the AstroTech C1000?"

"It is clearly the best option, but I doubt any of us will get it."

"Why not?" Chalk asked, wafting the smell from her nostrils.

"History dictates that one of the Veroselli or Garrangulars will land the best tech."

"Hardly seems fair. Who's deciding this?"

"Don't panic. I'm back now!" Professor Asimov rounded up the students and dragged the recent arrival before them. "Milton Barclay XVII," he announced. "Sagaroach. Specialisms: History of the Galaxy. Primaries: History of the Galaxy."

Chalk stared at Milton Barclay XVII. He looked incredibly similar to his father, the Sagaroach who had attended the Declaration of Interplanetary Inclusivity. But Milton Barclay XVII didn't stand with the same pride and confidence. He shifted uneasily from one spindly leg to the other. His pincers snapped as he took brief, frantic breaths. Reaching back, Milton pulled a strange object from a large canvas holdall he wore over shiny wings. It looked like a cucumber, but sickly yellow and dotted with dark, mushy patches. Taking a large bite, the horrific smell that invaded Chalk's senses became so bad she wanted to faint.

Most of First Cycle Aktari hurled objections at Milton. The Sagaroach looked utterly out of place, terrified and alone. His blue robes were shredded around the hem and one of his antennae drooped at a peculiar angle.

"I'd hate to be that guy's relay partner," Chalk grimaced.

Milton finished the rancid cucumber, attempted a smile, and waved his middle legs at Ripley. Chalk and Aida turned to the Revan.

"Shut up," Ripley said, noticing Chalk's smirk. "Just shut it."

"Enough, enough," Professor Asimov said, regaining First Cycle Aktari's attention. "If the smell of Milton's yuccagourds are overwhelming, your GI-VR sensitivity levels can be adjusted. Of course, this will reduce your sense of smell across the board. But be careful, a reduction to any of your senses could seriously impede your performance here at the Galactic Institute."

"That smell is going to impede my ability to breathe!" said one of the Garrangulars.

"Yeah, my lunch is already bolting for an exit," said another with a laugh.

"Okay, okay. That's quite enough vulgarity, hmm?"

"But I rely on my sense of smell to navigate," Aida protested, her voice lost in the commotion of students tapping their GI-VRs and sighing with relief as the noisome stench washed away. "This is highly unreasonable."

"I'll brave it with you," Chalk said, leaving her settings alone.

"That is immeasurably virtuous."

"And now, thanks to Lord Barclay, we are one point three hours behind schedule," Asimov said, pacing aggressively.

Milton shuffled over to Ripley.

He nodded, said nothing, and reached for another yuccagourd.

Bile rose in Chalk's throat.

"As I was saying, your eduhelper will be with you through all six cycles—if you make it that far—and will play a critical role in how you learn, how you revise, and how you graduate. Choose wisely, for not all is as it seems." Professor Asimov backed away from the eduhelpers, his arms trailing theatrically. "Oh, sorry," he piped up, jumping back to centre stage. "Forgot a salient snippet of information. Eduhelpers are chosen based on the results of the Data Drive Relay. Fastest goes first."

Chalk groaned. She'd taken ages, or so it seemed. Stupid Snider stalking her in the library stacks had cost her dear. She'd definitely beaten Milton, so she wasn't going to be last. Professor Asimov turned to a Veroselli with flawless mauve skin and waist-length crystal-white hair. She dripped with elegant robes, jewels and accessories.

"Princess Cressida Van Wyrm. Excellent time today. You have the honour."

Sure enough, Princess Cressida Van Wyrm chose the AstroTech C1000. The other Veroselli—Clementine Von Wax and Claridge Von Whump—congratulated her, clicking their fingers in a strange rhythm that Chalk surmised was the Veroselli equivalent of applause.

Krieg, a muscular Garrangular came next. He selected the AstroTech B420, a battle droid that looked like it could smash a hole in the spacetime continuum.

"Well, that is all the predictable decisions made," Aida said.

"And all the coolest tech gone."

"Not necessarily," the Tattorian replied. "Just because something is substantial and shiny and expensive does not mean it is the right choice for the individual. With the Veroselli and the Garrangulars, it is all about posturing and performance. I doubt they draw a fraction of the worth from their AstroTechs."

One by one the class made their selections.

"Miss Kromm-Nargulantis," said Professor Asimov. "Fourteenth fastest. What will it be?"

"The Chronos Abstract80," she replied without hesitation.

"Ah," the professor purred. "An excellent choice, hmm?"

Aida's eduhelper looked like a point-cut diamond floating a foot above the ground. All ten sides shimmered with a mirror-glaze that did not reflect its immediate surroundings. Aida pressed her claw to the side of the device and one of Asimov's layer screens turned blue.

The next round of students—including most of the Revans—plumped for the safety of TekTonik Touch tablets. Ironlung 8-47 received his Qwork, named Grimcrack, who shivered nervously as the large cybernetic student shook the translucent orb in greeting. Eduhelper choices became slimmer and slimmer. And, as the options dwindled, Chalk grew more and more anxious.

"We must have been incredibly slow," Chalk whispered.

Ripley grumbled. "Yeah, there was way more to it than I was told."

"You *knew* what was going to happen?"

"Not exactly. Each relay is unique, but loads of Revans have run it before, so—"

"Oh, yeah. Sure."

"First Earthling, huh?"

"Intergalactic guinea pig."

Ripley looked puzzled.

"And so, we come to the final three," Asimov enthused, but most of First Cycle Aktari had wandered off, inspecting their eduhelpers and chatting among themselves. "We have the St4rCr4ft™ 85R—a vintage reconnaissance droid, a Zenith buddy droid, and the mystery ball. Miss Hale, you were twenty-eighth fastest. Your choice, please."

"I beat Ripley?" she exploded. "Ha!"

Struggling to contain her amusement, Chalk considered each eduhelper in turn.

The St4rCr4ft™ 85R. Old, sizeable, and cumbersome.

The Zenith buddy droid. Cute, but badly damaged.

The mystery ball. A complete enigma.

"So, what are *you* thinking?" she asked the Revan.

"It's not my decision," he replied, arms crossed, his ego clearly bruised.

Milton stared over Chalk's shoulder, chewing nervously on a yuccagourd.

"You must have a preference," she insisted. "Or one you don't want."

"I'll take whatever," Ripley said, "but the mystery ball is a genuine gamble."

"I definitely came last," Milton said, his pincers firing tiny flecks of yuccagourd in all directions. "I'm the worst. I deserve the worst."

Chalk's heart ached for him.

"But which *is* the worst?" she said. "They all look like tricky choices."

"Of these," Milton replied. "The St4rCr4ft™ 85R is the oldest. Has the most damage. Its operating system is undoubtedly outdated and redundant. The user-interface is cracked. I guess that's mine."

Chalk frowned, arms folded. "You sure?"

"Categorically."

"Well, that decides it." She stepped forward and pointed. "I'll take the mystery ball."

Ripley gasped.

Professor Asimov nodded, fussed his moustache, and retrieved the eduhelper. The device was a touch bigger than a basketball with a smooth, black finish.

"What does it do?"

"You'll see, hmm?"

As the mystery ball fell into Chalk's hands, a tiny word in digitised lettering appeared on the side: INCUBE-8. A panel opened, displaying an unblemished touchscreen. Chalk pressed her thumb to the panel and the entire ball rippled with hoops of vivid orange light.

Every student looked over, the observation hall covered in long, vibrating shadows. And then, as quickly as it had come, the light vanished, and the ball returned to its original black preset.

"Here is its transportation rig," Asimov said, presenting her with a magnetised concave housing connected to shoulder straps. Chalk hoisted the straps over her shoulders. The mystery ball snapped into place. "It doesn't float or roll along on its own or anything exciting like that?"

"The mystery ball?" Asimov scoffed. "I shouldn't imagine so." He turned to Ripley. "Master Flinch?"

"Looks like I'm getting the battered barrel."

"The Zenith buddy droid!" the professor enthused. "An oldie, but a goodie."

The lopsided machine jolted to life, its bandy legs and arms—composed of chipped metal rods—stood to attention. Green lights on its lid spun in excited circles.

BING!

"I think he likes you," the professor said.

"Aw," Chalk said. "You've got a friend."

"I'd prefer the C1000." Ripley inspected the decals on his eduhelper. "Oh, it's an INFIN-8 droid."

"Is that good?"

"Yeah. It'll do."

URRRH! INFIN-8 buzzed loudly. Red lights glowed on the other side of its lid.

"You made it sad."

"I doubt it can feel," Ripley said, dropping to his knees and inspecting the damaged, hapless-looking machine.

"And Master Barclay XVII. For you, sir, I present the St4rCr4ft™ 85R."

Milton stared at the bulky box, its cracked screen a black mirror.

"The St4rCr4ft™ 85R!" Asimov said again, slamming a hand onto the lid as if to encourage it.

The box juddered and shook. The monitor pulsed with a flickering green glow. It honked aggressively. Four stubby legs ground into action and turned to face Milton. "A Sagaroach," the St4rCr4ft™ 85R moaned in a posh male voice consisting equal parts surprise and disdain. "One of my previous masters spent his entire life trying to eradicate you lot. It would appear he failed."

Milton pushed another yuccagourd into his face.

GAPSS
KNOWLEDGE
MAINFRAME

 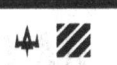

VEROSELLI
[SPECIES]

Homeworld: Zorik Minor, Lang. High Zorikian

An indigenous species from the Zorik System, the Veroselli
are elegant, erudite bipeds who regard power and technology
as central to their existence. They hold positions in every
critical department at GAPSS, are skilled engineers,
warriors, and Casters. The Veroselli are one of the three
oldest known civilisations in the SpiralVerse.

BANQUETING ROTUNDA

With every member of First Cycle Aktari designated an eduhelper, Professor Asimov led them across the observation hall and into yet another broken-down room. Two apertures punctuated the far wall, a foot above a raised platform. Pin lights, like those around portals, circled each. Green on the left, blue on the right.

A steady breeze swirled dust and lichen in mini tornados.

AGT WARNING . . .

"Warning?" Chalk said. "What are we in danger of? Mild windburn?"

"This is an anti-gravity transporter. AGT for short," Asimov explained. "Unlike portals, the AGT can take you to any place on campus without deconstructing and reconstructing your entire atomic make-up. Inside the AGT, you'll be propelled by our Tempest T7 wind-turbine system. Use your arms and body weight to alter your trajectory, much like avians or starfighters, hmm? I'm sure you do not need me to inform you that the AGT is omni-directional. Embarkation and disembarkation are gained through pods like the ones before you."

"What *is* this?" Chalk whispered.

"Not got an AGT on Earth?" Ripley replied.

"We have waterslides. Is it like that?"

"Slides. Boats. Is Earth made entirely of water?"

"Seventy-three per cent of the surface is."

"That's terrifying."

"Once you've traversed the embarkation pod, you'll descend into the hyperloop—positioned directly beneath us at the heart of Centurion H. From there you can access any destination on the Coin. Today, we are going to the banqueting rotunda where General Waxler and the rest of the school are waiting to welcome you."

Cressida's hair and gowns rippled gently as she edged towards the blue pin lights.

"Now, one at a time, step forward and hold the support rail."

Cressida swung herself through the opening. Her body levitated the instant she released the support rail and shot out of sight. Her C1000 bolted after her. Scrambling to be next, the remaining Veroselli and their eduhelpers vanished from sight.

"Good, good! Come on, everyone. We are already phenomenally late."

One by one, Pristina and Necrotta and Vitarus and the rest of First Cycle Aktari filtered into the AGT. Chalk fastened and refastened the straps to the mystery ball before following Ripley, Milton, and Aida to the foot of the platform.

The Tattorian hesitated as wind thundered by.

"Given the fact Aida cannot see, is this a smart idea?" Chalk said to Professor Asimov.

"I am fine," Aida told her admonishingly. "I can smell the banqueting rotunda from here."

"And she has a Chronos Abstract80. Incredibly handy for navigation!"

"Is that so?" Chalk said. "What is my mystery ball good for?"

The professor raised an eyebrow and turned to Aida. "Time to go, Miss Kromm-Nargulantis."

Aida stepped into the AGT and shot off like a rocket. Her Chronos Abstract80 buzzed along in hot pursuit.

Chalk mounted the steps, grasped the support rail, and glanced inside. Wind rushed by at an incredible rate. A strange pressure pulled and pressed against her, stirring the smell of hot rubber. She faltered, looked for Ripley, but the Revan had been overwhelmed by Spirit's incessant touching. INFIN-8 loitered beside him like a loyal dog.

"It's easier if you let go, Miss Hale."

Chalk refocused. "Like this," she said, twisting her hips and dropping backwards into the AGT.

"Miss Hale!" Asimov cried. "You're facing the wrong way!"

Engines and machinery, pipes and tubes, lasers and flickering diodes sped past at breakneck speed. Hoops of light shot around her, changing from blue to amber as she flew backwards, descending towards the hyperloop. Wriggling her hips, she managed to turn just as she emerged from the on-tube. Here, she burst into a huge space where students and staff and eduhelpers spun in an anti-clockwise direction, like ingredients in a giant cauldron.

Her vertigo spiked, logic insisting that she would drop out of the air and splat like a watermelon. Instead, she glided onward. Her jacket rippled. Pink hair flapped over one eye. By angling her arms and fanning her fingers, she found she could swoop and soar around the hyperloop, like a bird in flight.

The urge to squeal like an overexcited child fizzed on her tongue.

Cressida hurtled by, mounted on her AstroTech C1000 whose feet fired jets of white smoke. Chalk coughed and choked on the AstroTech's discharge. Gathering herself, she rose above the chaos and let the hyperloop carry her round and round until—

"Ouch!"

A cumbersome object clipped her shoulder and went careening into the centre of the hyperloop, where thick pipes and bulky tech rose from one side of the Coin to the other.

"Sorry," yelled Milton, tumbling end over end after his St4rCr4ft™ 85R like a rolled die. "I'm not good at this."

Ripley swept in beside her. "Well, this is not what I imagined I'd be doing today."

Chalk laughed. "Me either. I was all keyed up for a walking

tour and a thousand half-answered questions."

"Well, we got the half-answered questions bit."

"I guess so. Where's your … buddy?"

"INFIN-8? I'm not sure," Ripley said, gazing around. "He was reluctant to follow me but he'll be around here somewhere."

"Figured out what he's good for yet?"

"Nope. You?"

"The mystery ball? Not a clue."

"Miss Hale! Master Flinch! What are you doing lallygagging around in the hyperloop? I expressly informed *all* First Cycle Aktari to proceed to the banqueting rotunda." The professor expertly drifted between them, thrust all four palms into their backs and propelled them toward the outer rim. "Keep your eyes locked on the exit. Arriving in three … two … one."

Apologising to the professor, Chalk glided to the right and took the off-tube for the banqueting rotunda. Circles of amber light turned to green as they approached the disembarkation pod. Ripley and Chalk clasped the support rail and swung themselves out of the AGT.

Landing awkwardly, Chalk was completely unprepared for the change in atmospheric pressure. She tripped, knocked Ripley to the floor, and landed on top of him.

"Some practice needed, hmm?"

Chalk lay above Ripley, their noses fractions apart. "Sorry. I can be a real bonehead sometimes."

"No, clearly my fault."

Chalk's cheeks bloomed.

Slowly, she looked up.

Every optical was on them.

Cressida laughed first. The rest joined in. Everyone, that is, besides an irksome-looking Spirit whose face had turned to thunder.

The banqueting rotunda was packed with over seven hundred students from all six cycles. The waft of numerous challenging cuisines caught at the back of Chalk's throat. She glanced at her GI-VR. The compulsion to access her sense settings and dial the aroma down to zero was overwhelming.

Like the observation hall, rank and rusty walls rose on all sides, capped with a dome of filthy bio-glass. A halo of vivid light swept the circumference of the room, pulsing and humming gently. Twenty-four enormous circular tables were positioned evenly across the room. Thirty chairs orbited each. First cycle students from the other three chronotype shifts—Osmotrino, Zalazor, and Qantoculus—were already seated.

Asimov descended the disembarkation pod. "Welcome, First Cycle Aktari," he said, "to the banqueting rotunda. Leave your eduhelpers here, please. I'll have them transported to your dorm."

Students surged for the table.

"Now, now," the professor piped up. "Don't be hasty. Seating positions are dictated by the order you *ran* the Data Drive Relay, not who finished quickest!"

Krieg snarled.

Kiln and Kroket loomed imposingly behind him.

"Seat one, for example," Asimov said, turning and running his hand along the back of a numbered, beaten chair, "belongs to the first person to carry the data drive." He checked his layer screens. "Oh," he said. "My apologies, Master Krieg. This is your seat."

The indignant Garrangular ripped the chair from Asimov's hand and sank down. "Second was Sadler Arklan of the Vyshan Order, then Clementine—" Asimov swept around the table proffering each chair, but First Cycle Aktari quickly worked it out for themselves. Aida took her seat next to Cressida Van Wyrm with Chalk to her right, and Ripley beyond.

"Yes, yes, correct, perfect," Asimov purred as he scurried around the table, checking names and positions. He arrived behind Milton. "Ah, Lord Barclay," he said. "As you were the last to face the relay you had no one to pass the data drive to, hmm?"

Milton turned to face the muscular Garrangular beside him.

"So, we simply partner you with the first. Krieg, Milton. Milton, Krieg. Super. Perfect."

Before Milton could object, sections of table retracted, spun, and returned with a dented copper charger. Next, the centre of the table slipped away and half a dozen chrome-plated arms shot towards them. Chalk and Ripley shuddered in their seats as robotic arms placed smaller—but no less dented—tin plates and bowls loaded with food before them.

Steam rose from some. Others fizzed and smoked. Some *moved*.

Chalk got a simple plate of neatly sliced fruit, cubes of pungent cheese, and a garnish of leaves.

Ripley got a hot broth.

Yuccagourds appeared for the Sagaroach.

Strangely, Aida's charger remained empty.

The arms retracted. A sturdy column rose to face them. Metal projectiles fired out of barrels along the shaft, each skidding to a halt beside their plates. Chalk stared down. A knife, fork, and spoon. Sort of.

Another chrome-plated arm jangled goblets, glasses, and tankards towards them. Round and round it went, like the minute hand of a clock, until everybody had been provided with a beverage.

Except Aida.

Chalk sipped a heavily concentrated squash. She couldn't really tell what flavour it was. Perhaps an incredibly rare fruit from the jungles of Revus X, she imagined. Ripley got a hot drink that bubbled and fizzed like cola. Hovering in front of Milton, the machine took a moment to dispense a thick yellow-brown mush that spluttered and choked from the serving nozzle.

"Yuccagourd smoothie?" Chalk asked, her nose wrinkled.

Milton slurped it down in one.

The centre of the table rotated with napkins, additional cutlery, and baskets of bread, crackers, fruit, and stacks of things Chalk could not name.

Spearing a wedge of triangular fruit, she looked at Aida's empty charger.

"Where's yours?" she asked. "Is it … invisible?"

"Do not be absurd."

"Do you want me to go and get help?"

"No. It is fine."

"Seriously, it's not a problem," Chalk said, scanning the room for Professor Asimov.

"Sit down, Chalk."

"But they've forgotten your dinner."

"I … do not eat," Aida explained. "I mean, I do not *need* to eat."

"What?" Chalk said, returning to her seat. "You're not … hungry?"

Ripley and Milton leant in.

Aida seemed to sense their attention. "I am Tattorian. Yes, we are blind. And no, we do not eat. I understand you are all confused by this. I have a mouth, but no teeth. A throat, but no digestive system."

"So, you don't need to—?" Ripley began.

Chalk slapped him on the arm. "Inappropriate."

"No," Aida answered. "We produce no effluence, so have no need to—"

"So you're never hungry?" asked Milton, wide-eyed.

"Or tired?" Ripley added. "Thoden help me! Have you *never* thrown up?"

Chalk turned to him. Her eyes thinned.

"As Tattorians, we are born with all the energy we need to sustain ourselves. Like a fully-charged battery. We call it our lifeforce."

"That's genuinely amazing," Chalk enthused. "A finite lifeforce. Sort of like an existence warranty."

Aida huffed. "We are *not* manufactured goods."

"All life is," Ripley said. "To some degree."

Aida shrugged. "Just the way of life on Tattoraan."

"Do you—?" Ripley started.

"Is this another question about bodily functions?"

"Not at all."

"Proceed."

Giving Chalk a curious frown, Ripley asked, "So, you can decide? How you live, I mean. Slow and steady or all blasters blazing?"

"Very astute. And yes, small factions of Tattorian culture encourage this sort of behaviour. Many young Tattorians join our military, expecting to die in some horrific battle, and burn through their lifeforce on thrills and revelry. Some hibernate, decades at a time, and wake during times of change, learning new technologies and customs before returning to their incubations."

"You can … pause your life?" Chalk asked, her imagination overloading.

Ripley whistled approvingly. "That's incredible."

Chalk considered him again. "What about you?" she asked. "You look human, but you're not from Earth."

"Ugh," Princess Cressida Van Wyrm moaned, pointing a long knife at Ripley. "Enough already. He's a Revan, same as Dana Dune and the rest—descendants of thieves and murderers. Milton is a repulsive Sagaroach. Krieg and the other hairy louts are Garrangulars." She stabbed the large carving knife into the table where it juddered menacingly and shifted her gaze to Chalk. "I'm Veroselli. Erudite leaders and rightful heirs to the throne of Zorik Minor. And you're an incipient Earthling. Are we done with Astro Anthropology for today?"

"Erudite leaders? Rightful heirs?" Krieg yelled across the table. "Lies and falsehood!"

Kiln and Kroket were already on their feet, cutlery raised, poised for a confrontation.

"What is happening?" said Aida.

"The Roses and Grangs don't like each other," Ripley whispered to Chalk.

"You don't say."

"Zorik Minor is ours," Cressida seethed.

"You barely understand the nature of Zorik Minor," Krieg barked back. "You hide in your pale cities on perilous mountain tops. The heart of Zorik Minor is in the dirt and rock and stone."

"Caves and mines and jewels," Cressida scoffed. "The Garrangulan obsession with zorikanthium was the breaking of our world."

"Is that so?"

"It very much is."

"I very much doubt that."

"I very much doubt you have the mental capacity for a sliver of rational consideration."

"Why you—"

At this point, Krieg's voice became muted and replaced by—

INAPPROPRIATE LANGUAGE DETECTED . . .

"—on the crust of my heel!"

"Now, now, now! Calm down, everybody. We're still on appetisers," fired Professor Asimov, dashing down from the faculty platform and orbiting the table.

Cressida ripped the knife from the table and settled into her chair.

Krieg's entire body pulsed with rage.

"Please, Master Krieg. Return to your seat."

Snorting, the Garrangular coiled his huge fists around the hilt of two curved blades and lowered his massive body into the chair.

Beside him, Milton shook like a leaf. Ripley did nothing to calm his relay partner. Instead, he spooned steaming broth into his mouth and tapped absent-mindedly on his GI-VR. Asimov shuffled off, muttering to himself about the need for a much overdue full-system-diagnostic of the attitude easing atmospheric system.

Next, Chalk's plate bulged with a juicy nut roast. Ripley got a triple-stacked biletongue sandwich, while Milton's yuccagourd bonanza continued apace. Aida sat politely before her empty plate.

"Milton," Ripley said, eyeing the tower of putrid fruit. "At the risk of asking a stupid question, have you ever thought about trying something else? The smell alone is ghastly and I doubt you're getting much in the way of nutrients from those abhorrent things."

Milton ripped a yuccagourd in half. The middle oozed onto his plate like a slug's innards. "Look, I'm not trying to be annoying. Or different. Or interesting."

"You've succeeded at that," Ripley quipped, and Chalk elbowed his ribs.

"But Sagaroaches have an impossibly strict diet."

"Not as strict as Aida's!"

Chalk gave up.

"We're highly allergic," Milton said, "to anything, to everything, except the mighty yuccagourd. And you're right—"

"First time for everything," Chalk laughed, getting one back.

"—they contain barely any nutritional value. They're mostly water. As a result, we need to eat hundreds of them every rotation to survive."

The banqueting rotunda's halo light flashed amber, then blue. Everyone swivelled to face the faculty platform above the AGT.

"Welcome," General Waxler began, rising from the table. "Welcome back to those of you on the second cycle. I am sure it was a relief to avoid the Data Drive Relay prior to enrolment this year."

A murmur of agreement swelled from the second cycle tables.

"Remember," she said, earnestly. "This is your second cycle, your last chance to experiment with your Specialisms and Primaries before you solidify them for the start of the third.

Talking of which, everyone in the third cycle has now locked in your choices. A few have surprised me but I am satisfied for the most part. I am hoping to see great things as you progress through this cycle and into the next. Fours and fives, these are important rotations and phases for you. Hard rotations and phases. A strong work ethic, dedication, and determination are of paramount importance. The end may seem lightcycles away, but it will be upon you before you know it. Make sure you arrive prepared, equipped, and ready for the challenge. Sixth cycle students, I will say a small prayer to all the Gods and wish you well on this cycle of scrutiny, final examinations, and—the part I know you are all excited about—the Departure Relay."

Sixth cycle students grumbled.

"Just kidding, the *Orbit Strike!* tournament finals, of course!"

Students whooped and jeered, banging cutlery and chargers against the tables.

"And the biggest welcome of all goes to our first cycle. Well, what can I say? Good luck to each one of you. Go forth with open, curious minds. Discover. Question. Analyse … and have fun. You are only in the first cycle once. It gets much harder from here."

Excitement burbled in Chalk's chest. True, she was at school, but a school like no other.

"And, of course, I nearly forgot," Waxler added. "The GAPSS outreach programme has successfully enrolled their first-ever student from the Quora-13 System—a developing world known as Earth. I am sure you will make our first Earthling—and all the first cycle students—very welcome here at the Galactic Institute."

The entire student population clapped, clicked, honked, and tooted customary noises and gestures as General Waxler tipped her head. "Your cycle leaders will distribute timetables this evening. Be sure to check your GI-VR for updates, changes, and clashes. Report any issues to your cycle leaders."

She glanced at Chalk and the first cycle tables.

"That'll be Professor Mirage for Osmotrino, Professor Snider for Zalazor, Professor de Rema for Qantoculus, and all you First Cycle Aktari students have the pleasure of Professor Asimov."

INAPPROPRIATE LANGUAGE DETECTED . . .

GAPSS
KNOWLEDGE
MAINFRAME

CLASS SHIFTS
[CHRONOTYPES] [CONSTRUCT]

Students at the Galactic Institute are grouped into one of four class shifts [also known as chronotypes or sleeping patterns] designed to approximate rotation lengths observed on their homeworlds.

Class Shift	Waking Hours	Sleeping Hours	Mascot
Aktari	20	8	Fenray
Osmotrino	30	12	Niffinaglor
Zalazor	42	14	Sawtooth
Qantoculus	84	28	Flittermist

FIRST CYCLE DORMS

First Cycle Aktari snaked across the Coin inside the AGT. The transport tubes emerged above ground and barrelled arrow-straight across the surface of the Galactic Institute. Buildings and plazas zoomed by. Bridges and causeways looped overhead. Chalk rose sharply, orbiting a squat building that sprouted four massive towers with vast wrap-around windows. Regimented hexagonal portholes peppered the surface. Pipes and vents hissed with blue-grey steam.

The disembarkation pod was upon her before she'd realised what was happening. Thankfully, Asimov hung in the way, one arm coiled around the safety railing, the other three batting disorientated students like tennis balls.

"The AGT is *not* a toy," the professor said, landing softly and straightening his jacket. "Concentrate when using it. I'd hate to find any of you in a tailspin or catatonically circling the hyperloop. If you're unable to master the AGT or dislike the sensation, walkways and travellators are available."

"What about portals?"

"Master Flinch. Portals are dangerous and incredibly expensive devices. Portal travel from one end of the Coin to the other is not advisable. In fact, it's just plain lazy, hmm? And don't attempt anything until you've had your Introduction to Portals seminar with Professor de Rema or you could end up in a hundred billion pieces."

Most students had stopped listening and were exploring the

first cycle recreation room. Display shelves containing ceramics and potted plants semi-circled one wall, while a matrix of monitors occupied the other. News, sport, and entertainment channels from across the galaxy, along with student and faculty profiles flickered on each.

One read, *Danger Level*: FINE.

Asimov directed them to the first-floor landing where everyone gravitated to the huge, curved window that encompassed half the room. Endless questions battered the professor. "Maps and detailed information are available on your GI-VR," he fussed, waving away the interrogation. "Familiarise yourself. Tardiness will not be tolerated after phase one. Oh, and access to the Flipside—like the portals, Master Flinch—is prohibited until you've had your introductory tour. And once again, don't try to sneak around the security protocols. You'll end up in a huge heap of trouble … or as demanufactured plasma."

Chalk turned to Aida and Ripley. "Flipside?"

"Underneath."

"Underneath what?"

"Underneath the Coin."

"There's another side?"

"It is nicknamed the Coin for a reason."

Ripley pulled a face.

Chalk fired her best hate-smile. "What's on the Flipside?"

"Biomass speculators, geochemical labs, and hydroponics," said Aida.

"But to you and me," Ripley said, "parks, fountains, and woodland."

Many of First Cycle Aktari disappeared to investigate the bedrooms and lower levels while the rest breezed around the living quarters. Chalk, Ripley, Aida, and Milton stood side by side for a time, staring out over the Galactic Institute.

Blue lights flashed on each cycle's dorm tower. Students and eduhelpers fizzed through the exposed AGT pipes, climbing and diving through each quadrant, zipping about the campus.

As the Coin twisted through space, sunlight reflected off the observation hall at the centre. Beautiful double rainbows flared against the edge of the environsphere.

"Who's desperate to see where they sleep?" Ripley said eventually.

"And find out what our eduhelpers can do?" Aida added.

Chalk thrust an arm into the air as though she'd won a race.

Milton scoffed a yuccagourd and followed them upstairs.

On a wide oval landing, Chalk's GI-VR activated the door to room 28. Aida had the room to the left. Ripley, the right. Washed with cool blue downlights, Chalk's room widened—like a slice of cake—from the doorway to a high wall set with a hexagonal window. A double bed with crisp sheets and dark duvet lurked against the wall. A thin metal chest of drawers faced the bed while a desk, battered chair, and scuffed wardrobe with lopsided doors nestled either side. The patchwork of badly soldered treadplate had been replaced by a threadbare carpet. It lay wall to wall, spotted with stains and spillages of unknown origin.

Chalk kicked off her shoes and jumped on the bed. She stared through the hexagonal bio-glass at the Waterfall Nebula. The vast interstellar cloud bloomed before her. A sprawling cosmic web of gas and dust, surrounded by clusters of ancient stars.

Her skin rippled.

Her soul sang.

From her bedroom in 10 Downing Street, she could see the grey swell of the Thames and a rising, black smog. This was a vast improvement. She wondered where they were in the Milky Way—the SpiralVerse—and how far she was from home. Memories transported her to a time before the Hundred Hours War, to the banks of the Serpentine in Regent's Park, feeding birds, chatting with Kit, Bloue, and Zara, sipping flat whites and nibbling cinnamon churros. The yearn for home—for Mum and Dad and Grandpa Milo—tugged at her heart.

Chalk's suitcase was positioned behind the door. Upholstered in dark tartan, she'd accessorised it with canvas patches of skulls and band logos. She unzipped it and retrieved a stack of paperbacks. *The Adventures of Kaylor the Unknown*, *The Hunger Games*, *Angelina Angel: Interplanetary Detective*, *The Prisoner of Azkaban*, and the complete *Harriet Starlight* decalogy. Flicking through the pages, Chalk inhaled deeply. The musty smell of well-thumbed paper and ink charged her bones.

She'd only left this morning, but it felt like a lifetime.

She stacked the books side by side on the desk along with her Boba Fett bobblehead. Next, she turned to the chest of drawers. On top, nestled beside a strange miniature tree with vivid red leaves, was her eduhelper.

The Zenith mystery ball.

INCUBE-8.

Nervously lifting the black orb, Chalk spun it over and over, trying to decipher if she needed to press a button or a switch or solve a clue to operate the device.

What am I doing wrong?

The black ball vibrated beneath her fingertips.

Then—

INITIALISING . . .

Initialising what?

LOADING . . .

Loading what?

INSTALLING . . .

Chalk hardly dare breathe.

GENERATING PROFILE . . .

Her heart pounded like a galloping stallion.

ACTIVATE?

"Um—"

Her brain became scrambled, disorientated, scared and unsure.

ACTIVATE?

The word blinked again and again.

"Sure," she said. Every muscle tightened, primed to toss the ball over her shoulder and bolt for the door. "I mean, yes. *YES.* Engage. Um, activate. Make it so."

ACTIVATING . . .

Air whistled gently from an aperture around the circumference of the mystery ball. Instinctively, Chalk dropped it onto the bed and scuttled away. A thin white line formed a horizontal hoop. The top half rose, turned, hissed, then sprang open.

Chalk stifled a scream.

Her dimly lit room suddenly swarmed with glorious orange light.

Chalk shielded her eyes.

What is this? A lava lamp? A ball of light? Liquid-hot magma?

What sat inside truly astonished her.

It wasn't a lamp or a light or captured hellfire. But more curiously, it didn't appear to be a computer or a digital device either. Resting in the lower half of the mystery ball was a vivid orange amorphous blob. It undulated and pulsed, stretching and sprouting with long, jellified fingers.

Chalk gathered her limbs and pressed herself against the headboard.

The blob grew, changed shape, expanded and stretched. Part of it flowed onto the floor, the rest positioned on the bed. Chalk's eyes narrowed as the blob became defined. Fluctuating curves smoothed into angles and edges, legs and arms, a torso and a head.

It seemed to be sitting like Chalk.

It *was* Chalk.

A mirror image.

A face manifested on its globulous orange head.

A hand shot to her mouth as she looked back at her own horrified face.

"Wh-what are you?" she said, rolling off the bed and creeping nervously for the door.

The orange blob copied her every move, posing like the frightened girl.

"I am INCUBE-8."

"Wha—huh?"

Chalk hadn't expected a reply, much less to hear the eduhelper respond in her own voice.

"Stop that," she said, raising a flat palm. "It's creepy."

INCUBE-8 mirrored her, then dropped the hand to its side. "Sorry."

"The voice too."

"I did not mean to upset you," it said, now an androgynous teenager.

Chalk could barely believe her eyes. She'd been expecting a mechanical device. A robot, a cute little droid, perhaps a tablet, at least a pencil and paper, but this—

"Are you okay?" said INCUBE-8. "Your adrenaline levels are spiking and your heart rate is elevated."

"Huh?" Chalk mumbled, unable to force anything better out. She took a moment to steady herself. "I've been better."

"Perhaps I should introduce myself," it said. "And you can reciprocate. Having a mutual understanding of each other's strengths and weaknesses will significantly improve our compatibility and produce a much more effective study force."

A clump of pink hair swung across her face.

"Miss Hale?"

"Yes," she said, her mind reeling. "Activate. Proceed. Erm. Tell me about … you."

"I am INCUBE-8. Amorphous digital consciousness." It stopped for a moment. "Would you like the manufacturer-approved marketing spiel or something more candid?"

"Both," Chalk replied, surprised at her own response.

"U-hum," INCUBE-8 said, clearing a throat it did not have. The heroic sweep of strings and the rumble of drums erupted from somewhere inside the droid. "Behold! A SpiralVerse phenomenon! A first for the galaxy and the universe as we know it! IN—CUBE—EIGHT! You've heard the rumours, you've read the conspiracies, now *see* the truth! Zenith Industries brings you the first fully interactive amorphous … digital … consciousness. Smart. Fast. Reliable. Adaptable. Personable. *Product of the Century* says Spacetime Magazine. *Nothing short of a miracle* claims High-King Cillian Van Wyrm. *The Gods will hear of this!* wailed undisclosed Vyshan Order spokesperson." The music dropped to a low rumble. "INCUBE-8 … from Zenith Industries. It's … ALIVE!" A flourish of music exploded into the room, then quickly died. "Available at all good stockists."

"Most impressive," Chalk said, her face softening.

"Thank you," INCUBE-8 replied, pretending to crack its knuckles. "In simple terms, I am a gelatinous entity. A combination of fluid DNA and binary code. I am connected to the GAPSS Knowledge Mainframe, can perform any tasks you would expect from a TekTonik Touch, yet uniquely can transform into any shape, a feature you will find undoubtedly beneficial."

"INCUBE-8," Chalk said, drumming her bottom lip.

"Yes?"

"No, I mean, your name. INCUBE-8."

"It is somewhat descriptive, I must admit."

"It's a bit of a mouthful too."

"I do not think so," it said. "Your relay buddy, Miss Aidriendretta Kromm-Nargulantis' name is a mouthful."

"True." Chalk nodded. "But how about Inc? Or Cube? Or just Eight?"

"How about Nimrod or Balzarina?"

"Really?"

"What you decide to call me will not affect my ability to assist you in every matter, conflict, or problem you may encounter here at the Galactic Institute."

"I like Cube," Chalk said, clicking her fingers.

"Very well, Miss Hale."

"And you can call me Chalk."

"Yes, Miss Chalk—"

"Just Chalk."

UPDATING . . .

"It said in your marketing blurb that you're ... ALIVE! Is that true?"

"Salesmanship razzle-dazzle, I am sure. You see, I am conscious—which would denote I am alive—yet I do not breathe or possess what many refer to as a soul."

"Oh." Chalk nodded. "You're like a vampire."

RESEARCHING . . .

"I suppose so," Cube replied. "But without the desire to consume the blood of the living or to sire others into my brood."

Chalk giggled. "Can you be killed?"

"Are you planning to destroy me?"

"What? No. Don't be a bonehead. Of course not."

"What is a bonehead?"

"A stupid person, a numbskull."

"I am neither stupid nor constructed of bone."

"It's just an expression."

UPDATING . . .

"My gelatinous make-up is bound inside a construct of semi-permeable latex called gelarron. A manufactured composite susceptible only to xerillium, an element rarely found in the SpiralVerse."

"So," Chalk said as a grin crept across her face. "If you were to be submerged in a boiling vat of xerillium, then you would—?"

"Become irreversibly damaged and cease to exist. Expire. Die. Kick the bucket. End."

"Spoiler alert!"

"I beg your pardon?"

"Never mind." Chalk took a breath. "And you can transform into ... anything? Physically, I mean."

"Yes. Within reason."

"Can you just … *not* be *me*?" she asked. "It's giving me the wig."

"The wig?"

"The wiggins. Creeping me out. Making me uncomfortable."

UPDATING . . .

"I would hate to think I give you the wig," said Cube. "Is there a shape you would find more pleasing? Perhaps a vampire?"

"Nah. A dog, a cat, Grandpa Milo. I don't know."

Cube morphed into a playful Labrador with an orange tongue lolling from the side of its mouth. Then an Egyptian Blue, sat on its hind legs, a sour look on its face.

Chalk giggled again.

RESEARCHING . . .

"What is a Grandpa Milo? The GAPSS Knowledge Mainframe has no record of this creature."

"My grandfather. On my dad's side."

UPDATING . . .

"What's your default setting?"

"A sphere."

"Oh."

"It is the most efficient shape."

"That computes."

"But I can be a cube if you would prefer me to resemble my namesake."

"Take whatever shape you please." Chalk nudged the black orb. "So, what's this for?"

"My outer casing is used for storage and protection. Although I am self-charging, the outer casing does accelerate my regeneration, download, development, and processing speeds."

"You're a sort of snail," Chalk decided. "A digital vampire snail."

Cube considered this for a moment, then transformed into a gastropod with bulging eyes on the end of its long rubbery tentacles and the black outer casing balanced on its back like a shell.

"Does this form please you?"

Chalk laughed. "It's cute, but kinda icky."

"Icky?"

"Gross. Vile. Unpleasant."

UPDATING . . .

Cube returned to its default setting, curled inside the outer casing and pulsed gently, soothingly, like one of Grandpa Milo's Toydarian lava lamps.

"Better?"

"Affirmative."

GAPSS
KNOWLEDGE
MAINFRAME

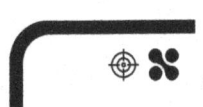 

GARRANGULARS
[SPECIES]
Homeworld: Zorik Minor, Lang. Garrangulese

An indigenous species from the Zorik System, Garrangulars are a proud and ferocious race of quadrupeds who honour tradition, loyalty, and strength. Garrangulars can be found throughout the SpiralVerse but many choose to live in a planet-wide cave system beneath Zorik Minor. They are passionate excavators, coveting precious gems and crystals. The Garrangulars are one of the three oldest known civilisations in the SpiralVerse.

VOID

Angry voices erupted. Cube retreated inside its outer casing with a breathy hiss. Activating the door, Chalk found a scrum of students struggling back and forth on the dormitory landing.

Cressida and Krieg stood toe-to-toe, their faces contorted. The slim Veroselli towered over the bulky Garrangular.

"I will not tolerate your vile and obscene words," she fired.

"I'm not asking for tolerance, you rancid filth!" Krieg bit back. "Zorik Minor is as much yours as it is ours. I'm demanding capitulation."

"Gracious Gods! That's a big word … for a grunt."

Aida stood beside Cressida, protesting diplomatically to the Veroselli, their eduhelpers locked in a frenetic data-exchange. Ripley and Milton had wedged their bodies between the two adversaries in a feeble attempt to defuse the confrontation. By the look of it, neither were particularly keen on the interspecies proximity.

Krieg surged forward. His huge arms toppled Milton like a bowling pin. The Revan caught a bicep in the face as Cressida effortlessly evaded Krieg's swipe and chuckled quietly to herself. Beneath the mop of knotted hair, Krieg's skin bloomed with rage.

"You mock me, Veroselli? I will destroy you!"

Garrangulars stormed around the curved landing, arms raised, voices bellowing. "Do it, Krieg. End her. Once and for all! Kill the Veroselli slime!"

The rest of First Cycle Aktari gathered nervously in their doorways. Some encouraged a fight. Others demanded an end to the madness. Aida's voice became lost in the commotion. Ripley and Milton struggled to detangle themselves from the escalating exchange of insults and attacks.

Chalk felt the urge to hide.

It would be easy to retreat and wait for the storm to pass.

Friends are like oxygen, came the voice of Harriet Starlight, *without them we are as good as dead.*

Chalk rushed headlong into the scuffle and shouldered Krieg aside. Normally, her paltry upper body strength would have zero effect on the stocky Garrangular, but she caught him off balance. Krieg's huge chest tipped over the bannister. His arms pinwheeled as he gawped at the living quarters far below.

Cressida laughed. "Taken out by an Earthling. That's adorable."

Krieg rallied, pulled himself up, and eyeballed Chalk. "Get out of my way!"

Chalk folded her arms. Her legs trembled. "There's thirty of us here. Not just Veroselli and Garrangulars. The dormitories belong to all of us. Revan and Pyramist and Genk and—" Chalk surveyed the other species but none of their names sprang to mind "—and Human alike. We all have to live together. As one."

Through ropes of Krieg's hair she found menacing eyes.

"Perhaps words would be a better solution than … violence?" she added meekly.

Cressida and Krieg stared at one another. Chalk tightened, convinced they were about to tear each other to pieces and crush her in the process.

Instead, they laughed.

"You know nothing of Garrangulan culture," Krieg barked. "And nothing of Zorik Minor."

A slender hand grabbed Chalk's shoulder and spun her about.

"Or Veroselli," the princess said, a wicked grin on her

elegant face. She flicked silver-white hair over her shoulders. "History between the Veroselli and Garrangulars is long, spiteful, and bloody. Perhaps time in the library would benefit your uneducated mind."

Krieg grunted. "Yeah, Mudder. Understand the rules before you play the game."

Chalk faced him. A smirk twisted on his lips. She wanted to take the last three minutes back. Powerlock her door shut and let all this nastiness pass. What had gotten into her?

"You've got a nerve, weighing in on Zorik Minor business," Krieg went on. "You mean to corral us? You? A Human?"

Cressida joined the bombardment. "What does your *civilisation* know of the socio-economic politics of a planet infinitely superior to your own? From what I hear, Earth is still hanging on the words of celebrities and actors when they should be honouring their scientists and educators. In spite of our differences, Zorik Minor outstrips your planet a thousand-fold."

"We could crush you in a heartbeat."

"Boom!"

"Like you never existed."

Chalk stood, baffled, terrified.

"The human race?" Cressida whispered. "Nothing but ticks and fleas clinging to the carcass of an unloved pet."

Kiln licked his grisly, yellow teeth. "Filthy Mudder."

"Castless parasite."

"Human garbage."

"Primordial waste."

A sizzling, green globule splattered at Chalk's feet. "Earthling!"

Laughter ricocheted round the landing.

"I'm—" Chalk began. "I'm … sorry. I didn't—"

Everyone dispersed.

Ripley rounded on her. "What did you just do? Milton and I had it in hand. Kind of."

Chalk's eyes flooded. Her bottom lip trembled.

"Are you going to cry?" he said. "Please don't cry."

Aida batted him away. "Chalk, come on. It is okay."

"No. It's not."

"Well, no," Aida conceded. "Getting involved in Zorik Minor business is less palatable than volunteering for the National Blazing Tar Wrestling squad. Honestly, I am surprised you got away with a verbal dressing-down. They could have pulled your arms out of their sockets."

"They're the dominant force in the SpiralVerse," Ripley told her. "You do not upset the Roses and Grangs. Any of them. You just ... don't. Okay?"

"But you were in the thick of it!"

"We were standing in the way when it started," Milton confessed.

"Believe me," Ripley added, "if we could have been anywhere else, we would."

"Well, thanks for the heads-up, guys. Great first lesson."

Aida took Chalk's arm. "Be careful," she said. "You made some dangerous enemies tonight. Try to sleep, maybe they will have forgotten all about it in the morning."

Chalk brightened. "Really?"

Ripley pulled a face.

Milton inhaled a yuccagourd.

Chalk groaned.

Chalk dimmed her dorm room lights, folded herself into the bedclothes, and stared at the Waterfall Nebula. She imagined herself rising out of the bed and drifting through the endless darkness of space, becoming lost in the nebula's mesmerising colours and texture and magic.

Snorting like a dragon, she woke in the middle of the night from a strange dream in which Harriet Starlight and Ripley Flinch were battling a monster made entirely of yuccagourds.

Cube rolled across the bed and nestled in her lap. Its lid opened a fraction, casting Chalk's face with warm light. "Are you okay?"

Chalk stretching irritably. "What time is it?"

"Twenty-three minutes past two."

"In the morning?"

"Your heart rate is heightened, and I have detected a slight drop in your serotonin levels. Are you having depressed or suicidal thoughts?"

"I'm not depressed. And I'm certainly not suicidal. I'm just a little ... sad."

"I understand."

"Do you?"

"I have detailed files on depression, seasonal affective disorder, anxiety—"

"I'm fine."

"Perhaps you should go for a run. Maybe eat some green vegetables or a high-fibre cereal. I am more than happy to order you a dopamine booster capsule if you would prefer."

"No. Really. I'm in a lull. Stop fussing."

"A lull?"

"A dip, you know. A slump. I'll bounce back."

UPDATING . . .

"Is there a reason for—?"

"Lots of things," Chalk admitted. "Homesick, I suppose."

"But you have been here for less than one rotation."

"Asimov took my iPhone. Being cut off from my family and friends sucks."

"The communication embargo is not always popular," Cube said, "but has proved highly successful in focusing the mind."

Chalk sighed. "I'd like to hear my mum's voice."

"The GAPSS Knowledge Mainframe does not hold such files."

Chalk unzipped her suitcase, rummaged inside, and held up the emerald fountain pen.

"That is a redundant tool."

"It was important to her."

UPDATING . . .

"She liked handwritten letters. Said it was a dying art."

"Perhaps you should write to her."

Chalk frowned. "Is there an intergalactic postal service?"

"No," Cube confirmed. "But the process of writing the letter, even if it is neither sent nor received, could give you a connection to your family and friends."

Chalk twirled the pen between her fingers. "Maybe later."

REMINDER SCHEDULED . . .

"Your timetable packet arrived while you were sleeping," Cube informed her. "Would you like to review it now?"

"Yes," Chalk said, swinging her legs off the bed. "But I'll need some tea. They have tea in space, right?"

"In the living quarters," Cube told her. "A beverage and snacks dispensary. You will find it beside—"

Chalk was already out of the door.

She returned with a fluted glass, rather than a cup and saucer, which she passed from hand to hand to avoid scalding her fingers.

"You found it without incident," Cube said. "Congratulations."

"Sure," Chalk muttered sarcastically, slipping the tea onto the nightstand and rifling through her suitcase for the pecan plaits and pain au chocolat. "Points for Gryffindor!"

The smell of sugary, buttery goodness overwhelmed her.

"What's Gryffindor?"

"Long story. About seven books' worth."

UPDATING . . .

"Most of the First Cycle are still up. Guess we're all a bit wired." She paused. "Means not tired. Awake due to over-stimulation."

UPDATING . . .

"Osmotrino, Zalazor, and Qantoculus students do not fall into your chronotype pattern."

"My chrono—?" she said. "I get the feeling Asimov mentioned this."

Cube's lid opened. Half of its gelatinous orange mass grew to display a graph of each chronotype pattern.

"Oh, right," Chalk said, analysing the data. "I get it. Looks like we're awake and asleep at different times, apart from every six rotations when we're all awake for around twenty hours, and every twelve rotations when we're all asleep."

"Exactly," Cube said. "The last one is known as the dark rotation."

"Crikey. I bet this timetable makes Asimov feel all warm and fuzzy inside."

"Talking of which," Cube said. "Would you like to review yours now?"

"I suppose so," she replied, sipping her tea and munching pastry. "Let's see what classes I can take."

ACCESSING . . .

Cube became a circular monitor. Transparent lettering appeared through an orange-tinted screen displaying a list of classes and subject areas. The eduhelper narrated as the lists scrolled.

"Timetable for Miss Harper Hale. First Cycle Aktari. You are required to attend a minimum of four classes each rotation. Classes last ninety-seven Earth minutes with a twenty-two-minute break. A refuelling period is scheduled between classes two and three and lasts forty-seven Earth minutes."

"I'm guessing not everyone in the galaxy uses minutes, hours, and days like we do on Earth?" Chalk said.

"Nobody does," Cube replied abruptly. "Every civilisation has their own denominations and perceptions of time."

"Space is tricky."

"Impossibly so."

Chalk hadn't even taken her first class and the dull throb of a tension headache had set up camp in her brain.

"Carry on."

"Classes are split into four areas. Study, Practical, Artistic, and Casting."

Chalk scanned the classes as they whizzed by.

"Are there any of interest to you at first glance? Would you like additional information or a more comprehensive list?"

"I've always enjoyed history and science."

"History of the Galaxy would be ideal. Emerging Physics and Chemical Cosmology too. Dark Matter is a challenging yet worthy pursuit."

"Conflict Engagement?" Chalk said. "Are those … fighting classes?"

"With words and weapons."

"Portal Theory sounds fun."

"If your definition of fun is toying with the most dangerous technology in the SpiralVerse, then yes. It is most certainly … fun."

"Narrative of Story?"

"An artistic class," Cube said. "Minimal credits."

"What about Casting?"

"You are from Earth."

"So?"

"Earth is bereft of Aether."

"So?"

"The possibility of anyone possessing a Casting ability from Earth is zero."

"Meaning?"

"You are registered: VOID."

"What?"

"VOID."

"Void?"

"VOID," Cube corrected. "Capital letters."

Chalk huffed. Flakes of pastry hit the bedclothes.

"What is Casting anyway?"

"Casting classes are split into three disciplines. Physical: the governance and manipulation of physical objects. Cerebral:

the governance and manipulation of thought and ideas. Elemental: the governance and manipulation of the natural world. Most Casting students have an affiliation with one of the three disciplines. Occasionally, a student will show an aptitude for two. No one has ever shown an aptitude for all three. It is believed impossible."

Chalk's mouth hung open. "You mean … Force studies! I can learn *The Force*!"

RESEARCHING . . .

"You are referring to the two-dimensional screen-projected space opera about the Skywalker family."

"Um, sure. And *Star Wars* is not two-dimensional. At all!"

"We do not refer to Casting as *Using the Force* although I can understand why you are making the connection. However, I am not permitted to elaborate further."

"Why?"

"You are VOID."

Chalk grumbled. "What about Aether? Can you tell me about that?"

"Same restrictions apply."

She folded her arms. "Seriously?"

"Yes," Cube said. "It goes against my programming."

"Okay. So … how do I become a Caster? How do I … *un*VOID myself?"

"Casting classes are conducted with the sole purpose of enhancing an ability. Similar to watering a seed so it might grow to become a tree. But those with no aptitude cannot acquire the ability to Cast. That would be like watering a stone. No recorded evidence of an acquired Casting ability has ever occurred at the Galactic Institute, or currently exists—or has ever existed—on the GAPSS Knowledge Mainframe."

Chalk's eyes thinned. "So, the chances of me—?"

"None."

"Percentage?"

"Zero. It is impossible."

"Are you serious?"

"Exactingly so."

Chalk grumbled.

As if to reinforce Cube's point, letters formed in the corner of her vision.

HARPER HALE . . .

CASTING STATUS . . .

VOID

GAPSS
KNOWLEDGE
MAINFRAME

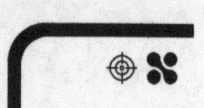 

WORLDGATE
[TECHNOLOGY]

Unlike portals, whose range rarely exceeds 100,000 lightcycles, worldgates were conceived as theoretical devices to transport entities between galaxies, universes, and even dimensions. Three worldgates were constructed and destroyed during the Spiral Wars. Two replicas remain today. The first in the lobby of GAPSS headquarters on Marstok and the other at the SpiralVerse military museum on Centurion H, the Galactic Institute.

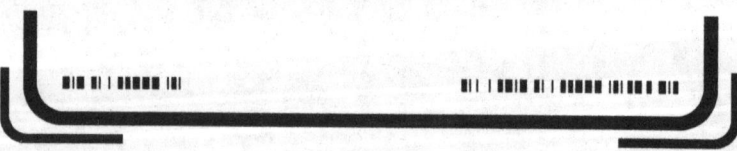

HISTORY OF THE GALAXY

Cube emitted a deafening siren. Its body, formed into long, swaying strands like a sea anemone, flashed vivid orange. Twisting in the sheets, Chalk kicked her way to freedom.

"WHAT … IS … THIS?"

"Wake up call," Cube replied. "Your History of the Galaxy trial class begins in thirty-one minutes."

"GREAT. THANKS," Chalk shouted over the siren. "CAN YOU—" Cube went silent. Its light blinked out. "TURN THE—" Chalk took a quick breath. "Noise down. Thank you."

"My files stipulate that the depths of human sleep differ wildly."

"But never that deep. Ever. You could have woken the dead."

UPDATING . . .

Chalk changed her T-shirt, spritzed herself with deodorant, and pulled on her boots. With Cube mounted on her back, she headed out. The AGT wrapped her in wondrous awe until she swerved into the wrong off-tube and found herself in a knot of tubes at the heart of quadrant three.

EXIT AHEAD . . .

INFIRMARY . . . PHARMACY . . . LOST AND FOUND . . .

Chalk stayed central as the AGT widened. The off-tube rose to her left.

EXIT AHEAD . . .

ADMINISTRATION OFFICES . . . STAFF HOUSING . . . BANQUETING ROTUNDA . . .

She took random exits, hoping the AGT would eventually return her to the hyperloop. After doubling back several times and almost causing a disembarkation pod collision, she emerged in the hyperloop.

Professor Asimov zoomed across her path slurping a tall glass of red liquid. Chalk followed as tiny droplets of the professor's red drink whizzed past like liquid meteorites. She trailed him into the sixth cycle exit and the off-tube for the SpiralVerse military museum. They broke the surface of the Coin and rose towards the roof of an enormous building where the AGT took a sharp left and plunged through the outer wall.

"Ah, Miss Hale. Our esteemed Earthling!" Asimov said as Chalk stumbled onto the disembarkation pod behind him. "How are you?"

"I'm fine, thank you, Professor Asimov."

"Fine?" he echoed, mildly annoyed. "You should be ecstatic and exultant at the thought of taking your first class at the Galactic Institute!"

"And I am," she said. "I'm just a little … overwhelmed."

"Overwhelmed?"

"There are so many classes. There's … too much choice."

Asimov almost choked on the steaming red concoction. "Too much? Too much! Never!"

"What is that?"

"Galaxian esophageal fire syrup. Mother always swore by it."

They descended the disembarkation pod and strolled along a wide corridor. An arch of light gathered at the far end, illuminating a series of turnstiles and a boarded gift shop. The air tasted stale. Rivulets of moisture ran through cracks and broken grout on the tiled floor.

"Well, this is C1-100-S. History of the Galaxy. It's a double class, Miss Hale. A great introduction to everything your planet doesn't know about everything else—historically speaking, hmm?" He fired up a layer screen. "Master Flinch, Princess Van Wyrm, Master Krieg, and a handful of other First Cycle Aktari students are scheduled to attend."

"Are Aida and Milton not in this class?"

Asimov ran his eyes over the layer screen. "Negative, Miss Hale. They … are … in … C1-100-C. Introduction to Casting."

"Milton's a Caster?"

"And Miss Kromm-Nargulantis."

"But Milton—the nervous Sagaroach with the yuccagourds—he's, sort of, magical?"

"Most students are, Miss Hale."

"Can I not, you know, go along with them and try out—?"

"Try out? One does not simply *try out* as a Caster. One simply is or is not. I'm sorry but you are VOID, Miss Hale. For now. For always."

Chalk's heart ached. Why couldn't they use something other than the V word?

VOID was so brutal.

"Professor?"

"Ye-es?"

"I'd been meaning to ask—"

"More questions," he said, and Chalk tightened, "are the cornerstone of any worthwhile education. If we do not question, we do not discover!"

"Yes. Exactly," Chalk said. The tension ebbed. "It's the, erm, condition of everything. And the smell."

Asimov turned his head as he walked. "I see where this is going, and yes, the Galactic Institute has been subject to a modicum of dilapidation. But the condition of her paintwork and treadplate should in no way hinder or adversely affect the incredibly high level of tuition on offer."

"I wasn't complaining. Just … curious."

"The Galactic Institute is funded by GAPSS, and GAPSS is run by politicians who are influenced by business moguls and oligarchs, who in turn are orchestrated by warlords and despots. Money trickles slowly to the bottom of the pond and, by the time it gets here, it's not much more than rusted pennies."

Chalk followed Professor Asimov through the broad arch and onto a platform that overlooked another perfectly round room. Here, the walls and floors were in better condition than anywhere else.

"The museum, while located on the Coin, is not technically part of the Galactic Institute. It does, however, generate a good income from tourists and visitors. That sort of thing always focuses GAPSS attention."

Chalk approached the lip of the platform and baulked at the stomach-churning drop that descended twelve or more stories. But what really drew her eye were the spacecraft and starfighters and battle mechs rotating down the centre of the room like an elaborate mechanical chandelier.

"Welcome," Professor Asimov said, "to the SpiralVerse military museum."

"Sponsored by AstroTech," Chalk read from the sign behind the professor.

"And we are unerringly grateful for their most generous endorsement."

A hubbub of activity emanated from a dozen students struggling through the turnstiles. Ripley arrived last. He glanced up from his GI-VR and gave her a friendly nod. INFIN-8 trundled behind, struggling to keep up.

"Gather round, gather round," Asimov ordered. "And stay away from the edge please, Miss Van Wyrm."

Cressida gave the professor a belittling look.

"So, History of the Galaxy," he began in earnest. "Current estimates stand at thirteen point eight billion cycles, so we probably won't cover *everything* in this lesson." He chuckled to himself. "However, a long tour of the museum should give you an excellent overview of the main talking points in recent military history." Asimov had clearly done this a thousand times and would do it a thousand more. "Here we stand, in the present. But, by descending the walkway you will find yourself stepping back in time!"

Chalk shook with excitement. Nobody else seemed bothered. Perhaps they were bored to death with the military history of the SpiralVerse in the same way her brain went into screensaver every time her online tutor mentioned the agricultural revolution, Parliamentary reform, or Theresa May.

"You wanna buddy up?" she asked Ripley.

"Sure," he replied, deactivating his GI-VR and giving Chalk his full attention.

"In groups of three if you would," Asimov added.

"Ugh, really?" Ripley groaned.

Krieg and Ironlung 8-47 were already standing together, leaving Spirit and Cressida as the only students without a group. Spirit beamed chaotically and darted for Ripley.

"Not so fast," Cressida said, hooking the Oneric's collar and shoving her aside. "I'm not teaming up with a Garrangular in this lifetime or the next!" She took two long strides across the platform. Her C1000 marched in lockstep. "Come on," she snapped, gazing down at Ripley and Chalk. "The sooner we're done, the sooner I can explore the recreation arcade."

"The what?"

"The recreation arcade," Cressida repeated. "Restaurants. Bars. Clubs. Don't you know anything?"

"It's my first day."

The princess rolled her beautiful eyes.

Professor Asimov marked Chalk, Ripley, and Cressida as one group. Krieg, Ironlung 8-47, and Spirit in another, then tottered away. "It's a double lesson, so take your time. Any problems, I'll be on the flight deck enjoying the gromit fish casserole at Gamma Ray's Grill!"

First Cycle Aktari descended through the museum. Chalk and Ripley gazed into display cabinets stocked with weapons from the Spiral Wars. Most were guns—handheld single shooters, pulse rifles, fully-automatic bio-blasters, and DNA-seeking torpedo launchers—but there were also electrified batons of various sizes, anti-personnel mines, shrike bombs, pew-pews, klackers, nims, and baldocks.

The armoured bodysuits were Chalk's favourite. They looked a lot like Cressida's C1000 and were exhibited alongside battle-weary helmets and visors. She marvelled at an AstroTech Bonecrusher (a twenty-foot humanoid remote-control battle droid) and a Chronos B5-Berserker which required zero explanation.

Tons of radar, echolocation, plasma-ray, and mind-boggling digital tech drew Ripley's eye. Cressida scoffed, making snarky remarks about the Veroselli's superior technology and how the museum served as nothing more than a tomb for ancient toys and gimmicks.

Between the displays, monstrous tech, and info monitors was a series of small platforms. Each rose a foot from the ground, topped with a silver-edged aperture. Inside, light shifted like a tiny disco.

"What are these?"

Cressida yawned.

As Chalk approached, a figure materialised atop the platform, constructed of flickering crystal light.

She lurched back. Her heart thudded in her chest.

"Well, hello there," the figure boomed, his eyes fixed on the middle distance. Clad in a bulky red and black battlesuit was a mean and determined-looking man of around sixty with a ragged white beard and scars drawn deep in his forehead. "My name is Admiral Xander 'Rumdog' Xenon. No doubt you've heard of me and seen photos of my achievements on the info screens." He waved a thick cigar in a three-fingered hand.

"Ooh, this is cool," Chalk said. "Dead man talking."

Cressida sighed. Her foot tapped impatiently.

"He *is* dead, isn't he?" Chalk asked.

"I died in the final rotations of the Spiral Wars."

"Knew it."

"But I played an important role in our victory against the Dark Trinity. Throughout the twelve cycle conflict, I flew with the Red Suffering, the Wind Whisperers, the Crying Shadows, the Swift Darkness, and even the Moon Riders. I survived many battles, most notably the Charge of Marstok and the Hunger Raid on Critterion 9. As the war entered its twelfth cycle, I took charge of the fleet and drew up plans to end the conflict once and for all."

"This guy is a stone-cold badass," said Chalk, watching the admiral suck on his cigar.

"He was also a bigot, a speciesist, and a heavy drinker," Cressida said. "And, like every other hologram in this forsaken place, he is dead. Can we move on?"

Cressida strode ahead with her C1000. Chalk and Ripley followed, scanning the cabinets arbitrarily and gazing over the central railing at the spacecraft and fighters twisting down the middle of the enormous room.

"That's a Red Thorn," Ripley said. "Single seater, quick and nimble, with twin laser cannons mounted on narrow wings."

Constructed of folded metal, the Red Thorn bore dirty blast marks on the cockpit, wings, and undercarriage. As the display rotated, a long, sleek, Splintered Needle approached.

"I want one of those!"

"The Splintered Needle was a great ship," Ripley replied. "Four-berth plasma-boosters, titanium cannons, reinforced rubinovium shell, slim forward thrusters, dead-lift brakes, intrinsic gear ratios, eye-popping acceleration. Incredible!"

Chalk stared at the Revan as he reeled the vital stats without pausing for breath.

"Erm ... well, you know, says it all here." He pointed to an info monitor. "Come on, Cressida's getting away."

A hologram of Field Marshall Tigor Ornassus, a celebrated Karmethian, told them about the Battle of Bolgar. A roguish commander called Belsoni Figoria led the charge at Westpoint

X7, while her sister, Andurus Figoria, conceived and executed the Drazden Illusion, a tactical manoeuvre that out-foxed the Dark Trinity in the final throes of war.

Another hologram flickered to life.

"For death and glory and the SpiralVerse!"

Chalk jumped.

Ripley laughed.

"That was the last thing I ever said," the hologram went on. "Hello. I'm Captain Dak Einhorn. Stingray Squadron second in command, *Yazanti* champion three years running, and company prankster."

He wore a grey flight suit and beige padded tunic with a dark console strapped to his chest. Tubes and wires ran to a slim pack threaded over his shoulders. In his hands hung a sky-blue helmet with a cracked, yellow visor. "I fought in many battles—the Blood Reign on Zantia, Seers Canyon on Corpus Morte, and the Battle of Lost Shadows—under the command of Dawn Chasers Squadron Leader, General Gertrude Prodigious Waxler."

"Ooh," Chalk said, excitement spiking. "He knew Waxler."

"Gertrude?"

"Prodigious!"

"For many cycles we battled the Dark Trinity, but never found a way to defeat them. They proved impervious to our bullets, our plasma shells, our xerillium rays. In the end the decision was made to expel them from the SpiralVerse, chase them into a place from which they could never return. Admiral Xenon came up with the plan. Behind you"—Chalk turned—"is a worldgate."

"Whoa."

At the bottom of the great chandelier hung blocks of complex tech, each pulsing with amber diodes, positioned like a huge clock. The colossal device spun in slow, mesmerising circles. A gentle hum spilled from somewhere inside.

"Three worldgates were constructed. One for each of the Dark Trinity. Positioned across the galaxy, I flew with General

Waxler, leading Miasma towards her fate. The battle was intense and devastating. We lost Stingray after Stingray. Pilot after pilot. Friend after friend. Until at last, our enemy was tempted through the worldgate and into the chaos dimension beyond. I was the last to fall, my Stingray destroyed in the final moments of battle as Miasma writhed and choked and vanished."

Chalk's eyes were out on stalks.

Worldgates. The Dark Trinity. Miasma.

"General Waxler was the lone survivor at the Battle of Lost Shadows," Captain Dak Einhorn continued. "It fell to her to unleash her xerillium missiles, destroy the worldgate, Miasma's only way back. The device you see today is a replica, based on Admiral Xenon's ingenious designs."

"Expensive-looking model," Chalk quipped.

"Yeah," Ripley added. "Shame it's not real."

Chalk laughed. "Did you hear that story? Would you keep a functioning worldgate kicking around after what happened? Technological destruction. The only sensible choice."

Cressida and the rest of the students had gathered round the hologram of Chief Strategist Proxima Proxalto who explained the finer points of the First Galactic War. Defying Asimov's instructions, Chalk and Ripley broke away from the group. They wandered around landcraft and life-size battlefield dioramas, along expansive corridors, across vaulted halls, and into the museum's subterranean theatres and art galleries.

The SpiralVerse had more wars than she could name. It occurred to her that, despite each one being uniquely different, they all came down to land border disputes, or political insurgency, or religious doctrines of one kind or another.

Except the Spiral Wars themselves.

Chalk couldn't find what the Dark Trinity wanted, where they came from, or why they were at war with every species in the SpiralVerse.

Perhaps they were one hundred per cent, eighteen-karat gold, diamond-cut evil. Accept no substitutes.

Gamma Ray's Grill hunkered between the museum and the flight deck. Professor Asimov sat studying a tower of layer screens and slurping his casserole when Chalk and the others arrived. "Gods below!" he said, feigning shock. "That time already. Come in, come in. Order something. Can't learn on an empty stomach."

Gamma Ray's Grill was an L-shaped room, oven-hot and flooded with mysterious aromas. A series of rubber booths queued beside the window. High-back stools faced a bar and serving hatch. Neon digital readouts showcased an array of indecipherable specials.

Chalk slid into a booth. She levered Cube off her shoulders and laid the black orb beside her. Ripley sat across, INFIN-8 beside him, and busied himself with his GI-VR.

"What you got there?" she asked, pointing at his wrist. "Best game in the SpiralVerse or something?"

"Huh?" He looked up. "This? Oh. Nothing. You know. Research."

"Research?"

"Private project. You know how it is."

"Oh, yeah. Sure. Private projects. Of course. Me too." Chalk drummed her lip. "How are you two getting on?"

"Me and INFIN-8?" Ripley shrugged. "Yeah, sure. He's … good."

"He?"

"Why not? Got a kinda slack, masculine attitude."

URRRH!

"Look at the way you're sitting."

URRRH! URRRH!

"Doesn't sound happy."

"He's fine."

INFIN-8 turned away like a sulky child.

"What does he do?"

"He's a buddy droid," Ripley said. "They hang out with

you. Get excited about stuff, sometimes moody. A constant companion."

"Oh."

"What about your mystery ball?" Ripley said, switching lanes.

Chalk's hand shot to the black orb.

"This thing? Still a … mystery. Can't figure out a way to open it. No way at all. Locked solid. Like a vault at Gringotts."

If Ripley wasn't sharing, neither was she. And anyway, Cube seemed like an incredible eduhelper, something the others might covet over their own.

"Give it here," Ripley said, reaching across the table. "I can probably—"

"No. It's fine," she said, rolling Cube out of reach. "I'll work it out."

"Touchy."

Chalk fussed her hair.

"You fancy sandwiches?"

"Yeah," she replied. "Cheese ones. Grilled if they do them."

Ripley ordered on his GI-VR and their food arrived via AstroTech Deliver-2-U, a uni-wheeled chrome droid with a flat head and square eyes. Inspecting her sandwich for any trace of slaughtered lifeforms, Chalk got a whiff of Asimov's esophageal fire syrup.

"How did you enjoy the museum?" the professor asked, loitering at the end of the table.

"I loved it," Chalk enthused. "Holograms are awesome. That Rumdog guy was cool. Dan Earhorn too!"

"Admiral Xander 'Rumdog' Xenon," Asimov corrected. "And Captain Dak Einhorn. Heroes and legends of the Spiral Wars."

"The Red Thorns were great. And the Splintered Needles. And the Dark Trinity. Wow. It was all just … amazing!"

Ripley scowled at Chalk's enthusiasm.

"And you, Master Flinch?"

"The worldgate was alright … despite being a fake. Neat bit of kit."

Asimov updated some layer screens and moved on to the next table where Krieg was methodically carving an entire roast Qwork in front of Spirit, Ironlung 8-47, and a pale-looking Grimcrack.

"Professor's pet," Ripley muttered.

Chalk sank into the squeaky seat. Arms folded.

"Oh, I love the amazing holograms and the inspiring vehicles and the terrifying stories of battle," Ripley mocked. "Power it down, Hale."

"I … genuinely loved the museum," she said, nibbling a fingernail. "Don't be mean."

Ripley cocked his head.

"Oh, my name's Ripley," Chalk retaliated, punching her GI-VR randomly. "I cannot take my eyes off the screen as I've found something more important than friendship inside!"

BING!

Ripley stared. Brows knitted.

A prickle of anxiety rushed her bones.

His mouth quirked. "Okay, okay," he said, snorting back a laugh and holding up his hands. "I'll be nicer. Okay?"

"Snagger."

"Bonehead."

BING! BING!

"Truce?"

"Truce. And be nicer to INFIN-8 too."

Ripley looked at his eduhelper. "Sure. No problem."

"Promise?"

"I promise."

BING! BING! BING!

GAPSS
KNOWLEDGE
MAINFRAME

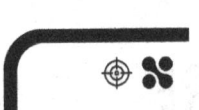 

SAGAROACHES
[SPECIES]
Homeworld: Xenothropod colonies, Lang. Gnix

Sagaroaches are the abundant species on the Xenothropod colonies. The average Sagaroach stands over six feet but moves fastest on all six legs. Their epidermis is constructed from a hardened protein compound called chitter which covers their abdomen, thorax, and wings. Unlike their near cousins on Earth, they are supremely intelligent creatures. Many of their number graduate into the fields of Emerging Physics, Quantum Thermology, and Dark Matter Manipulation. See also, Sagarachnids, Sagaflies, Sagafleas, Sagabeetles, and Sagamoths.

PROPELLOSPHERE

Chalk wiped her greasy, cheese-laced fingers along the bottom of the table, clicked Cube into its magnetic housing, and filed out of Gamma Ray's Grill.

As an extension of the museum, the flight deck was home to row upon row of decommissioned starfighters, battle mechs, and mountains of second-hand tech. A bio-glass ceiling arched high above, lofted skyward by vast iron struts like the roof of King's Cross Station. The whole place stank of plasma oil, burnt rubber, and hydraulic fluid.

Asimov was in full flow when Chalk caught up.

"—and of course, those of you who want to spend more time in the military museum are more than welcome, hmm? However, the flight deck is a dangerous place. We receive incoming and outgoing ships on a permanent basis so you must be supervised at all times. Commander Lasco will be here in … um … oh, three minutes ago."

Asimov looked down the flight deck. His fingers wriggled impatiently.

In the middle distance, a figure emerged.

"Ah!" the professor exclaimed. "Here he comes now."

Some students wandered back to the museum. Others to their next trial classes.

"You hanging around?" Chalk asked Ripley.

"Yeah," he said. "Let's see what this Lasco guy is about."

"Okay, gather round. This—when he finally gets here—is

Commander Hank K. Lasco. He is a seasoned pilot, war veteran, experienced engineer, and *runs* the flight deck. Do as he says, not as he does. Do not mess around. And stay close to one another. I will be checking in with the commander later so I *will* find out if anyone acts up."

Asimov turned to see what was taking the commander so long.

Lasco leant against the tail guns of a Splintered Needle looking decidedly unwell.

"One moment!"

While Asimov was gone, a new batch of students arrived.

"Aida," Chalk said, happy to see the diminutive Tattorian. "And Milton." Her enthusiasm not as high. "How was Introduction to Casting?"

"Informative," Aida said. "Snider gave us a brief, urgent overview of what he requires from us by the end of the first cycle. His expectations are challenging but well within my capabilities."

Milton appeared to be stress-eating.

Asimov returned with a pallid middle-aged Revan. He looked like he could do with a shower, a shave, and a good night's sleep. Perhaps something green to eat. "Here," Asimov said, pushing him towards the students, "is Hank K. Lasco. Commander, apparently."

"Kids," the commander opened with. Cressida snorted derisively. Necrotta flashed his pointy teeth. "Honourable Veroselli and Zillamoth too," he countered. "Welcome to the flight deck." Lasco swallowed hard and blinked several times as if to wake himself up. "This is a fully working—"

"I'll leave them with you, hmm?" Asimov interjected.

The commander nodded. He looked like he might faint. Throw up. Or worse. "As I was saying, this is a fully working flight deck. Ships and craft from all over the SpiralVerse dock here rotationally. We supply maintenance, refuelling, a complete interior and exterior valet service, upgrades, installs, and ammunition—licence permitting." He rubbed his stubble and took a long, steadying breath. "As I'm sure Franklin ... Professor Asimov has told you, the flight deck is extremely dangerous. This is *not* a playground."

"Are you okay?" Chalk asked.

"I'm fine, Miss—"

"Chalk."

"Miss Chalk."

"Just Chalk."

Lasco grasped his forehead. "Fine. Whatever."

"Would you like some water?"

Lasco declined and led them down the centre of the flight deck. The surface rose gradually underfoot. White lines cross-hatched the metal treadplate where recessed lights glowed amber and blue. On either side, squadrons of Red Thorns, Splintered Needles, and Stingrays faced the launch bay. Personnel carriers hunkered in the shadows, while the outlines of fifty-foot battle mechs skimmed the roof with the tops of their heads. Engineering droids bustled to and fro, coiling fuel hoses, reconditioning spare parts, and wheeling precarious transport containers filled with plasma oil and power cells.

"These vehicles have all been decommissioned," the commander explained, waving his hands expansively. "While they still contain engines, weapons systems, and guidance tech, all fuel, ammunition, and power cells have been removed. For safety's sake. We can't have some liberal-minded museum visitor jumping inside one of the AstroTech Gigantors and stomping around the flight deck, now can we?"

Chalk giggled.

Ripley shook his head.

Cressida muttered quietly to her C1000.

Commander Lasco wandered over. "Neat bit of tech." He whistled. "First to pick, huh? Nailed the Data Drive Relay, I presume? Impressive."

Cressida eyed him suspiciously as he circled her droid.

"Have you named it?"

"It responds to its model number."

"Had a Zenith Industries XCLER-8 when I was a student … did a whole bunch of cool stuff. Called him Ace. Cracking little droid. Still got him tucked away in my workshop. Power cells for those old models are as rare as zorikanthium."

As they walked, Lasco inspected INFIN-8 who *BING!*ed gleefully under the commander's attention before turning to Necrotta's Equinox ATAK-ATAK: a weaponised eduhelper capable of transforming into swords, blasters, and fighting batons. Chalk could feel Lasco's eyes on the mystery ball, but he did not comment.

At the end of the flight deck, the white lines and recessed lights spread in a wide V, running parallel with the gaping mouth of the launch bay.

WARNING . . .

"Are we in danger?"

"Yes," replied the commander matter-of-factly. "This is undoubtedly the most dangerous place on the Coin." He stopped several metres before two parallel yellow lines. "Between us and the infinite oceans of space is the propellosphere. An invisible anomaly generated by a matrix of iridian stones positioned inside the launch bay."

"How can stones be dangerous?" asked Chalk.

"Anyone heard of iridian stones?" the commander went on.

"They are ancient and rare and can manipulate the laws of physics."

"That's right, Miss—?"

"Kromm-Nargulantis."

"Iridian stones block dangerous solar rays and dark matter from breaching the flight deck. If anything enters the propellosphere and fails to resonate with an iridian spectographic signature—standard issue on all GAPSS spacecraft—then it gets crushed like a kraken-weevil and spat out into space."

Lasco fished a broken Touch3 from a stack of disused tech.

"Stand back," he said and promptly tossed the device into

the air. It collided with the edge of an enormous magnetic field that bloomed around the Touch3, rippling like vivid green water.

WARNING . . .

PROPELLOSPHERE BREACH . . .

DANGER OF DEATH . . .

It swallowed the device. Crushed it to the size of a grape. Then fired it into space. An arc of crystal light trailed in its wake.

"So," Commander Lasco said, turning to look at their petrified faces. "It's dead simple. Do not cross the yellow lines. Or you're … dead."

"Good health and safety tip," Chalk said, legs trembling.

"How did you all enjoy the museum?" the commander asked, leading them away from the propellosphere. "Any of you got plans to join the Galactic Elite when you graduate?"

Milton raised a spindly arm, but Lasco failed to notice.

"Oh, well," he went on, directing them between two Stingrays. "Military life isn't for everyone. It's routine and discipline and devotion. It's … well, it's bloody hard work."

They passed a huge personnel carrier whose top half was entirely see-through while the hull had been scored with long, black indentations.

"What *are* your plans after GI?" Lasco said to the group.

Necrotta double punched his chest. "A warrior for the Zillamoth Empire."

"My father owns the Marstok Meteors *Orbit Strike!* team," Spirit said, walking close to Ripley, "so I'll probably end up managing them."

"I would like to become more than my programming," Ironlung 8-47 declared.

"Once I succeed my mother and rise to Queen Cressida Van Wyrm, I will overhaul the courts on Zorik Minor, vanquish the Garrangulan pestilence, and rule supreme."

"Probably something to do with languages," Ripley said, half-heartedly.

Lasco's gaze fell on Chalk. "And how about you?"

"Haven't decided," she admitted. "Still working it out."

Lasco sat on the toe of a rusty battle mech. "That's some lofty ambitions," he said, looking at everyone in turn. "Marstok Meteors, eh? More of a Revus Roughnecks fan myself."

"The Roughnecks came bottom of the league last season."

"And, as for you, Miss Chalk—"

"Just Chalk."

"Not knowing who we are and what we want to be is the reality of billions. Don't let these career-driven high-fliers make you feel bad. We're different every rotation. And every rotation brings a new challenge. Right now, I'm commander of the flight deck at the Galactic Institute. But I've woken as a pilot in a Stingray Squadron. As a spy for the SpiralVerse Resistance. As a boy with a dream of escaping Revus X and reaching the stars."

Ripley looked up. "You're from Revus X?"

"Yeah, Fifth District. Couldn't wait to escape the heat."

"Twenty-third District," Ripley told him. "Right on the edge of the jungle."

Hank Lasco pretended to wipe his brow.

"Are we done here?" Cressida asked, bored.

"Sure," the commander replied. "I was about to take you into my workshop if you're interested—"

"But it's not part of the introductory tour?"

"No, but—"

Without a word, Cressida turned and marched away, her C1000 close behind. Necrotta and Ironlung 8-47 made disinterested noises and marched after the Veroselli.

The remaining students followed the commander to the edge of the flight deck where a wall of square windows rose from floor to ceiling like a giant, frosted chessboard. The commander tapped a pressure pad and a panel juddered to one side. "In we go."

The students hesitated.

"It's perfectly safe," Lasco said. "Or do none of you want to have a look at the flight simulator?"

Chalk was elbowed aside as the others fought to be first through the door.

A huge workbench dominated Commander Lasco's workshop, cluttered with tools, circuitry, and half-built eduhelpers. A shelving system of metal girders and wooden slats ran end to end, piled with monitors and cannon mountings, steering columns and gear plates, fighter helmets and storage crates overflowing with wires and cables and control shafts. Cans of oil and lubricants and cleaning products were jammed into every remaining inch of space.

"Commander!" Spirit screamed. "There's a horrible Qwork in your workshop."

Sure enough, a Qwork sat in the middle of the workbench staring at them.

Lasco moved past Spirit and swept the creature into his arms. "This is not a *horrible* anything," he said. "Yes, she's a Qwork. And her name is Cozy."

"Like Ironlung's eduhelper," Chalk said. "Grimlock or Grimmel or something."

"G-g-grimcrack," said Cozy, shy and timid.

"Cozy was supposed to be the eduhelper of another Cylesian," Lasco said.

"What happened?"

"Software malfunction during the Data Drive Relay," Lasco explained. "There were … some deaths." Cozy shivered. "So, rather than sending her to a Qwork farm, I offered to keep Cozy here to help out in the workshop."

"Did *you* dress her?" Spirit asked.

Cozy wore a red and white striped tunic.

"She chose it herself. I think it rather suits her."

"Whoever heard of dressing a Qwork?"

The commander ignored Spirit, fussed Cozy's big ears and

returned her to the workbench. "If you're studying Empirical Mechanics or advanced engineering then you'll be in here with me, pulling tech apart and trying to fathom out how and why it works."

"Where's the flight simulator?" Chalk asked, unable to contain her excitement a moment longer.

Lasco directed them past a wall of framed photos, through an archway, and into an antechamber where a series of six wheel-less go-karts faced one another on a huge circular track. Each device had been mounted with massive springs that connected it to a metal ring and a huge ball bearing, secured with dozens of axles and dynamos.

"Thoden be praised!" Ripley enthused, completing a speedy circuit of the room.

"Made by my own hands," Lasco said proudly, "but you'll need to pass Conflict Engagement into the third cycle before I can grant permission for flight."

"You're kidding me?" Chalk exploded.

"Are they … safe?" Spirit asked, nudging one with her elbow.

"Of course. Well … pretty safe. It's a proper flight simulation. Not the kind of thing GAPSS would endorse. Let's put it this way: you won't die, but you will gain a solemn appreciation of what it takes to fly one of those old fighters out there."

"That's not very reassuring," grumbled Milton.

"How do I get in?" Chalk said, wasting no time at all. She placed Cube on a tool chest and struggled to hoist herself into the cockpit.

"No getting in, Miss Chalk."

"Seriously?"

"Third cycle and above only."

"No one will know," Chalk said. "I won't tell. Promise on my life."

"Been burned by that one before."

Chalk clung to the amazing device as a tornado of frustration swirled inside. "I guess I'll have to take your classes then."

"Good," Lasco said, helping her down. "Do you have an aptitude for strategy and battle, for mechanics and engineering?"

"Um," Chalk replied. "Snider said I'm a fast runner. Quick, like a Horned Sagamoth."

Spirit sniggered derisively.

"Well, I'm sure that'll come in useful," the commander encouraged. "Right, come on. I need to brief you on some important workshop safety precautions—"

"Hey," Ripley said, turning Chalk by the shoulder. "Ignore Spirit. She's your typical privileged Oneric and not worth worrying about."

"I wasn't worried." Chalk smiled. Her fingers shifted covetously over the smooth bodywork of the flight simulator. "Were *you* worried that I was worried?"

"What?"

"Ignore me," she said. "I want a go on this. Bad."

"I know a bit about mechanics and whatnot," he told her. "I'm pretty confident we'll ace this class."

"Really?"

"Yeah."

"Promise?"

"Sure," he said casually. "You'll be hurtling through simulated space at faster-than-lightspeed with your hair on fire before you can say interdimensional-quadraphonetic-bicuspids!"

GAPSS
KNOWLEDGE
MAINFRAME

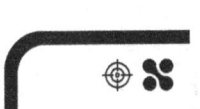 

REVANS
[SPECIES]
Homeworld: Revus I-XII, Lang. Galaxian

Revans are an oviparous mongrel species with DNA from all thirty-five known worlds. Spawned from the millions of criminals held on the Revus prison worlds, Revans have no specific history and prefer to find comfort in family over tradition and culture. Most Revans take a predominantly bipedal form, and many have complex digestive, respiratory, cardiac, and dermatological systems. It could be argued that no two Revans are physiologically alike [although a conclusive study has not been undertaken due to financial restrictions].

ORBIT STRIKE!

Following an afternoon of Metaphysical Mathematics, where Chalk's brain became knotted by Professor Dustenberg's analysis of algerhythmic vortecies, gravitational trigonometry, and topological linear spaces in time, she joined Aida, Milton, and Ripley in the recreation arcade.

The arcade squatted beneath a dilapidated canopy surrounding the observation hall. Every other panel seemed to have come loose, gone missing, or promised to fall, trampling some unwitting student to death. It reminded Chalk of a disused seaside pier, minus the smell of salty chips and the caw of opportunistic seagulls. Hordes of stores and food trucks lingered between gaming galleries, colonnades, restaurants, bars and cafes. Admission to The Math Addicts, the Garrangulan Battle Dancers, the Quantum Leapers, the Mechanical Marvels, the Veroselli Operatic Choir, the *Yazanti* Foundation, and dozens more advertised in warped neon on digital billboards.

Holographic salespeople made Chalk jump every time they materialised, welcoming students inside. Tech stores offered the latest deals on Zenith, TekTonik, Chronos, and AstroTech products, while travel outlets advertised end-of-cycle breaks to popular destinations across the SpiralVerse. Confectionery drew her nose with wafts of sticky sweetness. Clothing appeared to be sold by species, size, and number of limbs, while souvenir shops peddled Galactic Institute apparel, merchandise, and Spiral Wars commemorative plaques, plates, and holographic badges.

A wide shopfront with a floor-to-ceiling curved bio-glass facade contained smooth desks in a brightly lit showroom. Staff busied themselves on the latest TekTonik tablets while shiny new AstroTech and Zenith buddy droids twisted and turned beneath warm spotlights like exotic dancers.

"What's this?" Chalk said, as they shambled by.

"Upgrade and customisation outlet," Ripley said, glimpsing inside.

"For eduhelpers?"

"Of course," Aida said. "Some impetuous students obliterate their study loans on upgrades and custom decoration. I understand the desire to purchase your eduhelper more processing power or personality filters, but some of the add-ons are an irresponsible waste of quasoids."

"Quasoids?"

"Currency," Milton said helpfully.

"You do have a financial system on Earth?" Aida asked, looking faint.

"Oh, sure," Chalk said. "I bet the pound to quasoid exchange rate is lousy."

"Hey, you guys want to catch an *Orbit Strike!* match?" said Ripley, pointing towards a huge domed building.

"What exactly is *Orbit Strike!?*" Chalk said as the Revan herded them across the busy concourse. "And why is there an exclamation mark in its name?"

"Enough with the questions," Ripley said, heaving the doors open. "All will be revealed."

Inside, Chalk sank into a deep, red carpet. Reconditioned air gushed from boxy vents smelling of polish, resin, and glucose. At the bottom of a dozen steps spread food and drinks dispensaries and row upon row of gaming tables and betting machines. Digital monitors dripped from the ceiling advertising the latest odds.

They zigzagged between tables and overstimulated students, through a doorway in an undulating silver wall, and into the darkness beyond. Screams of excitement bounced around a cavernous chamber. The air was palpable with nervous tension. Chalk's footfalls rang on metal stairways as she climbed to a high platform that overlooked a giant, transparent sphere. "Where am I?" she said. "Disneyland Jupiter?"

"This," Ripley said, arms wide, "is an *Orbit Strike!* arena."

Chalk gripped a curved rail at the edge of the viewing platform. Students sat below sipping long, colourful drinks and bouncing excitedly in the seats.

"And that," Ripley continued, "is the playsphere."

A giant, transparent sphere hung before her. It rotated slowly, spinning in one direction, then another. End over end over end. Dramatic lights throbbed and flashed and zoomed around inside. A digital air horn blasted directly above, rattling the fillings in her teeth. Chalk stumbled onto a stool as the top of the playsphere retracted and ten figures dropped into the anti-gravity arena. Five wore lurid green, the others blood orange. Both teams flaunted bulky body pads, their helmets emblazoned with fluorescent team logos.

Students whooped and hollered as the players whizzed around inside the playsphere, tumbling and somersaulting, propelling themselves at stomach-churning speeds.

"Yes!" hooted Ripley. "The Marstok Meteors *and* the Karmethian Comets! Reserve teams obviously ... but still!"

"Is that good?"

"Good? They're only two of the best teams in the SpiralVerse!"

Three cylindrical droids burst into the playsphere. Lights blinked as they manoeuvred into preordained orbits.

"What are—?"

"Refbots."

"So, what happens—"

"Molluscs and Bipeds," boomed a deep voice, "Hexapods and Octopods, Ancient Civilisations and New, welcome to the first *Orbit Strike!* exhibition match of the season. The mighty Marstok Meteors, eight-time SpiralVerse champions, take on the seven-time champions, the Karmethian Comets! Are ... you ... ready ...?"

"YES!"

"Are ... you ... set ...?"

"YES!"

"Then ignite the abyss ... and let chaos commence!"

Chalk's eyes were out on stalks, skin fizzing, intoxicated by the sensory overload.

The *Orbit Strike!* players hovered at the edge of the playsphere. A spinning black vortex materialised at the centre, crackling with bolts of energy. The air horn fired again and two spheres—one blue, the other pink—burst into the playsphere and orbited at colossal speed.

"What in the name of—?"

"Those are holoballs. Only two allowed inside the playsphere at any time," Ripley yelled, pointing, as the noise swelled. "Blue is worth one point, green two, pink three. And that's the abyss in the middle. The scoring zone."

The air horn blasted once more and the game began.

"The Comets begin in attack, Alendi chasing a blue for a single score ... Noric and Syla on the far side, juggling a pink back and forth, confusing Marko from the Meteors as he patrols the abyss ... Jespar is trailing the scoring switch for the Comets, Brant in hot pursuit, eager to turn the tide ... And it's Alendi, rocketing a blue into the abyss! One point to the Comets!"

A mighty roar erupted. Hands, claws, and pincers punched the air.

"A green holoball enters the game, Maia and Pongle leave their defensive duties and converge on Loje ... There's a gap, Syla and Noric ricochet a pink towards the abyss, but it's blocked by Reiss who spins in deadly circles knocking Syla against the edge of the playsphere. That's gotta hurt!"

The crowd winced as Syla slammed into the playsphere and fell into a listless orbit like a rag doll.

"Is she okay?" shouted Chalk. "This is utter madness."

"I know," Ripley said. "Brilliant, isn't it?"

"What are the rules?"

"It's quite simple," he explained. "To score, you launch one of the holoballs into the abyss. Any way you can. One team attack, the other defend."

"Okay. When do they swap? At half time?"

"Half time? What's that?"

"Doesn't matter."

"You see that?" Ripley said, his finger trailing a circular disc that zoomed in manic patterns against the inner edge of the playsphere. "That's the scoring switch. You punch that, kick it, smack it with your head, and the teams switch. Defenders become attackers, attackers become defenders."

"Jespar has the scoring switch covered, but Brant will not quit ... Alendi shoulders a green to Loje, who spins and drops beneath the abyss ... and scores! Two points to the Comets! But Brant has overpowered Jespar—that looked nasty—and he's going for the scoring switch!"

A dark chromatic flourish tore through the speakers.

The lights switched from green to red.

"The Meteors are on the attack! Marko and Brant guard the scoring switch while the rest of the Meteors charge through the playsphere, bouncing holoballs to one another, and they shoot! ... Maia scores with a blue, Reiss with a pink, Pongle arcs high, dodging body slams from Alendi and Noric ... and scores! Comets four, Meteors six! What a start!"

Chalk sat, mouth open, as the players propelled themselves around the spinning orb, hurling holoballs towards the abyss, and battering one another senseless.

"This is insanely brilliant!" she said, as the Comets hit the scoring switch and turned their attention to attack. "I love it so much. How *do* they decide a winner?"

"First to pass one hundred points," Ripley told her. "Although, *Atomic Orbit Strike!* has a whole different set of rules."

"*Atomic Orbit Strike!?*"

"There are loads of variations. This is standard gameplay."

"I want a go," Chalk said, bouncing on her stool. "Looks intense ... and painful ... but so much fun."

The Comets scored four points on the next play, deflecting two green holoballs against Syla's unconscious body.

"Well, you'll have to wait," Ripley said, "for the third cycle."

"First the flight simulator," Chalk grumbled. "*Now Orbit Strike!* You have to be joking?"

"GAPSS rules. No one would be foolish enough to break those."

As one holoball disappeared into the abyss, another shot into the playsphere. The scoring switch got battered repeatedly as the balance of play shifted. The game raced on, tightly contested, the scores separated by no more than a handful of points.

"Noric and Jespar move to the edge of the arena, shoulder to shoulder, a pink passing back and forth ... Brant and Reiss get steamed into the playsphere ... Jespar ducks behind his teammate, arms interlocked, and goes spinning in a tight loop beneath Marko, over Pongle ... And Noric releases the pink in an opposing trajectory to Jespar ... The pink is up, Jespar is down ... but he rises once more, catches the pink and thunders it home, through Maia's despairing, outstretched hands, and ... SCORES!"

The crowd erupted.

"One hundred and two points ... Karmethian Comets win!"

With the glorious fever of *Orbit Strike!* ringing in her ears, Chalk followed Ripley, Aida, and Milton out onto the arcade where long sleepy shadows stretched across the Coin.

"What's next?" she said eagerly.

"Next?" Aida replied. "I do not know about you, but I plan to study."

"Study?" Chalk moaned. She looked at Ripley and Milton, but they seemed to be siding with the Tattorian.

"I do not wish to fall behind," Aida said. "We can attend the welcome ball at the end of phase one. It would be agreeable to stay later then."

"Pah!" Chalk groaned, as her endorphin-high stalled before it had time to ignite. "That's ten rotations away!"

"And you should probably spend that time going over your notes from Dustenberg's Metaphysical Mathematics class. It is only going to get harder."

"Isn't there a basic maths class? I'd even settle for an advanced one?"

"Advanced mathematics? That is for children."

"Space is hard," Chalk huffed. "I'm ten cycles behind. At least."

"You'll catch up," Ripley assured her.

Milton nodded, chewing loudly.

As they approached the AGT, Krieg and his bulky droid stormed past.

Ahead, Cressida and her C1000 stood waiting.

Sensing another confrontation, Chalk slowed and hissed at the others to hide in a souvenir shop doorway.

Cressida blocked the steps to the embarkation pod.

Krieg stared at her menacingly.

"What is happening?" whispered Aida.

"Looks like an old-fashioned stand-off," said Chalk.

"What is old-fashioned about it? Are they dressed as Knights of the Old Dominion?"

"No," Chalk said, swivelling to look at Aida. "It's … never mind."

Krieg, clearly growing restless, forced Cressida aside, but the Veroselli stood her ground.

"Been at the *Orbit Strike!*, have we?" the princess sneered.

"What of it?" Krieg fired back.

"Base entertainment for base lifeforms."

"*Orbit Strike!*? Base? Clearly, the finer points of the galaxy's best-loved sport have been lost on your … kind."

Cressida scoffed. "You should try *Yazanti* or *Tigero*. Recreational pursuit passed down the generations by erudite minds." The Veroselli coiled her silver hair behind her pointed ears. "Quaffing GanyMead while others hurl holoballs and punches! Not exactly inter-dimensional astrophysics, is it?"

Krieg grasped the Veroselli by the throat and raised her off the floor. Cressida's eyes bulged as a strangled scream whistled past her lips. The princess twisted, coiled tight, then slammed her knees against the Garrangular's midriff.

Krieg fell back, winded.

A sharp alarm sounded. Burning beams of light descended on the scuffle. Cressida and Krieg retreated, standing six feet apart, chests heaving from the encounter.

"What is happening?" Aida whispered, more insistent.

Several droids, clad in black armour and red visors, rose from concealed holes in the ground and rolled on single wheels to the scene of the fight.

"Enforcers," Milton whispered, nervously.

Chalk shuddered.

"Nothing to see here," Cressida said.

"Just a brief disagreement," Krieg added.

"All fine now."

"Best of friends."

Professor Snider barrelled out of the AGT. His black robes flapped behind him like bat wings. "What is the meaning of this?" he cried, descending two steps at a time. Spinning in the space between the Veroselli and the Garrangular, he put his hands on his hips, a sour look on his face. "Well?"

Neither spoke.

Snider waved the Enforcers away. "I understand the complicated history you two share," he began, turning from Cressida to Krieg, "but that is a matter for Zorik Minor, *not* the Galactic Institute. Violence, of any kind, will not be tolerated on the Coin or the Flipside or anywhere in-between." His eyes looked cold and unforgiving. "Do you understand me?"

Cressida bowed, yet an air of defiance lingered in her stance.

Krieg grunted and straightened the huge metal bracelets around his neck and wrists.

"It is settled then," Snider said, spying Chalk and her friends in the shadows. "We should *all* be moving along. It is late and I am sure many of you have a mountain of revision to do … even after a single rotation."

Chalk trailed Ripley and Milton towards the embarkation pod.

"Miss Hale," Snider said, hooking her by the shoulder with a long finger.

"Yes, Professor?"

He stared at her for a moment. His sharp features twitched. He looked as though he was attempting to fathom an impossibly complex problem.

"Your Jedi mind tricks will not work on me," she said nervously.

Snider frowned. "You're such a … peculiar creature," he whispered, his large watery eyes seeming to drink her in. He sniffed sharply, flicked a tear aside, and nodded towards the AGT. "Go. Now."

Chalk didn't need telling twice.

GAPSS
KNOWLEDGE
MAINFRAME

YUCCAGOURDS
[FRUIT]

A soft subterranean cylindrical fruit with a porous rind
cultivated on the Xenothropod colonies. The yuccagourd
is the only source of nutrition for Sagaroaches, many of
whom suffer fatal reactions to all other foodstuffs.

See also, Grimagourds.

INTRODUCTION TO PORTALS

The following morning, Chalk made her way to a trial class of Domestic and Interspecies Languages. Professor Hypocrates Balefire made them deactivate their GI-VR language modifiers. Trying to understand what anyone said became an obnoxious commotion. Revan languages were similar to those spoken on Earth, a mix of vowels and consonants. The Tattorian dialect made Aida sound like she had a gobstopper lodged in her throat while Milton's voice was nothing more than a series of clicks and wheezes.

Galactigraphical Routemaps came next.

"Of the three-hundred and seventy-six billion, one hundred and ninety-eight thousand, five-hundred and twenty-three stars in the SpiralVerse, only thirty-six are orbited by planets containing intelligent life," Professor Sigma-Sontos informed them. "However, thousands of other worlds contain bacteria and amoebas, viruses and parasites which, under the GAPSS *Parameters for Intelligent Consciousness Report*, do not qualify as *intelligent*."

Cressida put up a hand. "Do Garrangulars meet the requirements?"

Half the class burst out laughing. Krieg ripped a half-eaten yuccagourd from Milton's claws and hurled it at the Veroselli.

At lunch, Chalk sat with Ripley, Aida, Milton, and their eduhelpers on a purple faux-lawn garden in the shadow of the Casting citadel.

A broad stone stairway unfolded to their right. Its steps bowed at the centre from centuries of wear. Above, a gaping arch of battlements and crenelations connected three mighty towers topped with flags that cracked as if under the spell of a wicked storm. The entire structure felt completely out of place. It was almost as if someone had teleported Castle Grayskull off the surface of Eternia and accidentally dropped it on the Coin.

"Come on, Aida?" Chalk urged. "Tell me something about Casting. Anything."

"For the twenty-third time, I cannot share Casting knowledge with you. Suffice to say, it is difficult and dangerous, even to those with an aptitude. Plus, you need Aether to Cast, and that stuff is closely monitored and as rare as Tattorian teeth. Teaching the Castless and the VOID is irresponsible and goes against every law in the SpiralVerse."

"That's a strong no, then?"

"Professor Snider had us thumb-sign more than a dozen layer screens."

"*Casting is for Casters*," Milton added. "Snider's mantra."

"Elitist, uptight, joyless snagger!"

"What did you expect?" Aida said. "He is a Shadow Seer."

"A *what* now?"

"A Shadow Seer. He can sense those with Casting abilities."

"And those without," Milton added helpfully.

"Like a witch-smeller?"

"What is a witch?"

"Doesn't matter."

"Very few become Shadow Seers," Aida explained. "It only occurs to Casters when they become too powerful, obtain too much knowledge. Professor Snider was a master of both Cerebral and Elemental Casting. Now he has nothing but the power to see the abilities of others. I would imagine it must be agony. A neutron star gazing across infinite space at its former, supermassive glory."

Chalk took a moment. "He was ... powerful?"

"Legendary."

"And I'm VOID," she mumbled. "Capital letters."

The final class of the rotation was Introduction to Portals. Professor de Rema materialised in the chamber adjacent to the observation hall via the portal itself.

Like Professor Asimov, Gabriella de Rema was a hexapod from Marstok, but she was much younger than the other professors. De Rema's dark hair flowed onto her shoulders in thick waves where flashes of emerald shone in the flickering light. Her flawless skin glistened like honey tea. She wore an earth-tone Galactic Institute fitted bodysuit. A dark jacket with orange stripes and stiff collar.

"Right," she said, after signing everyone in and slipping a Touch10 into a shoulder bag. "Introduction to Portals. Pretty exciting, right?"

Her enthusiasm got a mixed response.

"Oh, come on," the young professor enthused. "I know it's the end of the rotation and you've probably had enough of dusty lecturers blithering on about paraxial neutron density and inverse adverbs. You probably want to see your friends and eat Karmethian jellob, drink some GanyMead, and watch an *Orbit Strike!* match."

The class perked up a bit.

"This," she said, turning to the portal, "is a Chronos P950—patent pending—and is part of the Galactic Institute's integrated portal system. This means it's hard-wired into the dominant and auxiliary power grids—when those aren't on the blink—and can transport you to any of the six portal sites on the Coin. Now, I know what you're thinking. Why do we have portals when the Coin is only two kilometres in diameter, and we have the hyperloop and the AGT? For a start, some of the professors are very old and refuse to walk far, plus some stomachs cannot handle the gravitational pressures of the AGT. There have been some ... *unfortunate* accidents."

Chalk giggled.

Aida shook her head disapprovingly.

"Portal Systems are an instantaneous way to move from one point to another across the SpiralVerse, but the process is complicated, dangerous, and therefore restricted. Because of this, portals are only to be used under the scrutiny of an officially licensed portal administrator, as a last resort, or in case of an emergency. GAPSS regulations. Galactic Institute rules. Do not break them. The consequences are extremely unpleasant."

Krieg grumbled impatiently.

"However," de Rema said, raising a black-nailed finger, "during Introduction to Portals we have special dispensation." Chalk smiled, catching the professor's eye. "Miss Hale, you look like a keen, bright-eyed student. Perhaps you'd like to be first—"

"I will go first," said Cressida, barging Chalk and Ripley aside.

The professor frowned. "Very well, Miss Van Wyrm. Have you used a portal on your own before?"

"Of course I have," the Veroselli scoffed. "We have technology on Zorik Minor far superior to anything GAPSS and the Galactic Institute can boast. Our portal system is activated by personalised DNA sequences and uses a hydroplasmic—"

"How nice," de Rema said, cutting the princess off. "So— for the sake of the class—the large circular section of the portal is called the threshold. These cumbersome looking drums at the base contain power cells. They rotate the threshold while syphoning and regulating the power surge needed to activate a temporal doorway—the black filmy stuff—while the keypad at the side is ... well, it's just a keypad."

Chalk sketched a diagram of the portal onto a blank layer screen.

"The Terrazuma Treaty dictates that portal travel be exclusively limited to biological materials, other than a three point one four per cent tolerance for clothes and GI-VRs. This means your eduhelpers will have to remain behind. Cressida, I trust your C1000 will be suitably proficient in guarding them for us."

Cressida looked bored but ordered her droid to remain behind. INFIN-8 gave a disgruntled *URRRH!* as Ripley deposited him next to Cressida's imposing AstroTech.

"Now, hundreds of thousands of portals exist through the SpiralVerse, all accessible with the right keyphrase—encrypted passcodes or retinal scans are occasionally required too—and the swipe of an official, approved, personalised passkey."

Unzipping the top of her body suit, Professor de Rema tugged out a white card and let it dangle from a lanyard. The professor's face and details were printed to one side, a jagged flash of hexachromatic film on the other. As she ran the card over the keypad, the edge of the threshold bloomed with amber lights. The power cells emitted a low thrum.

She looked at Cressida. "Okay then, Miss Van Wyrm. Scan your GI-VR and type: GI002." The Veroselli complied. "Hit the blue square at the bottom." A temporal doorway appeared. A rippling black sheet. "Okay. Good. Now, one at a time. Follow Miss Van Wyrm. And keep moving on the other side or you'll trip over one another."

Chalk let Aida go ahead. Ripley and Milton followed. They found themselves standing on a platform overlooking a busy kitchen. Mouth-watering and insufferable aromas enveloped them, like a bowl of truffle-ganache glazed yuccagourds.

"Are we all here? Yes, yes. Good. Okay, so, this is Portal Site GI002," de Rema instructed over the noise from the kitchen. "This is one of the busiest portals on the Coin as deliveries of fresh produce and ingredients arrive constantly. Before us is the preparation hall and kitchens for the various cuisines available at the Galactic Institute."

"I'm next," Krieg decided, looking at the portal. "Let's get this over with."

"Of course. No rush. Does anyone want to look around the kitchens before we depart? Everyone gets a chance. This *is* a double class!"

With no takers for a kitchen tour, the professor returned to the portal. Under de Rema's guidance, Krieg scanned his GI-VR, punched in GI003, and hit the blue square. They filed onto the flight deck where Commander Lasco sat against a stack of dismantled eduhelpers.

"Is the commander okay?"

"He's fine," de Rema told Chalk, shepherding the class back towards the portal. "Just having an afternoon nap, I shouldn't wonder."

Chalk and Ripley exchanged glances.

Professor de Rema invited the Tattorian next. Using a voice-activated upgrade on her GI-VR, Aida verbally entered GI004 and transported them to a windowless room in the basement of the lecture theatre complex.

"An emergency exit," the professor informed them, "and quick access for masterclass tutors and external, last-minute substitute professors."

Necrotta took them to GI005, a mirror image of GI004 at the other end of the complex. Ripley went next. GI006 was situated in the lobby of the laboratories and study halls that rose several stories, constructed of sleek architectural patchwork of bio-glass and sculpted metal sheets. Stairways criss-crossed overhead; doorways and corridors vanished in all directions.

"Excellent work," said the professor. "Just Lord Barclay and Miss Hale remaining. Perhaps one of you would like to take us back to the portal chamber beside the observation hall."

Chalk stepped up.

She scanned her GI-VR. The keypad turned blue, her name and digitised photo appeared in the top corner. Chalk typed GI001 and pressed the blue square. The temporal doorway opened and, after some corralling by Professor de Rema, everyone filed through.

"Hang on, First Cycle Aktari," de Rema said as the class began to disperse. "Not everyone has had a chance to use the portal."

Milton shuffled nervously. His eyes flicked towards the threshold, the power cells, and the keypad. "Don't panic, Lord Barclay," the professor encouraged, swiping her passkey. "It's quite simple. First, scan your GI-VR—"

Krieg and Cressida exchanged spiteful words.

Leaving Milton at the keypad, the professor rushed away to deal with the situation. "What is occurring?"

"The Veroselli was casting shade upon the Garrangulan horde," Krieg erupted, spittle forming around his mouth.

"I was stating facts gathered at the last Zorik Minor gloomsday census," Cressida replied. "No harm in that."

"I will have no more of this," de Rema told them. "This is the Galactic Institute, not the Killing Fields of Zorik Minor." Frowning, she urged them back to the portal chamber where Milton stood looking decidedly unwell. "Now, the choice is yours, Milton. Take us to any of the six portals on the Coin. Simply type: GI00 and then any number from one to six."

"Right. Sure," said the Sagaroach. "Think I've got it."

The threshold spun. Turned blue. A sheen of rippling black materialised.

With Cressida and Krieg hissing insults at one another, de Rema forced everyone through the temporal doorway.

Chalk had only taken a single step out the other side when a sense of dread swept through her. Rather than finding herself in one of the portal chambers on the Coin, she fought for balance on an uneven pile of crumbling stone. Dark wind swirled through broken walls. Skeletal towers loomed above. Ragged pennants and banners whipped viciously on blood-stained poles.

INAPPROPRIATE LANGUAGE DETECTED . . .

Professor de Rema stumbled through, still wrangling Krieg and Cressida whose argument had escalated to hair-pulling and eye-gouging. All three stopped and took in their surroundings. The professor looked ill. She did a full circuit of the threshold, which, by some miracle, had survived these desolate surroundings.

The power cells fizzed and sparked. Black smoke belched from one end. The temporal doorway spluttered and vanished. Blue light turned amber and blinked out.

They stood for a moment in the gathering dark, staring at the dead portal.

"What is happening?" said Aida.

No one answered.

"Have the climate controls failed?" she asked. "It is uncommonly cold."

"No," de Rema told her. "We're not at the Galactic Institute anymore."

"Where are we?" Chalk asked, zipping her jacket.

Professor Gabriella de Rema's eyes were wild with fear. "I have absolutely no idea."

Cressida levelled an accusatory finger towards Lord Milton Barclay XVII. "The stupid bug messed it up!"

Milton backed away, tripped over the defunct power cells and landed awkwardly on his wings. "Razabelle help me!" he screamed, scrambling to his feet.

"What is it?"

On the ground, wedged between heavy slats of fallen stone, were two strange skeletons. Chalk's skin crawled as she found the area littered with hundreds of skulls, bones, and weapons. Above, a star-smattered universe rotated. Vast and terrifying.

"What in God's name—?"

Cressida groaned. "I think I know where we are."

All eyes turned.

"This is Zorik Major."

"Impossible," Aida said. "Zorik Major was destroyed."

"True," Krieg added reproachfully. "But … chunks … remain."

"Chunks?" Milton said, reaching for a yuccagourd.

"We're standing on a chunk?"

"Of a destroyed planet?"

Necrotta ground his teeth.

"I do not mean to highlight the obvious," Aida said, her voice unaffected by the dire nature of their predicament. "But if the planet has been destroyed, then the gravitational field and therefore the atmospheric pressure would have eroded too. The fact we're breathing at all is nigh on imposs—"

"Look, it's quite simple," Cressida began hotly. "Veroselli—"

"And Garrangulan," Krieg added.

"—technology has been implemented on several of the larger remnants—like the Shield of Zorik and Zorikania—to support life. It works in much the same way as the environsphere surrounding the Coin."

"Ah, of course," Aida said, satisfied by the explanation. "Makes perfect sense."

"Sense? Sense!" Milton spluttered. "We're on a chunk of rock hurtling through the galaxy to goodness knows where."

"We are not hurtling anywhere," corrected Cressida. "We are in a wide orbit around Zorik Minor, tethered by the gravitational pull from the Shield of Zorik. Most of you are far more likely to die of dehydration than anything truly concerning."

Chalk nudged a pile of bones with her boot. "Who did these belong to?"

"Victims of the Zorik conflicts," said Necrotta.

"Veroselli," said Cressida, her voice low.

"And Garrangulars," Krieg added triumphantly.

"What about this one," said Ripley, kicking over a much smaller skeleton.

Cressida sneered.

Krieg spat on the arid ground.

"Sevantes," they said in unison.

"Who?"

"Vicious cut-throats," Krieg rumbled.

"Turncoats and betrayers," Cressida added. "Loyal to none but their own."

Krieg and Cressida set off in opposite directions to count their fallen dead.

Professor de Rema ran her hands over the threshold, opened the power drums, and inspected the dead cells inside. Her once impeccable demeanour had gone to hell. She shook with panic. Sweat beaded her forehead. "I just ... I think ... If I could only get—" she muttered, fiddling with wires and cables.

Chalk and Ripley hunkered beside her while Milton found a large crumbling pillar to hide behind.

"I can't be responsible for getting us stuck on Zorik Major," de Rema bleated, looking at Ripley. "It's only my second cycle at the Galactic Institute. The first was shaky, but I made it through the ridiculously challenging GAPSS staff assessment programme. But this"—she blinked at the cables hanging from her hands like dead snakes—"could be the end of me."

Ripley placed a hand on the professor's shoulder. "I can sort this."

"I doubt that. You're in the first cycle! I graduated from the Galactic Institute with seventeen X grades. The highest achievement *ever* ... at the time. I have ten cycles of field work and laboratory experience, and a masterwork certificate in Emerging and Improbable Physics to rely on. These power cells are dead, Master Flinch. Are you an Elemental Caster? Can you regenerate the power cells without Aether? If so, I've never heard of such a thing." The professor's eyes became wild. Her hands shook. "But ... really? You can fix this?"

"I think so."

"You think?"

"You think?" Chalk echoed.

"Well, it looks like the power cells have overloaded. If we reroute the power through the keypad—which should have its own localised backup power source—we might be able to generate enough energy to send one person back."

"One person?" the professor wailed, dumping the cables on the cracked earth. Her entire body convulsed. "I mean, I could have come up with that. What good's sending one person back? There's eight stranded here!"

"Well," Chalk said, coming to Ripley's defence, "one person could raise the alarm, get Waxler or Asimov to figure out a way home."

"Gods! No!" de Rema exclaimed, pacing now. "If news of this finds its way to any of the faculty members—especially General Waxler—then my career is as dead as this portal. Over. Kaput. I'll be upgrading VR devices and replacing cracked monitor screens on Florian XIII before you can say—"

INAPPROPRIATE LANGUAGE DETECTED . . .

"Calm down, Professor," Ripley said. "My idea is … different."

"Different? How?"

"Well, if I can find a way to generate enough energy to send someone back, it's equally probable I can bring someone through."

The professor stared at Ripley. "So, instead of having eight lost souls, you mean to make us nine?"

"The new person can bring things to help."

"Who?" the professor asked.

"Lachrymosa? Dana Dune? Not … Spirit?"

Ripley shook his head. "INFIN-8."

"Your … eduhelper?"

"That broken battered barrel with the wonky legs?" de Rema moaned.

"Hey," Ripley said. "As Asimov once said, not everything is as it seems. INFIN-8 is quite resourceful."

De Rema shook her head. "But, as I explained, temporal doorways are only configured to allow a three point one four per cent tolerance for manufactured elements. If you send your eduhelper through, it'll be reduced to nothing but atoms. Configuring the portal to allow one hundred per cent manufactured materials is immeasurably complicated. Temporal doorways are not configured to displace and replace that level of manufactured properties. It's a simple matter of Improbable Physics, Master Flinch. Not to mention it goes against the Terrazuma Treaty. What you're advocating is an act of war!"

"War? What war?" Cressida said, returning. "Are we any closer to getting out of here?"

"Yeah, what's the timeframe?" added Krieg, shouldering her aside.

"Are you in a rush?" Aida said.

"Well, I do not mean to be alarmist," Cressida said, "but a new dilemma has arisen."

"New dilemma?" Aida asked.

"I can officially confirm that we are on a chunk of Zorik Major."

"Yes. So—?" Ripley said.

"Bad things happened here," Krieg told them.

"We can see that."

"Yes," Cressida said. "I believe this *ruin* is Fort Van Murk."

"Get to the point."

Cressida looked decidedly awkward. "The Battle at Fort Van Murk was won by … the Sevantes."

"Did we ever find out who the Sevantes were?" Chalk asked.

The Veroselli turned and pointed to a series of red flaming beacons that had ignited on the distant rocky horizon. "I think that's some of them over there."

"More are congregating on that escarpment," Krieg added, pointing a huge finger.

"And dozens more appear to be swarming down that ravine."

Chalk stood. Mouth open.

"They will not tolerate us on their turf."

"Blimey."

"We need to leave," the princess urged. "Right now!"

GAPSS
KNOWLEDGE
MAINFRAME

TATTORIANS
[SPECIES]
Homeworld: Tattoraan, Lang. Moon Whisper / Telepathic

Tattorians are a small, blind species with soft claws and large heads. Unlike other lifeforms in the galaxy, their existence is predetermined by a lifeforce—the precise length is unknown and differs from one Tattorian to the next. They are an incredibly intelligent species, revered Casters, can communicate telepathically, and sense their surroundings through echolocation.

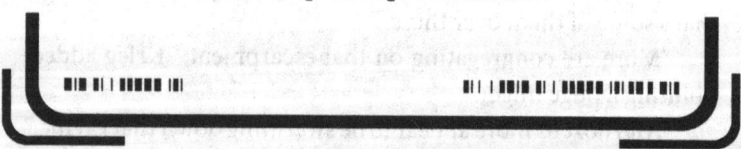

ATTACK OF THE BONES

Ripley whizzed through dozens of layer screens, adjusted his settings and code, then fired off a message. "If all the relay stations between here and the Galactic Institute are functioning correctly, INFIN-8 should be getting his instructions about … now. He'll signal when he's ready to come through."

"That's a big *if*," Cressida sneered.

"How long will he take?" Chalk said, shifting closer to the threshold.

"Well, he has to reach the flight deck, source some compatible power cells, load them up, and take them to the nearest portal chamber."

"And what about an official passkey?" de Rema said, waving hers in front of Ripley's face. "Your droid won't be able to access the portal without one."

"He's going to … borrow one," the Revan replied.

"Borrow?" she baulked. "How? From who?"

"I'm hoping the commander is having one of his … little rests."

"Lasco?"

"Makes strategic sense," Aida told them. "GI003 is adjacent to the flight deck."

"This also presumes that no one stops to ask what he is doing," Milton added.

"Quite," Ripley said. "Could be five minutes, could be five hours."

Cressida looked rattled.

Chalk found it reassuring that something could shake the Veroselli's cool exterior.

"Can your droid just ask Lasco to help?"

"He only speaks in *BINGs* and *URRRHs*."

"You failed to buy him a vocabulary upgrade?"

"Obviously, I could ask him to relay a message to Commander Lasco's GI-VR, but Professor de Rema wants to keep the circle close … for the sake of her career."

"What about the sake of our lives?" Cressida fired. "You clearly have no idea who my family are or the power they wield. If I die here, my family will kill you all."

"If you die here," Chalk told her smugly, "then we're dead too."

"Well, *Earthling*, they'll hunt and assassinate everyone and everything you ever loved," she bit and spun away.

Necrotta returned with handfuls of crude melee weapons. Everyone except Ripley and the professor selected one and swished it amateurishly through the air.

Aida stood facing the glowing red lights. "I would estimate the Sevantes will be in range in … eleven minutes."

"You're able to sense that far?" Chalk said.

"It is an open space," she replied. "Vibrations are easier to read when there is less environmental clutter."

"How many are there?"

"That is harder to deduce. They are grouped together," Aida told her. "But perhaps we should operate on the irrefutable fact that we are too few to prevail."

"Code: Bleak!" Chalk said with a grimace.

"Your frivolous approach to danger and hardship are both astounding and infuriating."

"Standard human defence mechanism. It's laugh or cry!" Chalk's explanation just seemed to infuriate Aida further.

Squabbling once more, Cressida, Krieg, and Necrotta clambered over the rubble to the edge of the fort. Chalk watched them duck behind a low wall to observe the advancing enemy.

Ripley dug through the mess of cables while the professor rerouted power from the keypad to the threshold, dumped the spent power cells, and cleaned the blown connectors. Nervously, Ripley tested the device. The faintest trace of amber flickered around the threshold. "This might just work."

Chalk smiled. Fear and relief writhed inside like duelling serpents. "I thought your Specialisms were Languages and Anthropology."

"That's my ... Yeah, sure. But, you know, I like to dabble in physics too," Ripley replied, opening the end of the keypad and retrieving a clutch of wires. Connecting them to his GI-VR, he fired up a stack of layer screens and began typing.

"You *dabble*?" de Rema said, her eyes wild. "What are you doing now?"

"Re-formatting the temporal doorway to receive one hundred per cent manufactured materials," he replied, not looking up. "It's just a matter of increasing the atomic density and using an eight trillion node algorithm to digitally adjust and randomly predict—"

"That'll never work," the professor said. "You're asking the device to make a one in eight trillion estimation. A blind guess!"

"It'll be a better guess than if I do it myself!"

"But your eduhelper could get dematerialised!"

"Yep."

"And it's against the law!"

"Better ideas welcome."

Professor de Rema swallowed hard. Her eyes flicked towards the reddening skies. "Hurry up."

"What I need from you is a swipe from your passkey and the Galactic Institute integrated portal system access node for our journey home."

"Yes. Of course," the professor said, fiddling with her GI-VR to retrieve the details. "I cannot give these to you directly. They're confidential."

"I thought as much," Ripley said. "Just have them ready!"

With everything set, Ripley, Chalk and the professor stood, poised, ready for INFIN-8's message. The skies became choked with red smoke. The noise of the approaching Sevantes grew. Cressida arrowed between the fort wall and the portal, demanding answers and timeframes, her anger and frustration on full display. Krieg and Necrotta remained at the wall, weapons in hand, as though eager for the confrontation to swallow them like a crimson wave.

Chalk scanned the fort for Milton. She found him skirting the outer wall, concealed in shadow. "You okay?" she asked, creeping closer.

"Leave me."

"What kind of talk is that?"

"I've gone and gotten us killed."

"Not yet you haven't. I'm still breathing."

"It's only a matter of time."

"You made a mistake," Chalk told him. "It's no big deal. I've made tons of mistakes."

Milton turned his strange eyes to her.

"There was this one time," she continued, "when I made tea for the Ambassador of Antarctica, and I accidentally used salt instead of sugar. He spat the lot all over a painting of Prime Minister Boris Johnson."

Milton chuckled and threw a fresh yuccagourd into his mouth.

"How many of those things do you have?"

"Nearly run out."

"How long can you go without them?"

"Milton Barclay XI once went for twenty-two hours without one. That's a colonies record."

"What happened to him?"

"Starved to death."

"Grisly."

"I don't want to be beaten to a pulp," Milton said. "Or die of starvation."

"That is no one's dream day out," Chalk replied. "Let's hope Ripley and the professor can work some magic and portal us the hell out of Dodge!"

They returned to the portal as a gossamer temporal doorway etched the threshold. Ripley muttered to himself, frantically making adjustments on his GI-VR until the doorway darkened. Everyone watched in silence as the flimsy film stuttered and shook, promising to fail.

And then—

INFIN-8 came marching through.

"Yes!" Ripley yelled, punching the air.

BING! BING! BING!

Ripley lifted INFIN-8 and spun him in joyous circles. Placing the droid next to the portal, he flipped INFIN-8's lid, reached inside, and retrieved the power cells.

One, two, three, four—

Chalk watched on, amazed.

It seemed impossible that INFIN-8 could hold—

—five, six, seven, eight.

Diving shoulder deep, Ripley retrieved huge coils of cabling and plonked them on the crumbling ground.

"How in the Mary Poppins are you doing that?"

INFIN-8's lid snapped shut. The buddy droid scuttled away.

Ripley inspected each of the power cells. He discarded several incompatible units until he had two contenders. Dropping them into the drums beside the threshold, de Rema attached the cables and tightened the locking nuts.

At the fort wall, a desperate cry rose on the swirling wind. The red glow of the Sevantes' fire beacons had consumed the sky. Cressida came barrelling over, a curved blade in her hand. "He made it," she said, gawping at INFIN-8. "The tin can actually made it!"

"We're almost ready," Ripley said, standing and re-setting the keypad for anatomical portal travel. "Okay. Got it. Get Krieg and Necrotta and let's go!"

Cressida paused. "But we could just—"

"We are *not* leaving them behind," de Rema said angrily.

Cressida didn't move.

"Fine," Chalk huffed. "I'll go."

She hopped from one fallen wall to the next. Hurdling skeletal remains, she glimpsed the wailing, fiery red horde rushing towards her.

"It's go time!" she wailed, mounting the wall and wishing she'd said something better.

Krieg and Necrotta looked disappointed but dashed back to the portal where Professor de Rema swiped her passkey and punched in the GI access node.

The power cells fired.

The temporal doorway ignited, strong and true.

"Go! Go! Go!" Ripley yelled.

Behind Krieg and Necrotta, a torrent of screaming creatures vaulted the outer wall.

Milton pushed his way to the front and dived through the portal, Aida a close second. Ripley forced the professor through next, grabbing Chalk by the shoulder and turning her to face the threshold. "See you back home," he said, urging her forward.

The Sevantes had gained significant ground.

Krieg and Necrotta were engaged with more than a dozen emaciated creatures. Their skin looked malformed, thin, plastered in dirt. Bright red paint smeared their sunken cheeks. In their hands swung weapons cast from bone and sharpened stone. Cressida ducked the blow from one Sevante, vaulted another, then attempted to trip Krieg. The Garrangular lurched at Cressida, who simply laughed, dived past Chalk, and swept through the temporal doorway.

"Go," Ripley urged. "I'm right behind you!"

With the crunch of bone on bone, the roar of Krieg and Necrotta engaged in mortal combat, and her heartbeat thundering in her ears, Chalk came to a skidding halt on the floor of the portal chamber adjacent to the flight deck.

Commander Lasco was hunched over Professor de Rema.

He glanced up and smiled.

Krieg emerged, Necrotta close behind, weapons in mid-swing. The Garrangular raised his weapon again and sprang towards Cressida. Both went tumbling to the ground. Fists and hair and curses flew. Lasco wrenched them apart.

Chalk's breath caught in her chest as she stood, waiting for Ripley to materialise.

He clattered through moments later, landing awkwardly. Two Sevantes erupted into the portal chamber. Commander Lasco spun, grabbed both by the shoulders and launched them, screaming, back to Fort Van Murk.

Ripley frantically activated his GI-VR.

Stabbed a layer screen.

The temporal doorway fizzed.

Stuttered.

Closed.

The chamber fell silent.

Ripley spun, chest heaving. "Are we all here?"

"There should be eight of us," de Rema managed. "Make sure there's eight."

"Hush, Gabriella," Lasco said. "What in the name of Arcadian's Third Eye did you do?"

"Nothing," the professor told him, her eyes fierce with warning. "Nothing. At. All."

Chalk quickly counted. "Yeah, we're all here. All eight of us," she confirmed, then looked to Ripley. "What are you doing?"

The Revan was at the keypad, unplugging the device and attaching his GI-VR.

"Ripley? It's done. We're all here. We're all safe."

He looked at her. "And what about INFIN-8?"

Chalk's stomach dropped. She pictured the wobbly-legged droid stuck on Zorik Major surrounded by hordes of Sevantes, their haunting screams, and their bludgeoning weapons.

Surely it was too late.

"I just have to reconfigure the device for one hundred per cent manufactured materials," he said, fingers flying over multiple layer screens. "Increase the atomic density. Activate my eight trillion node algorithm. And … press … the … blue square."

The temporal doorway developed.

Everyone gathered round, pushing in.

Ripley consulted his settings.

The doorway rippled slowly, calmly.

"It's too late," Cressida hissed. "The tin can is lost."

"You'd like that, wouldn't you?" Krieg snapped.

"I'll rip that vile tongue from your repugnant throat."

"Shut up," Ripley yelled. "All of you."

Silence.

No one dared breathe.

Ripley's gaze darted from his GI-VR to the keypad to the temporal doorway. His gaze fell on Chalk, a look of utter confusion and dismay on his face.

And then …

INFIN-8 burst through.

The burning remnants of Sevantes' limbs and weapons clung to the buddy droid for an instant then dematerialised into ember and ash on the buckled treadplate.

INFIN-8 staggered, spun, and collapsed with a hollow *clang!*

Ripley brushed the steaming residue away and pulled his eduhelper close.

A tear escaped Chalk's eye.

A swell of relief in her heart.

Phase one—the approximation of ten Earth days—passed with considerably less drama than her trip to Zorik Major. However, ten straight rotations of trial classes proved exhausting. She found herself being pulled from dreams about mind-boggling physics, fiddly robotics, and tongue-twisting languages by the more refined alarm system Cube had adopted.

The tension between Cressida and Krieg remained palpable, but both gave Chalk a slither of respect in the rec room. A snort. A shallow nod.

On the morning of the eleventh rotation, all classes ceased. Taking the initiative, Chalk went through her notes. She made a list of what she liked and disliked about each topic, trying to fathom which to add to her permanent timetable.

Her door buzzed.

Cube slipped inside its orb as Aida and Milton entered.

"What are you up to?" the Tattorian asked. "Choosing an outfit for the welcome ball?"

"Not a chance," Chalk said. "Working out the next six cycles of my life."

"Finally," Aida said. "Are you any closer to deciding what you want to do with your existence?"

"If anything, I'm further away." She reduced her layer screens and slumped on the bed. Aida took the chair while Milton loomed in the doorway.

"When does Asimov want your timetable decision?"

"Today, I think. He said by the end of phase one, but I get confused whether that includes the two-rotation break or not. Phases, rotations, cycles. Boils my noodle."

"He probably meant yesterday," Milton added unhelpfully.

Chalk groaned. "Shall I flip a coin?"

Aida and Milton looked concerned.

"Not the actual Coin. A coin. A physical unit of currency. We still have them on Earth, although they're rarely used anymore. My ... grandpa collects them."

Aida touched her hand soothingly.

"I'm okay," Chalk said. "Just missing a few people. That's all. Mum, Grandpa, my friends. And have you seen Ripley lately? He's gone all ... distant again."

Aida took a deep breath. "His energy has changed," she said.

"Nothing bad. A different sensation surrounds him now."

"Sensation?"

"Correct."

"Something to do with Zorik Major?"

"Undoubtedly."

"I saw Professor de Rema," Chalk added. "She was all composed and authoritarian again, her clothes and hair immaculate. But I can't forget that look in her eyes. That mad, primal fear."

"Ripley probably needs some time to deal with what happened."

"Yeah, maybe."

"We should go and ask him," Milton said. "Direct questions would be better than all this speculation."

"I've tried," Chalk said. "He says he's researching private projects and has *a lot going on.*"

"Probably missing home too," the Sagaroach said, reaching for a snack. "Not that I can appreciate what that feels like. My family couldn't wait to ship me off to the Galactic Institute."

Milton's St4rCr4ft™ 85R appeared in the doorway. "At last," it honked miserably. "Those stairs are savage beasts. My legs can barely reach. Any sign of an upgrade in my future?"

Milton shrugged. "Sorry. I'm totally cut off. Not a single quasoid in sight."

The St4rCr4ft™ 85R moaned, lowered itself and powered down.

Chalk rolled the mystery ball towards her and gave it a reassuring squeeze.

GAPSS
KNOWLEDGE
MAINFRAME

GALACTIC INSTITUTE GARDENS
[THE FLIPSIDE] [RECREATION]

The Galactic Institute gardens, colloquially referred to as the Flipside, consist of large green spaces on the opposite surface of Centurion H to the Galactic Institute. The gardens are open to the student body, faculty, and visitors, encouraging exercise, exploration, and positive mental and physical well-being. As well as a phalanx of research buildings, monoliths, follies, and fountains, the Flipside is home to millions of non-lethal plants, animals, and insect life from every corner of the SpiralVerse.

WELCOME BALL

Aida and Milton helped Chalk complete her timetable. Galactic Culture, Domestic and Interspecies Languages, and History of the Galaxy had gone in easily. She'd highlighted all Professor Mirage's art classes but had to sacrifice Plasma Sculpture and Five-Dimensional Puppetry as they clashed with Biodiverse Medical Science and Metaphysical Mathematics which Aida insisted Chalk *had* to take, even though they filled her with the most severe incarnations of dread.

She took a couple of practical classes—Conflict Engagement and Empirical Mechanics—explaining to Aida that the need to defend herself or repair robots had become more than a distant possibility and had nothing to do with her ambition to pilot Commander Lasco's flight simulator in the third cycle. At all. Against her better judgement, Chalk chanced her arm at Emerging Physics, Chemical Cosmology, Dark Matter, and Galactic Law, too.

The first cycle was a time for experimentation after all.

No matter how terrifying it seemed.

Scrolling down the layer screen, her fingers hovered over three empty boxes. "I still don't know what to put for my Specialisms and Primaries. Or my Career Target."

"Specialisms and Primaries can be changed any time before the end of the second cycle," Aida told her.

"What are yours again?"

"Specialisms: Cerebral Casting. Primaries: Interplanetary

Politics, Anatomy of the Species, and Galactic Culture," Aida reeled off. "Career Target: Diplomatic Communicator."

"History of the Galaxy," Milton said. "For both. Keeping it simple. History is just about remembering dates and names after all. No lateral thinking required."

Chalk's fingers twitched, wondering what this moment meant. It felt substantial but she had two cycles to change her mind. She typed History of the Galaxy and Conflict Engagement into Primaries, and Narrative of Story into Specialisms. She had no idea if she'd be any good at those, but they certainly were the most enjoyable.

Typing quickly, she entered her Career Target.

"What's a ... Jedi Master?" Milton asked, peering over her shoulder.

"It's aspirational," Chalk told him. "Something to aim for."

"Good for you."

"Right, who else could use some recycled air?"

First Cycle Aktari living quarters teemed with students. Cressida and her Veroselli friends loitered around the beverage dispenser sipping long, clear drinks. The Vyshan Order cloistered together, hoods drawn, shrouded beneath red cloaks. Necrotta sat alone, digging dirt from his claws with curved, glistening fangs.

Deciding to go elsewhere, they descended to the rec room. Students from all chronotypes stormed, slithered, and floated about. Chalk hadn't spoken to any students from Osmotrino, Zalazor, or Qantoculus yet, or discovered what strange worlds they were from. Trying to take in everything in Aktari was enough for now.

She swiped a cheese sandwich from the dispenser and, rather than riding the AGT, they took the stairs, passed the gym—where Krieg, Kiln, and Kroket were engaged in combat training—and out onto the Coin.

Paths led in all directions on the uneven surface. Heated patches of coloured resin broke up the monochromatic facade, where the conjoined Traxa twins lounged, and the vulpine Karmethian Renix played a non-contact game with balls and discs with Spirit. They took the ring road: a six-kilometre path along the edge of the Galactic Institute. Squat circular buildings of the lecture theatre complex loomed to their right in shades of grey, ringed with peeling orange and blue hoops.

Hundreds of windows had gone dark. Classes on pause.

Chalk could feel the pulse and gentle hum of the environsphere against her left cheek, and the draw of infinite space beyond.

Milton wandered to the edge, peered over, and regretted it immediately.

"You cannot fall," Aida told him.

The Sagaroach grumbled, feeding his face.

"What's over there?" Chalk asked.

"Ultimately," Aida replied, "the Flipside."

"I know that," Chalk said. "But if Milton falls? Is he thrown back or swept over or … something else?"

"Are you proposing we find out?"

Chalk clapped excitedly.

"You are *not* throwing me over the edge of the Coin as part of some experiment."

"Spoilsport."

"The chances of you being hurt in any way are almost zero," Aida told him.

"The risk is too high," he said, and scampered away from the edge.

Pristina, the poison-breathing Moxi, jogged by, gasping through her breath-diffuser while Vitarus trundled along behind like a golden hamster in a liquid ball.

They passed the second and third cycle dorms, arriving at the study halls and the towering research laboratories beyond. Lights inside the tower, like the lecture theatre complex, were all out.

Except one.

At the top, where the patchwork exterior wrapped the building like decorative ribbons, shone a single light.

Who works on the rotation break? A professor probably, catching up on research or study plans. Maintenance droids perhaps, industriously moving through the building.

But, as she watched, a silhouette appeared at the window.

They appeared to be talking to someone. Someone she couldn't see.

Chalk stared, convinced she recognised the silhouette.

It wasn't a professor, or a droid, or even General Waxler.

She couldn't be sure, but it looked just like Ripley Flinch.

By the time they'd reached the fourth cycle dorms, Milton had sore feet and a cramp in his thorax. Aida and Milton returned home via the AGT, while Chalk zipped to the museum. She paced the descending spiral walkways, nodding courteously at the holograms of Admiral Xenon, the Figoria sisters, and Captain Dak Einhorn. She read a batch of info screens she'd missed the first time and sat through a twenty-minute instructional video on the correct use and maintenance of the Gigantor battle mech.

Back in her room, Chalk read from *Harriet Starlight and the Cosmic Boneyard*. Cube listened as Harriet Starlight discovered her father was actually Daj Villannious—the flamboyant space warlock—and had to escape the homeworld she loved before his pernicious magic eviscerated her fragile human brain.

Snapping the book shut with satisfaction, Chalk smiled. Cube had a bunch of questions about the story, but there wasn't time for book group.

She pulled on a pair of tight-fitting black trousers with pink double stripes on the hem, a *Star Wars* T-shirt Grandpa Milo had given her, and heavy boots. Rolling bracelets over her wrist, she applied a shimmer of cherry lip gloss and edged her eyes with dark pencil. She inspected herself in the mirror and groaned. "I should probably wear a dress."

"You look highly presentable," Cube told her.

"Presentable?" she said. "That's not exactly flattering."

"How would you like to look?"

"Cool. Mysterious. Edgy." Chalk kicked off her boots and yanked down her trousers. She rummaged in her suitcase—as she hadn't bothered to unpack properly—and fished out two dresses.

One black. The other dark grey.

She raised a questioning eyebrow.

"The one on the right," Cube said.

Chalk took the other, whipped off her T-shirt, and pulled it on. She twirled like a ballerina in front of the mirror. The pleats bloomed pleasingly.

"Better?"

"Different."

"Thank you. That's very helpful."

"I am programmed for education and research. My knowledge of Earth's fashions, styles, and oeuvre are much maligned. Upgrades are available at the recreation arcade."

Chalk ignored Cube, stuffed her feet into the heavy boots and twirled a gossamer pink pashmina, embellished with tiny black skulls, around her neck.

"I'm calling it cyberpunk-goth-chic."

UPDATING . . .

Chalk stopped suddenly, catching her reflection in the mirror on the back of the door.

You've come so far, Harriet Starlight told her. *Adventure is to therapy, as time is to wisdom.*

"I should have gone to my end-of-year party with Kit, and Bloue, and Zara," Chalk replied, fussing with the pashmina. "I'll make up for it tonight."

Deciding her outfit was as good as it was going to get, she punched the keypad and the door retracted into the wall.

On the other side stood Ripley Flinch.

The Revan wore an off-white jumpsuit draped with a long blue cape and high collar. A silver chain circled his neck with a pendant concealed beneath. He'd painted black streaks around his eyes and smothered holding wax through his hair to make it stick out in a dozen sharp points.

"Hey," she said. "I didn't expect to see you."

Ripley looked puzzled. "Erm, really? Pretty sure we'd agreed we were both going to the welcome ball."

"Yeah," she muttered. "It's just, you know, you've been …"

"Busy?" he finished. "Yeah, sorry. Come on, everyone else is queuing for the AGT. Aida and Milton are saving us a spot in line."

The hyperloop swirled chaotically with strange fashions, peculiar hairstyles, and overwhelming perfumes that Chalk concluded were probably all the rage in some far-flung star system. Rising through one of the busy off-tubes, she clattered into Ripley again as they hit the disembarkation pod.

"I'll stop doing that one day," she told him, laughing.

Ripley straightened his cape.

Music struck their ears.

Chalk turned, gasped. The observation hall had been transformed into a cavern of swirling lights, lasers, and billowing smoke. At the centre, surrounding the rickety elevator, were enormous screens projecting footage from drone cameras that buzzed overhead. On a platform that circled the elevator, danced an iridescent octopod. She appeared to be selecting music from a sphere of layer screens that spun round her like a giant globe.

"Thoden be praised!" Ripley said. "We've got Octomica."

"Octommy-what?"

"Octomica," he enthused. "She's only one of the best audio manipulators in the SpiralVerse. Must have set GI back a stack of quasoids."

Aida and Milton joined them at a crescent of tables.

"What music is this?" Milton asked.

"Marstokian dirge," Ripley told him, bobbing gently to the angular beat.

Milton scowled, clearly unimpressed. "We have different music on the colonies."

"I'm sure Octomica will play some bug beats!"

"I quite like music," Aida said, tapping her foot. "It is sonic arithmetic after all."

"Right," Chalk said. "But bleak and distorted!"

Octomica switched sounds and a tidal wave of Garrangulars launched themselves onto the dance floor.

"The Grangs like music?" Chalk said.

"They have souls after all," Milton joked.

"It's a tribal fighting song," Ripley informed them. "Gets them in the mood for battle."

"Highly irresponsible."

A group of professors snaked through the tables, nodding at students and sipping shallow glasses filled with steaming green liquid. Asimov and Snider stepped aside to reveal General Waxler behind. She wore a long red qipao-style dress beneath her usual fitted jacket and high collar. Her hair had been curled tightly and hung majestically beside her sharp chin.

"Miss Hale," she said, approaching their table. "Master Flinch, Miss Kromm-Nargulantis, Lord Barclay." She gazed around the room. "What do you think?"

They nodded enthusiastically.

"This is quite the party," Chalk said. "I missed the last one at my old school."

"I remember. The night of the Declaration, yes?"

"That's right."

"Well, if you had gone to that party then you might not be here now."

"I guess not."

"Do you regret it?"

"No," Chalk said. "Just missing home a little, that's all."

"Ah, yes. The ties that bind," Waxler went on. "Many new

bonds to make and others to break. GAPSS and the Galactic Institute are overjoyed to have you. We hope you are happy too." She smiled. "Have a good evening."

The general rejoined Asimov and Snider and vanished into the crowd.

"Remind me to make you watch *Battlestar Galactica*," Chalk said, turning, but Ripley had moved away. She spied him talking with Professor de Rema who was flexing all twenty fingers and looking highly agitated.

"What was that about?" Chalk asked when Ripley returned.

"Come on," he said, grabbing her hand. "I love this song."

The Garrangulars stalked away as an upbeat tune filled the room. Chalk followed Ripley's lead, dancing to the strange sounds.

"Is this a Revan song?"

"Revan?" He laughed. "No chance. There's no indigenous music on Revus X. We listen to whatever they pipe in."

The song ended and another began. Slower, mid-tempo. Ripley and Chalk swayed along, their eyes finding one another's. He brushed past. Their arms touched momentarily as smoke swirled through beams of coloured light.

Chalk's skin rippled.

Her breath caught in her chest.

The music slowed again. Necrotta's tail unbalanced Chalk, sending her pirouetting into Ripley's arm. He caught her expertly but didn't let go. Instead, they spun, moving gently to the music. Pale light dappled their skin as the sound coiled around them, smooth and comforting. Feeling Ripley's breath against her neck, powerful emotions bloomed in her chest. Happiness and confusion, excitement and fear. The room seemed to spin in the opposite direction. Her vision stretched into long ribbons of vibrating light.

"Are you okay?" he asked.

"Yes. I'm … great," she replied. "How is everything?"

"Chalk?"

"With you, I mean."

Ripley's fingers found her waist. "Me?"

"Yeah. I'm … that is … we're worried about you," Chalk said, nodding toward Aida and Milton who were joined by some classmates.

"I'm great too," Ripley said, his eyes studying her face.

"It's just … Zorik Major," she said. "And the last few rotations. And just now with Professor de Rema …" Ripley frowned. His grip loosened. "And …" She faltered, wondering if she should ask him if he met someone in the research labs on rotation break.

"And what?"

Chalk's arms fell to her side. Her bravery dwindled. "Nothing. Nothing at all." She stopped dancing. "We're your friends, Ripley. We … care about you."

Cressida sailed past, her long arms locked around the neck of a sixth cycle Veroselli. She raised a sardonic eyebrow and whipped her hair over her shoulder.

"Whatever's going on," Chalk said. "We're here if you need us."

Ripley frowned again, shrugged.

More students poured onto the dance floor as the music transitioned into a high energy stomp. Spirit materialised through the smoke, her eyes sparkling like adamonte crystals. She ran her hands seductively over Ripley's chest before circling him in a series of vulgar dance moves.

"I guess I'll go and see how—" Chalk began, but Garrangulars swarmed the edge of the dancefloor, their eyes filled with menace. "They're at it again," she said, grabbing Ripley and looking for Cressida and the rest of the Veroselli.

Spirit shot death-eyes at Chalk as her dance moves became increasingly lavish.

"That's their business," said Ripley.

"We've got to do something before a full-scale riot breaks out."

"What do you suggest?"

"You're the guy with the plans."

"This isn't a matter of portal dynamics, Hale. This is age-old hatred, passed down through generations."

"But isn't there some sort of atmospheric environmental thingiemawotsits to stop them ripping each other to pieces?"

"Supposedly," Ripley said, "but look around. Everything is on the wrong side of broken, outdated and in need of replacing. Why should those devices be any different?"

Garrangulan arms smashed through the crowds. Students screamed. Some fell to their knees and claws and socket joints, scrambling and crawling to escape.

Across the dance floor, Veroselli stood their ground.

There were twenty or more on each side, Roses and Grangs from every cycle.

The elder Garrangulars led the charge, bellowing and pounding their chests and thighs. Krieg and Kiln and Kroket followed, a look of wild hatred in their eyes. But the Veroselli appeared unfazed, as though they'd seen the behaviour a million times. They stood, posed, sneered. A chair launched from the Garrangulan side. It tumbled through the air, heading directly at Prince Castor Van Wyrm.

But the chair never connected.

Instead, to Chalk's amazement, it froze in mid-air.

The music died.

The conflict alarm sounded.

Lights flooded the observation hall like an operating table.

Professor Dustenberg stood on the dance floor between the two rival factions, her hands raised towards the spinning chair. Asimov, Snider, and de Rema were quickly at her side, eyeing both sets of students. General Waxler swept in and circled the professors, her long cape whipping viciously.

"What is the meaning of this?" she said coolly. "This is a party, not a Qwork fight on the lower decks of a smuggler's starship." She studied each Veroselli in turn. "Master Van Wyrm. Castor. I have never had a sliver of trouble from you in over five cycles," she said, still pacing. "Why now? Why this?" Before the Veroselli could answer, the general eyeballed a sixth cycle Garrangular. "You too, Krantos? There have been years of peace between your two races on Zorik Minor and here on the Coin. Why this? Why now?"

The Garrangular grunted, her arms locked, muscles swelling to engage.

General Waxler's boots clicked against the mismatched treadplate.

No one spoke.

No one dared.

"This party is over," she announced. "Blame your Veroselli and Garrangulan classmates for curtailing the fun." Looking at each species, her eyes shook with a silent fury. "Go!"

GAPSS
KNOWLEDGE
MAINFRAME

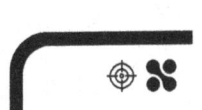 

ONERICS
[SPECIES]
Homeworld: Gaia 15, Lang. Galaxian

Onerics are never truly awake nor asleep. They exist in a
dream-like state for their entire lives, flitting in and out of
consciousness. Some Onerics are believed to move through
alternate consciousnesses, realities, and dimensions but
no evidence has ever been ratified by GAPSS.

MISSING

Mum. This place is amazing and ~~insane~~ somewhat confusing. The Coin is huge, crammed with hundreds of buildings, and surrounded by the most fantastic nebula. They have transport tunnels you can literally FLY down and portals that zip you off to any place in the ~~Milky~~ SpiralVerse. I think I love the military museum the most. It's full of starfyters and battle meks and holograms of fallen war heroes. But the whole place is broken and looks nothing like the digital brochure you showed me. I do have my own robot, like R2-D2, but made of orange goo. ~~I'm eating a lot of cheese~~. General Waxler and the rest of the faculty seem okay. Classes are WAY harder than anything I've studied before, and no one understands my pop culture refs. I've made a few friends. ~~And a few enemies~~. There's my relay partner Aida, and a six-foot insect called Milton, and this one boy, a Revan, called Ripley. He's cool and smart, but a little stand-off-ish. Yet, despite their friendship, I'm still kinda alone. I'm an Earthling. The only one. I guess to them … I'm the alien. Everyone else has people from their homeworlds. They understand the history. The culture. The way things are done. There's violence here. An ancient, vicious hatred. It scares me. How are you? Any word about Dad? I miss you so much. I love you. Tell Grandpa Milo—

Chalk sat in bed, fully clothed. Her mother's emerald fountain pen hovered over her notebook. The warm glow from Cube illuminated the room as memories of the confrontation at the welcome ball tumbled through her mind.

Krieg's enraged face.

Cressida's holier-than-thou smile.

Waxler's dominance.

They'd been escorted back to the dorms by Asimov and half a dozen Enforcers. The professor looked ragged and distraught. Chalk had tried to spark a lively discussion with him but, contrary to his trademark chatty nature, he'd had none of it.

Enforcers rumbled by outside.

Chalk wriggled deeper into her bedclothes.

"This is madness," she whispered, staring at the corroded system of pipes and vents on the ceiling.

"Your adrenaline levels spiked several times this evening," Cube informed her. "You experienced a huge rush of endorphins too. You are also mildly dehydrated."

"Why do the Veroselli and the Garrangulars hate each other so much?"

"Would you like to hear their entire biological, socio-economic, and military history?"

Chalk shook her head. "Just the highlights."

"Bathed in the glory of Zorik Prime," Cube began in an authoritarian tone, "the inhabitants of Zorik Major—known collectively as Zorans—lived in peace for millennia. But over thousands of years their genetics became fractured and broke into three distinct factions."

"The Veroselli and the Garrangulars are related?" Chalk said, amazed. "Hang on, *three* factions?"

"The erudite, the powerful, and the scraps," Cube explained.

"The Veroselli, the Garrangulars, and—?"

"—the Sevantes."

"Holy tragic trilogies! The Sevantes are related to the Veroselli and the Garrangulars?"

"Correct."

"But—" She let the rest of the sentence hang in her mind, unsure what it meant.

Cube continued. "The Veroselli and the Garrangulars used

politics and diplomacy for governance and control of Zorik Major. But, when Clod Van Wyrm and Krull became opposition leaders, a calamitous accident—involving an exuberance of illegal zorikanthium mining—brought about the destruction of their homeworld."

"Ah, so that's how Zorik Major became chunks!"

"Mutually assured destruction," Cube said.

"What's zorikanthium?"

"A crystal," the eduhelper said. "Phenomenally unstable."

"Intriguing."

"During the devastation, many escaped to Zorik Minor—the largest moon of Zorik Major—which now shelters behind the Shield of Zorik, a vast asteroid field created from the remnants of the destroyed planet."

"Ah, yes. I've read about that. It's one of the nine phenomenological wonders of the SpiralVerse."

"In the shadows of their dead world, the Zorik Wars escalated. Both the Veroselli and the Garrangulars enslaved the Sevantes, mercilessly wasting them over decades to furious fighting. But, once in every four hundred and thirty-two rotations, Zorik Minor breaks cover from the Shield of Zorik and bathes in the light of Zorik Prime. On this rotation, and this rotation only, the Veroselli and Garrangulars are at peace."

"Jeepers," Chalk said. "So, the light from their sun has a calming influence?"

"Perhaps," replied Cube. "The science is inconclusive."

"What about the Sevantes? Cressida and Krieg never mentioned they were descended from Zorans."

"The Veroselli and the Garrangulars are ashamed of their relationship to the Sevantes. They are small, slight, and thought to be dull of mind. But the Sevantes are highly organised. They rose up and turned their weapons against their masters."

"So, the Sevantes weren't some aggravated force. They were … slaves?"

"Quite so, but they broke their bonds and won their freedom.

All surviving Sevantes migrated to Zorik Pol, a distant, frozen moon, where they live in relative peace."

"But there were Sevantes at Fort Van Murk."

"There shouldn't be. It's a restricted, unstable land mass inside the Shield of Zorik."

"You don't say!"

Chalk wondered how many other civilisations had such a twisted, violent, and bloody history as those from the Zorik System. She couldn't help but think of Earth's own barbaric history and wondered if it was a matter of time before they met the same fate. She slipped the pen and notebook onto the bedside table, closed her eyes and, in Cube's embryonic glow, drifted into dreams.

Chalk rose early. The trundle of Enforcers had gone. Stony silence dominated the dorms instead. She gazed through the window, expecting to look upon the calming beauty of the Waterfall Nebula but, to her dismay, it had gone.

In the living quarters, the thin-skinned Sadler Arklan and avian-featured Olivia Hondrax of the Vyshan Order whispered beside the drinks dispenser. Revans Marcy-Kate Scythe, Rani Romesh, and Dana Dune sat crossed-legged on the sofas reading quietly.

"What's going on?" Chalk asked, hurrying downstairs. "Where are the Enforcers? And what happened to the Waterfall Nebula?"

The Revans shrugged.

The Vyshans ignored her.

Chalk descended to the rec room and boarded the AGT. She took the off-tube towards the administration lobby, clattered unceremoniously through the disembarkation pod, and approached the front desk.

Agitated voices bled from a room behind reception.

The waft of Asimov's throat remedy hung thick in the air.

"Hello," Chalk called timidly. "Anybody here?"

As she was about to give up, Asimov glanced out and caught her eye. He disappeared for a moment then strolled over, straightening his waistcoat, a mawkish smile buttered across his face.

"Yes, Miss Hale," he said quickly. "What brings you here on rotation break?"

"I can come back if—"

"But you're here now," he said, smiling wider.

"I … um … sent my timetable yesterday," she told him. "I got a reply instructing me to come and thumb-sign my approval."

Professor Asimov nodded, reaching for his Touch10.

"History of the Galaxy, hmm?" he said, eyebrows raised. "Excellent choice. I'll see you in phase two, rotation one, where we'll be delving into the furthest reaches of time." He perused the rest of her timetable choices. "Yes, yes, good. Oh, interesting. Good luck with *that*. And *two* art classes, Miss Hale, hmm? Well, it is the first cycle. Experimentation is encouraged."

Chalk smiled wanly.

Raised voices bounced out of the back room.

Asimov's face darkened.

"Triple D, if you would."

She pressed her thumb to the pad. "What's going on, Professor?"

"Faculty matter," he admitted, rather than the denial she'd been expecting. "Little to concern yourself with."

"Oh, right. It's just that no one's around, and the Waterfall Nebula isn't—"

Professor Asimov looked directly at her. Twenty fingers drummed the counter. "We're finished here, Miss Hale. Yes?"

Chalk's mouth hung open.

"Good."

"Professor?"

"Ye-es?"

"I keep forgetting to collect my iPhone from you."

"iPhone?"

"iPhone Firebird."

Asimov looked blank.

"My communication device from Earth. Harriet Starlight decals. About yay big. You confiscated it on the first rotation?"

"Ah, yes. I recall now," he said, patting his pockets. "I had it here, just the other rotation. Give me a minute, will you? Is it important?"

"Extremely," she said. "Please tell me you have it."

Just when Chalk thought the professor had misplaced it, he sank one of his hands into an impossibly deep inner pocket and retrieved the device. "Is this it?"

Chalk almost squealed.

Asimov bent towards her. "Your device narrowly passed the *Galactic Institute System-Wide Threat and Corruption Diagnosis Protocols.*"

"Narrowly?"

"I'm afraid some of the *functions* have been deactivated."

"Deactivated?"

"Just be thankful I returned it at all. Now, I must be going. See you tomorrow," the professor said curtly. "And bring that wonderful human brain of yours!"

Chalk unlocked her iPhone and scanned the apps. There were considerably less than before. Most of the games had gone.

"Fun police," she muttered, climbing the steps to the AGT.

She opened the camera roll and lingered on her favourite photos of Kit, Bloue, and Zara. Mum and Grandpa Milo. Her dad. An emotional avalanche burbled behind her eyes.

The resin walls of the AGT brushed against her arms as she went careening into the hyperloop. Chalk pressed the iPhone Firebird to her chest. She knew it wasn't the same as holding her loved ones in her arms, but having their photos and videos soothed her mind.

Back in the dorms, Chalk loitered inside the door to Aida's pristine room.

"Hello, Chalk," Aida said, swivelling on her chair. "You have been to see Asimov. Has your timetable been approved?"

"How did you …? Oh, the red stuff."

Aida wrinkled her nose.

"Well, yeah, all done. Got my iPhone back too."

Aida returned to her work.

"Weird thing though," Chalk said. "It's dead quiet today and Asimov is in a strange mood, and there were a whole bunch of professors congregated in some room behind the front desk. I guess it's the fallout from last night."

"It is also the dark rotation," Aida said. "Qantoculus are asleep for the entire twenty-eight hours. Osmotrino and Zalazor half that. It is unlikely you will see any of them today."

"Oh, yeah. Of course. I forgot. Final rotation is basically a ghost town."

"If you mean deserted, then yes," Aida said. "Like you, I imagine Asimov is probably in deep conversation with the other professors over the matter of our friends from Zorik Minor."

"And," Chalk went on, looking towards the window, "the missing nebula."

Aida stopped working. "I beg your pardon?"

"Um … the Waterfall Nebula. It's not there anymore. I guess we've spun around or something."

Aida frantically launched a fresh batch of layer screens. Her mirror-edged eduhelper spun faster and faster as it processed information. "Well," Aida said, looking up. "It appears we are not in Pylon-Maximanox Tendril-7 of the SpiralVerse anymore."

"What … Who … Um, where are we then?"

"I do not know," Aida said. "But we appear to be … moving."

"Oh, cool."

"No. Not cool. Not cool at all. The opposite of cool. Uncool. The Galactic Institute has not moved in over seventy cycles."

"I have a really bad feeling about this."

"Your assumptions are astute," Aida went on. "Galactic Institute code 348-Q states: *Space Station Centurion H*—that is the Galactic Institute to you and I—*will remain in permanent stasis inside the neutral zone, adjacent to the Waterfall Nebula in Pylon-Maximanox Tendril-7.* Core GAPSS directives issue only three reasons for departure from its designated residence."

"I presume you know—"

"*One. Irreparable damage to a degree that could compromise Centurion H or lead to its ultimate destruction.*"

"I mean, the place is broken, but it cannot be that bad."

"*Two. Insurgence. Compromise of Centurion H to an enemy—foreign, domestic, viral, or trans-dimensional—that would necessitate full and complete evacuation or surrender.*"

"Um … and the third?"

"*War.*"

Cube's alarm shook Chalk from another batch of questionable dreams. She'd spent the rest of the dark rotation creating wild conspiracy theories with Ripley and Milton about the change of location. Aida became agitated at their antics, refused to engage in speculation on such a serious matter, and buried herself in homework.

Tiny amber LEDs orbited the face of her GI-VR, signalling an urgent message. Swishing her hair aside, she hitched herself against the headboard and tapped the screen.

GENERAL WAXLER: Your first classes have been cancelled. All students report to the observation hall.

Chalk wiped the sleep from her eyes, blinked, and read the message again.

Activating the door, she found Aida, Ripley, and Milton on the other side.

"Eager beavers," she said, smiling.

"What's a beaver?"

"Doesn't matter."

Conversation buzzed in the first cycle rec room as students

queued for the AGT. Chalk zoomed down the on-tube, round the hyperloop, and up to the observation hall. Traces of the welcome ball had been stripped away yet row upon row of chairs faced the platform around the elevator.

General Waxler and the entire faculty were seated, staring solemnly into the middle distance. Students filed in. The room hummed with excitement, confusion, trepidation. More theories raced down each row. Chalk caught snippets of Sadler Arklan insisting he'd heard the Coin's power system had utterly failed and they were floating aimlessly through space. Spirit became agitated by the idea of a killer bacteria finding its way onboard which would force the entire student body into quarantine. Even Necrotta had heard that Maximanox A—the supermassive black hole at the centre of the SpiralVerse—was due to collapse and mercilessly consume every molecule in the galaxy.

General Waxler rose, quieting the room with her mechanical hand.

"Exciting," whispered Chalk.

"Exciting is hardly the word I would use."

"Students of the Galactic Institute, it is with sad news that I, and my fellow faculty members, appear before you today." Discontent rumbled. "As I am sure you are all aware, a confrontation between the Veroselli and Garrangulan population occurred at the welcome ball two evenings ago. While this in itself is a despicable act—the likes of which has not been seen at the Galactic Institute in aeons—a far more serious event has transpired in its wake." Chalk and Ripley looked at one another. "It is our solemn regret to inform you that a First Cycle Aktari student has gone missing—"

Gasps rose from the student body.

"Presumed dead."

Chalk's stomach dropped.

Everyone searched the crowd, craning their necks to discover who was missing. Chalk could see Sadler and the other members of the Vyshan Order. Necrotta, Marcy-Kate, Spirit,

Renix, and Saffron Été. Krieg, Kiln, and Kroket were hunched together gazing around too. Ironlung 8-47, Pristina, Vitarus, and Lachrymosa. Claridge was here, Clementine too, and—

"What is happening?"

"During the small hours following the welcome ball, Princess Cressida Van Wyrm's GI-VR went dead, her signal lost." Chalk's eyes shot to the Garrangulars. "A thorough investigation is currently underway into her whereabouts and the events leading to her disappearance."

Questions and confusion washed through the student lines. Veroselli stood waving their fists at the Garrangulars who barked insults back. Enforcers surrounded them.

"Quiet!" General Waxler ordered.

The Enforcers pushed in.

"Classes will continue as usual," she said. "If anyone knows anything, please approach your Head of Cycle immediately. Anybody taking matters into their own hands will be dealt with by me personally. I trust you all understand what this means." She surveyed them for a moment, her eyes raking each row. "We will have this atrocious act dealt with swiftly. Life at the Galactic Institute *will* continue as normal." General Waxler took a long, considered breath. "Now, get to class."

GAPSS
KNOWLEDGE
MAINFRAME

ANTI-GRAVITY ELEVATOR
[AGE] [TECHNOLOGY]

Personal vertical transportation. Powered by a variety of manufactured wind-turbine systems, AGEs simulate the effect of anti-gravity with high-pressure air flows inside vertical shafts constructed of membrane resin. Many AGEs are connected to a central gyrosphere—situated inside a perpetual centrifuge—where gravitational fields are disrupted and reconfigured allowing swift travel to multi-sided non-planetary constructs such as spacecraft and space stations.

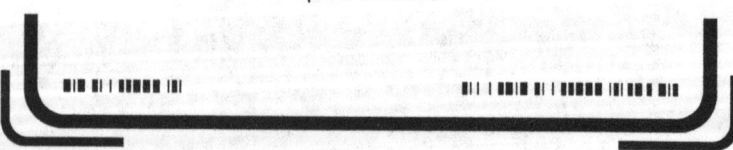

THE FLIPSIDE

"Get to class? What is she thinking?" Chalk grumbled as they stepped inside the lecture theatre complex.

"Exactly. How could anybody concentrate after finding out that Cressida has been kidnapped, or murdered, or worse?" Milton added, walking past a bank of monitors displaying: *Danger Level:* CAUTION.

And he was right.

Professor Dustenberg had a torrid time keeping her class focused on every Metaphysical Mathematics problem she put before them.

"Do you think she's dead?" whispered Chalk when Dustenberg shuffled to the other end of the room.

"Kidnapped, surely," Ripley said.

"Gone," Aida said. "Vanished from the Galactic Institute."

"How's that possible?"

"Portals?" Milton suggested. "How else?"

"Without a passkey it's impossible to activate one," Ripley told him.

"Are you suggesting Professor de Rema took her?"

"Well, she's not been the same since Zorik Major. She was a nervous wreck. Looked capable of anything!"

Chalk crossed her arms. "That doesn't mean she'd abduct a student and do unspeakable things to her. And for what reason?"

"My quasoids are on the Garrangulars," Ripley said, looking at Krieg and his crew. "Who else could be responsible?"

"Seems too obvious."

"Based on what?"

"Doesn't feel right. Has Krieg got it in him to kill Cressida—"

"Yes," hissed the other three.

"Or the smarts to transport her off the Galactic Institute?"

"Perhaps he sliced her into ribbons, or stashed her under the treadplate, or threw her over the side, or—"

Chalk's skin bristled. "Abduction and kidnapping are nothing to joke about."

"I'm not joking."

As they whispered amongst themselves, all three Garrangulars trooped towards the door. Professor Dustenberg intercepted them, inspected their GI-VRs, then stepped aside.

"Told you," Ripley said. "Waxler's questioning them first. Makes perfect sense."

Biodiverse Medical Science held Chalk's attention for less than fifteen minutes before she drifted into dark memories. Professor Cricklock—a wire-haired, purple Marstokian octopod—squirmed through the aisles. He idled beside Chalk and looked at her layer screen. "Remind us again what Hempenstall-Chua says about the reverse blood flow and cell regeneration in jemima jerks, Miss Hale?"

Blinking, Chalk scanned the layer screen, noticing she had the wrong information in front of her. "He's … against it?"

"*She*," the professor corrected, "holds quite the opposite opinion." Cricklock considered Chalk for a moment. "Thanks to Miss Hale, you're all to write a ten-layer screen essay on the advantages and drawbacks of the jemima jerk regenerative system. Extra credit for three-dimensional diagrams."

After lunch, Chalk and Ripley joined Commander Lasco for double Empirical Mechanics. Sitting around the huge workbench, Chalk struggled to rewire a floating desk lamp. All eight bulbs fizzed and exploded, showering the desk with electric shards and flaming filaments. The commander stamped on a power-breaker and the device died. Beside her, Ripley quickly moved on from his lamp, reconditioned the digital visor settings on a starfighter helmet and began dismantling an automated camera drone.

Lasco opened his layer screens.

"Master Flinch," he said conversationally. "Perhaps I'm wrong, but I don't have you registered for this class. Have you made a last-minute switch and forgotten to inform Professor Asimov?"

Ripley didn't look up. "I had a free class," he said, simply. "Just thought I'd pop along and keep Hale company."

"Pop along?"

"He likes to … *dabble*," Chalk told the commander.

"Well, as long as it's not interfering with your"—he checked his layer screens—"Domestic and Interspecies Languages and Astro Anthropology classes then I'm more than happy for you to do as much *dabbling* as you like." The commander watched Ripley work. "Perhaps you should consider switching your Specialisms."

"I'll think about it."

The Revan disappeared quickly after class. Alone, Chalk checked her GI-VR and noticed Aida and Milton had double Casting so she took the opportunity to visit the library. On the way she did a double take as a C1000 marched by.

"Is that … Cressida's eduhelper?" she whispered, tightening Cube's straps. "Where's it going?"

"One of the C1000's primary protocols would be to locate its owner," Cube informed her.

"So, if I went missing, you'd come find me."

"Affirmative," it said. "Unless you instruct me otherwise."

"No, no. If someone runs off with me—"

"Do not worry," Cube said. "I will find you."

Chalk smiled.

"However, the probability of your abduction, even in light of Cressida's disappearance, is less than half a per cent."

"Thanks, buddy," she grumbled. "Good to know."

Situated in quadrant two, the Galactic Institute library

and study halls were utterly empty. MAXXX, the automated librarian, seemed both pleased and surprised to see her. The spindly droid towered over Chalk, painted in flaking Galactic Institute orange, with a long, see-through head—like one of Grandpa Milo's spaghetti tins—packed with circuit boards, data drives, and whirring, optical components.

"MAXXX does not rrreceive many visitorrrs," the droid said, his voice gruff, syncopated and utterly robotic. Most of the robots on the Coin sounded almost biological. She guessed MAXXX must be from another era. "All inforrrmarrrtion storrred in the librrrarrry is available on yourrr GI-VRrr."

"I know," Chalk said. "But libraries have a cool smell."

"MAXXX can assurrre you the entirrre facility has been thorrroughly cleaned and sterrrilised."

Chalk laughed. "No. It's the books that smell. The paper, the pages, the ink."

"MAXXX has neverrr taken the time to smell the books."

"Add it to the laterbase!"

"It would take MAXXX five-hundred and eighty-fourrr cycles to smell the ninety-seven million, fourrr-hundred thousand, seven hundrrred and twenty-thrrree books in the arrrchive."

Chalk struggled to contemplate this. "Why so many?"

"Physical backup," MAXXX bleated. "GAPSS dirrrective TK-124."

Leaving the rigid librarian at the front desk, Chalk sauntered through the cavernous halls, scanned her notes, and tried to make a homework plan. Her mind drifted from layer screen essays, to Cressida, and down into shadowy memories of her own abduction. Not the theatrical one on Revus X, but the real one on Earth during the Hundred Hours War. The one where her life had hung by a thread. The one she'd spent with her father, gagged and bound. The one where she came home. And her father vanished.

Abandoning all thought of essays and research notes,

Chalk took several long breaths, slung her feet on a desk and read the opening chapters from *Harriet Starlight and the Age of Armageddon*.

The following rotation, Chalk tried her best to engage with Professor Balefire's lecture on the galaxian alphabet. But once again, she failed. Miserably.

Emerging Physics forced Chalk's mind to stall as Professor de Rema extended the virtues of simulated astral projection and particle kinesetics. She set them an exercise on each for homework. Chalk forgot to write any notes but made a mental note to badger Ripley for help later.

With a free double lesson looming, she signed up to one of Professor de Rema's guided tours of the Flipside.

A palpable swell of tension clouded the observation hall as Chalk arrived. The Garrangulars stalked ahead, while Clementine and Claridge stared at them spitefully, seeming less assured without the princess. Enforcers trundled beside them as they approached the ramshackle glass elevator at the centre of the room where Professor de Rema waited.

"We're going in *that* thing?" Spirit said, looking nervous.

"Thought it was out of commission," said Dana Dune.

"Hoped, you mean!"

"Looks like a deathtrap?" added Spirit.

Several others murmured their distrust.

"The anti-gravity elevator is perfectly safe," de Rema told them. "Nobody is in any danger."

"Tell that to Cressida," hooted Krieg, and the other Garrangulars snorted. Clementine and Claridge turned to retaliate, but an Enforcer swivelled, its eyes burning red.

"That's quite enough," de Rema told them. "If this hostility persists, none of you will be getting an introductory tour of the Flipside this side of the mid-cycle break."

The rest of the students moaned, urging them to cool off.

Chalk was curious about the Flipside. She knew it to be some kind of green space, but hoped its condition was better than the Coin. The idea of the Flipside being some overgrown, neglected allotment, swarming with insects and parasites was all too likely.

She could already feel her allergies spiking.

In her pocket, she crossed her fingers and whispered a tiny prayer.

"The AGE—"

"Anti-gravity elevator," Aida whispered to Milton.

"I know!"

"—works in a similar way to the AGT, although you won't be moving forward." The professor paused, tension building for dramatic effect. "You'll be falling."

"Falling?" wailed Milton.

Spirit gasped and fanned her face.

"It's a controlled fall. The initial reduction in gravity will plunge you through the centre of the Coin to the gyrosphere which, as the more astute of you may have noticed, is located at the centre of the hyperloop. Here, gravity becomes fractured and inverted."

"Aren't there any stairs we could use?" Spirit asked.

Professor de Rema ignored her. She held her GI-VR to a digital reader and the AGE's doors squeaked open. Like the AGT, strong winds emerged, ruffling the professor's perfect hair. "Come along," she said. "One at a time. Scan your GI-VR and step off."

"Step off?" Chalk asked.

"Yes."

"And you're sure this is totally safe?"

"Of course."

She peered over the lip of the AGE. Below, a vertical tunnel fell away into darkness. A seemingly bottomless drop.

Chalk looked at the professor. "Is this a joke?"

"Do you see me laughing?"

"It's a leap of faith."

"It's hard science, Miss Hale."

Chalk took a deep breath.

Closed her eyes.

And stepped off.

She expected an immediate fall of some kind but, instead, found herself hanging in mid-air, legs pin-wheeling. "Ah, okay. I feel like Wile E Coyote—" The gravity field around her shifted and she dropped like a stone.

Eyes streaming, fear tore through Chalk as her friends vanished and she arrowed down the black tube. The fall was far longer than she imagined. She braced, half expecting her legs to splinter upon landing, but found herself slowing with incredible force, like a bullet into water.

The skin on her face tightened as she bounced around inside a massive sphere. She was pulled in a thousand directions and pushed in a thousand more. Her insides were keen to become her outsides, spinning end over end, until she lost all sense of direction. Giddy and disorientated, she was suddenly gripped and propelled upwards at an alarming speed. She strained her neck, convinced Ripley, or Milton, or even Krieg would crash into her, feet first, but she rose higher and higher, slowing all the time until she emerged over a wide expanse of parkland, shrubs, and trees.

Doors appeared. Chalk floated towards them, grabbed a handle and stepped quickly onto solid ground.

One by one the others appeared, staring around in amazement.

Professor de Rema stepped expertly off the AGE and smoothed her hair.

"Welcome to the Flipside," she said, ushering everyone together. "You are now standing on the other side of the Coin. Some would say you're now upside down, but space has no right way up, does it? We are currently in the centre of the Flipside, an expanse devoted to extensive parks and grasslands. Around the edge you'll find a ring of forests and woodland, fountains, floral displays, and a cornucopia of wildlife. There's also a vast web of research facilities including biomass speculators, geochemical labs, and hydroponics. Please observe the signs and GI-VR warnings where you see them. I'll be monitoring you. Don't try anything silly. We'll meet here towards the end of the class. You have approximately eighty-eight minutes."

The professor took a seat on a bench beside the AGE and turned her attention to a swell of layer screens.

Most scattered in their friend groups.

"What a strange sensation," Chalk said, strolling beside Ripley. "I don't feel like I'm at the Galactic Institute anymore. This looks and feels, even smells, a lot like being on Earth."

Ripley adjusted his settings and took a long sniff. "Freshly cut grass, summer flowers, lavanuts, solar rays, jactar bees, Krieg's back sweat."

"I think you turned it up too high!"

Two black-and-white-striped creatures scuttled into view, observed Chalk and Ripley curiously, then vanished into the undergrowth.

They walked in silence.

Ripley seemed content to gaze at the swaying ferns and flowers as a multitude of colourful insects buzzed and flitted around his head. He tapped his GI-VR from time to time, sweeping layer screens away.

Chalk tried to summon the courage to ask him about the other night. To answer the questions he'd evaded on the dance floor.

"This place is amazing," she said, slipping her jacket from beneath Cube's straps and folding it over her arm. "I could spend all rotation here."

"Yeah, sure. It's lovely."

Chalk felt awkward. Her mouth dry. "Are you okay?"

"Me? Sure."

They took a dozen steps.

"You're always asking that," Ripley said. He appeared to sense her apprehension. "Why?"

"It's just … your behaviour …"

"My behaviour?"

"Yeah, I dunno. Maybe it's a Revan thing …"

"A *Revan* thing?"

"Um."

They walked beneath the entrance to a corridor woven from lush green Wistorian creepers.

"You blow hot and cold around me, and you're amazing at Emerging Physics, and Empirical Mechanics, yet your Specialisms are languages and anthropology which, to be honest, you're no better at than me."

Ripley picked a leaf from the creeper and twisted it between his fingers.

"Since Zorik Major you've spent loads of time alone, and—"

"And what?" he said defensively. "Didn't realise this was character assassination 101 with Professor Bonehead."

Chalk withered a little. "I wasn't trying to be mean," she said. "Just honest."

"Go on then," he said, avoiding her gaze. "I know you're desperate to say whatever this other thing is."

She paused. Stared at her boots. "The research laboratories."

Ripley sniffed. "What?"

"You were there. Right?"

"You were there too," he replied. "Introduction to Portals. Just before Milton sent us spinning halfway across the galaxy."

"But you were there another time."

"Doubt it."

"I saw you."

"Can't have."

"The afternoon before the welcome ball."

Ripley went quiet, his gaze on the crumbling leaf.

"It was you, wasn't it? I was quite far away, but …" she said, giving him an out.

"Look." Ripley stopped and turned to face her. "I'm clearly useless at keeping things to myself." His face hardened. "I don't want the entire Galactic Institute to know my business, okay?"

"Okay."

"It's …" He threw the creeper to the ground. "It's my brother."

Chalk stumbled as her brain forgot how to work her feet. "Your—?"

"Dante," he said, kneading his hands. "During the Revan Solstice—"

"What happened?"

"He … died."

"What? No!" Chalk put her hands on his. The Revan felt warm and soft yet shivered as though in the thrall of some terrible fever. "How?" she said, then backtracked. "Sorry. That's none of my business."

"Terrorist strike," Ripley explained. "Revus X is a dangerous place. You've been there. Authority is thin, almost non-existent. I … I'm struggling with it to be fair," he confessed. "Some days are better than others. Some days I want to be around you. And Aida and Milton, of course. Even the Veroselli, the Garrangulars, the Vyshan Order, and everyone else."

"Even Spirit?" Chalk asked, and immediately regretted it.

"Erm, sure," he said. Her heart trembled. "It's a distraction, a good distraction. But most days I want to sit and lose myself in study … or stare into the void."

"Ripley," she said, pulling him close.

He didn't resist.

"What about your parents?" Chalk's mind paddled at a thousand miles per hour. "How are they—?"

"My foster parents have been amazing, the rest of my foster family too."

"Do you miss them?"

"Obviously."

"This communication embargo with our homeworlds is kind of barbaric," Chalk said, running her hand down the Revan's chest and outlining the pendant beneath his shirt.

Ripley pulled away. "I need time."

"Sure, of course. Whatever you need."

"And space."

"There's infinite quantities of that!"

Chalk's joke fell flat.

"Sorry."

Ripley wiped his nose with his sleeve. "It feels good to talk."

"You can tell me anything," she said, offering a determined smile.

Ripley nodded, slow and grim.

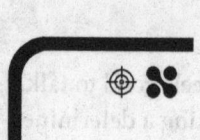

GAPSS
KNOWLEDGE
MAINFRAME

GALAXIAN ESOPHAGEAL FIRE SYRUP
[RECIPE]

Ingredients:
3 giant lava beans
2 roasted firebat wings [de-boned]
1 kritten tail
1 thermoslug
6 fever bulbs
1 sachet of flame-smoked volcanus sauce
300ml Qwork milk

Method:
Blend ingredients and heat until scalding.
Consume immediately.

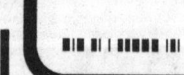

TURNCOATS AND BETRAYERS

The next morning, as Chalk and Ripley headed to History of the Galaxy, they passed Cressida's C1000 again. Rather than its authoritarian march, the droid had quickened its pace, scurrying along the wide, airy hallways of the lecture theatre complex like an anxious kraken-weevil.

"Do you think it's possible for eduhelpers to go mad if they cannot finish a task?" she asked.

"They're machines. Driven by core-directives and sub-routines," he told her. "The stupid thing is probably stuck in a loop, searching for a signal from Cressida's GI-VR."

"You still got the Garrangulars in number one slot?"

"Sure," he said, shrugging nonchalantly. "Only serious choice."

"But Asimov cleared Krieg and the others last night."

"Might not be first cycle Garrangulars," he said, shaking his head. "Could be a bunch of sixth cyclers, hell bent on reigniting the Zorik Wars!"

"Really?"

"Cressida *is* a princess of the Veroselli royal family," Ripley said. "The Roses and the Grangs have never needed much of an excuse to obliterate one another. Cressida's disappearance gives the Roses a mandate to bomb the hell out of the Grangs. Sadly, I think it's only a matter of time."

Enforcers patrolled every major cross-section on campus. Chalk and Ripley passed one at the foot of a sweeping stairway.

Its gleaming red eyes whizzed and whirred at everything that passed.

To Chalk's dismay, History of the Galaxy had been moved from the SpiralVerse military museum to one of the brightly lit oval lecture theatres. To make matters worse, somebody far less malleable than Professor Asimov stood at the head of the room.

"Come on, Miss Hale, Master Flinch. Find a seat," Professor Snider urged, gazing at his GI-VR and tapping his foot irritably. "Now, as Professor Asimov is embroiled in collating information about the disappearance of Princess Van Wyrm, I shall be handling your historical education."

Students grumbled.

"That's quite enough. Please scroll to layer screen fifty-four in *An Expansive Galactic History* and silently read chapters three through eight on Astronomical Agriculture. There will be a test in rotation seven."

"Is he going to make us read for the whole double lesson?"

"I said *silently*, Master Flinch!"

Chalk trawled through a dirge of information about arable and animal farming methods on Tattoraan, Marstok, Gaia 23, and a dozen more.

Halfway through, Sadler, Clementine, and Spirit returned from their meeting with Asimov. Volgar, Ironlung 8-47, and Necrotta were up next.

"At this rate, Asimov will summon us right in the middle of dinner," Chalk complained.

"Always thinking with your stomach."

She wasn't far wrong.

Asimov's message arrived ten minutes before the end of Domestic and Interspecies Languages. Professor Balefire authenticated their absence, promising to send homework exercises immediately.

Chalk and Ripley met Milton and Aida in the administration lobby. They took a traditional elevator to the third floor which juddered and shook horribly. A solitary light flickered and died several times during the journey. As they rose, Chalk hoped they'd get stuck and avoid whatever waited for them, but the elevator opened with a joyless *ping!* on a particularly destitute-looking corridor.

"How come we have amazing technology like the AGT and the hyperloop, but still suffer the indignity of a vertical elevation system?" Aida muttered, more to herself than anyone else.

"You could always use the stairs," Ripley told her.

"Waste of lifeforce," the Tattorian muttered, drifting along as efficiently as possible.

Outside Professor Asimov's office, sat back from the arched corridor and lined with monitors in various states of decay, was a waiting nook. Information about the disappearance of Cressida Van Wyrm scrolled across several screens while the rest transmitted various channels including the Qwork News Network. Half a dozen resin chairs were set around a low table which was mounted with colourful potted trees. Worn-out tape and pins jutted from dirty-white walls where posters and notices had been displayed. Recessed bulbs seemed indifferent to providing any substantial light, while the smell of Asimov's throat cocktail circulated through the life-support system like a persistent ghost.

Marcy-Kate emerged from the professor's room, closing the door behind her.

"How was it?" Chalk asked.

The Revan girl shrugged. "Fine. I mean, I don't know anything, so—"

"Oh."

"Waste of time, if I'm honest. *And* I missed Languages." Marcy-Kate made a genuinely discontented groan, fussed her hair, and trudged off.

Aida's GI-VR buzzed. "It would appear to be my turn."

The others sat in silence.

Chalk flexed her fingers.

Ripley tapped.

Milton chewed.

Aida wasn't with the professor long. The Tattorian came out, her Chronos Abstract80 floating gently behind. She stopped and considered Chalk. "I sense tension," she said. "You do not … know anything, do you?"

"No," Chalk said. "Of course not. I get nervy when things get … serious."

"You should take everything seriously, Chalk. I fail to understand any opposing worldview."

Chalk's GI-VR buzzed.

MEETING WITH PROFESSOR ASIMOV . . .

ENTER NOW . . .

Professor Asimov's office sent a cold, damp chill to Chalk's bones. A messy desk and two chairs sat in the centre surrounded by lopsided monitors on water-damaged walls. A mesh of wires and cables looped across the ceiling, flowering with fibre-optic spindles.

Data drives hummed gently.

The professor looked agitated, tired. Dark rings laid siege to his eyes.

"Miss Hale," he said, attempting a smile. "Lovely to see you as always."

Chalk beamed back, hoping it would buoy his drowning demeanour.

Asimov cradled another bowl of his terrible smelling red liquid. His fingernails drummed lightly against the smooth glass. "So," he started, then took a sip. "The last few rotations have been quite exciting, hmm? I cannot imagine you'd have expected this level of drama during your first cycle at the Galactic Institute."

Chalk stroked her thighs. "I'm not sure what I expected," she answered truthfully. "I definitely underestimated the diversity of the student body. So many languages and cultures and diets and sleeping patterns. Earth is packed with history and knowledge, and I barely know a fraction of it. Being at the Galactic Institute feels a thousand times more complicated."

"But you have a GI-VR," the professor said. "And an eduhelper."

"Yes." Chalk nodded, running a hand over the mystery ball. "That helps with the language barriers. The cultural ones ... not so much."

"Is anyone in particular making life difficult for you?"

"Um," Chalk stalled. "The Veroselli and the Garrangulars are ... complicated."

Professor Asimov tapped his Touch10.

"It's not that we don't get along," she said hurriedly. "I mean, at first we didn't. Cressida and Krieg had an altercation outside my room and I jumped in to protect my friends."

"Really?" Asimov said. "That sounds ill-advised?"

"Exactly. It started with some unpleasant name calling ... and then they gave me a pass. I think. First human and all that."

"You're lucky," Asimov replied. "The Veroselli and the Garrangulars are not known for their second chances, tolerance, or patience."

"And now things on their planet are ... problematic?"

The professor choked on his drink. "Are you suggesting that the civil unrest on Zorik Minor is a direct result of your intervention in a ... dorm room scuffle?"

Chalk fidgeted in her chair. "I angered them both. Maybe that led to—"

Asimov waved away her interjection. "Zorik Minor has been on the brink of open war for centuries. Miss Van Wyrm's disappearance is just another spark in an already lively blaze. And, as such, that leads us to why we're here today, why I'm conducting these interviews with everyone in First Cycle Aktari, hmm?"

Chalk crossed her legs. Knitted her fingers.

"My suspicions about you being involved are almost zero."

"Almost?"

"But if we could go over the events of the last few rotations and highlight any interactions you had with the princess, that would be most helpful."

Other than the hostile exchange of words between Cressida and Krieg in the dorms, the confrontation after the *Orbit Strike!* match, and the fight at the welcome ball, all Chalk could think of was their illegal expedition to a chunk of Zorik Major and Ripley breaking the Terrazuma Treaty.

Had anyone spilled this information to Asimov?

Cressida couldn't, obviously. Aida, despite her lawful-good nature, wouldn't betray her friends. Ripley faced expulsion or worse. De Rema's fear of losing her job would quieten her lips and Lasco was probably on his last chance in a long line of last chances. Krieg and Necrotta seemed the most likely if pushed, but she doubted Asimov had the skills to intimidate either of them.

She paused on Milton.

How much browbeating would the Sagaroach take before he let the whole story come flowing out of him like yuccagourd vomit? Not much. He'd probably succumb to tickling.

"Um, no. Nothing," Chalk said. "I mean, I don't know much. Other than what's already common knowledge on the Coin, of course."

Professor Asimov leant back. He sighed deeply, distracted.

"Why do they hate each other so much?" Chalk asked. "I know they were once Zorans and evolved into three factions."

"You've heard about the—?"

"Sevantes."

"It's not on the curriculum."

"Or in the museum," Chalk added, an eyebrow raised.

The professor curled his fingers around his drink. "Political pressure," he admitted, loose-lipped as ever, his voice low. "Representatives from the Sevantes cannot be found working for GAPSS, in the faculty, or any of their number enrolled as a student at the Galactic Institute."

"Seems horribly unfair."

"Right, hmm?" Asimov agreed, a finger waving. "It *is* unfair. Prejudiced. Speciesist. A travesty. How did you hear of them?"

"Cressida mentioned the Sevantes when we were—" Chalk began, caught in the moment.

"Ye-es?"

"In the museum."

Asimov stared over his glasses.

Chalk could feel her cheeks redden. "The … she … told us, that's Ripley and I, about the Sevantes. Not much, I'll admit. Said they were turncoats and betrayers. Loyal to none but their own."

"Is that so?"

"Definitely." Chalk doubled-down. "True story. Facts."

"Seems strange that she would offer this information without provocation. Talk of the Sevantes is something the Veroselli and Garrangulars prefer to keep in the shadows. Just like their mating rituals and that ghastly obsession with zorikanthium."

Chalk's legs jigged nervously.

Asimov made a note on his Touch10 and slurped his drink.

"So, any other concerns, Miss Hale? I only ask as you are our first human … our first Earthling … and we're keen to make sure you're settling in."

Chalk took a moment to consider his question, a tactic she wished she'd employed two minutes earlier.

"Everything else is fine," she said. Then added, "Well, it's nothing really, but several of us have seen Cressida's C1000 wandering about. Is it okay? It might know something about her disappearance."

"Yes, others have mentioned this. And don't worry, I had her eduhelper in for a full diagnostic and system reboot as soon as news of her disappearance surfaced. The droid has no knowledge beyond its last recorded interaction after the princess left her room in the early hours to visit the bathroom. She did not return. Anything else?"

"Don't think so. Everything else is fine. I mean great. I'm having a great time ... experience ... here at the Galactic Institute."

"Good, good."

"Actually, one more thing," she said, waving a single digit.

"Yes?"

"My eduhelper. The Zenith mystery ball. Turns out it's an ... INCUBE-8."

The professor smiled knowingly. "That's an incredibly special, expensive, desirable piece of tech, Miss Hale."

"I thought so."

"I'd keep it close," Asimov said. "You never know when you might need it."

"Quite right."

"Except when travelling through portals, obviously," he added, dismissively.

Chalk froze. "Yes, of course not. Because of the ... um ... temporal doorways have a three point one four per cent tolerance for manufactured materials."

"Professor de Rema has taught you well."

"She's the absolutely brilliantly excellentist best."

Professor Asimov frowned, waved her out of the room, and returned to his layer screens.

GAPSS
KNOWLEDGE
MAINFRAME

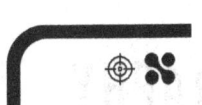 

QUASOIDS
[UNIVERSAL CURRENCY]

Every civilised world in the SpiralVerse has its own complex system of local, national, and international currencies and financial institutions. Intergalactic money transfers, sales, investments, and taxation are conducted in quasoids: a universal numeric dividend monitored and authenticated at Credit Continuum—an independent body of representatives from all thirty-five civilised worlds— housed at the GAPSS headquarters on Marstok.

PRACTICAL TOPOGRAPHY

Chalk left Ripley and Milton outside Asimov's office, slunk back to the dorm, and collapsed into bed. Cube positioned itself beside her. Closing her eyes, she sank into anxious dreams about the pipes and vents on her ceiling descending towards her, the ends snapping like rabid krittens. She woke with a start, quickly checked the pipes were still pipes, and swung her feet to the ground.

The conversation with Asimov swirled through her head. Did he know about their portal adventure to Zorik Major and the breaking of the Terrazuma Treaty? She buzzed for Ripley and Milton, hoping they could quell her nerves but when neither answered she hurried to Aida's room, her mind in freefall.

"Where are the boys?"

"As you can see, they are not here," Aida said, beavering away at her desk. "And to be honest, I am quite thankful for it. The Emerging Physics essay this phase is lethal. Even for me!"

"It's been over two hours," Chalk said, checking her GI-VR. "Something's happened. Something bad. I know it."

Aida dropped from her chair. "They have probably gone to watch an *Orbit Strike!* match or partake in several quarts of GanyMead, or indulge the Revan's obsession with that depraved biletongue."

"Would they?" Chalk said urgently.

"They *are* boys," Aida said. "No matter what galaxy, star system, or backwater planet, the male of the species does have a tendency towards self-mindedness. It is not necessarily a bad thing," she prattled on. "Just coded into their genetic make-up. I wrote a thesis on it a few cycles ago." Aida loaded a handful of layer screens for Chalk to digest.

"It's fine, Aida. I'll go and look downstairs. See if anyone knows anything."

"You could just message them," Aida said.

Of course! What a bonehead.

Chalk had barely opened a layer screen when the fetid stink of yuccagourds invaded her nostrils.

"Where have you been?" she hissed, hanging over the bannister.

"With Asimov," Ripley said, climbing the stairs. "Are you okay? You look ill."

Chalk fussed her hair and rearranged her face. "It's been two hours! What happened? Are you—? Did you—?" She dragged them into Aida's room. The door swooshed shut. "Zorik Major," she blurted, as though she could barely keep it inside any longer. "Did Asimov ask about Zorik Major? About us portalling there? Did you tell him? Did you sense that he already knows? Tell me!"

"Calm down, Hale," Ripley said, gripping her shoulders.

"Okay, *Flinch*," she fired back, shaking him off.

"Asimov asked a bunch of questions and I told him what I knew about Cressida ... which is nothing."

"But what took two hours?"

Ripley looked at the Sagaroach.

"Milton?"

"I didn't ... It's just that ... Look, I'm struggling. Okay?"

"Struggling? With keeping secrets? Just keep your pincers zipped!"

"No," he snapped. "Struggling with ... life at GI."

"So?" Ripley fired.

Chalk punched his shoulder.

"Pressure from my homeworld builds every day," Milton went on. "Mostly for me to fail. You should see the messages I get."

Ripley glanced at Milton's GI-VR. "Whoa … Thoden's eyes … That's savage!"

"You get messages from home?" Chalk cried. "No fair!"

"Indirectly," he moaned. "They reroute them through Sagaroaches in the fifth and sixth cycles. It's cruel and demeaning and utterly without end. They'd love me to fail and have an excuse to extricate me from the family. Finding the courage to talk to you lot about it is incredibly difficult, current exchange included!"

Ripley folded his arms. "What did you tell him?"

"Everything."

"*Everything*?"

"Not *that* everything. *My* everything. The pitiful story of a useless Sagaroach that achieved his claim to the Barclay fortune and dynasty through underhanded, cowardly acts during the Spawning."

"Fortune?" Ripley said. "How much are you worth?"

"Ripley? Seriously?" Chalk turned to the Sagaroach, her fingers shaking. "The Spawning?"

"A traditional, sadistic event in which the spawn of each Sagaroach Lord engage in a brutal fight to the death," Aida explained. "Hundreds of thousands of Sagaroach infants are involved."

"What's cowardly about that?" Ripley said.

"I hid," Milton admitted, "until all but one exhausted Sagaroach remained. I simply eased her passing and claimed my Lordly titles."

"Razabelle be merciful!"

Chalk shook the visual images away. "Is that all you told him? Nothing about the portals and Zorik Major. Nothing about Fort Van Murk and the Sevantes?"

"No. Nothing. I might be a coward, but I'm loyal to the end."

"Hale, you're being weird."

"Am I?"

"He is right," the Tattorian said. "You are panicking when you should be strategising."

"Look," Ripley whispered. "That excursion to Zorik Major was a mistake. Milton *somehow* typed in the wrong co-ordinates and I had to break a couple of laws to get us home. All you did was survive."

Chalk took a breath.

"Sit on the bed—" Ripley started. "Why isn't there a bed in here?"

Aida aimed her visor at him.

"Oh, right. Lifeforce. Do you just ... power down?"

"In a sense," she said. "It is more akin to hibernation."

"Fancy."

"I've always been keen to ask—" Milton began.

"Not now," Aida said. "Take Chalk to her room. Her aura is unsettled. It would appear we are in for a bumpy couple of phases."

Ripley obeyed.

"Want me to tidy up a bit?" he said, gazing at the mess on Chalk's floor.

She pushed him away. "Nah. I'll do it."

"Will you?"

"Nope."

Ripley rubbed the back of his neck. "Okay, well, I've got an unfathomable stack of essays to write and layer screens to stare at."

"Can't you stay?" she asked, crawling under the bedclothes. "We can form a study group. It'll be fun. And more productive than if we—"

"I can't."

"Why?" Chalk said, sticking out her bottom lip.

He looked at her knowingly.

"Oh, sure," she said. "Of course. Stupid Chalk. Dante, right? Whatever you need. Sorry. Later, yeah?"

"One hundred per cent."

"Five by five!"

Ripley frowned. "One rotation you'll have to explain what all your references mean."

"Sure thing. Christmas. I mean, mid-cycle break," she said. Then, before her brain had time to dissuade her tongue, added, "You could … come to London. Meet Mum and Grandpa Milo. I'll make you watch *Star Wars* and *Buffy* and *Harry Potter* …"

Ripley smiled awkwardly.

"Too much?" she said. "But seriously. Could be fun. Think about it?"

Ripley nodded.

Vanished.

Chalk opened *Harriet Starlight and the Frozen Dark* and skipped to the chapter where Harriet gets trapped inside Daj Villannious' space freighter with Cosmo Mackensie and the two girls have their first kiss. Absent-mindedly drumming her lip, Chalk wished she could be gifted and courageous like Harriet Starlight. Sadly, she knew she wasn't ever going to be the ultimate hero. She'd love to be Rey Skywalker, but in her heart she knew she was—at best—Chewbacca. Even the Sorting Hat at Madame Tussauds' "Hogwarts Ultimate VR Experience" had put her in Ravenclaw when her heart knew her to be Gryffindor. Ripley was the real hero. A boy, after all, with an aptitude for droids and engineering, a twin, an orphan with dead parents. Classic backstory.

Being Chewbacca in Ravenclaw isn't so bad, she thought. *At least I'm not Jar Jar Binks in Hufflepuff.*

A palpable tension surrounded Chalk as she plodded through phase two and three. Ten rotations of arduous classes were mind-crushing. Her thoughts were starting to unravel by rotation eight. The promise of a much-needed siesta couldn't come soon enough.

Ripley stuck with her through the tough classes and continued to show up in Empirical Mechanics even though he had no official reason to be there. They studied together some nights and practised Conflict Engagement moves in the gym, which were routinely scoffed at by Krieg and Necrotta. Ripley sank in and out of introversion, disappearing from his room, uncontactable on his GI-VR. Despite her best efforts, Chalk had no idea where he went. The Coin was vast. She'd barely explored a fraction of it herself. But relief always flooded her chest when he appeared in class the following rotation.

Narrative of Story and Conflict Engagement were fast becoming her favourites. History of the Galaxy was a close runner-up, even with Professor Snider at the helm. Professor Mirage and Commander Lasco made their classes entertaining, challenging, and the time whizzed by. Conversely, Dustenberg's Metaphysical Mathematics made Chalk feel as though she'd crossed the event horizon.

A consuming quiet filled the dark rotation at the end of phase three. Chalk woke in the middle of the night after a confusing dream about herself, Ripley, and Harriet Starlight that she would never share with anyone.

Ever.

She flicked through the images and videos on her iPhone. The faces of her family and friends always raised her spirits. She dug through the functions on her GI-VR too and, as well as fiddling with the digital dials to increase or reduce her senses (and then restore them to factory settings), she stumbled onto the interactive map that she'd not touched since her ordeal on Revus X.

Firing up the application, every square inch of the campus was displayed in a holographic, three-dimensional wireframe. She flicked the lip, spinning the map like a turntable. Aida's, Milton's, and Ripley's GI-VR transponders were still in their rooms. Probably asleep or hibernating or whatever Aida did to stem the consumption of lifeforce.

Deactivating the app, she rolled over and tried to sleep. Her mind reeled with a million questions surrounding Cressida's disappearance, the chaos brewing on Zorik Minor, and why Asimov didn't appear to be any closer to discovering the truth.

Was there something Chalk could do that the professors or Enforcers or Cressida's C1000 could not?

She doubted it.

She was, after all, only a Mudder.

Human Garbage.

An Earthling.

Insomnia rising, Chalk tiptoed to Ripley's door. His room wasn't locked. She slid the door aside gently, expecting to find him working away at his desk or sound asleep in bed.

"Ripley?" she whispered. "Hey? You home?"

But there was no sign of him.

Drifting in, she opened the wardrobe and scanned his clothes. A typical ensemble of fitted jackets, striped trousers, and vests. She sank her head into the fabrics and breathed in. Hydraulic fluid, plasma oil, biletongue, and linen soap. An aroma distinctly him. She ran her fingers over a stack of tech on his desk and lifted a pile of photographs from the bedside table. The images were of an older couple, his foster parents she guessed, and a bunch of kids and teens. They were huddled together, smiling, laughing, in an oval living room. Some sort of party, a birthday perhaps. There were three pictures of a cute blonde girl, about the same age as Ripley. At the bottom she found a picture of him and his twin, Dante. To the casual observer they were identical. However, she could instantly tell which was which. Ripley's playful grin was evident a mile away. His brother looked more serious, solemn. His clothes neatly pressed. Hair perfectly combed. He looked annoyed that someone had the audacity to take his—

"What are you doing with those?" Ripley said, knocking the photos from her hands. They scattered across the carpet. The picture of the twins landed face up.

Shocked, Chalk backed away. "I ... I'm sorry," she said. "I was looking for you."

"And when you realised I wasn't here," he said breathlessly, a light sheen of sweat coating his face, "you thought you'd have a snoop through my stuff?"

"Not at all," Chalk protested. "Admittedly, yes, I did have a quick look at your photos … and I sniffed your clothes. I don't know why I did that. I'm *so* sorry. I don't know what came over me. It's just … you weren't here, and I thought you were, so I came in and—" She stopped. "Where *were* you?"

"That is none of your concern," he said, then softened. "I was getting a drink."

Chalk looked at his empty hands.

"They'd … run out." He shouldered her aside. "Look, I'm busy working on something."

"You're sweating."

"There are lots of steps."

"I'm sorry. I really am."

"It's fine."

He slumped into a chair, his back to her.

"Is it? Fine, I mean?"

Ripley looked at her in the mirror. "Yes."

Chalk took a quick breath. "It's just … I like you."

"I like you too."

"Who is … the pretty blonde girl?"

"Really?"

Chalk wrinkled her nose and went to leave.

"Madeleine," he said, as she placed her hands on the door frame. "Dante's girlfriend. *Was* Dante's girlfriend."

"Oh," she said happily, then, more sincerely, "Right. I see. How is she?"

"You don't care about her," Ripley said. "It's fine. She misses him, obviously. We all do."

Chalk watched the Revan in the mirror. His eyes looked sad and hollow, scarred by a loneliness that would never heal. "And like I said before, I'm here if you want to talk."

"I know."

"Right."

"Right."

Chalk fell face first onto her bed.

INAPPROPRIATE LANGUAGE DETECTED . . .

Cube became a balloon and floated above its black orb. It bobbed playfully in mid-air, refracting warm orange light against the wall.

"You are sad."

"Duh," she replied. "Made a bonehead of myself."

"Again?"

"Hey!"

"I'm attempting a variety of humour called sarcasm," it said. "How did I do?"

"Ten points for effort. Two for timing."

UPDATING . . .

She wriggled onto her back and opened the interactive map. Sure enough, the amber hoop of Ripley's GI-VR transponder hovered over his room. Chalk sank into her pillows and stared accusingly at Ripley's signal as it pulsed gently, curiously, in the dark.

Phase four. Rotation four. Chalk's classes began with double Dark Matter, then double Galactic Law. At lunchtime she wandered towards the banqueting rotunda, convinced she'd picked the hardest subjects imaginable and believing her imminent failure and dismissal from the Galactic Institute—and shameful return to Earth—were only a matter of time.

She could see the newspaper headlines now.

Space Reject.

Astro-Naught.

Harper Fail.

Knowing Cube was already putting together a list of her body's atomic reactions to every flicker of anxiety and depression, she tried to kickstart her rotation by ordering a huge slice of raclette and an entire Marstokian baguette.

Munching steadily through the enormous meal, Chalk's

thoughts bounced back to the Revan, his stack of photographs, and what he'd *really* been doing last night. Growing up in Number 10, she'd been surrounded by lies and half-truths her entire life. She could sense them a mile off. The body language. The eyes. The way fingers fidgeted and skin glistened.

Ripley Flinch was up to something.

Chalk knew it.

She opened the interactive map. His transponder pulsed in the first cycle dorms. They both had a double free lesson, so she zoomed around the hyperloop for a while, before heading home.

As she slowed for the disembarkation pod, Ripley and INFIN-8 launched into the AGT ahead of her.

Chalk flapped her arms.

Indecision coated her in a blinding, paralysing fever.

With a will of their own, Chalk's legs propelled her away from the resin wall and over the safety handles of the disembarkation pod. Warning lights flashed as she blustered through the embarkation area, clattered into Dana Dune, and almost wiped Lachrymosa clean out.

"Sorry," she cried, racing past Dana.

"Hale! What in Kyzon's Abyss are you doing?"

What *was* she doing?

She knew Aida and Milton would tell her not to overreact, but she was genuinely worried about the Revan. If she followed Ripley and found him visiting one of the holy centres to think about his brother, or to praise his God Thoden, or feed that peppered biletongue addiction or—her heart ached—to meet another girl, at least she'd know he was okay. That he was safe.

And if he never found out, what harm could it do?

Ripley and INFIN-8 took a quarter lap of the hyperloop—

Joyless snaggers!

—and rose towards the recreation arcade. Barrelling towards the sixth cycle dorms, Chalk lost sight of him. She took the next exit and emerged further down where shops and restaurants were in the throes of the lunchtime stampede.

She stumbled off the disembarkation pod, searching through the crowd for any sign of Ripley and INFIN-8, but the noise and chaos of the arcade made it impossible.

Chalk walked in an anti-clockwise direction and opened the interactive map. She kept the layer screen small, discreet. Zooming in, she navigated to her current location where a white hoop pulsed with Harper Hale digitised below. She pulled back, expanded the search zone, but Ripley's signal had gone. She skimmed to the first cycle dorms and there, hovering over his bedroom, pulsated an amber hoop, accompanied by the name Ripley Flinch.

Chalk reduced the map and slumped against the railings of a GanyMead drinks outlet.

She scanned the crowd again. Her eyes moved distractedly over wave upon wave of strange student lifeforms. Conflict spiked through her. Maybe the map *was* right. Maybe he'd forgotten something and had to double-back to the dorm. Maybe he *was* sweating from climbing the stairs the other night. And maybe the drinks dispenser *had* run dry—

And then, there he was.

Ripley Flinch.

Walking out of an eduhelper upgrade store.

His purple eyes staring directly at her.

GAPSS
KNOWLEDGE
MAINFRAME

QWORK
[SPECIES]

Homeworld: Gaia I–XII, Lang. Various.

A predominantly docile quadruped with large ears and elongated proboscis, a hairless or fine-haired body, burrowing claws and long, thin tail. Qwork skin and pelage come in all manner of tones, however black, brown, and white are most common. Weighing on average ten kilograms, Qworks were initially taken as pets as their interaction with intellectual life revealed an incredible aptitude for language and learning. While many still serve as pets and hunting companions [and a source of nutrition in some regions], Qworks are employed by GAPSS in a variety of roles from janitorial and hospitality work to positions of authority.

CHEMICAL COSMOLOGY

Ripley waved and strolled over. INFIN-8 hurried behind. A thousand wild stories and botched explanations rolodexed through Chalk's head.

"Hey. What are you doing? Queuing for ... GanyMead?"

"What?" she replied, as though he'd asked in High Wistorian.

"GanyMead," he repeated, pointing to the drinks outlet behind her. "Never had you pegged as a Meadhead. Want to share some?"

"Um, yes. Of course," she said dismissively. "I'm trying new things."

"I wasn't accusing you of anything," he said, turning a vulpine Karmethian in a branded apron. "What's good here?"

"GanyMead Best is the most popular—thick and malty," the seller said. "Veroselli Vanguard and Tattorian Tribute are light and sweet: your daytime tipple. Revan Pale Ale, which I'm sure you're accustomed with, is fruity and full bodied, while Garrangulan Grog is a chalky, dark stout with undertones of bloodberries and chaosfruit."

"And these are all ... *alcoholic?*" Chalk asked, trying to remain cool.

The Karmethian laughed. "Alcohol? In a drink? What planet are you from?"

"Um—"

"Alcohol?" Ripley whispered. "That'll kill you quicker than a rabid Qwork bite!"

"Obviously," Chalk said. "Just checking."

"We'll try a quart of each."

The seller poured the drinks from branded nozzles and slid them across the counter. Ripley positioned them, lightest to darkest, on INFIN-8's head.

The battered droid didn't seem to mind.

Veroselli Vanguard had a butterscotch-peach colour. Revan Pale Ale, a swirl of orange and gold. GanyMead Best resembled a dark green smoothie while the black gloopy Garrangulan Grog sparkled with filaments of red and purple.

Alternating who went first, Chalk found them highly palatable. "Favourite?" she said, the tension in her body easing as they goofed about.

"I guess I'll be patriotic—despite patriotism being actively discouraged on Revus X—and stick with the Revan Pale Ale," he said. "Veroselli Vanguard, a close second."

"Yeah, I couldn't drink more than a quart of the Garrangulan stuff. It's like a meal in a glass!"

"So, what are you *really* doing here?" he asked, catching Chalk off guard. With the last of the Vanguard to her lips, she drained the glass as slowly as she dare.

"Just," she started, wiping froth from her chin, "taking in the sights."

Ripley looked around at the ramshackle arcade. "Clawswoggle!"

"Huh?"

"I don't believe you."

Chalk pointed at the glittering sky above. "I'll never grow tired of that view."

"Oh," he said, frowning. "You know, the stars are visible from the window in your room?"

Which is where your GI-VR transponder says you are right now, she thought. But went with, "What's better than taking in the wonders of the SpiralVerse with a quart or two of GanyMead's finest … with a good friend."

"You're being dead weird, Hale."

URRRH! buzzed INFIN-8 as condensation from the Garrangulan Grog trickled down his sides.

"Sorry, buddy." Ripley wiped the droid with his sleeve. "Only just got you upgraded and now I'm getting moisture in your circuits and gears."

"Upgraded? What did he have done?"

URRRH!

"New limbs," Ripley said, eyes wide. "Can't you tell?"

"Oh," she said, catching on. "They look sensational!"

BING!

If anything, they looked better. To be fair, they couldn't have looked much worse. INFIN-8's new arms and legs were made of silver-alloy and sported chunky joints at the knee and elbow. Chalk was glad those flaky yellow limbs had gone. They'd looked ready to buckle at any moment.

She recalled how Ripley had pulled not one but eight power cells and a dozen metres of cabling out of INFIN-8 on Zorik Major. The droid looked incapable of holding five yuccagourds.

"He deserved a treat after ... you know what!"

BING! BING!

"He seems pleased."

"Better be. Cost enough. Got some system upgrades too," Ripley said, fanning a handful of data drives. "We'd better get these installed. What do you say, buddy?"

BING! BING! BING!

As he worked, Ripley talked her through the upgrades. Power regeneration and file management software. Processing upgrades. Enhanced night-mode capabilities. He installed a basic language decoder which allowed INFIN-8 to express himself through a selection of single word statements. It might have been Chalk's imagination but, once Ripley had finished, INFIN-8 seemed to stand taller, proud even.

"Where did you get the quasoids for all this?" she asked. "It can't be cheap."

"Did some extra work for Lasco," Ripley explained. "The commander's way behind with his maintenance, and Waxler is breathing down his neck. Asked me to help out."

"Oh," Chalk said, her senses easing. "Of course. What sort of thing?"

Ripley fussed with his droid. "Reconditioned some tech, changed some filters, replaced a whole batch of power couplings," he told her, then leaned in. "I shouldn't be doing it. It flies in the face of Galactic Institute rules, but the extra quasoids come in handy. Look, it's totally off the record, so don't say anything. Especially not to Lasco. Think he feels bad having to ask for help."

Was it true? Or a load of clawswoggle?

Chalk couldn't tell. His story made sense and he explained without missing a beat. Perhaps she was the one in the wrong. Sneaking around after him. Firing loaded questions. Stalking him on the interactive map. That was the sort of thing she expected from Spirit.

Trust is like a shooting star, said Harriet Starlight. *Rare and irretrievable.*

Chalk's eyes switched to the happy, gleaming eduhelper.

"So, what are you going to do with INFIN-8 when you come to visit me in London?" she asked, grinning nervously.

"So, I'm coming now, am I?"

Chalk angled her head. "Travel and adventure not your scene?"

"I don't remember ever agreeing to anything. Adventurous or otherwise," he said, now buffing INFIN-8 with a fibrous cloth. "But …"

"Ye-es?"

"Okay. For a bit," he conceded. "I want to go home and see my family too."

"Of course."

He stopped fiddling with the droid. "Maybe you could come too."

Chalk fanned a hand across her chest. "Moi?"

"Alright, Hale. Don't get overexcited. There's still plenty of time for me to go off you."

Chalk swung a playful fist towards him, but Ripley caught her hand in his. Their eyes locked. Fingers knitted together. His skin warm and calm. A thrill rushed through her, a light-headed yearning. The opposite of homesickness.

UN-COMF-TABLE buzzed INFIN-8.

With no fluctuations to the climate on the Coin, autumn didn't wither into winter and there was no spring or summer to look forward to. Every rotation passed with the same pleasant, appealing normalcy.

Chalk would have streaked across campus for a smattering of rain.

Chomped down a gut-full of biletongue for a thunderstorm.

As usual, Commander Lasco's Conflict Engagement lesson was the highlight of the phase. Despite the irritable eczema that followed, she relished the chance to lock horns with Ripley or Dana or the conjoined Traxa twins in Garrangulan strangle holds, Pyramist staring stances, and Montizoan voice punches.

To balance the universe, Galactic Law followed.

Later, Professor Mirage led an ever-growing Narrative of Story class into the morally grey, murky realms of the vast and unyielding religious systems that weaved throughout the SpiralVerse.

Dark Matter had become a surprisingly speculative class. Snider seemed inexplicably baffled by the subject himself, proposing new theories every time they gathered, and obliterated most of the lesson by reading from *The Mystery of Dark Matter and Other Impossible Pursuits* by Morgana Moonshadow.

Biodiverse Medical Science informed Chalk of the eighty-seven known breeds of Qwork, the loneliness and lethal nature of the Sagafly, and the combined digestive and reproductive system of the giant kraken-weevil via a hands-on practical lesson with Professor Cricklock.

Chalk wondered if she'd ever get the smell out of her hair.

Professor de Rema helped her keep up with the rest of the Emerging Physics class as they worked steadily through the seven hundred layer screens of *Entropic-Magnetism, Terminal-Dynamics, and Inverse Metamotion Phenomena* by Yeniffer Onkan-Spleen.

Bewildered and exhausted, Chalk dragged herself along to Professor Krazkow's class at the end of phase eight. Inside, she found the Garrangulan professor's desk loaded with glimmering rocks and crystals. Most were positioned on stands, but one had been set inside a secure display case. As students orbited the desk, Professor Krazkow stomped into the room and shooed them away like irritating bugs.

"Come on, come on, come on!" he bellowed. "Be seated. Master Krieg, put Spirit down! Thank you. Right. Ready? Enormously busy lecture today!"

Chalk and Ripley bumped shoulders as they crashed into the curved seating along the edge of the room. Krazkow circled his desk, tapping attendance numbers into his Touch10. "Full class!" he said, sounding amazed. "Normally one or two would have wilted under the pressure by now. Very good. Very good indeed. Highly durable first cycle we have here!"

He slammed a hairy fist against the table, making everyone jump. "Crystals," he boomed, indicating the glimmering rocks before him, "are beautiful, are they not?"

"Yes," said Spirit, who'd escaped Krieg's massive hands and taken a seat on the other side of Ripley. "I have dozens of them in my room on Gaia 15. They're good for healing and peace of mind. Plus, they're beautiful … in a lonely, static sort of way."

"Incorrect!" barked the Garrangular. "Ninety-seven point three per cent of all crystals in the SpiralVerse are exceptionally *dangerous* and should not be handled or displayed in a domestic setting." He towered over Spirit. The Oneric looked distraught. "I'd suggest you see Professor Asimov and ask him to contact your parents after class."

"I'll do it now," the Oneric said and tore out of the room.

"Where was I?" Krazkow rattled on. "Crystals and death, yes of course. So, who can tell me the eleven base crystal formations found in the SpiralVerse?"

Chalk glanced at Aida, expecting her to reel them off, but it was Milton who spoke first. "I don't know them all," the Sagaroach said, "but there's monoclinic, triclinic, trigonal, metrogonic, hexagonal, domestic, dynamic, and cubic."

"Excellent, Lord Barclay. You only missed orthorhombic, millasant, and mortaneous." He made a note on his Touch10. "I'm impressed, Milton. Other faculty members have been rather scathing of your progress thus far."

Milton looked like he might dash after Spirit.

Krazkow slammed his hand on the desk again.

Everyone jumped.

"Chemical Cosmology is more than mere science and astronomy. More than elements and molecules and structure and behaviour. It's about reaction and interaction. How galaxies and consciousness are one and the same. How the universe exists because we—the physical, the emotional, the living—perceive it to be. How we are part of the stars, and the stars are part of us."

An excited shiver prickled Chalk's bones.

"The relationship between one crystal and the next is the same as the relationship between one life form and the next. Their properties have fused and formed in the depths of planets and meteors over billions of cycles. They all share the same origin, evolution, and ultimate fate as the universe herself." His gaze landed on Chalk. "Miss Hale. Can you name any of the crystals displayed before you?"

"Honestly?"

"Of course."

"Not a chance."

"Have you done *any* pre-lesson preparation?" Krazkow asked, folding his muscular arms.

Chalk looked around the room. Twenty faces stared back. "Some," she said. "Just not on … crystals. I didn't think it would be such a big deal."

Clearly irritated, Professor Krazkow moved along the line. "Miss Dune?"

Dana looked perplexed.

"Master Renix? Nothing? Miss Pristina? Miss Lachrymosa?"

Sighing as though every crystal in the galaxy were housed on his broad shoulders, Krazkow returned to Milton. "Lord Barclay? I don't suppose you—"

"The red crystal is crimsonite, cubic construction found on Pyramax."

"Yes, indeed!" the professor said. "From your homeworld, Miss Lachrymosa."

"The bluish one is knotglass, a trigonal crystal from Gaia 23."

"Correct again!"

"The next two are both from Marstok. The amethyst one is heartstone, a crystal of hexagonal construction. The white crystal is wintershard—sometimes known as angel tooth—and is cubic like crimsonite."

"Correct on both counts!" Krazkow said excitedly. "Extra credit for knowing angel tooth, Master Barclay!"

"And the strange, black one inside the case is …"

"Go on," Professor Krazkow enthused, his fingers wriggling as if to pull the answer from Milton's insect brain. "Four out of five so far. Very good indeed. Don't stumble now."

Chalk and Ripley looked at Milton in utter astonishment.

"Is it … borelium?" the Sagaroach asked. "A metrogonic crystal from Eos Yol."

Professor Krazkow's face fell.

Milton withered.

"Incorrect!" the Garrangular roared, slamming his giant

hands together, "but excellent work today, Lord Barclay. If we still had a house points system I'd give you a hatful." The professor scoured the rest of the class. "Anyone know what the final crystal is? No one? Not a single soul? Not even students descended from the forefathers of Zorik Major?"

Krazkow stopped in front of the two Veroselli.

Clementine raised her hand slowly. "Zoranite?"

"Zoranite is yellow, Miss Von Wax." He turned to Claridge. "Master Von Whump?"

"It cannot be zorikanthium because—" he began, but the professor spun on his heels and slammed both hands onto the desk.

"Correct-a-mundo!"

Milton gasped.

The professor scurried around the desk like a Garrangular possessed. "And who can tell me about the properties of zorikanthium?"

Nobody answered.

Not the Veroselli.

Nor the Garrangulars.

"It's from Zorik Major," Milton said. "A mortaneous crystal. Believed extinct, destroyed at the same time as the planet itself."

"What else?"

"Many theories suggest zorikanthium is to blame for the tension and ill-feeling between"—he looked nervously across the room—"the Veroselli and the Garrangulars."

"Continue."

"Some say proximity to the crystal bestowed unusual powers, like luck and wisdom," he went on. "But those powers came with devastatingly violent side effects."

"Indeed," Krazkow said. "The Crystal of Shadows some call it, after the dark gas that moves and swirls inside, searching for a way out. It's true, not a trace has been found since the destruction of Zorik Major, yet the Veroselli and the Garrangulars are still at each other's throats, even now on Zorik Minor"—he swept past Krieg and Kroket and Kiln—"and here on the Coin. Who knows? Perhaps a crystal or two have survived!"

"Professor?" Milton said, pointing. "You have zorikanthium right there. On the Coin? Isn't that—?"

"—immeasurably irresponsible," Aida finished.

"These five crystals are the most dangerous in the SpiralVerse and, as such, are banned from the Galactic Institute," Krazkow declared. Students fidgeted nervously. "I couldn't imagine the sort of devastation that would occur if they were to fall and smash, releasing their hypnotic, hallucinogenic, poisonous gaseous centres. Why, we'd all die the most horrible of deaths."

At this point, the professor tripped and careened head first across the desk.

Dana Dune and Marcy-Kate screamed. The Vyshan Order huddled together in prayer. Chalk and Ripley scrambled out of their seats. Ironlung 8-47, Pristina, and Lachrymosa didn't move an inch but watched events unfold with morbid curiosity.

"That's quite enough," Krazkow said. "Return to your seats."

Everyone turned to look.

Astonishingly, the crystals hadn't crashed to the floor or polluted the ship. Instead, they wobbled and fizzed, disappearing and reappearing, as the professor swooshed his hands through them playfully.

"Holograms," he said. "Nothing more."

INAPPROPRIATE LANGUAGE DETECTED . . .

"That's quite enough, Lord Barclay, or you'll undo all your good work." The professor punched a layer screen and the holograms vanished. "Right then, open *Crystal Caverns of the Cosmos* by Maddette Réticule and start reading. Fastest wins."

Chalk concluded phase eight in a determined fashion. The promise of Christmas seemed to put an undiluted energy source in her plasma engines.

In the evening of the dark rotation, Ripley appeared.

"What's new, Hale?" he said, leaning against the doorjamb.

"Layer screens, essays, cheese sandwiches. Life's glorious cornucopia!"

Wandering in, he gazed at her homework.

"You know, if you partition the inverse power-ratios and reroute the residual photons through a cubit matrix, then you—"

"It's okay," she said. "I'll work it out."

"But it's just—"

"*Flinch*. I'll do it."

Ripley fanned his hands and stepped back. "Well, you'll need to do it later."

"And why's that?"

He slipped his fingers over hers. "Because I've got something for you."

"For me?" she said. "An early Christmas present?"

"What's Christmas?"

"Doesn't matter."

From the observation hall they descended the AGE to the Flipside and wandered along the outer paths. Dense congregations of trees hunkered beneath the rippling sheen of the environsphere.

"Where are you taking me?" Chalk said, growing impatient. "Nothing out here but trees."

The Revan stopped beside a shallow pond where colourful birds chased one another in wide arcs. "Look up," he said, opening a layer screen and tapping feverishly.

"What am I—?"

But Chalk's words caught in her throat as a billion stars slowly evaporated and the environsphere became ice blue and dotted with fluffy clouds.

"Ripley. This is amazing."

The Revan raised a slim digit and tapped the layer screen once more.

Chalk could not believe her eyes. For nine phases—one

hundred and eight rotations—the sky had been starry and black, the world illuminated by ambient light alone. A winter sky hung above her now. The temperature dropped. Her skin prickled, throbbed. A single tear pooled in the corner of her eye, then froze against her cheek.

She couldn't believe it.

"How did you—?"

"Insider secrets."

"We're not dressed for this," she told him.

"Don't worry," Ripley replied. "The environmental settings will counteract my changes soon enough."

Snowflakes fell across the Flipside.

They drifted happily on the manufactured breeze, pirouetting like graceful ballerinas, coating plants and trees. Some students squealed with delight. Others sprinted for the AGE in alarm.

Chalk turned in circles, arms outstretched.

Her heart raced as snowflakes nestled on her nose and eyelashes.

She pulled Ripley close, his body warm and comforting. Her fingers coiled into his soft jacket, traced the pendant beneath his shirt, and brushed his soft skin. She eased back and looked deep into his hypnotic purple eyes.

"If Krazkow's right," he said, "then every snowflake is made of stardust."

Chalk nodded, her chest alive with nerves and excitement. "Who share the same evolution and ultimate fate as the universe herself."

"They're part of the stars."

"Just like you ... and me."

GAPSS
KNOWLEDGE
MAINFRAME

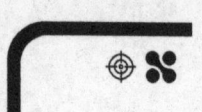 

ZORIKANTHIUM
[CRYSTAL]

A crystal of mortaneous construction formed in the mantle beneath Zorik Major. The crystal itself is clear but filled with a poisonous black vapour—giving it the nickname the Crystal of Shadows. Zorikanthium was mined by both the Veroselli and the Garrangulars—who believed it brought great power—and used for ornaments, weapons, and jewellery. There are no known resources of zorikanthium remaining in the SpiralVerse. The last known traces were believed lost during the untimely destruction of Zorik Major.

BROKEN WINGS

Chalk couldn't remember much of phase ten. She'd definitely been to classes, read hundreds of layer screens, and written dozens more. Her mind was transfixed on that beautiful moment beneath the winter sky on the Flipside.

The snow.

The Revan.

The kiss.

She had barely unpacked, so it took her no time to prepare for the return trip to London. Bouncing on her suitcase, she reached down and yanked the zipper. Her dorm room looked alien without clothes strewn mercilessly across the floor and paperbacks stacked precariously on the bedside table.

Cube poised on the unmade bed. Its gelatinous orange mass shifted into various geometric shapes. "You are halfway through the first cycle," it said. "How does that feel?"

Chalk stamped on her suitcase. "Somewhat impressed by myself. Although, I do feel like I'm sprinting all the time. Pretty sure that's unsustainable."

"Well, you were certainly not sprinting in phase ten."

Chalk frowned. "What's that supposed to mean?"

"You have been sent several correspondence pertaining to your conduct."

"Really?" she said and opened her GI-VR. Cube highlighted a stream of unread messages. "Where did these come from?"

"If you will permit me to paraphrase," Cube began.

"Professor Dustenberg says you were: *Physically present, intellectually absent.* Professor Sigma-Santos writes: *Miss Hale had the potential to be one of my best students.* Professor Mirage insinuates you have been possessed. By what or whom, she does not stipulate. And Professor Snider simply writes: *Hale has the look and fortitude of a lovesick fool.* Should I continue?"

"Nope. Got it."

"Perhaps what you need is a good long break," the eduhelper said. "To rest and relax and recuperate and recharge and—"

"Yeah, that's the plan."

Cube hid as the door buzzed and the gentle rush of air caressed the back of Chalk's neck. Spinning, she found Ripley framed in the doorway, a travel trunk dumped beside him.

"This still happening?"

Chalk coiled her hands round her hips. "'No' is always an option," she told him. "I mean, London isn't all that. Loads of old buildings and dirty streets and gang crime."

"Sounds like home."

"Come on. I bet the queue at the portal chamber is longer than a celestial worm's digestive tract."

Hundreds of students and eduhelpers, loaded with travel-packs and hover-trunks, swirled around the hyperloop like ingredients in a blender. Riding the off-tube, they disembarked at the observation hall. The enormous room bulged with long, snaking queues.

INAPPROPRIATE LANGUAGE DETECTED . . .

"This is going to take forever."

"What's the hold-up?" Chalk asked.

Lachrymosa angled her bony face towards them. "There's a temporary halt on portal travel," the Pyramist said, her eyes swimming in bilious, watery pools.

"A halt?"

"Something to do with Cressida," crackled Pristina, through her breathing apparatus. "Asimov is wandering about quoting GAPSS security protocols."

"What does that mean?"

"Right now?" Lachrymosa droned. "We wait."

Nothing happened for over an hour. Chalk and Ripley sat on their bags, chatting to Lachrymosa and Pristina about their mid-cycle plans. By all accounts, the Pyramist had a strict schedule of chanting ahead, while the Moxi was excited to remove her breathing apparatus and enjoy the poisonous air of Cyanol 7.

Chalk's GI-VR buzzed.

Every GI-VR buzzed.

Frustration cannoned around the observation hall.

GENERAL WAXLER: Due to unprecedented events at the Galactic Institute, GAPSS have embargoed all portal travel beyond the confines of the school until further notice. I know many of you were looking forward to returning to your homeworlds and families at this time, for that I apologise unreservedly. You will be advised if the situation changes.

Chalk wallowed for several rotations. She shut herself away from Aida and Milton—even Ripley—losing herself in *Harriet Starlight* and *The Hunger Games*. Cube got the sharp end of her tongue when it tried to advise her to eat or exercise or take a shower.

She wrote in her notebook to her mother, to Grandpa Milo, and her friends. Chalk felt closer to them with the emerald fountain pen in her hand. But, no matter how many words she scribbled, she remained stuck, thousands of lightcycles away.

Emerging, she looked for Ripley.

An apology was definitely overdue.

Chalk wasn't prone to high-level strops and found it hard to believe she could be annoyed at spending Christmas on an enormous space station on the other side of the SpiralVerse. It always bothered her how Harry, Ron, and Hermione could ever want to spend Christmas anywhere other than Hogwarts. Her eight-year-old self would have drunk a gallon of unicorn blood for the chance.

She buzzed Ripley's door. No answer. Chalk stopped herself from forcing it open and wandering in. He'd probably gone for something to eat or to upgrade INFIN-8 or help Lasco with more tech repairs.

The rotunda and the arcade were a bust. Chalk took the AGT to the flight deck. She marvelled again at the powerful starfighters and battle mechs that lined the edge, facing the launch bay and the propellosphere beyond.

Lasco's workshop door hung open. She poked her head inside. "Hello? Commander? Cozy? Ripley? Anyone here?"

The nervous Qwork appeared. "Miss H-Hale," she said, her fingers coiling into her striped T-shirt.

"Hey Cozy," she said breezily. "Where is everyone?"

"I'm h-here," the Qwork replied. "C-Commander. Asleep."

"Siesta, huh? Very continental."

Cozy wrinkled her trunk.

"Ripley not about?" she asked, casually inspecting each corner of the workshop and glancing covetously at the flight simulator.

Cozy frowned. "M-Master Flinch?"

"Yeah."

"Not since," Cozy said. "E-E-Empirical Mechanics."

Chalk did a full lap of the workbench and checked the tiers of broken tech in more detail. "Are you expecting him later?"

"Expecting?" Cozy said. "G-Galactic Institute shut. Mid-cycle b-break."

"I know," Chalk said, then, "but Ripley told me about the extra work he's doing for the commander. Helping out with the backlog of busted tech."

Cozy tilted her head.

"I know it's all on the hush-hush," she said, putting a finger to her lips. "I won't say a word. Promise."

"Miss Hale?" the Qwork said, following her around the

workbench as though caught in a tractor beam.

Chalk stopped. "Ripley. Master Flinch. He's been coming down here to help the commander, yes? He told me about it. It's fine."

Cozy shook her head.

"After class? During lunch break? Late at night?"

Several crates clattered to the ground as Commander Lasco stumbled into the workshop and pulled a shirt over his head. "Miss Hale. What are you doing here?"

Chalk didn't know anymore.

Her head spun.

Her legs felt weak.

She clasped the edge of the workbench.

"Miss Hale? What is it?"

"Nothing. It's nothing. Nothing at all."

"M-master Flinch," Cozy said.

"What about him?"

"He l-l-l-l—"

"Don't say it."

"—lied!" Cozy finished.

"About what?"

"It's nothing. Really."

Tears broke through her defences.

"Chalk," Lasco said. "Sit down. Tell me."

She turned her sore eyes towards the commander. He looked as off-colour as ever, but perhaps her water-logged vision wasn't doing him any favours. "He told me … He said that … Was he here?"

"Here?"

"Helping you fix stuff. Reconditioning tech and gear for the Galactic Institute."

Commander Lasco pulled back.

"Well?" she pressed, more urgent. "Was he? Did you ask him? Tell me!"

"Chalk. Students cannot—"

"But he said you paid him. He upgraded INFIN-8 with the quasoids."

"Ripley is an exceptionally talented engineer, but I haven't … I cannot … employ him."

Tears came hard now.

"I wish I could," Lasco said conversationally. "He'd be an excellent asset to my department."

"That's not helping."

Commander Hank K. Lasco looked a thousand lightcycles out of his comfort zone. He patted Chalk gingerly on the shoulder. "I'm sure he didn't mean to mislead you."

"Yeah. Sure." She nodded. "Just a simple misunderstanding."

"Exactly."

"He told me lies. *Lies.* To my face … and I believed them! Then he went and made it snow, and he kissed me, and said so many wonderful things."

"Now," the commander said, taking Chalk's quivering hand, "I'm a relative emotional wasteland—"

Chalk snorted. Tears and snot mingled on her top lip.

"—but I always feel immeasurably better with a fast ship under my bones and a control yoke in my grasp."

Chalk dragged the tears across her face. "Wh-what?"

Lasco spun a sparkling blue starfighter helmet in his hands. "Wanna fly?"

Lasco helped Chalk into the flight simulator. A complex series of cables jutted from each side, connected to an array of trunking on the ceiling. Punching a matrix of buttons on a panel behind her, the simulator became taut, rising several inches. A peculiar sensation rocketed through her—like she wasn't connected to the world in the usual way.

"Excuse me if I'm teaching you how to boil a Predorian gromit fish, but this is the control yoke," he said, indicating the long joystick-style column in the centre. "It governs pitch and roll. Button on the front fires the blasters. Button on the top drops the bombs. Left foot rudder is the yaw. Right foot is thrust. Questions? Good!"

Commander Lasco mounted the simulator to Chalk's right, donned a red helmet with orange starbursts, and ignited the power units. "Are you ready?"

Chalk nodded.

"For death and glory and the SpiralVerse, right?"

Sniffing down a torrent of gloop, Chalk opened her mouth to echo the commander's battle cry, but her heart wasn't in it.

Lasco flicked a dial on his console. A visor snapped over Chalk's face. Darkness consumed her. Stars materialised before her. Golden, three-dimensional letters faded into existence.

SHIP SELECTION . . .

Four vessels hovered side by side.

Red Thorn.

Splintered Needle.

Stingray.

Black Emperor.

Lasco's voice crackled over the intercom. "Best stick to Red Thorns for our first outing."

Chalk did as she was told despite her gaze being drawn to the cool lines of the Splintered Needle and the enigmatic presence of the Black Emperor. She didn't remember seeing any of the latter in the museum or the flight deck. Perhaps none had survived whatever war they'd flown in.

Chalk's vision filled with a hyper-real environment. Glowing buttons, switches, and readouts spread beneath a slim viewport and a galaxy of stars. It felt good to be somewhere else, somewhere new, somewhere beyond the confines of the Galactic Institute.

The Red Thorn bobbed and shuddered as it glided through space. Solar flares glinted off her screen. She could feel the push of the simulator forcing her spine into the seat as she eased her foot on the thrust. Her hands, encased in digitise leather gloves, coiled around the control yoke.

Her brain knew this was software.

Her senses assured her otherwise.

It's just like playing Green Death *on my Hagrid beanbag back home.*

"Squadron Leader reporting," said Commander Lasco. "All souls come back."

"Captain Chalk reporting."

"Captain, eh?" Lasco said. "We'll see."

"H-homebase receiving. Loud and c-c-clear," Cozy replied on the intercom. "Incoming report. C-critical intel. President of the F-f-foundation. Colonial B-buildings. B-B-Berklon III. Search and d-d-d-destroy."

"Okay, Hero Squadron. Wings up. Follow my lead to Berklon III. We'll scope the terrain, test our hardware and weapon systems, before conducting a strategic strike."

Commander Lasco's Red Thorn roared into view, forming the head of a diamond with software-generated non-playing characters on either side. Chalk squeezed the control yoke and gave the ship a generous shake. The Red Thorn lurched dynamically from side to side. Her hips smashed into the edge of her seat. Her lips quirked.

"Faster-than-light drives are up."

"Engage!" yelled Chalk, becoming overstimulated.

"Yeah, sure," Lasco said. "Go for FTL travel."

Chalk took a deep breath and whispered, "Make it so."

Her display became elongated. Her hands pinched into infinity. Chalk's world flashed white for an instant, then everything snapped back. A large planet with green continents and blue oceans shot towards them and stopped on a dime. A huge space station circled the globe. Small, personal transports buzzed around loading bays, while larger commercial vehicles hung in launch bays undergoing maintenance or waiting for departure.

"Berklon III," Lasco said. "Black market trading hub, refuge for criminals and outlaws."

"A wretched hive of scum and villainy!"

"Yes, Captain Chalk. Very colourful."

"Location c-c-confirmed," Cozy piped up. "Colonial b-buildings. Jardox c-c-continent. Sending c-c-co-ordinates."

Lasco's fighter began its descent. Chalk and the NPCs followed, flying in vague formation. Her Red Thorn rattled and shook as they passed through the atmosphere. Flames licked the viewport. The tip of her ship glowed white hot. Clouds spun past. Rivulets of moisture hissed over the screen. Chalk bounced excitedly as her Red Thorn pitched from side to side under each delicate adjustment.

"Okay, let's see what you've got," Lasco said, blasting towards a range of sandy mountains. "Stay in formation."

Commander Lasco's Red Thorn threaded its way into a deep gorge where a river meandered between divorced clumps of bracken and brush. Chalk pulled in behind. The NPCs' line astern.

Sun-baked rock whizzed by. Trees became a green smudge. Lasco accelerated and Chalk baulked at the level she had to open the thrusters to stay close. Her shoulders pressed hard into the seat. Sweat bubbled on her top lip. Eyes wide as saucers. The terrain closed in, the valley walls no more than a ship's width on either side.

Lasco turned hard, his Red Thorn at right angles. Chalk followed, flying on instinct. They slammed left, curved hard, dived low to avoid a rockfall. Chalk had to remind herself to breathe as her arms shook under the force of each violent direction change.

The valley widened and Lasco dropped low. The tips of his wings skimmed the surface of the river. Chalk followed, misjudged her elevation, and dumped her rear thrusters into the crystal-clear water.

ENGINE STALL . . .

Warning buttons flashed on her dashboard. The engine guttered and bucked like a donkey. The acrid stink of plasma exhausts filled her head.

"Engine re-fire," said Lasco calmly. "Green button. Next to the altimeter. No, that's your warning lights. Your other green button."

Chalk's engine fired, pushing the ship nose-first through the water and into the sky.

"That was too close."

Lasco looped his Red Thorn over mountain peaks and rocketed across an open salt plain where dark boulders nestled upon a cracked, barren landscape.

"Weapons training," he said. Slithers of blue light erupted from his wing-mounted twin-blasters, reducing the nearest boulder to smoking ruins. He swooped effortlessly between one boulder and the next, destroying five, six, seven, before spinning skyward.

"Seven to beat, Captain Chalk."

"Easy pickings."

She flew low. Skimmed the deck. Eased her index finger onto the trigger. As she connected, a cross-hatch target appeared in her retinal display. Chalk's Red Thorn sprayed an arc of white crystals into the air as she blasted one, two, three boulders, swung wide to avoid a pair blocking her path, then soared over the top of another.

Chunks of rock and ash rained onto Chalk's fighter, knocking it against the planet surface. Sparks and debris scattered in all directions.

"Yee-haw!" she screamed euphorically, despite a spike of pain between her shoulder blades and the throbbing ache in her heart.

Chalk let rip.

Four boulders. Five.

"Easy does it," came the commander's voice. "Push everything from your mind. Focus. Breathe."

But the cross-hatch target faded.

Ripley's face replaced it.

She couldn't help it.

Bile sloshed in her gut.

Salty tears found her lips.

Her fingers shook on the control yoke as boulders nicked the Red Thorn, throwing the fighter into chaotic undulations.

"Chalk," the commander said, his voice a strict warning.

Struggling to correct the ship, she bobbed erratically.

Boulders came thick and fast.

She weaved intuitively, fired again.

Grazed the edge of one boulder, missed the next.

She tried to blink the tears away, but it was no use.

"Chalk? What's going on—?"

She unleashed dozens of laser blasts. Fingers jabbed angrily at the fire button. Hands shook dangerously. Chin trembled. Boulders exploded all around. Tornados of salt and dirt rattled horribly against the ship. Her vision eroded.

And yet she kept firing.

Again and again and again.

Until—*BOOM!!!*

PILOT DOWN . . .

GAPSS
KNOWLEDGE
MAINFRAME

SEVANTES
[SPECIES]
Homeworld: Zorik System, Lang. Galaxian

An indigenous species from the Zorik System, the Sevantes are a mutant race constructed of outcast genetics and corrupted DNA who were enslaved by the Veroselli and the Garrangulars for thousands of cycles. Following their liberation, the Sevantes live a peaceful, yet untrusting existence, on Zorik Pol. The Sevantes are one of the three oldest known civilisations in the SpiralVerse.

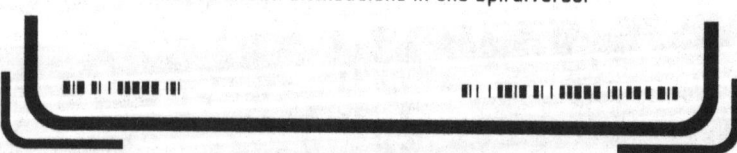

MISCHIEF MANAGED

"W-w-what happened?" Cozy said, as Chalk scrambled out of the cockpit and bolted for the door. She raced across the flight deck, behind the defunct battle mechs, eyes streaming, a hollow ache in her chest. Skidding into the portal chamber, she dropped to the treadplate and curled into a ball. Chalk begged the universe to swallow her whole—like one of a trillion stars, blinking, unnoticed, out of existence.

Commander Lasco wheezed by a moment later. He disappeared into the museum where his voice rebounded into fading echoes.

Chalk fired up the interactive map.

The pulsating, amber hoop of Ripley's transponder hovered over the dorms.

"Fraking clawswoggler."

Her head slumped against the damp, metal wall.

The amber hoop throbbed.

I should confront him. Ask him outright. Look him in those purple eyes—

But the thought of hearing a fresh set of lies made Chalk shiver.

There must be a way to—

And then it hit her. She'd had the solution the entire time. Standing, she wiped her face, fixed her hair, and pulled her iPhone Firebird from her pocket.

"I need to activate the GPS transponder and link it to the Galactic Institute mainframe so it registers on the map," she told Cube, in the safety of her room. "It must be possible. I'm sure Ripley would be able to do it in a heartbeat."

"Why do you not ask him?"

"Because," she said impatiently, "I'm going to use the iPhone to follow him."

"Well," Cube said, "I should robustly advise against hacking the Galactic Institute mainframe and adding foreign devices. Those actions constitute a breach of campus policy, a flagrant disregard for school ethics, and an invasion of personal and private data."

"And your point is?"

"This is highly irresponsible."

"Thanks, *Aida*."

"And dangerous, considering the current state of affairs at the school," Cube added. "Some might regard your actions as suspicious."

"Well," Chalk said, "Ripley is being suspicious too. I'm only being suspicious because he's being suspicious."

"That is incredibly immature."

Chalk glowered at Cube who'd transformed itself into a palm tree. "You're my eduhelper," she told it. "So eduhelp me!"

"You want me to break every Galactic Institute data law and pair a foreign device to the mainframe?"

"If you could."

"Why?"

"Does there need to be a compelling reason?"

"Acts of criminal intent are usually driven by—"

"Look," Chalk told Cube, "I know what I'm asking is wrong, but sometimes people do the wrong things for the right reasons."

"Is this human logic?"

"One hundred per cent."

UPDATING . . .

"Ripley is involved in something. I don't know what. He lied to me about where he'd been, about what he was doing. Part of me wants to forget about him. Let him go on all his snaggerific late-night wanderings and wallow in all the private projects he wants. Let him suffer the consequences of his own mistakes." Chalk dropped onto the bed. "But I care for him. I think I—" She sniffed and rolled onto her side. "I think he's doing something dangerous."

"Something to do with Princess Van Wyrm's disappearance?"

Chalk bit her lip. "Gods. I don't know. That's why I need to add the iPhone to the network. So I can see where he goes. Find out what he's doing. Make sure he's safe."

Cube morphed into a sphere, expanding and retracting as though breathing. "I am against this course of action," it said.

"But—"

"Categorically."

"Cube—"

"Your logic and reasoning are illogical and without reason."

"Noted."

Her GI-VR pinged!

NEW USER PROFILE CREATED . . .

A green circle appeared on the interactive map beside her own, the iPhone serial number written beneath.

"Yes!" Chalk said gleefully. "This is amazing."

"And unlawful," Cube said. "I could be dematerialised."

"I'll protect you."

"Would you like to assign a name for this device?" Cube asked. "AP856U9X1187 is problematic to pronounce in any language."

Chalk highlighted the serial number and typed a replacement.

"What's *PADFOOT?*"

"I can solemnly swear I am up to no good!"

Chalk reduced the layer screens.

"You do realise that your actions amount to stalking?"

"Operation: Chalk-Stalk engaged!"

Buzzing for the Revan an hour later under the pretence of hitting the food dispenser, Chalk found him soldering a stack of bulky tech.

"What is all this?" she asked, a tightness in her chest.

"Oh, some old tech I'm reconditioning and repurposing."

"Looks … complicated."

"Just power cells and data drives."

"For the commander?" Chalk asked, unblinking.

Ripley looked away. "Yeah, sure. But, you know, keep your voice down."

Chalk wrestled with the urge to vomit everything out at once.

"You need a break?" she said breezily. "I want to introduce you to pizza."

"Pizza?"

"Dough, red sauce, cheese," Chalk said, layering one hand above the other. "Toppings are dealers' choice."

"Toppings?"

"Yeah, like mushrooms or pineapple or that vile peppered biletongue stuff you're obsessed with."

"An open sandwich?"

"Um, kind of, but it's all crispy and melty and yum."

"Crispy *and* melty?"

"Come on," she said, inching through the mini towers of tech and pulling his sleeve.

INFIN-8 followed them to the living quarters where they picked up the pizza from the serving hatch. Chalk tried to steer Ripley away from sitting with Milton, but the Sagaroach was eating alone. Reluctantly, they joined him.

Ripley devoured his pizza in no time, wiping his mouth on his sleeve, and leaning back in his chair. "That was outstanding, Hale," he said. "Why haven't you introduced me to pizza before? Honestly, what other Earthly wonders are you holding on to?"

"You had Angel Delight?"

"Obviously not."

"Get me one too," she said, smiling. "Butterscotch. With whipped cream. And chocolate sprinkles."

Ripley scooted over to the food dispensary, tapping his GI-VR as he went.

Chalk pulled the iPhone from her pocket, dived across the table, and grabbed INFIN-8.

URRRH! URRRH! URRRH! the droid protested.

She prised his lid open and tossed the iPhone in.

VI-O-LATED!

INFIN-8 shook irritably as though swallowing a gallon of disgusting medicine.

"What in Razabelle's name are you doing?" Milton said, yuccagourd dribbling onto the table.

"Not a word," Chalk said, zipping her lips.

"But—?"

"That's a word," she told him. "None. Silence. This is our secret."

"Is this something I should—?"

"Milton? What's wrong with you?" she said. "You saw nothing. I did nothing. Nothing is all you know about the nothing you saw."

"But you—"

"And that is why we stay silent."

INFIN-8 shook wildly. Red lights flashed on his lid.

"That goes for you too," Chalk told the droid. "It's for his own good."

URRRH! INFIN-8 blared again. Then, *BING?*

Butterscotch Angel Delight arrived in two fluted sundae glasses with long, silver spoons. Ripley was less impressed with the dessert but promised he'd provide Chalk with a vegetarian Revan-inspired menu soon.

Sitting on her bed alone with the map open, Chalk stared desperately at the two circles pulsating in Ripley's room.

The amber ring of his GI-VR.

And the green hoop of *PADFOOT*—the iPhone Firebird inside INFIN-8.

She sat and watched for hours.

Nothing happened.

Perhaps he wasn't going anywhere today. Maybe INFIN-8 had ratted her out or perhaps the plucky droid didn't go with him on his travels. It was a risk to put the iPhone inside INFIN-8, but her options were slim. Ripley would definitely notice if she stuck it in one of his pockets or tried to conceal it in his bag.

Sleep took Chalk. She dreamt of soaring inside the AGT as light beams fizzed by in long white ribbons. Of pizza and butterscotch Angel Delight. Of Ripley. And of all the secrets the future held.

She woke with a start.

Curiosity coursed through her veins.

It was almost three in the morning.

Chalk opened the interactive map. The amber hoop still pulsated in the middle of Ripley's room. But the green ring had gone!

Fanning her fingers, she expanded the map and scoured the campus.

Chalk couldn't find the green transponder anywhere. Perhaps it had sunk so far down inside INFIN-8—like all those power cells and cables—that the signal had become lost. She was about to collapse the display and bury her face in the pillows when she flicked the edge of the map.

Inverting it.

Zooming in, her heart rate doubled, her breath became ragged.

The iPhone's emerald-green locator appeared, strong and true.

The word *PADFOOT* detailed below.

Ripley was on the Flipside.

Descending the AGE, Chalk stepped into dusky, twilit gardens. Long shadows yawned effortlessly across swaying grey grass.

She checked the position of her iPhone, of INFIN-8, and hopefully the Revan too. They were heading into the forest of quadrant three. A part of the Flipside she'd not explored before.

Getting her bearings, she marched along the zigzagging paths, ignoring all the strange night life that scurried beneath the marauding bushes and borders. Ornate fountains spiralled with dancing jets of moonlit water. Chalk gave them an urgent glance but pressed on to the outer wall.

Guilt clawed the inside of her skull.

Guilt about tracking Ripley, following him on his secret, personal excursions.

Cube threw warnings and alternate suggestions at her, but Operation: Chalk-Stalk was green-lit. No bugging out now.

The iPhone's transponder plunged deep through the forest, somewhere to her right in the thick woodland borders. Chalk skirted along the treeline, one eye on roots that broke the path, the other on her GI-VR. The iPhone signal appeared to stop, pulsating one hundred and fifty metres inside the trees.

She shouldered her way through the dense bracken. Branches bent as she forged onward. She ducked and clawed at the increasingly difficult terrain. What was Ripley doing in here? What was hidden inside the woods? Surely the trees just formed a protective barrier. A living fence around the edge of the Flipside.

She checked the map once more.

The green circle was no longer at the edge.

It was moving.

Fast.

Directly towards her.

Chalk dithered, unsure.

"He's coming," Cube told her.

"I can see that."

"The prudent thing to do would be *hide*. The gallant thing—"

"I understand my choices."

The green ring approached, moving much faster through the trees than Chalk thought possible. Yet, in her indecision she became rooted to the spot. Mind churning like a smoothie blender.

"Visual confirmation in less than ten seconds."

Chalk's hands shook.

Her stomach somersaulted.

"Eight seconds. Seven. Six."

"Enough!"

Chalk raked the woodland. He'd be here any second. Ripley and INFIN-8 would be here imminently. She checked the interactive map again. The iPhone inched closer and closer.

"He's ten feet away," Cube said. "Six feet, four."

"That can't be. That's right in front of me!"

"I assure you it is right."

"Then you're not reading it right!"

Sure enough, for a moment the two coloured hoops occupied the same space. "How? What? I don't understand," Chalk said. "That's … impossible."

Her skin crawled, as though a ghost had walked through her. Chalk's focus shifted from the interactive map to the knobbly, tree-routed ground beneath her feet.

"Gods below!"

"What is it?"

"He's underneath me."

"I beg your pardon?"

"He's *inside* the Coin!"

GAPSS
KNOWLEDGE
MAINFRAME

KRITTENS
[SPECIES]

A small, hairless, hardy, reproductively rapid species of quadrupeds found in every civilised world in the SpiralVerse. They are considered a pest and a nuisance by most cultures, but all plans to eradicate them have proved fruitless. Krittens live in large family units and appear to be driven by mischief and chaos, an activity that researchers believe brings them no benefit other than joy.

BETWEEN THE FLOORBOARDS

"The inside of the Coin," Cube informed Chalk as they moved through the dense brambles and thickets, "is strictly off limits to students and teaching staff. The lower decks are primarily designated for engine rooms and auxiliary systems that include, but are not limited to: environsphere, anti-gravity transport and elevator, life-support system, integrated portal system, environmental controls, mains power and distribution, attitude easing atmospheric system, security, lighting, heating—"

"Enough already. I get it," Chalk snapped, crashing towards the outer edge of the Flipside. Sharp twigs and thorns pulled at her clothes. Nicked her jacket. Cut her hands. "Did you find anything ahead?"

"There are a number of small buildings. Fifty-five metres at twenty-three degrees to your right."

Chalk stormed on. Her gaze drove through the brown and green, looking for a shiny metal doorway, a hatch, any means of descending into the engine rooms below.

But what came through the trees was truly unexpected.

The dense undergrowth thinned to reveal bulky green hedges rising high above her head. Five archways led to shadowy passages beyond. "What's this?" she said. "A ... maze?"

A grim holographic figure, wrapped in black flowing robes that hid all but the tip of his nose, suddenly materialised. "Welcome," he hissed. Chalk almost collapsed from shock. "To the mazeoleums!"

"Mazeoleums?" she echoed, regaining her composure.

"Five entrances stand before you," the holographic figure continued. "Each marks the start of a befuddling labyrinth that lead to the burial grounds of mighty historical figures."

"What in the name of …?"

"Behold!" the hunched, pallid hologram went on. "Through these mazes you will find the resting place of Obit Venk Tyllimens (founder and first Headmaster of the Galactic Institute), the Crypt of the Unknown Engineer, Sepulchre of the Vanquished Starfighter, Burial Grounds of Astrologer Klark Klarkksson, and the Remembrance Halls of Extinct Civilisations (New and Ancient)."

"Which one did Ripley take?" Chalk asked, but the hologram continued its scripted spiel. She stamped out of frustration.

"Any ideas?"

"Billions," Cube said.

"About our current predicament?" She groaned. "Five doorways. Twenty per cent chance of success."

"Eighty per cent chance of failure," Cube advised. "It is not a healthy gamble."

"Which one is which?" she asked the hologram again, who now regaled them with stories about the first headmistress, Noxious Ranx, who commissioned the mazeoleums and oversaw their construction at the end of the Thousand Moons War.

Chalk shook her head. "Tyllimens, Engineer, Starfighter, Klarkksson, Extinct Civilisations? He said them in that order, right?"

"Affirmative."

"So, seems to follow that the doorways would be positioned in the same way."

"It is a definite possibility," Cube said. "Which are you leaning towards?"

"If Ripley is in the engine rooms between the Flipside and the Coin," she said, turning to the second doorway, "then Crypt of the Unknown Engineer seems logical."

Chalk opened the interactive map. The green iPhone signal was approaching the AGE, scurrying through the bowels of Centurion H.

The mazeoleum was tight and claustrophobic. Chalk walked on instinct, making quick turns and losing her sense of direction. She backtracked, hoping to return to the start, but found herself in a new tangle of crossroads and forks that occupied far more space than known physics allowed.

"This is nuts," she said, colliding with another dead end and twisting around. "Do you have any information about the solution for these mazes?"

"The presence of the mazes are hidden in deep folders on the GAPSS Knowledge Mainframe, but no information about the specific paths through the puzzles have been supplied."

"Glorious," she muttered, taking a series of random turns. "We're going to lose him, aren't we?"

"I would be more concerned about losing yourself."

"That's not very reassuring."

"It is, however, accurate."

"Agreed. But sometimes, especially in anxious moments such as this, positivity and encouragement would be preferable to brutal truth."

UPDATING . . .

Chalk pressed on, looking for a crypt or, failing that, a way out. And then, when hope hung by a Sagarachnid's thread, the maze opened to reveal a grey stone building. Strange icons and hieroglyphs glowed on its sides in complex, alien tongues. Her GI-VR quickly translated.

CRYPT OF THE UNKNOWN ENGINEER . . .

"Hoo-Ha!" Chalk yelled, punching the air. "Let's hope this is the right one. I don't have the strength to get out of here, much less conquer four more mazeoleums."

To Chalk's relief, the door hung ajar. She wrapped her fingers around the burnished metal and heaved. It moved steadily and, as she leant into the gloom, an intoxicating blend of heat and chemicals rose to meet her.

"I am detecting hazardous conditions. Incapacitating heat and poor air quality. Without protective equipment you will survive approximately seven to nine minutes."

Chalk ignored Cube and moved quickly, descending into the sweltering dark.

The stairs ended at a metal door. A damp, rusty wheel sat in the middle like the bulkhead on a battleship. Chalk could feel the immense heat coming from beyond.

"Last chance for reason," Cube said.

Chalk gripped the wheel and turned. It shifted a fraction, sticking in the housing. The mechanisms inside groaned and complained. Eventually, it let out a dull clang! and the door swung wide.

A billowing wave of boiling vapour consumed her. She gripped the walls and staggered forward, her eyes watering like an upset Pyramist. Walkways circled left and right off an impossibly long corridor, each brimming with panels of tech, flashing diodes, corrugated silver tubing, and chaotic cables and wires. Charcoaled roots broke through from the woodland above. Droplets of moisture sizzled as they exploded against the machine-turned floor.

An acrid, chemical stink consumed Chalk's senses.

Her head spun.

A grinding, churning noise rattled her skull. An amalgamation of every piece of kit and device and engine melded together in a riotous cacophony.

The heartbeat of the Galactic Institute.

Perspiration bubbled on her forehead. Rivulets trickled down her back.

"Your temperature is approaching critical levels," Cube said. "Brain processes and motor functions are dramatically reduced."

"Anything else?" Chalk said, moving as fast as she dare.

"Dehydration is imminent."

Grumbling, she pressed on, trying to ignore Cube's constant commentary. The corridor ran for half a kilometre to a large circular room with five additional entranceways. Large openings in the floor and ceiling were surrounded by a busted safety rail. Without warning, a huge torrent of steam exploded from below and suffocated the room.

Chalk fell back.

Her skin like fire.

She dragged herself to the edge and used a button panel to claw herself to her feet. Her vision doubled. Body swayed dangerously. She dived into the nearest corridor, desperate to be away from another wave of scalding vapour.

But she tripped.

Slammed against one wall. Then another.

Her sight failed to improve.

Her legs felt like semi-digested yuccagourds.

Darkness closed in. Her head became light.

Chalk crashed to the ground.

Her sight flickered, promised to fail.

Hot treadplate sizzled against her cheek. Several pairs of feet ran towards her. Footfalls reverberated through the floor. Hands pressed against her body. Alarmed, muffled voices rang.

Everything went dark.

Chalk woke on a green rubber sofa in a darkened room. A faint glow sliced the floor, creating a hypnotic gauze of three-dimensional light. Piles of tech surrounded her. A square resin table and chairs were arranged beside a pitiful-looking kitchenette, stacked with dirty pans and cutlery. A workbench—much like Commander Lasco's—dominated the space. Dented boxes rattled noisily, throwing cool air into the room. Chalk could feel herself reaching towards one, her skin alive with prickly heat.

"She's awake," said a voice.

A familiar face emerged from the shadows.

"Chalk," Ripley said, relief thick in his voice. "You're alive."

"Looks like it."

"You're such a—"

"Bonehead?"

He tried to smile, but his frown won the battle. "What in Thoden's name are you doing down here?" he asked, holding a cup of water to her lips. "Are you following me? And how? I'm guessing you worked out that I've bypassed the GI-VR transponder system and remotely affixed my location."

Chalk nodded confidently. Her eyes drifted towards INFIN-8. The buddy droid sat on the workbench, his shiny legs dangling.

URRRH! he said. *URRRH! URRRH!*

"Clever girl," Ripley said, rounding on her. "You put something inside him."

"My iPhone."

"What's an iPhone?"

"Doesn't matter."

Two figures appeared through spears of warm light.

"She okay?"

"Yeah," Ripley replied, not looking back. "She'll be fine. Got a little poached in the atmospheric pressure release chamber."

Chalk squinted into the gloom. "Who are your ... friends?"

Two women came into focus. Both smeared with grease and bandages.

"This is Esme and Spanners."

"Y'know I hate that name," Spanners said. "It's Briana Blaze."

She wore baggy orange overalls rolled to her waist, revealing a lean, muscled torso beneath a tight black vest. A chunky belt laden with tools and pockets hung from her hips. Her skin was pale, her hair lank, white-blonde and shot through with a streak of blue.

"Major Esme Silverside," the other woman said, her eyes shining like fire-lit emeralds. She wore a threadbare flight suit embroidered with squadron patches, her thick hair in a bun, except for a single coil that spiralled to her shoulder. "And you're either a lovesick fool or a catastrophic imbecile."

Chalk blushed instantly. "I'm … just—"

"Cool your thrusters," Esme said, then looked at Ripley. "You need to get her out of here."

"Where is *here* exactly?" Chalk said, finding some strength. "And who are you?"

"Well, you're in the engine rooms of the Galactic Institute," Ripley said.

"Between the floorboards," Spanners added. "With the dirt and the filth and the Gods-damn krittens."

"The restricted, extremely off-limit decks of Centurion H," Esme added. "As I said, you need to go."

"But why are *you* here?" Chalk asked Ripley.

Spanners took the question as her own. "We work 'ere. We're engineers."

"I wouldn't have guessed," Chalk replied sarcastically.

"Don't be smart," Esme waded in. "Every light, device, and door you use is activated by the power cells and engines and data systems down here. Every mouthful you eat and every breath you take is a result of the tireless, dangerous work we do."

Chalk tried to moisten her tongue. "How many of you are there?"

Esme and Spanners looked at one another and laughed.

"As flesh and blood goes … it's just us."

"We 'ave a bunch of droids and reconditioned eduhelpers, but the heat tends to burn 'em out faster than we can fix 'em."

"And *him*?" Chalk said, nodding at the Revan.

"He's … helping out."

"Really?" Chalk said. "Heard that one before."

Ripley angled his head.

"Isn't he ... aren't *you* ... a student?"

"He's gettin' extra credit for ... what's that class you're takin' again?"

"Empirical Mechanics," Ripley said helpfully.

"He's not taking that class," Chalk said. "He gatecrashed it. Apparently, to keep me company. He's supposed to be in Domestic and Interspecies Languages and Astro Anthropology!"

Esme rolled her shoulders and wandered over to the kitchen where she absently moved some dirty cups around. Spanners grunted and fidgeted with her tool belt.

"So, what's the truth, Ripley Flinch?" Chalk asked, decommissioning Operation Chalk-Stalk and filing it in the catastrophe drawer. "You're not helping Lasco. I checked. And you're definitely not getting extra credit by helping down here."

Ripley stood and looked at Major Silverside.

"Your call," Esme said. "If she bleats, we'll deny all knowledge you were ever here."

"To paraphrase our Tattorian friend," Chalk said, staring at the Revan. "What the bloody hell is happening?"

Leaving Cube with Esme and Spanners, they snaked through a labyrinth of corridors that hissed with torrents of steam. Ripley circled left, right, through a large chamber that rose and fell several storeys, and down yet more corridors. Chalk's legs were still like jelly, her mind less solid. But somehow his voice and touch made the pain slip away.

"Here. Wear this," he said, adhering a digital bio-mask to her skin. "Filters out the chemicals. It'll keep you alive for the time being."

A deafening roar shook the room like a passing starfighter.

Chalk gripped Ripley, ducking to avoid whatever had caused the sound. The Revan slapped the bottom of a large grey tube that swept in and out of the ceiling. "AGT," he yelled over the noise. "The engine rooms are built around it. Or the AGT was built through them. Hard to know."

Chalk touched the soft resin. The rush of passing students rippled against her fingertips. Ripley led her through an arched door and into an antechamber.

Here, amber lights flickered gently around a shape she recognised immediately.

Her breath caught in her throat.

"It's a—"

"Portal," he finished. "No Sagaflies on you."

"Did you … make it?"

Ripley laughed. "You flatter me. No, this is the engine room portal. According to Esme and Spanners, it's been broken for a couple of cycles. I just … fixed it up."

"I am made of questions."

Ripley placed his hands on her shoulders. "Professor de Rema said the Galactic Institute integrated portal system consists of six portals, but I found more. This one. Waxler's got a private one. And who knows how many others. After what happened on Zorik Major, I got a little … fascinated."

"Fascinated?"

"Well, yeah. Think of the possibilities," Ripley said, gazing at the gently humming tech and pulsating lights. "It's seductive." Chalk didn't see the appeal, but understood the pull of desire. "I made a clone of de Rema's passkey and the Galactic Institute access node when we were—"

"You did what?"

"You'd have done the same if you'd thought of it."

"I most certainly would not have."

"Come on. It's not that bad."

Chalk fidgeted with the itchy face mask. She wondered how Pristina lived like this all the time.

"That's why de Rema was talking to you at the welcome ball, wasn't it?"

Ripley smirked. "She'd noticed additional portal usage on her account. If Waxler found out that an unauthorised person had access to her card she'd be fired in a nanosecond. I told her I knew nothing about it, but she wouldn't let it go. I've ghosted the travel locations. A casual inspection will just indicate that she's been zipping lavishly around the Coin, nothing more."

Chalk stared at him, agog. "You're … *using* it?"

"Well, what did you think I was—?"

"What about the portal embargo? The unimaginably serious GAPSS portal embargo? We're not in London right now with Mum and Grandpa Milo because of it. Everyone has been stuck on the Coin for the entire mid-cycle break. And all this time you've been zipping about all over the galaxy!"

Ripley appeared to be searching for the right expression.

"Gods. I thought—I hoped—you were just fixing it!"

Ripley sighed. "I've sorted loads of stuff for them actually, but the portal was the one thing that got my blood pumping." Chalk stared at him incredulously. "Commander Lasco's lessons are fun and all, but I wanted a challenge, something that gave me the same feeling I got on Zorik Major."

"That was *fun* for you? This *is* fun for you?"

"No. I mean, yes. In a way. Sure, it was terrifying, and we could have died, but I solved the problem. I got us home. I did something de Rema couldn't."

"You also violated the Terrazuma Treaty," Chalk said, now pacing in sweaty circles. "Cloned the professor's passkey, stole access nodes, and broke God knows what additional Galactic Institute laws. Don't get me wrong, I'm grateful to be breathing, but I don't understand why you'd risk your place at the Galactic Institute chasing some technological high in this oven with the engineering sisters."

"They're not sisters," he said. "I think they're … Look, I know what I'm doing is risky, illegal even, but if no one finds out, what's the problem? I'm not hurting anyone. If anything, I'm helping to improve the Galactic Institute … for free! And I've totally covered my tracks. I'm basically invisible."

"But *I* found you," Chalk said, sticking out her chest. "And if I can do it, then people far smarter than me—like Asimov or Snider or Waxler—can find you too. They're all experienced war heroes and Casters. And I'm VOID."

They stared at one another for a moment.

"So, now what?"

"Now," he said, "you have several options."

"Tell me."

"Go back to the dorms and forget any of this happened."

"No chance."

"Run to de Rema and Waxler and spill your guts."

"Tempting. Option three?"

Ripley grinned. "Come with me."

"Where are you going?"

"Anywhere you like."

GAPSS
KNOWLEDGE
MAINFRAME

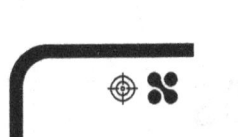 

SHIELD OF ZORIK, THE
[PHENOMENON]

The Shield of Zorik is the largest remaining fragment of Zorik Major, encompassing eighteen per cent of the planet's original crust and is on average 117 kilometres thick. The Shield of Zorik resides in a sun-synchronous orbit between Zorik Prime—the system's central star—and its neighbouring planet Zorik Minor, blocking all natural light to the planet for most of the cycle. Viewed from the surface of Zorik Minor, the Shield of Zorik is one of the nine phenomenological wonders of the SpiralVerse.

OUTERWORLDS

Chalk emerged on a stone dais. A dark landscape sliced the horizon. Elegant buildings with sloped roofs jutted from a shadowy mountainside, misted by the cool haze from a mighty waterfall.

Ripley appeared beside her.

INFIN-8 too.

"Where did he come from? And how did he—?" Chalk said, pointing at the plucky droid.

"Oh, I've written a new algorithm that allows both biological and manufactured materials to travel freely through the portal at any time," Ripley said breezily.

Chalk's eyes widened.

"Had a few errors with some test droids, but Spanners assures me she can put them back together."

BING! BING! chimed INFIN-8, clearly more at home here than in the stifling heat of the engine rooms.

"Does the Terrazuma Treaty mean anything to you?"

Ripley shrugged. "Broke it once already. I can't imagine a couple dozen more makes much difference."

"That is not the point," Chalk began. "A couple of dozen?"

"Have you read the Terrazuma Treaty?"

"No," she replied irritably. "Obviously not."

Ripley laughed. "Me either."

"Where are we anyway? Darkest timeline Rivendell?"

"This is Zorik Minor. And you don't need your face mask

anymore." He hopped off the dais and merged into a steady flow of Veroselli who drifted beneath swaying street lamps and elegant canopies.

"I thought you were going to show me, and I quote, 'The most wondrous sight in the SpiralVerse!' Or was I mistaken?"

"Patience. I have a few things to do first. The girls need some stuff. Kinda payment for the use of their portal … and their discretion. Won't take long, and look, this place is beautiful. Soak it up, Hale."

Chalk couldn't deny that. The Veroselli city resembled a vast elven kingdom populated by pastel-skinned creatures and their mechanical companions. Like Cressida, most of the Veroselli had C1000s—or droids that looked indecipherably similar—in a range of colours and finishes. Some sported upgrades she'd seen advertised in stores around the arcade, including the shoulder-mounted laser cannons and shimmering silver jetpack of a Zenith PowerDread TX Weapon System™.

"This is Clodvorg," Ripley said as they strolled. "Capital city of the Veroselli. Home of the royal family. Named after their greatest leader Clod Van Wyrm."

"Wasn't he the guy who destroyed Zorik Major?"

"The Garrangulars would have you believe that, but the Veroselli lay the blame at the door of Krull. No one knows for sure."

"Bet the Sevantes do."

Ripley grabbed Chalk's hand as they entered a wide plaza bordered by high-windowed boutiques and eateries. Rows of market traders filled the central courtyard, selling everything from baked goods to precious gems. "Wait here," Ripley said, disappearing into a second-hand tech shop with INFIN-8. He returned minutes later. "Okay, let's go."

"What? That's it?"

"In Clodvorg? Sure."

"Oh," Chalk said. "Why is the market open in the middle of the night?"

"Ah, well, it's not actually night, is it?"

"Isn't it?"

"That's what I want to show you."

Puzzled, Chalk followed the Revan along wide promenades and into narrow, twisty streets. Species from every denomination mingled on corners and conversed in cafes and restaurants. The Veroselli towered above them all, walking with an air of supremacy. It only occurred to her after a while that there were no Garrangulars. Not one.

They took a long flight of stairs cut into the side of an enormous inverted bone-white pyramid. Chalk's vertigo bloomed as they emerged on a lookout point high above the sprawling city.

"There you go," Ripley said, staring up.

Chalk turned her gaze skyward. A thousand emotions overwhelmed her. Her legs became Karmethian jellob as her place in the universe shrank, becoming more inconsequential with each passing second.

Floating beyond the clouds, filling the entire sky, loomed a colossal haunch of rock haloed with a billion stars. Solar winds wisped by, bouncing off Zorik Minor's atmosphere. Precious gems and ancient crystals glittered and shone as the huge celestial object twisted slowly, impossibly, in the heavens.

"Behold! The Shield of Zorik."

"It's beautiful," Chalk said, gawping at the Shield of Zorik and thousands of pieces of debris that orbited like a colossal windmill. "Yet, brutal and violent."

She watched as its jagged edges shone with the blood-red radiance of the system's central sun, Zorik Prime. "I can't look away," she said. "It's … utterly captivating."

"There are eight other phenomenological wonders of the SpiralVerse."

"Are they as beautiful as this?"

"Not been yet," he replied. "We could … go together?"

"Now?"

"Afraid not. Got more collections to make."

"Seriously?"

Ripley nodded and pulled up a layer screen. "Let me see, I need three vials of dark mercury from Eos Yol and half a dozen girders of rubinovium from Gaia 23. The girls want polonium crystals too. A quick hop over to Zorik Pol and we're done."

"Mercury? Polonium? Aren't they incredibly dangerous?"

"Power cells don't run on hope and promises, Hale."

Ripley transported them to Eos Yol where Chalk wore the face mask again. They trekked through a ramshackle village hidden beneath a thick smog and surrounded by vast arid deserts. Mercury, in all its forms, seemed to be the stock and trade for the entire settlement. Ripley bartered with several merchants before exchanging some reconditioned tech for a clear orb filled with curling white smoke above liquid dark mercury. He slipped the orb inside INFIN-8 and headed back to the portal.

Gaia 23 was a pleasant relief. Chalk could breathe freely while standing in luscious green valleys topped with jaw-dropping snow-capped mountains. Rubinovium, which Ripley obtained from a rosy-cheeked seller in a twee cobbled marketplace, turned out to be a dark red metal. "This place may look picturesque," he said, sliding half a dozen nine-foot girders inside INFIN-8 and marching back to the portal, "but this stuff is some kind of composite metallic element ... fused with blood."

"Bloodmetal?" Chalk wailed. "Whose blood?"

"I didn't ask. And I'm not going to," he replied. "But, essentially, it's alive!"

Inside a large, purple tent, Ripley activated the temporal doorway and they stepped through.

A deathly cold instantly snapped to Chalk's bones. Through vast, frost-edged windows, the surface of Zorik Pol disappeared in an endless sheet of ice. Colossal spears studded the landscape like the frozen blades of ice giants.

Chalk approached the window, awed by the sight while Ripley talked to two Sevantes. Unlike the ravaged, destitute creatures that had attacked at Fort Van Murk, these wore plain robes, entwined by golden belts and floral decorations, their hair fixed in long, neat plaits.

"Chaperones are non-negotiable," he explained as they walked. "They have an extremely superstitious, untrusting culture."

"I'm not surprised."

The Sevante chaperones took them through snow-lined hallways. Great arched windows displayed frozen vistas of the planet in all directions. Beneath the planet surface, accessed via a broad descent, they emerged on yet another thriving marketplace. Here, troupes performed upbeat, lively music. The smell of baking, caramelised sugar, and roasted meat spiralled through the air. Chalk turned, wide-eyed, amazed that an atmosphere like this could exist on such an inhospitable, frozen waste.

"What are you getting again?" she asked, hoping he'd say pain au chocolat or carrot cake or maple syrup pancakes.

"Polonium crystals," Ripley whispered, his hand masking his mouth.

"What's with the secrecy?"

Ripley's eyes thinned. "Tell you later."

They approached a large tent selling hand-carved wooden furniture and trinkets. "Wait here," he said, leaving Chalk with the chaperones and ducking inside. After a swift discussion with the dealer, Ripley vanished through a curtain at the rear of the store.

Chalk's nose and toes turned numb. A puddle of anxiety began to ripple in her stomach. "Is everything okay?" she asked the chaperones.

"Negotiations take time."

"The best deal is hard won."

As Chalk tried to decipher exactly what that meant, Ripley and INFIN-8 emerged. The Revan looked shaken and distressed, his fingers flexing and coiling rhythmically.

"Um … You okay?"

"Yeah," he said. "Let's go."

"Got the—?"

"Just move."

Back at the portal, the chaperones nodded evenly at Ripley and Chalk before departing.

"Come on then," she said, as they faced the threshold. "Spill it."

"When we're back," he replied, activating the temporal doorway and ducking through. On the other side, the infernal heat clung to Chalk's skin. She unzipped her jacket, threw her hair back, and slipped on the bio-mask.

"What gives?" her voice crackled.

"The seas on Zorik Pol are ninety-three per cent polonium— hence the name—and are kept stable by the incredibly low temperatures."

Chalk stared at INFIN-8.

"Don't worry," he said, heading for the workshop. "The crystals are safe inside INFIN-8. For now."

"And the ill-favoured look?"

"Polonium is high in … radiation."

"Radiation! Are you serious?"

"Do you pay any attention in class?"

"Ouch."

"Small exposures are fine," he told her confidently, retrieving the pendant beneath his shirt. Elegantly cast in silver, it tapered like an incisor. A strange swirl of green and purple vapour danced around it. "Plus, I have this."

"What *is* that?"

"Protective amulet."

"Very Dungeons & Dragons."

Back in the workshop, Chalk took a seat next to Cube on the rubber sofa. Ripley conversed with Esme and Spanners at the workbench and unloaded the items. Spanners lifted the rubinovium, turned it in her gloves and slammed it against the desk. The bloodmetal rang like a death bell, high and long. To Chalk's amazement, she tore the girder in two as though it were clay.

"Fantastic stuff this," she said. "Living metal. Who knew?"

Esme took the other items and stored them in pressure vaults and lock boxes. "You took longer than I thought," Esme said, unscrewing the lid of her water canteen and taking a long draught.

"Bit of sightseeing," Ripley said. "Shield of Zorik."

"Bet that never gets old."

Chalk looked up. "I can still see it now. Breathtaking."

Spanners elbowed Esme. "Come on," she said. "We need to go see it. Specially as the Veroselli and Garrangulars look set to blow the livin' hell out of one another again. Who knows what'll be left this time."

Esme bristled. "When we get vacation time and raise the quasoids for a transport to Zorik Minor, I'm totally there."

"You know that'll never happen," Spanners said. "Vacation time? Quasoid windfall? Are you kiddin' me?"

Chalk frowned. "Why not just—"

Esme looked embarrassed. "I don't trust it."

"The … portal?"

"Utter molecular destruction and reconstruction," Esme said, shuddering. "More dangerous and unpredictable than dark matter or zorikanthium. I like science that I can see and touch and smash into working order with my bio-wrench."

"Then I guess we're stuck 'ere," Spanners said, feigning heartbreak.

"You can go," Esme said, but her voice wasn't in it. "Let the Revan take you."

Spanners squeezed Esme's hand. "I'd never go without you. It wouldn't be the same."

Ripley pushed INFIN-8's lid shut and hoisted him off the workbench. "Ladies," he said, bowing. "Pleasure as always."

Esme and Spanners bid them farewell. Ripley took the lead

as they left the air-conditioned workshop and weaved through the boiling outer rooms and corridors towards the Crypt of the Unknown Engineer.

Chalk's shoes scuffed on the hot floor. Sweat beaded on her lip. Exhaustion hit her like a Garrangulan death punch. Was it the heat? Was it the hour? Probably both.

Approaching the bulkhead at the bottom of the stairs, metallic footsteps rang in one of the side tunnels. Chalk and Ripley stopped dead.

"Someone's here," she said. "Between the floorboards."

"Can't be," Ripley replied.

"Someone that's not you or me, Esme or Spanners."

A long shadow fell over them.

Eyes burned red through the gloom.

Was this real? Was she having an exhaustion-induced T-1000 hallucination?

By the look on Ripley's face, reality had come calling.

They backed away from the bulkhead door as Cressida's C1000 emerged from the shadows.

GAPSS
KNOWLEDGE
MAINFRAME

POLONIUM
[CHEMICAL]

A highly flammable, corrosive chemical found beneath the
frozen oceans of Zorik Pol. Due to its unstable construction,
GAPSS directive SF-69 forbids the mining and removal of
polonium from its indigenous homeworld, and classifies the
act as a threat to the SpiralVerse.

Crystalline polonium: Order 12 - Risk to biological life

Liquid polonium: Order 15 - Risk to biological life

Polonium vapour: Order 23 - Lethal to all biological life

TRIPLE THREAT

"What in Thoden's name is that thing doing here?" Ripley asked.

"Is it ... scanning us?"

"Hello?" he said, waving a hand in front of the C1000's face. A mechanical arm shot out and grabbed his wrist. "Hey! Get off!"

"Princess Cressida Van Wyrm," the C1000 said. "Do you have a location?"

"No, of course not," Ripley said, yanking his wrist. "How did you get down here?"

"I followed the Earthling's heat signature," the C1000 said, releasing Ripley, "and the aroma profile of coagulated milk protein."

"He's saying you stink of cheese."

"I know what he's saying and I don't care for it one bit!"

"I have powerful sensors."

"Yet you still cannot find your owner."

"Princess Cressida Van Wyrm is not upon the Coin or the Flipside. I have failed to locate her in the engine rooms. I shall begin my search again."

"Not here you won't," Ripley said, nodding towards the door. "We can't have rogue eduhelpers wandering around between the floorboards."

"I will go where the data leads me," the C1000 said.

"Then I will have you decommissioned."

The C1000 grunted, then marched through the bulkhead

and up the stairs. Chalk and Ripley traipsed along in its wake.

The Flipside came as a welcome relief.

Chalk removed the mask and gulped down lungfuls of cool reconditioned air.

Ripley closed the door after INFIN-8 and followed the C1000 through the maze. To Chalk's surprise, Cressida's eduhelper led them effortlessly through the walls of knotted vegetation and on towards the AGE.

Plunging the depths of the gyrosphere, Chalk clung to Cube's straps and waited for the energy-sapping, stomach-churning encounter to be over. She hauled herself onto the treadplate of the observation hall as the C1000 sped away.

"Wonder where it's going now?"

"Who cares." Ripley shrugged. "We're going for breakfast!"

In the banqueting rotunda, Chalk fought to stay awake despite the huge stack of pancakes before her. Ripley ate his body weight in pizza. Joy sparked in Chalk's chest, knowing that she'd got him thoroughly hooked.

She collapsed onto her bed an hour later, stomach full, head lighter than helium. Her dreams came in snippets of sound and vision, transitioning one to the next, faster and faster, until they spread like oil on water.

She woke to the familiar sound of Krieg, Kroket, and Kiln battering one of the dorm room doors.

Chalk watched for a moment.

"The Veroselli have barricaded themselves inside," Spirit said, slouching against her doorjamb. "You going to run in and save them again?"

Ripley emerged.

The smell of yuccagourds followed.

"More of this?" the Sagaroach grumbled.

"Aren't the atmospheric sensors supposed to negate this sort of thing?"

"There's something funny going on with the system," Ripley said. "Glitchy, apparently."

Chalk looked at him knowingly. "So, how is the system *supposed* to work?"

"Well," he said, scowling, "I'm no expert—"

"Just a *dabbler*," Chalk said, wrinkling her nose.

"—but the attitude easing atmospheric system generates an algorithm computed by equating the number of students, the diversity of species and genders, chronotype, weight, casting requirements et cetera in any given location, and feeds a cocktail of chemicals into the environment to stimulate or discourage certain emotional states."

"Stimulate or discourage?"

"It's supposed to boost concentration receptors and quell excessive rage. But, as I said, it's glitchy."

"What we need is the light from Zorik Prime," Milton decided.

"Yeah," Ripley nodded. "Got any of that on you?"

Krieg and Kroket attacked the door, making it shake horribly.

"Typical," the Sagaroach went on. "If it's not the portals sending us to dangerous places, the busted AEAS is bringing danger to our doors. Literally. If I didn't know better, I'd say someone has smuggled zorikanthium onto the Galactic Institute."

Ripley and Chalk frowned at the Sagaroach.

Enforcers spilled out of the AGT and roared up the stairs. "Cease," said the first to arrive. "Immediately."

Krieg and the others paid no notice, hammering and smashing Clementine's door as though possessed. The rest of First Cycle Aktari gathered to watch.

"This is insane," Chalk said. "Krieg looks like he's going to murder someone."

"Damage to Galactic Institute property can lead to fines and prosecution," a second Enforcer said.

"You can't damage what's already broken," mocked Sadler Arklan. The other Vyshans laughed drily.

Spirit looked like she was about to faint.

Lachrymosa raised a sardonic eyebrow.

"Injury or death caused to another student will lead to expulsion and criminal charges," the Enforcers urged.

This seemed to spur Krieg on. He slammed his head against the door and screamed.

INAPPROPRIATE LANGUAGE DETECTED . . .

The Enforcers changed stance. Wheels back, tilted, suppression darts trained on their targets.

"Last chance for reason."

Spirit and Milton let out woeful squeals as all three Garrangulars dropped to the floor with a dull *thud!* The Vyshan Order moved in, peering between the broad shoulders of the Enforcers for a closer look.

"Are they ... dead?"

"Tranqed. Should be fine."

"Jeepers," Chalk said, steadying herself against the wall. "That was intense."

"Imagine how it was for Clementine and Claridge," Milton said as the door buckled, was wrenched aside, and the two nervous Veroselli peered out.

Sadler and the other Vyshans quickly surrounded the Veroselli, congratulating them on their survival and condemning the Garrangulars.

Spirit coiled her fingers around Ripley's arm and pressed her head on his shoulder. "What is going on?" she implored dramatically, pulling him tight. "I was terrified for my life. I actually thought the Garrangulars were going to kill us all."

"Good job the Enforcers response system is extraordinarily reliable," Ripley said.

"And you," Spirit went on. "I'm calmer when you're close."

He managed to detach the Oneric when her attention shifted to the unconscious Garrangulars being carted downstairs.

"What'll happen to them?" Spirit asked. A hand fluttered over her mouth.

"Melt them down for fuel," Ripley joked. But seeing Spirit's expression, added, "Just kidding. Probably get banned from the arcade for a phase or two."

The Oneric withered away, plaguing Dana, Marcy-Kate and Saffron for their affections and platitudes.

Chalk returned to her room and sat on the bed.

Ripley followed, his silhouette framed in the doorway.

"You need to talk?" he said. "About … everything?"

"No," she said. "I don't think so. I mean, yes of course. But—"

Ripley moved into the room. "I'm sorry."

"Don't lie to me again. You don't need to."

"I was trying to protect you."

"I'm going to worry about you, okay. Down … *there*. Between the floorboards. In the dark and heat with Esme and Spanners. You could get kicked out of here … or worse."

"I'll be careful."

"I'm being selfish," she told him. Ripley smiled. "I want you here, at the Galactic Institute, for the next however many cycles I can hack the pace."

"Me too."

"Just go and do something about the atmospheric system thingie. We don't want any more near-death experiences on the dormitory landing."

He nodded.

"And, I don't want to be *that* girl, but …" Ripley tipped his head. "Tell Spirit to keep her hands to herself."

The portal embargo remained in place and the mid-cycle break concluded without any major disasters. The Garrangulars returned from a dressing-down by General Waxler and were forced to make a verbal apology to Clementine and Claridge. None of them did it with much sincerity.

Chalk floated through phase eleven, an aura of confidence

beginning to flower. She chatted with the Revan girls Dana Dune, Marcy-Kate, and Saffron who were incredibly friendly, but rarely dwelt on anything other than their studies, or career prospects, or a fourth cycle Oneric called Dream. By all accounts, he was not only devastatingly handsome and hailed from a wealthy family, but Marcy-Kate heard a rumour that Dream had an aptitude for two of the three Casting disciplines. The others looked like they might faint.

With phase twelve looming, Chalk buried herself in work. Her iPhone Firebird rested beside her with rotating pictures of Kit, Bloue, and Zara, while cranking out her *Space Vibes* playlist. She'd stopped wondering what Ripley was up to at night. She knew where he was—*roughly*—but it didn't quell her anxiety. He popped in during the small hours to reassure her that he wasn't in trouble or getting expelled or torn to pieces by vicious alien civilisations. His lips found hers, kissing more passionately each time, while her fingers brushed against his soft skin.

But every time he returned, he looked more ill, gaunt, less like the boy she'd met on the playing fields of Revus X. She couldn't help but worry about the long-term effects of his exposure to polonium. Did that silver pendant around his neck truly offer any protection? And how did Esme and Spanners sleep, knowing they were putting him in harm's way?

As the dark rotation embalmed the Coin, Chalk suffered a turbulent night of wretched dreams in which Ripley succumbed to radiation poisoning. She watched as his body degraded into a pus-oozing slab of pustules and corruption. In the wake of his death, Aida and Milton shunned her friendship, Professor Snider gave her detention for the rest of her natural life, her mother sent a message informing Chalk she was no longer welcome back on Earth, and Grandpa Milo died from a broken heart.

Chalk sat up with a start, sticky, shaky, anxiety sloshing in her belly.

Her GI-VR flashed with an incoming message.

Cube spun to face her, its gelatinous body formed into an

inverted, spinning pyramid. "Just exercising," it said playfully, quickly shifting into a diamond, a sphere, a cube, and then retreating inside its orb. "You are perspiring heavily. Your hypothalamus is firing. Cortisol and adrenaline levels are above normal."

Chalk kicked the bedclothes away. "A nightmare," she told it. "Multiple."

UPDATING . . .

Still fully clothed from working late on Professor Cricklock's paleo-ingestinal magnetism essay, Chalk checked the message.

GENERAL WAXLER: First classes have been cancelled this morning. All students report to the observation hall.

As before, the huge room bulged with hundreds of chairs, the faculty mounted on a raised platform in front of the AGE.

The general waved her hands, quieting the students. "I've brought us together as turmoil and trouble have spread through the halls of the Galactic Institute once again. In my tenure as headmistress I have never overseen such a breakdown in order and discipline."

Chalk held Aida's pincer to stop it from shaking. The Tattorian's skin felt warm and soft and turned from mauve to plum as Chalk's fingers tightened. Her eyes shot to Ripley. Had they found out about him? Had his portal adventures been discovered? Were Enforcers on their way to detain and expel the Revan?

"As you know, Professor Asimov has been conducting a series of interviews with students from all six cycles. He has established a timeline of events and a picture of what happened to Princess Cressida Van Wyrm in her final hours at the Galactic Institute. Last night we were close to pinpointing a suspect—"

"But—?" Chalk added to herself.

"—a series of new, far more terrible events have transpired."

Those around her muttered.

"A second student has gone missing."

Heads turned. Gasps rose. Accusations flew past Chalk.

"It is with regret that I inform you that the second student to go missing from the Galactic Institute is Master Krieg of Zorik Minor."

A Veroselli gone … and now a Garrangular!

"Please," General Waxler said, more forcefully than ever. "There is more." Most settled instantly but the Veroselli and Garrangulars continued a barrage of heated, verbal squabbles. "During the night, the Veroselli took credit for the disappearance of Master Krieg." A venomous hiss rose from Clementine and Claridge and the rest of the Veroselli cohort. "Moments later, the Garrangulars answered in kind, owning the fate of Cressida Van Wyrm as their handiwork."

Barks tore through the crowd.

Students dived for cover as chairs took flight.

Enforcers circled the students. Red eyes glowed menacingly. Suppression darts loaded. General Waxler leaped from the platform, her cape billowing in magnificent waves. She swarmed into the fight, her arms raised. Chairs froze in mid-air. Waxler's hands twisted and sent them arcing safely towards the outer rim. Several older, more experienced Veroselli and Garrangulars backed away, but Kroket and Kiln, Clementine and Claridge continued to hurl threats and abuse, ignoring the presence of the headmistress.

As venomous words soiled the air, General Waxler seemed overcome by an aura of calm. Her cape rippled gently, settling over her shoulders and down her back.

Her palms turned up.

Her eyes diluted to solid white.

Voices of the Veroselli and the Garrangulars slowed, becoming low and drawn. Their arms drooped to their sides. Bodies ground to a halt as their torsos tipped like toys with dying batteries.

Chalk's eyes were wide as saucers.

The entire room stood frozen in self-induced wonder.

"Classes continue as normal," the headmistress instructed. She blinked.

Her eyes returned to normal.

"Although, I fear life at the Galactic Institute is going to change. And soon."

Chalk sat in a stupor for most of the curtailed Metaphysical Mathematics class. Biodiverse Medical Science barely registered in her memory. Commander Lasco made her run dozens of laps in Conflict Engagement before assigning her a fractal dehumidifier to strip and reassemble in Empirical Mechanics. When she was done, the device kicked out lethal ice fragments instead of cool air.

"Too much power routed via the thermostat, Miss Hale. It's closer to a weapon than a dehumidifier," the commander said, switching the device off. "But we're done for today."

"I'm done until summer break," Chalk moaned.

She trooped along with Ripley and the others to the embarkation pod, fussing her eczema. Spilling out into the rec room, the rest of the first cycle were congregated around the monitor wall. Each screen displayed one of the many intergalactic news channels. Reporters and anchors were in full flow, wearing serious faces and repeating long desperate headlines in a mounting cacophony.

Chalk's GI-VR struggled to authenticate, decode, and translate each one before the next raft of news bulletins arrived. Superimposed behind the reporters were darkened cityscapes exploding with plumes of orange fire and billowing smoke.

"What is happening?" asked Aida, returning from Casting.

They moved closer to the monitors. Ripley manually tuned his GI-VR to one of the news stations and sent the link to Chalk.

Punching her GI-VR, she stood in awe as the report bled into her ears.

"Zorik Minor is in disarray!" a hexapod journalist yelled, as munitions detonated around her. "From what we can tell, the truce between the Veroselli and the Garrangulars has eroded, and military engagements are escalating. I'm currently standing"—a missile flew into shot behind the reporter, reducing a building to rubble and crushing several vehicles on its way to the ground— "in the Garrangulan capital of G'hrak where, as you can see, warheads are raining from the sky." The picture shook violently. The reporter struggled to stand. "No additional information has been forthcoming from either side. Speculation grows around a breakdown of communication"—*KaBoom!*—"and the reigniting of the Zorik conflicts!" The hexapod grasped the device strapped to her ears, listening intently. "As I say that, sources inside GAPSS have issued me with—" But before she could finish her sentence the feed became distorted, crackled, and died.

The channel cut to the news anchor who tried his best to appear calm and authoritative. He too seemed to be receiving information.

Chalk's gaze shifted to the adjacent monitor.

The words *Danger Level:* CAUTION vanished, replaced by *Danger Level:* EXTREME.

Spreading his hands, the anchor sat up straight.

"Breaking News just in."

He looked pale and apprehensive, like he was about to throw up.

"Zorik Minor ... is at war!"

GAPSS
KNOWLEDGE
MAINFRAME

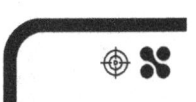 

DARK TRINITY, THE
[MALICIOUS ENTITIES]

Antagonist of the Spiral Wars. The Dark Trinity possessed the minds of more than half the SpiralVerse, turning families and friends against one another in a horrific twelve cycle conflict. The three entities—known only as Graven, Oddrax, and Miasma—appeared suddenly. Their motives, other than the unadulterated destruction of the SpiralVerse, are unknown. Banished through worldgates to unmonitored chaos dimensions, the current status of the Dark Trinity remains a mystery.

LOCKDOWN

Emergency lights flooded the rec room. Monitor feeds shrank to black. A piercing alarm shook Chalk's eardrums. She landed on her backside as Necrotta and Kroket elbowed her aside, heading for the stairs.

"What is happening?"

"Lockdown!" Marcy-Kate said, hauling Chalk to her feet.

"What's that?"

"No one in," Saffron told her, following the others upstairs, "and no one out."

"Get to your room," Dana Dune instructed. "Now!"

Enforcers poured through the AGT. Blue lights sank to amber, then blood-red.

Chalk took the stairs three at a time, skimmed across the landing and into her room. The door hissed shut. She removed her stinking T-shirt and kicked her Converse into the corner. Her eczema stung like hell. She badly needed a shower, some epidermal cream and an antihistamine, but she wasn't getting them anytime soon.

What the heck-fire is going on? What did Marcy-Kate call it? A lockdown?

Chalk stabbed the door activation pad. It didn't respond.

She tried again.

Same outcome.

"What fresh hell is this?" she said, trying the door a couple more times.

"The Galactic Institute is in lockdown," Cube said, taking the form of Harriet Starlight.

"Is that supposed to fill me with a sense of calm?" she said, looking at the translucent orange reconstruction of the space wizard. Cube had based its depiction more on Ophelia Olsen's indulgent portrayal in the expansive Netflix original holographic series than the nervous, whimsical, wide-eyed characterisation in D K Gramplin's books.

"Is it working?"

"Not really."

UPDATING . . .

Cube became Sirius Black, then Gaius Baltar, and finally Chewbacca.

"You've been researching. Nice try."

"I am quite the fan of the Harry Potter stories," Cube told her. "Although I am not overly keen on Sirius myself, but I understand why you like him."

"I need a shower and meds," Chalk said, shaking her arms irritably. "I smell like death and itch like a flea colony."

"The bathrooms—like all public spaces on the Coin—are currently restricted."

"What do you mean *restricted?* What if I need to … *go?*"

"You cannot *go* anywhere?"

"Not go go. I mean *go go!*"

"Are you malfunctioning?"

"You're malfunctioning!"

Chalk dumped her towel on the floor and threw on some deodorant. Scratching at the eczema now rising around her wrists and in the fold of her elbow, she bounced across the bed and stared out the window.

For phase after phase there had been nothing but endless space. Chalk missed the ancient twists and spirals of the Waterfall Nebula that had hung beyond her window like a priceless painting.

Today, however, there was something new.

She stared disbelievingly, her hands and nose pressed to the bio-glass.

A dazzling ball of light shone above a huge broken sphere of vast rocky continents separated by a black sea of stars.

"The Shield of Zorik."

Cube, now rising beside her in the form of Willow Rosenberg, agreed.

"So, that's Zorik Prime," she said, nodding towards the sun. "And Zorik Minor is at the centre of all that debris." Chalk stared at the massive sheets of planetary crust and mantle. It looked like the Death Star paused mid-detonation. "I can't see it."

"It is there," Cube assured her. "Hidden. In shadow."

"I know," she said. "But how did it get *in* there?"

"Zorik Minor was the largest orbiting moon of Zorik Major but, unlike your own moon of grey crumbling rock, Zorik Minor is a planet with an atmosphere and ecosystem of its own. The force of Zorik Major's destruction disrupted Zorik Minor's orbit, sending it blasting through space. But, as it stabilised and found a new trajectory around the sun, the dead pieces of Zorik Major were pulled towards its gravitational field, forming what you see before you. An almost improbable anomaly found nowhere else in the galaxy. One planet inside the destroyed shell of another. It is quite something."

"Why are we here?"

"That information is not available."

"What's happening down there?"

"War. Destruction. Death."

"Over Cressida and Krieg?"

"It would appear so."

"But why are we in lockdown? It's not like we can go anywhere. There's no way off the Galactic Institute, unless you have one of those passkey thingies like Ripley."

"A ship is approaching."

"A ship. Who?"

"Galactic Enforcers. GAPSS interrogation committee.

Representatives from Veroselli and Garrangulan families. Some droids. Would you like the ship's complete passenger manifest and cargo?"

"No, that's fine."

Cube morphed into a tall, imposing figure, draped from head to toe in flowing cloaks, its face hidden behind a strange mask.

Chalk's eyes bulged. "Who is this?"

"GAPSS interrogation committee. Informal apparel."

Chalk's attention snapped to the window as light from Zorik Prime glinted off the sleek mirror-glazed hull, narrow wings, and propulsion arrays of a GAPSS personnel carrier. Accompanied by a squadron of Black Ghost starfighters, the personnel carrier disappeared from Chalk's sight, heading for the flight deck.

"We need to go and see that thing!"

"You are forgetting the Galactic Institute is in lockdown."

"Scud!" she bleated.

Chalk slumped onto the lip of the bed and frowned at the remains of Zorik Major. A Black Ghost flashed by. Somewhere down there, in the thick shadows, war raged. And Chalk still couldn't shake the thought—no matter how narcissistic Asimov thought it might be—that she was partly to blame.

After writing in her notebook and reading a dozen chapters from *Harriet Starlight and the Runaway Universe*, Chalk dozed off. She woke to heavy footfalls on the landing. Before she had time to wipe the crust from her eyes, the door opened and three people stooped beneath the curved frame.

Inside its black orb, Cube raised the light levels.

Chalk found herself staring at the imposing figures of the GAPSS interrogation committee. As Cube had demonstrated, they wore long dark robes, their faces concealed behind sculpted silver masks, cast with dour-looking expressions.

"Miss Harper Hale," said the first, his voice ministerial and old.

Before she could answer, General Waxler elbowed her way into the room. "What is the meaning of this, Constantine?"

The figure turned to the headmistress. "I am here under the jurisdiction of the GAPSS interrogation committee," he told her sharply. "I have no need for the interference of a government-funded educator."

"Is that so?" Waxler spat. "Miss Hale is in the first cycle."

"Meaning?"

"Galactic Institute representation is required should you wish to question her on *any* matter."

"Representation?" The man twitched. "You?"

"What happened to Professor Asimov?" Chalk asked. "I thought he was leading the investigation."

Constantine laughed. He sat in Chalk's chair. The other interrogators took positions either side of the door. One facing in, the other out.

"My name is Counsellor Constantine Van Wyrm," he said, his silver mask glinting with sunlight from Zorik Prime.

"Oh," she said. "Are you related to Cressida?"

"That is no concern of yours," he told her bluntly. "I am Lead Interrogator and High Judge at GAPSS, and have been for forty-seven cycles. My word is law. My findings are final. Professor Asimov has done a … *satisfactory* preliminary enquiry. But it's time this matter be taken into more *skilful* hands."

Chalk's senses hiked to red alert. Her mind raced. Her skin itched. The smell of dirty laundry and grubby armpits rose to meet her. She shot a look at General Waxler. The headmistress returned a reassuring, yet grim smile.

"Sounds like you have an important job."

"The *most* important," the counsellor told her.

"My grandpa always said that being a teacher was the most important job."

"Your forebear is a fool."

Chalk's fists twisted into the sheets.

"Personal insults will not be tolerated," Waxler told Constantine.

"My notes inform me you have a Zenith Systems INCUBE-8," the interrogator went on, ignoring Waxler's interjection and eyeing the eduhelper. "How did you come to obtain such a device? You came twenty-eighth in the Data Drive Relay. A poor effort by even the most average of candidates."

"No one else wanted it."

"An INCUBE-8?" Van Wyrm roared. "Lies. Anyone with half a mind would have chosen that above all others. It's more valuable than a dozen C1000s." He angled his head. "Did you Cast something? A mind cloak perhaps? A cerebral disruption?"

"Cast? Me? No," Chalk said quickly. "I'm … VOID. With capital letters. I took a risk on a mystery ball and found Cube inside. Got lucky, I guess."

"Cube?" the high judge scoffed. "You *named* your eduhelper?"

"Is any of this relevant?" said General Waxler, becoming impatient. "Sounds to me like you are harassing Miss Hale. Is there a question any time in our future?"

Slowly, Constantine removed the silver mask. Beneath, his face was classic Veroselli. Slender and sculpted. Dark eyes. Long pointed ears. But unlike Cressida's mauve skin, the counsellor's was dark red. A rich, aged claret.

Was this Cillian's father—the Veroselli from the welcome committee—and Cressida's grandfather? Were the Van Wyrms members of the Veroselli royal family *and* heads of all the government positions too? Chalk wondered what life would be like on Earth if King William and Queen Catherine were left to run the country.

"What *is* this about?"

"Like you do not know."

Chalk drew a blank.

Intertwining his long dark red fingers, Constantine leant forward. His shadow swallowed her whole. "As you know, Zorik

Minor is at war. I fear no truce this time. No accord to fuse our two races in symbiotic unity." He pointed towards the window. "Down there, beyond the broken shell of our mother world, chaos and destruction reign, brought about by events here, at the Galactic Institute." His dark eyes shifted between Chalk and General Waxler. "Two students have gone missing. Abducted? Killed? It matters not. War is here and many more will suffer because of what has been allowed to unfold."

"Are you accusing Miss Hale of something?"

"Someone inside the Galactic Institute is to blame."

"For Cressida and Krieg?" Chalk asked.

"Of course," he bit. "And the resulting war on Zorik Minor!"

I was right, Chalk thought. *This is all my fault.*

"But the Veroselli and the Garrangulars took responsibility for—"

"Of course they did," he snapped, a look of exasperation on his face. "Do you think either would allow themselves to appear weak in front of the other? What would happen to the pride of every Veroselli on Zorik Minor if one of their number had been abducted or killed by anything less than a Garrangular? Spirits would crumble and the future of our world would fall into ruin."

"I don't understand," Chalk said. "I thought the Veroselli and the Garrangulars hated one another."

"I do not have time for this," Constantine said. "Miss Hale. You are new here. You are from a world that was hastily chosen for inclusion in GAPSS. Your species has a bleak history of confrontation, persecution, and prejudice. You, like the Revans and the Xenothropods, still worship Gods and Divinities. A pathetic crutch for understanding and reason."

"I'm an atheist," Chalk said, unsure of the relevance.

The counsellor looked at her paperbacks and snorted derisively. "Yet you waste your mind on fiction! A whimsical, worthless pursuit."

"Constantine!" General Waxler broke in. "I already told you that personal attacks will not be tolerated. This is your last warning. One more and I will have you removed."

"My apologies, Miss Hale," he said, his eyes burning with disdain. "You, like every odd, strange, low creature on the Coin, will be under the closest scrutiny by me and my advisors. One or more of you have done this dire thing. One or more of you will be discovered and convicted. When all is said and done, I shall be the one to execute the final order."

"You're scaring her," Waxler told him. "I warned you."

"Master Flinch."

Chalk's skin turned to ice. Had Constantine conjured the winds of Zorik Pol?

"W-what about him?"

Constantine stared, saying nothing.

Emotions bloomed in Chalk's chest. She thought of the Revan breaking the Terrazuma Treaty on Zorik Major, his override of the location transponder, his secret missions in the engine rooms, and his adventures through temporal doorways to a multitude of worlds across the SpiralVerse.

"Tell me about your friend," Constantine purred. "Tell me what you *know* of him."

Disorientation clouded Chalk's mind. She felt numb, raw, like her nervous system had been turned down, her willingness to fight and survive reduced to its lowest level. Her eyes became heavy. Her vision wavered under the deep glare from the high judge.

Yet, something stirred. A resistance. A defiance. It rose swiftly and commanded her mind, pushing the strange sensation away.

"No," Chalk said.

"Yes," he hissed.

Chalk folded her arms. "I said no."

"Miss Hale," Constantine whispered. "I will not be denied."

General Waxler's gaze burrowed into Chalk.

"Tell me about the untrustworthy, deceitful Revan."

"Ask him yourself."

"Tell me the secrets you've shared."

"I'd never betray my friends."

Constantine rose, head bent towards her.

"What about the cunning, loathsome Tattorian? Is she involved too?"

"Loathsome? Aida? Involved in what?"

"And the Sagaroach?" Constantine pressed, shaking with frustration. "Lord Milton Barclay XVII? A substantial underachiever. Quite the embarrassment to his forebears."

"Milton's lovely. Leave him alone!"

"Much like you, the Sagaroach is nothing but a snivelling coward. A worthless academic. A castless VOID!"

"That's not fair, Milton's not here to defend himself."

"Quite true," General Waxler added, standing. "It's time you left, Constantine."

Counsellor Van Wyrm grunted. His hands dropped to his sides. Disbelief raged on his dark red face. "I'd be more concerned about your own circumstances, Earthling!" he hissed, venomously. "And don't worry, I will be dealing with your rebellious *friends* soon enough!"

GAPSS
KNOWLEDGE
MAINFRAME

STASISSTATION10
[TECHNOLOGY]

Criminal activity is rife throughout the SpiralVerse. To house criminals, GAPSS designated the Revus planets as colonial prison worlds, although only Revus V continues to serve as a long-term detention facility. High-level criminals—such as warlords, genocidal psychopaths, and threats to the galaxy—are now incarcerated at StasisStation10; a cryogenic, reconditioning laboratory. Location: classified.

JEDI MIND TRICK

Constantine Van Wyrm withdrew from the room in a dramatic flurry. General Waxler remained, a dark look in her eyes. "What is it?" Chalk said, her voice soft, fragile. "I'm in trouble, aren't I?"

"Do you know what you just did, Miss Hale?"

"I didn't *do* anything," she insisted. "Just refused to let a bully force me into betraying my friends. They'd do the same."

"I meant about the mind probe?"

"The ... mind probe?"

"A cerebral Caster's gambit."

Chalk frowned.

"The high judge is a powerful creature, Miss Hale. I have never seen anyone withstand a cerebral interrogation like that. Not now. Not ever."

"But I'm ... VOID."

"Yes. You are," Waxler said, an eyebrow raised. "But, as I told you in London, I sensed something in you. A feeling. A knowing."

"I—"

"Rest now, Miss Hale. You will feel better in the morning."

Light pierced Chalk's eyes hours later when the locking mechanisms were released and dozens of feet stampeded for the bathroom.

Her door activated and three faces peered inside.

"Hey," she said, sitting up. "Did you all get—?"

"Constantine Van Wyrm?" Aida said. "Affirmative."

The boys nodded.

"Did he do that mind—?"

More nodding.

"Why does he think we have anything to do with Cressida and Krieg?"

"I am not convinced he does," Aida said. "He is employing a fairly standard interrogation strategy."

"Seems like a complete waste of time," Milton grumbled, eating his breakfast. "None of us are hiding anything, right?"

Ripley caught Chalk's eye.

"What have I missed?" the Sagaroach said. "All secrets on the table. I told you mine, including the time I ate grimagourds by mistake at a royal banquet and was sick from both ends."

Ripley snorted. "I hadn't heard that one!"

"Messy business."

"Look, Counsellor Van Wyrm can do all the Jedi mind tricks he likes," Chalk said. "He'll find nothing here."

Dana Dune and Marcy-Kate wandered past, chatting animatedly. They peered inside, frowned, pointed, then continued on their way.

Chalk rolled out of bed and joined her friends on the landing.

Lachrymosa slouched against the bannister, eavesdropping on various conversations. Necrotta hunkered in his doorway, stretching his muscles while the remaining Veroselli and the Garrangulars spilled out of their rooms and surged towards Chalk.

"Hey, Earthling!" barked Kroket. "What've you been saying?"

"What did you tell him, Hale?" Clementine added.

First Cycle Aktari students moved her way.

"Nothing," Chalk said, standing between Ripley and Milton. "He just asked questions. Same ones he asked you. Probably."

"But what did you tell him?" said Dana.

"Come on, Hale," added Necrotta, his reptilian arms folded. "Spill it all."

"What did the counsellor wring out of you?"

Questions battered her from all sides. Hard questions. Spiteful questions. The room began to spin, nausea swirling. She gripped her friends for balance as the floor seemed to rise and drop away in dizzying swells.

Ripley was first to her defence. "Hale has nothing to do with this. You all know it. The interrogators are trying to turn us against one another."

"He assured me Earthlings were inexplicably untrustworthy."

"Worse than Revans!"

"Is that even possible?"

"He implied that the human race harbours a great hatred for GAPSS."

"They plan to enslave us all," Necrotta said, laughing. "I'd like to see them try!"

"He told me humans could conceal their Casting abilities."

"Make us *think* they were VOID!"

"Then use their powers to manipulate us all."

"I *am* VOID," Chalk said. "I wish I were a Caster, but I'm not—"

"That's enough," Ripley bit. "Hale is innocent."

Spirit pushed to the front. "Perhaps it was *you*," she said, jabbing a finger to his chest. "I've seen you sneaking off in the dead of night. I've followed you, thinking your heart had led you into the arms of another lover."

Ripley stared, aghast. "We … are *not* lovers."

Spirit thrust both hands onto her slender hips and cocked her head.

"It was him. The *Revan*," she said viciously. "I *know* it!"

"Me too," growled Kroket. "Never trust a Revan!"

Clementine and Claridge hissed venomously. "Or an Earthling!"

"The Revan and the Mudder are in it together!"

"You are dead," Clementine hissed. "Your entire family too."

"This is crazy!" Chalk shouted, pushing Ripley aside. "Flinch would never do that. Neither would I. Use some common sense. All of you!"

"See? She's doing it now. Trying to use her filthy Earthling powers on us."

"Nonsense," Chalk wailed. "Utter nonsense."

"They killed Cressida," Kroket said smugly.

"And Krieg," Claridge added spitefully.

"That's a filthy lie!"

Spirit gasped, her hands pressed to her cheeks. "And I thought the galaxy had something special planned for us, Ripley Flinch!"

Kiln massaged his knuckles.

The Veroselli fired up their GI-VRs.

Lachrymosa watched the scene unfold with a dark grin.

The Vyshan Order gathered in silent curiosity.

"The Revan's a secret Caster!"

"Clawswoggle!"

"All Casting abilities *must* be declared," Spirit spat. "It's the law!"

"But I'm not a Caster," protested Ripley. "I'm just like Hale. Totally VOID."

"Lies," erupted Spirit, bitterly. "I've seen you. You thought no one was watching, but I was there … in the shadows."

"No one's taking this lunatic seriously, are they?"

"I saw you," Spirit said, her face streaming with tears. "In the laboratories at the end of phase one. You shouldn't have been there … but you broke in. Used some secret code to force the lock. You met someone."

Goosebumps prickled Chalk's skin. "Who did you meet?"

"Secrets, see." Spirit laughed spitefully. "He hides things, even from Hale."

Ripley looked from one girl to the other. "No one."

"No one?"

"She's clearly unstable," Ripley said, nodding at Spirit.

"Maybe. But—" Chalk whispered.

"But what?" Anger mounted in Ripley's eyes.

"*I* saw you too."

Disbelief crossed his face.

Chalk thought about all the nights Ripley spent alone in his room. His clandestine excursions across the Coin, his time in the engine rooms with Esme and Spanners, his missions to the other side of the SpiralVerse. He'd explained all those away, but through everything she'd almost forgotten about the time she'd seen him at the laboratory window the day of the welcome ball.

"So?" Chalk pushed. She didn't want to. She could see the desperation and sadness on Ripley's face, but she needed to know. They all did.

"Did you … take them?"

"Cressida and Krieg?"

Chalk swallowed hard, nodded.

Ripley looked different then. His face creased with hurt and betrayal. His playful smile replaced by a thin hard line.

"That rotation in the laboratories was a personal matter," he uttered so only Chalk could hear. His hands gripped her shoulders. "Something for me. Not for you. Not for sharing with the entire class." He pushed her away. "How can you think that of me? After everything—*EVERYTHING!*"

He stared, unblinking.

Chalk flooded with regret.

"And you," Ripley said, his gaze on Spirit. "Stay away from me! Far away from me. You got it?"

He shouldered through the crowd and disappeared into his room.

Questions flew at Aida and Milton. Accusations of compliance and conspiracy. Wild theories and interwoven plots. Paranoia, anxiety, and fear.

First Cycle Aktari grew restless and disbanded, quarrelling

amongst themselves, taking sides over the matter of Ripley Flinch, Harper Hale, and their missing classmates.

Chalk shook.

Quivering fingers threaded her pink hair.

Aida waited patiently beside her.

"Hey," Chalk said after a while.

"Are you okay?"

"Dunno."

"Makes two of us."

"I'm his friend," Chalk said. "Maybe more than that. I can't believe he'd do ... anything bad."

"You do not have to decide his guilt or innocence."

She nodded, letting her hair cover her face.

"That is up to Counsellor Van Wyrm and General Waxler."

"I don't trust that man."

"He is a rather blunt weapon."

"He told me the Veroselli and the Garrangulars only *claimed* to have taken Cressida and Krieg. A political move. If that's true, then the real culprit could be among us."

Aida's soft claw stroked Chalk's arm.

"Counsellor Van Wyrm used the mind probe on everyone in First Cycle Aktari," the Tattorian said. "Pulling secrets and planting lies. Making everyone suspicious of everyone else. Except me obviously. Tattorians are immune to cerebral Casting."

"Well, he got nothing from me."

"Impossible," Aida said. "You are human. You are VOID."

"I know," she replied, still not happy about the V word. "But Waxler said I withstood his interrogation. She seemed ... impressed."

Aida adjusted her visor.

"I can't believe I accused Ripley."

"That was surprising."

"I'm an idiot."

"A bonehead of the highest kind, quality, and order. Supreme."

Aida and Milton ushered Chalk to her room. Her eyes shut the instant her head hit the pillows. Her mind spun. Pulling the bedclothes over her head, she prayed that when she surfaced, somebody, somewhere, would have straightened this all out. And Ripley would be her friend once again.

Even in the darkest reaches of the universe, whispered Harriet Starlight, *Hope lights the way.*

Ripley Flinch failed to attend classes that rotation. Luckily, Aida and Milton were on hand to distract Chalk from dwelling on his absence. As she slogged through the final minutes of Languages, where Professor Balefire made them compile lists of Garrangulan inverse feminine pre-nouns, a message arrived.

GENERAL WAXLER: All students report to the banqueting rotunda after classes. Thank you.

"Why the banqueting rotunda?" Chalk said. "Is this a last supper?"

"Why General Waxler cannot send important information via GI-VR is beyond me," Aida exclaimed.

"I think she's addicted to giving speeches," Milton mumbled.

In the banqueting rotunda, there were three empty seats now at the First Cycle Aktari table.

Chalk peered over her shoulder hoping the Revan would fall out of the AGT and join them. On the faculty platform, General Waxler and the other professors were joined by Counsellor Van Wyrm and his advisors. The high judge entertained the faculty with boisterous anecdotes. Snider sniggered darkly. The others fiddled with their cutlery.

"Students of the Galactic Institute," General Waxler said, standing at the railing. "As some of you may have noticed, we are graced this evening by the esteemed presence of representatives from GAPSS. May I present Counsellor Constantine Van Wyrm—Lead Interrogator and High Judge—and his advisors

Colson Ven Wyndigo and Climp Von Wyggle."

The three guests nodded respectfully.

"News of the war on Zorik Minor will not be a shock to you." Jeers and abuse trickled through the air. "Counsellor Van Wyrm and his advisors are here to determine the other matter that pertains to the Zorik System—that of Princess Cressida Van Wyrm and Master Krieg."

The general surveyed the entire school, her posture dominant, austere.

"Professor Asimov has conducted an excellent *initial* investigation, but the counsellor will now bring his considerable experience and expertise to hand and draw this matter to a swift conclusion."

Constantine rose. His dark, ominous robes hung from his body like sheets of necrotic flesh. "Thank you, Headmistress," he said. "Thank you for welcoming me back to the Galactic Institute, a school where I, and many of my colleagues from the multitudinous offices of GAPSS, studied and toiled and shaped ourselves into the powerful leaders we are today."

Chalk listened with growing concern.

"The Galactic Institute was once a proud and noble school—a paradigm of educational excellence, a monolith to the founding knowledge and supremacy of the SpiralVerse. But, as I look around now, I see nothing of its former glory. Its deterioration is a slight upon the great legacy GAPSS has fought to build, and now jeopardises your future and the futures of us all."

Galactic Enforcers edged into the banqueting rotunda. They were bigger and more fierce than their counterparts. Two took position by each entrance. Half a dozen more around the AGT.

"It is with great sadness that I perform this next act."

Chalk swallowed hard. Her fingers tingled.

"Never have two students from the Galactic Institute been taken from under the noses of its leaders, professors, and fellow students. Responsibility starts at the top and trickles down. You are all culpable for the loss of Princess Cressida Van Wyrm and Master Krieg. One of you, maybe many of you, know what happened. I *will* extract this information and uncover the fate of our missing cohorts. But for now, General Waxler"—the counsellor waved a hand in her direction—"will be removed from office and placed in StasisStation10 until this matter is concluded!"

Roars of contrition and disapproval billowed into the domed ceiling.

The halo light blinked from white to amber.

"Ineptitude of this magnitude cannot go unanswered," the counsellor bellowed. "Take her away!"

———

GAPSS
KNOWLEDGE
MAINFRAME

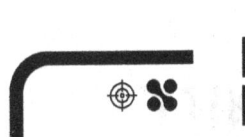 

GENKS
[SPECIES]
Homeworld: Gaia 23, Lang. Genkanese

Genks are a soft-skinned, high-minded, industrious species. While many of their population tend to fields and livestock and reside in close-knit communities, a fraction of their number—predominantly those displaying Casting abilities—seek careers beyond the Gaia systems. Genks have a high tolerance for pain and disease, living on average two-hundred to three-hundred cycles and procreate, on average, a dozen or more offspring.

THE DARK TRINITY

Three rotations passed. Shock paralysed the Galactic Institute. General Waxler had been at the helm for more than a decade and now she was gone, tossed into a holding cell on StasisStation10. Chalk decided against asking Cube exactly what that entailed. She had enough dark images rolling around her head to last a lifetime.

A team of maintenance droids swarmed the Coin. With Counsellor Van Wyrm and his advisors overseeing the installation, the Galactic Institute received an influx of updated tech, including: motion-sensitive cameras, biometric sensors, and covert GI-VR screening. Random spot checks were introduced, demanding students to report to campus locations and thumb-sign their attendance.

Chalk had been summoned three times already. Once to the Visitor Centre, then to hydroponics on the Flipside, and most recently to the detainment centre which hunkered in the shadow of the enigmatic Casting citadel.

But the strangest change of all came with the announcement of their new headmaster.

Chalk and Aida were convinced the high judge would take the role for himself. Others cited Professor Krazkow and Professor Balefire as surefire candidates, but most opted for Professor Snider as his sycophantic behaviour might hold sway.

But no.

The announcement came at lunchtime on the third rotation.

"Asimov?" Chalk said, reading the news to the others in the First Cycle Aktari living quarters. "He's a tablet tapper, not a fierce leader."

"Is ferocity a prerequisite of good leadership?" Aida asked sagely.

Chalk pulled a black beanie over her ears. "No. Not really. Administrative skills and speech-giving are probably just as useful. Look, Asimov is fine. I like him, but he's not right to lead us. Especially when civil war is raging on the other side of the bio-glass and students are disappearing into thin air."

"Maybe that is the point," Aida said. "Steady the ship. Put someone in charge who knows the Galactic Institute from top to toe. Steer us through the next few phases while the interrogation committee sort out the unpleasantries with Cressida and Krieg."

Chalk slumped in her chair, arms folded. "Maybe."

Aida seemed to be watching, which Chalk found strange, considering the Tattorian was utterly blind. "What is it?"

"You are plotting something."

Chalk leaned in. "What if that was the plan all along?"

Milton's bug eyes widened. His pincers clicked.

"Explain yourself."

"Abduct some students, blame it on Waxler, get her replaced with someone they can ... *manipulate?*"

"Manipulate?" Aida said. "Why on Tattoraan would they ... Hold on a moment, who are *they?*"

"I don't know," Chalk said. "The enemy, the Big Bad, maybe ... GAPSS."

"GAPSS?" Milton blurted. "That's preposterous."

Chalk hushed the Sagaroach, adding, "Who are the most powerful races in the SpiralVerse?"

"The Veroselli and the Garrangulars," Aida replied, cottoning on.

"So, if they were to obliterate one another, who would benefit?"

Milton looked lost.

"Other prominent civilisations and species."

"Exactly," Chalk said impatiently. "Like—?"

"Zillamoths, Karmethians, Sagaroaches, Pyramists, the Vyshan Order, even … Tattorians," Aida said. "But we have no desire for galactic supremacy. The Karmethians are a kind-hearted, peaceful civilisation. Pyramists are preposterously gloomy and self-involved. It is the Sagaroaches and the Zillamoths and the Vyshan Order you want to worry about."

"Hey," Milton said. "I'm right here."

"What about Revans?"

"A sprawling mongrel species. DNA from every conceivable life form in the galaxy. Driven by family, not civilisation and power."

"It also makes Revans unpredictable," Chalk said. "An unquantifiable … um … quantity."

"Not unlike Earthlings."

Chalk nodded tentatively. "Perhaps that's why Counsellor Van Wyrm is looking at you, me, Milton, and Ripley."

"You think one of us is a spy?" Milton said.

"Course not," Chalk replied, half-seriously.

"Necrotta is far more likely. He's a Zillamoth. Big and tough and angry."

"What about the Vyshan Order?" Aida said.

Chalk scanned the room, but none of the red-robed students were around. "Ox is a Zillamoth and in the Vyshan Order."

"True," Aida said. "But the Vyshans are a religious sect."

"Religion is a strong motivator for war," Chalk told them. "Most conflicts on Earth were over which Gods are real and which are not. And it's still going on … just like soccer. No one will ever finally win."

"Soccer?"

"Doesn't matter."

"The Spiral Wars were also about belief … and power," Aida said. "And ignited by the Dark Trinity. Those that followed saw them as Gods. But that was more to do with the Dark Trinity's powerful cerebral Casting, rather than the free will of their disciples."

"Crikey," Chalk said. "The galaxy was ... brainwashed?"

"I cannot speak to that," Aida said. "As you know, we Tattorians are immune."

"We've got a free double lesson next," Chalk said. "Let's hit the library—"

"There's a library?" Milton said, pulling a particularly squishy-looking yuccagourd from his bag.

"—and learn more about Waxler and Spiral Wars and those brain-washing super powers. I'll bet every quasoid I have there's a secret reason they wanted her gone."

"You again?" the animatronic librarian MAXXX said derisively. "And it appearrrs you have brrrought frrriends?"

"Knowledge is power," Chalk said, smiling at the lanky droid.

"Corrrerrrct," he replied. "Can MAXXX dirrrect you to anything in parrrticularrr?"

"General Waxler and the Dark Trinity," Milton announced.

"Yes," Chalk countered, throwing him a dirty look. "We're ... um ... doing an essay on famous military battles. Thought we'd start there."

"Yet again," the robot said, "all this informarrrtion is available on yourrr Gl-VRrr."

"We understand," Chalk said. "Yet again, we just love the smell of books."

Old circuits and dials whirred and fizzed inside the librarian's head. MAXXX wheeled about and directed them to the fourth floor where thousands of volumes of military history were stacked in perfect order on towering shelves.

Milton groaned as they stepped out of the vertical elevator. "There must be a billion books in here." His voice echoed against the curved, marble-effect floors. "Why can't we use our GI-VRs again?"

"As I told you in the hyperloop," Chalk reiterated, "we need to go analogue. The counsellor is definitely having all our search data monitored. If anything off-curriculum or suspicious comes up, it's getting flagged."

"So, I probably shouldn't be looking at—"

Chalk raised a hand. "I don't *even* want to know."

Following MAXXX's directions, they walked through the curved bookshelves to the opposite end where long research tables and hovering desk lamps were situated on a raised platform. Chalk placed Cube on the table while Aida used her Chronos Abstract80 to scan the shelves. Milton slumped in a chair. His St4rCr4ft™ 85R was probably still making his tortoise-like way across the Coin.

With its triangular sides open, thin arms extended from Aida's Chronos Abstract80. The eduhelper retrieved weighty tomes from the highest shelves and slipped them effortlessly onto the table. Aida opened one and set the Abstract80 to translate through an audio application on her GI-VR.

Chalk attempted the arduous task of reading. However, her book was written in High Zorikian and therefore could only make out the odd word. She slid the book to Cube.

"*The Spiral Wars: A Struggle for the Dark* by Closette Von Wist," the eduhelper read.

Aida's visor snapped towards Cube.

"Are you finally in communication with your eduhelper?" Aida said.

Chalk panicked. "Me and …? Um, yeah. Sure."

"What is the mystery of the mystery ball?"

"Well, it's just that," Chalk said timidly. "Black, shiny, rolls around a lot."

"I mean inside," Aida asked, and Milton's interest piqued. "Does it have TekTonik hardware? A closed-circuit interface? Eco-learning software? Explain yourself."

Chalk pulled the device closer. "It's … well … a sort of orangey goo."

"Do not make false claims."

"I'm not!"

"Really?"

"The absolute realest."

Aida's mouth fell open. "A gelatinous digital consciousness?"

"Um …"

"Are you steaming my visor?" Aida seemed all of a dither. "At best I was expecting a NextGen processing unit or an experimental, collapsible humanoid … but a gelatinous digi—"

"Alright, don't shout about it or we'll draw a crowd!"

Milton gazed around the cavernous hall.

"Chalk," Aida whispered. "You are talking about something entirely theoretical. You cannot even pre-order them on the off chance someone might invent one. How did …? Why did …? I am so—"

"Aida. Seriously. Calm down."

The Tattorian took several soothing breaths.

"Asimov said I was lucky to have it," Chalk continued. "That I should keep it close."

"That is an immeasurably understated piece of advice," Aida said. "Can I … have a look?"

"Um," Chalk muttered. "Cube?"

"It is called Cube?"

"Short for INCUBE-8."

"This is overwhelming."

"Cube. You can come out."

"I thought I was supposed to remain secret, concealed, camouflaged, hidden from those who would covet me over their own eduhelpers."

"Aida and Milton are friends," Chalk said. "I think it's time you met."

The mystery ball hissed, opened. Cube rose above the table, spinning slowly like the playsphere at the *Orbit Strike!* arena.

"By the Eyes of Loras!"

"Razabelle swallow me whole!"

"Cube, this is Aida and Milton. Aida and Milton, this is Cube."

"Astounding."

"Can I … touch it?"

"No," Chalk said, looking at Milton's yuccagourd-smeared hands. "And this is our secret. You, me, and Aida."

"And Ripley, obviously."

"No, I haven't … I didn't—" Chalk faltered. "Look, this research isn't going to do itself. Start reading."

While Aida busied herself with a dozen or more volumes, Cube listed chapter headings from Chalk's book, but nothing sounded useful. She grabbed the next. Aida worked through her stack at an impressive speed, sweeping volumes aside as they failed to serve anything helpful.

Milton, with no eduhelper to assist him, stared blankly at the endless pages of cryptic text, his attention only spiking when he found black-and-white etchings of breathtaking battle scenes.

"We should periodically access some class-related information," Aida told them. "GI-VR silence could be just as suspicious as searching for the precise location of StasisStation10?"

Milton spun a huge book to face Chalk. "Doesn't that look like the world door thing from the museum?"

"It's a worldgate," Chalk said, taking the book from him and gazing at a perfectly etched drawing of the Dawn Chaser squadron and Miasma engaged in deadly combat.

"Didn't Waxler fly with them?"

"That's right, Milton. This could be it!"

Chalk flipped the page. Cube read aloud. "After twelve years of brutal warfare, the Dark Trinity were vanquished at three locations across the SpiralVerse. Commander Crossfield Croft engaged Oddrax at the Assault on Blood Springs. General Gordon Sardothian vanquished Graven at the Skirmish of Black

Falls. While General Gertrude Waxler led her Dawn Chasers against Miasma at the Battle of Lost Shadows (pictured over). With the Dark Trinity drawn through worldgates, the Spiral Wars were officially declared over. GAPSS claimed a historic victory, yet only Commander Croft, General Sardothian, and General Waxler returned, their entire squadrons lost to the eternal dark."

"No one else made it back. Just the squadron leaders. Does that seem a tad suspicious to you?"

"I will admit it is unlikely, but not suspicious," Aida said. "They were three of the greatest pilots the galaxy has ever known."

"Is that it?" Chalk asked Cube. "Nothing more to this story?"

"No," it said. "At least, nothing written in this book."

"But that's the same story as the one in the museum!"

"I guess that's what happened then," Milton said.

Chalk pushed the book away. "I thought there'd be something else ... something *more*. Something deleted or hidden from the GAPSS Knowledge Mainframe, but alive in the pages of a book. A reason someone might have targeted Waxler and got her removed from office."

"Maybe there is nothing to your theory," Aida said. "Maybe the Veroselli and the Garrangulars did abduct one another and start a civil war. It is quite possible that General Waxler is collateral damage."

"No," Chalk said, folding her arms. "Constantine admitted that the Roses and Grangs only took responsibility for Cressida and Krieg as a political move. He's actively seeking the true culprit. Whoever it is, they're here, with us, somewhere on the Coin!"

"But why is it up to us to work this out?" Milton moaned. "I've got enough problems without getting involved in political espionage."

"Well, even if we can't discover the culprits," Chalk said, "we need to prove that it's not us."

This sharpened Milton's attention.

Chalk's GI-VR buzzed. "I've got Empirical Mechanics now." She collected up the other books, slid them towards Aida, and froze.

"What is it?" Milton asked.

"I'm an idiot."

"Comparatively speaking."

Chalk frowned at Aida. "No. Empirical Mechanics."

"You are losing me."

"It's with Commander Hank K. Lasco."

"That is correct."

"General Waxler wasn't the only person on the Coin that flew with the Dawn Chasers in the Spiral Wars."

Milton's antennae wobbled.

"Lasco did," Chalk announced.

"That would account for the drinking," Aida said.

"I've seen photos in his workshop," she continued, giddy with excitement. "Maybe he was there. At the very end. And, if I'm right, and there's more to the Battle of Lost Shadows than what's displayed in the museum and written in these books, then Hank K. Lasco just might be our golden ticket!"

GAPSS
KNOWLEDGE
MAINFRAME

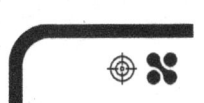 

PYRAMISTS
[SPECIES]

Homeworld: Pyramax, Lang. Ichorian

Pyramists inhabit the perpetually dark, storm-ravaged planet Pyramax. They are a powerful civilisation, with advanced technology, and gifted Casters. Pyramists are naturally morbid and morose creatures. They have pale, rangy bodies; languid, watery eyes; and dress exclusively in black.

ZORIK PRIME

Chalk stared at the empty bench beside her in Empirical Mechanics. When a bleary-eyed Commander Lasco enquired about Ripley's whereabouts, Chalk could only shrug.

In the following Conflict Engagement class she was forced to partner with Spirit.

"How is Ripley?" the Oneric asked devilishly, as Chalk bundled her to the ground. "No one's seen him for days. It's all your fault."

"Shut up, Spirit," she replied, taking an elbow in the ribs. "You accused him too."

"I may have thrust the blade," Spirit grunted. "But you twisted it."

"He's my friend. I wouldn't do anything to hurt him."

"Friend, huh? I think that starship has flown."

"—and don't think about Casting!" yelled Lasco, circling the students. "You know the rules, Sadler." The commander checked his GI-VR. "Okay. That's time. Break it up! Put her down, Kroket! KRO-KET!"

Spirit threw a malicious smile at Chalk as she wriggled free and stormed down the flight deck.

"Miss Hale," the commander said, helping her back to her feet. "Class is over. Time to leave."

"Do you mind if I stay?"

"Whatever for?"

"I have a few ... questions."

"Questions?" the commander asked, heading for his workshop. "Did Asimov send you?"

"Not at all."

"This isn't about that business with Professor de Rema and the portal in phase one because I assured her that—"

"No," Chalk said. "Not that either."

"Oh," he said. "Questions about ... Conflict Engagement then?"

"In a way."

Lasco heaved the workshop door open. Chalk made a beeline for the commander's photo gallery. "I want to ask about these."

"My pictures?"

"Yes. I wanted to ask about the battles you flew in. What you saw. The danger, the excitement, the friendships. And how the Spiral Wars ended."

The commander fidgeted with his jacket pocket.

Chalk couldn't simply pull the pin and detonate her theory about General Waxler. If the commander knew anything, he might clam up or accuse her of an acute case of hydralunas syndrome. "Some of us think the history books are keeping ... secrets."

"Secrets?"

"Well, we've been studying famous battles and I'm fascinated by General Waxler and the Dawn Chasers." Chalk's gaze danced over group portraits and candid shots of revelry and camaraderie. The young Hank K. Lasco was quite the specimen. Lean and clean-shaven, with thick auburn curls swept off his chiselled face. "The bravery these pilots needed to face Miasma is awe-inspiring."

Lasco rubbed his stubbled jowls. "Okay, Chalk. What are you after?"

"Well," she said, spinning away from the photos. "You were there, right?"

"Miss Hale—"

"You flew with the Dawn Chasers during the Spiral Wars, didn't you?"

He grunted an affirmation.

"But were you there? At the very end? At the … Battle of Lost Shadows?"

Commander Lasco shot her a steely glare.

"Professor Snider taught us that the Dawn Chasers led Miasma through the worldgate and into a chaos dimension." The commander didn't flinch. "And the only person to survive the encounter was General Waxler." Lasco's gaze became distant. "What happened to the others?"

The commander pulled a flask from his pocket and took a long pull.

"And … where were you in all that?"

"Do not go down this path, Miss Hale."

"Are the history books wrong?" she said, ignoring his warning. "There's no mention of any survivors except General Waxler and the other squadron leaders—"

"Are all Earthlings like this?"

"Like what?"

"Persistent. Stubborn."

"You mean *determined*."

Wimbam's Finest Retrograde dribbled over his bottom lip. "Sure, there's more to this story than you'll find in history books and layer screens and the GAPSS Knowledge Mainframe." He took another feverish gulp. "But don't look into this. For your own sake. Sometimes the truth is worse than the lie."

"But I—"

"Chalk. Don't." Calloused fingers coiled round her arm. "I like you. You're a great kid."

The last word rattled her bones.

"If I could, I'd tell you. But I'd hate to see you in trouble."

Chalk nodded.

"Class is over," he said, attempting a smile.

Chalk inched for the door. "Obviously, it's none of my business," she said, turning to face him, "and I know it's hokey as all hell, but Grandpa Milo used to tell my father that the secret to happiness wasn't hidden at the bottom of a bottle."

The commander froze, mid-swig.

"I'd hate to see you in trouble too."

In the dorm, most of First Cycle Aktari had gathered around the monitor wall. Nervous energy burbled through the air. A news anchor appeared on screen. A digital composite of Veroselli and Garrangulan combatants was inset to his right.

"The Zorik Civil War continues apace! Hundreds now confirmed dead in both capital cities, while rural Veroselli strongholds and Garrangulan outposts burn. Negotiations for a ceasefire—first called for by high-ranking GAPSS officials— have been met with angered vitriol and promises of utter annihilation from opposition leaders. As we move into another night of strategic bombardment and speciated decimation, news crews and journalists are pulling back to the Galactic Institute, currently in orbit around Zorik Prime."

"The Galactic Institute is going to war?" Milton asked.

"Not at all," Aida corrected. "Centurion H—like all GAPSS vessels—is a neutral zone, governed by intergalactic law."

"We're Switzerland?"

The inset graphic faded and a photo of General Waxler replaced it. She wore her usual white robes, but her hair had been pulled off her face, making her look more fierce and uncompromising than ever.

"The recent and turbulent removal of Gertrude Prodigious Waxler—former headmistress of the Galactic Institute and war veteran—has led to this offer of sanctuary aboard the Galactic Institute; a move that would otherwise have been littered with political tripwires and bureaucracy under Miss Waxler's turbulent command."

"That's a lie," Chalk spat. "Waxler would never do such a thing!"

Milton chomped nervously.

"Counsellor Constantine Van Wyrm, Lead Interrogator and High Judge at GAPSS, has taken control of a media sanctuary aboard the Coin, while continuing his daily commitments and spearheading an investigation into the porous security protocols and fractured leadership that led to the disappearance of his granddaughter Princess Cressida Van Wyrm and a Garrangulan student named Krieg."

"They're making him out like some sort of hero."

"This *is* Qwork News."

"Run by GAPSS."

"Financed by the Veroselli."

Life in Downing Street had taught her that corruption and self-service festered at all levels of politics, but this was something else. Was Counsellor Van Wyrm somehow mixed up in all this? Cressida and Krieg's disappearance, the start of the Zorik Civil War, and Waxler's fall from grace? And for what? To position himself higher in GAPSS? For power and money and legacy? At the cost of hundreds, if not thousands, of his own people and those of their symbiotic cousins? Where did Constantine's ambition end?

"Sentencing of the disgraced childless spinster Gertrude Prodigious Waxler was read this morning by the high judge himself, after a swift yet comprehensive hearing," the anchor read, unblinking.

"Sentencing?" Chalk erupted. "But there hasn't been a trial."

"Took place this morning," Marcy-Kate said. "Lasted thirteen minutes."

The inset of General Waxler morphed into a video. She looked tired yet resolute. A lonely figure stood inside a sealed bio-glass cell. Members of the GAPSS judicial command sat around her in low sweeping arcs.

Mounted on a central platform loomed Constantine.

His silver mask offered no emotion.

"It is the ruling of this court that Miss Gertrude Prodigious

Waxler, being of sound mind, did underestimate and overlook the threat of abduction and mortal injury to the students in her care. She actively ignored the protestations of faculty members, abusing the trust and power of her position to allow the most severe events to transpire. Miss Gertrude Prodigious Waxler will be stripped of all titles. She will be sentenced to a minimum of one hundred cycles in StasisStation10 where she will undergo personality reconditioning. Once complete, she will labour in the Tar Pits on Revus VII until she is physically unable. Her medals of valour and courage will be revoked. Her name will be stripped from history. She will be blacklisted, removed, forgotten."

Silence filled the rec room.

No one dared breathe.

"They can't do that?" Chalk whispered.

"They just did."

"Thoden help us."

Qwork News let the film run as Galactic Enforcers led Waxler from the courtroom, her biological and mechanical arms bio-bolted behind her back.

"One hundred cycles. Personality reconditioning. Tar Pits!" Chalk wailed. "This is barbaric."

"What did you expect?" snapped Necrotta, pushing past.

"I don't know," Chalk called after him. "Reason. Irrefutable evidence. Due process."

"From GAPSS?" He laughed, tail swishing. "Think again, Earthling."

Qwork News sidestepped into a rolling news cycle, flip-flopping between the Zorik Civil War, Waxler's sentencing, and a mawkish biopic on Constantine Van Wyrm.

Students disbursed.

Chalk lingered.

Anger burned in her chest.

Her mind in free fall.

"I am sensing distress," stated Aida.

"We need to go to the beginning."

"Of time?" Milton asked. "I don't see how that is going to help. And time travel is more a Ripley thing, so—"

Chalk sighed irritably. "To the beginning of the first cycle. We've missed something. A clue. A reason. Whatever it is, it's out there. And I plan to find it."

Chalk escaped the idle chatter, baseless accusations, and hot takes from First Cycle Aktari by dragging Aida and Milton to the recreation arcade. They nestled on picnic tables in a shaded courtyard adjacent to the observation hall. Without thinking, Chalk bought three quarts of Tattorian Tribute then realised she'd have to drink them all herself.

"We need to make a plan," she said, drumming her fingers eagerly on the table. "I'll be in charge of ideas. Aida, you take research. Milton can be moral support."

"Chalk. Stop," Aida said sternly. "You cannot go against Counsellor Van Wyrm and the whole of GAPSS."

"Why not?"

"Because you are just one person, and a VOID person at that," Aida said.

"Ouch."

"GAPSS are thousands. Tens of thousands. They are government, and military, and law."

"So, I'm on my own?" She folded her arms. "Fine with me."

Aida and Milton looked blank.

"What about you?" Chalk directed her question at Cube.

"I am your eduhelper," the black orb replied. "I can advise and instruct you about the laws surrounding these events and calculate the probability of you getting yourself in trouble. Or worse."

"Go on then," she urged. "What are the—?"

"High. Extremely high."

Chalk finished the first glass of GanyMead and pulled the

others close. "Cube and I are getting to the bottom of this. With or without you."

Aida fidgeted with her visor. Chalk had never seen her look this disgruntled. "I am your friend," the Tattorian said evenly. "Your relay partner. You have kept your sensors set to normal despite the horrific wafts from Milton's yuccagourds."

"We have suffered together."

"Hey," Milton complained. "I'm right here!"

"But this goes against everything I set out to achieve," Aida continued. "My time at the Galactic Institute was to be measured, and calm, and conducted with the most stringent, calculated use of lifeforce. But since meeting you, and the Sagaroach, and *that* Revan, my plans have degraded exponentially."

"So, what you're saying is—?"

"I am in," Aida groaned reluctantly. "Obviously, I am in. What sort of relay partner—what sort of Tattorian—would I be if I let a well-meaning hot-head with ill-conceived plans go barrelling head first into danger by herself?"

"I'm not alone," Chalk said, her hand on Cube.

"Just so we are clear, I intended to out-live the lot of you. By aeons. Please do nothing to bring about my premature expiration or condemn me to the same objectionable fate as General Waxler."

Milton wiped his pincers. Vile mucus dribbled down his sleeve. "For what it's worth, I'm in too," he said. "I can't bear the thought of you having fun without me."

"Classic FOMO."

"What's—?"

"Doesn't matter."

"Additionally," Aida said, "you are yet to inform us on your findings with Commander Lasco."

"Oh, total bust." Chalk sipped her drink. "*Sometimes the truth is worse than the lie.* His words, not mine."

"What does that mean?" Milton asked.

"The commander believes we are better off not knowing," Aida said.

"Or he's been told to keep schtum," Chalk grumbled irritably.

"We should start with Cressida and Krieg," Aida said. "The general's incarceration all stems from their infighting and disappearance."

"There have been six notable occurrences of confrontation involving the Veroselli and the Garrangulars since the start of the cycle," Cube informed them. "In the entirety of Galactic Institute history, Veroselli and the Garrangulan interactions on the Coin have never been so hostile."

"Ripley's sure there's something wrong with the attitude easing atmospheric system," Chalk added. "But when he hacked in and ran a diagnostic the results came back normal."

"Well, that may be true. Equally, Ripley lied. And before you defend him, he has lied about a great many things."

"He's a snagger *and* a clawswoggler. I get it," Chalk said. "Let's presume for the moment that Ripley isn't lying about the AEAS. If that's working fine, then what's setting them off?"

Chalk rolled her shoulders and stared at the endless black beyond the environsphere. The broken shell of Zorik Major swarmed around the war-torn planet within. Light from Zorik Prime bounced off its manufactured biosphere in colourful waves.

"Zorik Prime," Chalk whispered, then looked at Aida and Milton's blank faces. "Zorik bloody Prime!"

"What about it?"

"That's why we're here," she said. "Why we're not in the neutral zone anymore."

Aida stared.

"Once in every ... four thousand and ... I forget. Cube?"

"Once in every four hundred and thirty-two rotations, Zorik Minor breaks cover from the Shield of Zorik and bathes in the light of Zorik Prime. On this rotation, and this rotation only, the Veroselli and the Garrangulars are at peace."

"A calming light," Aida said. "To quell the hostilities."

"Well, if that rumour is true, it's clearly not working," Milton said.

"Exactly."

"What?"

"Even here, bathed in the calming light from Zorik Prime, the Veroselli and the Garrangulars are still going at one another."

"Meaning?"

"Meaning there must be some unknown or unauthorised atmospheric issue or element or toxin causing their violent tendencies," Aida concluded.

"Like zorikanthium," Milton said.

"Zorikanthi—what?"

"Zo … rik … an … thium," he said more carefully. "You know, the exceptionally hazardous geological crystal. Formed in the mantle of Zorik Major. Rumoured to have all kinds of weird properties. None of them good."

Chalk frowned.

"We covered it with Professor Krazkow in Chemical Cosmology," Milton went on. "The Crystal of Shadows? One of the five most dangerous crystals in the SpiralVerse. The ones banned from the Galactic Institute."

"How long have you been sitting on this information?"

"You were both in that class!"

"I have been in numerous classes," Aida informed him. "The study of crystals was fourth from bottom on my long list of low-level topics."

"Okay, look," Chalk began. "Most of the occurrences took place here on the Coin, which would lead anyone to believe the AEAS is to blame. But they were at each other's throats at Fort Van Murk too."

"But that chunk was once part of Zorik Major," Aida said. "The home of zorikanthium."

"No trace of zorikanthium has been detected since the destruction of the planet," Milton corrected.

"So—?" Chalk said.

"Somebody had zorikanthium on them."

"You mean … *has*."

"On Zorik Major. *And* here, on the Coin."

"Why would anyone do that?" Milton asked. "That stuff is lethal."

"For all the reasons we're having this conversation," Chalk explained. "To enrage the Veroselli and the Garrangulars. To create a disturbance, a smokescreen for Cressida and Krieg's disappearance, to spark civil war and remove General Waxler."

"Suppose this is all true," Aida said, waving her claws. "Who was present at all these events? The list cannot be long."

"Other than Cressida and Krieg themselves," Cube added helpfully, "the only persons present at all the disturbances were Aidriendretta Kromm-Nargulantis, Harper Hale, Lord Milton Barclay XVII, and Ripley Flinch."

"That cannot be right," Milton said. "What about Necrotta?"

"He was not there after the *Orbit Strike!* match."

"Kroket and Kiln?"

"They weren't on Fort Van Murk. Same for Clementine and Claridge."

"Professor de Rema?" Milton tried.

"Serious suggestions only," Aida snapped.

They sat in silence, brains whirring.

"Well, it most certainly is not me."

"Nor me."

"It's Ripley," Chalk said, her lip trembling. "Isn't it?"

Aida and Milton's silence was deafening.

"The probability of Ripley Flinch obtaining a shard of zorikanthium and smuggling it onto the Coin is—"

"Although," Chalk rallied before Cube could deliver the odds. "It *could* be me. I mean, I'm from Earth. I have Earth bones and DNA and clothes made from human-made fibres and glues and loads of things that could be setting them off. It doesn't necessarily mean it's this zorikanthium stuff. This … Crystal of Shadows."

Chalk knew that Ripley had left the Coin during the first cycle. He'd certainly had the time to obtain whatever zorikanthium remained in the galaxy.

But why?

The best thing to do would be to ask him.

Wouldn't it?

But, even if he *had* found one of the rarest and most deadliest crystals in the galaxy *and* found a way to get it onto the Coin, he'd never admit it.

Especially now.

Their friendship was already balanced on a knife-edge.

Another accusation would cut to the bone.

GAPSS
KNOWLEDGE MAINFRAME

ATTITUDE EASING ATMOSPHERIC SYSTEM
[AEAS] [TECHNOLOGY]

Most prevalent at schools and colleges—due to the changeable nature of young adults—the AEAS is a time-sensitive self-optimising system designed to diagnostically adjust the chemical balance of the environment to accommodate species from all thirty-five civilised worlds. While the AEAS is reported as substantially successful, many suffer adverse reactions to chemical imbalances. These range from skin irritations and digestive disarray, excessive infatuation and desire, to psychological breaks and bloodlust. The AEAS is crucial to the smooth running and moderated attitude on all mixed-species environments.

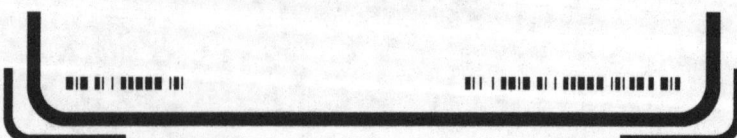

BLOOD FOR BLOOD

Chalk slept through most of the dark rotation. She'd stayed up reading *Harriet Starlight and the Quantum Resistance*, playing *Yazanti* with Cube, and staring at the pieces of Zorik Major that bathed in the calming warmth from Zorik Prime. It had done nothing for the anger and self-loathing that simmered inside.

Her GI-VR buzzed in the early hours. She woke from anxious dreams, her face stuck to the pillow crusted with snot and tears. Flipping the bedclothes aside in disgust, she sat up, and dimmed the window.

The mystery ball rested by her feet.

Orange and blue hoops orbited its smooth exterior.

No sound came from the dorm, save for the gentle hum of power units. First Cycle Aktari were either sleeping or studying quietly.

Her GI-VR buzzed again.

Wiping the sleep from her eyes, she tapped the device.

The message icon flashed.

A message from Ripley!

Chalk couldn't bring up the layer screen fast enough.

Where was he? In his room? Between the floorboards? Trading dark mercury or polonium somewhere across the SpiralVerse? These past rotations she'd felt the furthest from the Revan—physically and emotionally—since the moment they'd met on Revus X.

RIPLEY: Emergency. Flipside. Mazeoleum. Bring help.

Chalk blinked.

Read it again.

CHALK: On way!

Anxiety now consuming her waking state too, she yanked on her jacket and drove her feet into her Converse without bothering to tie the laces.

Bring help, she thought. *Did he mean Aida and Milton? Or some sort of weapon?*

No time to weigh it up.

She found the Tattorian in the middle of her room, her body folded into a ball.

"Aida," Chalk hissed. "Ai-da."

She did not move.

"AIDRIENDRETTA!"

Aida unfolded. "What is happening?"

"Ripley."

"Inevitably."

"He's in trouble."

"This is hardly enlightening information," Aida said. "And why is this *my* problem?"

Chalk found Milton asleep inside a nest built from shed wing and thorax membranes. The smell in his room was devastating.

"Milton." Chalk gagged. "MIL-TON!"

When he failed to rise, she grabbed a yuccagourd from an open crate and launched it. The noxious fruit glanced off Milton's head, propelling him from a deep sleep into a vicious defensive pose. "Who goes there? Who dares to wake a lord of the colonies? I'll pull your arms from their sockets!"

Chalk stifled a scream.

"Oh, it's you," Milton said, relaxing slightly. "Sorry. Instinct kicked in."

"Your instinct is to … dismember?" Chalk took several deep breaths.

"You've clearly never been to the Xenothropod colonies."

"I'll be sure to book holidays elsewhere."

"Please do," Milton agreed. "Although, the weather is sumptuous."

"Sorry to wake you," she said. "But we have to go."

"Go?"

"No time for questions!"

They soared into the hyperloop, tore across the observation hall, then plummeted into the chaos of the gyrosphere. Clamouring for the exit on the Flipside, Chalk dug her feet into the resin paving slabs and sprinted towards the forest at the outer rim.

She glanced back.

Her heart warmed to see Aida and Milton disembarking the AGE and pelting to catch up. She knew how preoccupied the Tattorian was with preserving her lifeforce. How she walked and talked. Used the most efficient movements. Right now she darted along behind Chalk as fast as she knew how. Milton had dropped onto all six legs, scuttling in a way she hadn't seen before. He looked dangerous, fearsome even.

"Where are we headed?" he urged, catching up.

Chalk pointed as they passed the outer wall of the Flipside gardens and made for the trees. She used her forearms to lever the knotted branches aside. Brambles and thorns pinched her clothes, hair, face.

"Let me," Milton said, letting his hardened, shell-like wings smash a hole through the undergrowth. Chalk followed, urging Aida to hurry.

"Mazeoleums?" he read. "What in Razabelle's name is this?"

"Resting places," Aida told him, clearly much further ahead in History of the Galaxy than anyone else. "Memorials to the fallen."

"Great," the Sagaroach said. "Is this a cultural day trip?"

A commotion swelled on the other side of the hedge, moving closer.

"What in the seventeen moons of—?"

Ripley and INFIN-8 came flying out of the mazeoleum

of the Unknown Engineer. The Revan's face looked gaunt and sallow, coated in sweat and grease, his hair slick against his skin.

"Find a weapon!"

"What for?"

"Protection."

"From who?"

"We need to break them up."

"Again ... who?"

Before he could answer, a dozen Sevantes poured out of the maze. But these weren't the rag-tag emaciated Sevantes they had encountered on Fort Van Murk with sticks and bones. These were Sevantes from Zorik Pol. Healthy, strong, determined. And armed to the teeth.

Defying his recent display of aggression, Milton wailed and sprinted into the maze for the Remembrance Halls of Extinct Civilisations (New and Ancient). Ripley rounded on the Sevantes as they bottle-necked in the entranceway and pelted them with rocks and stones.

"Go, go, go!"

Chalk pushed Aida into the Sepulchre of the Vanquished Starfighter maze while she took Burial Grounds of the Astrologer Klark Klarkksson.

Unlike the maze to the Unknown Engineer—constructed of high, grassy hedges—this puzzle had been moulded with smooth metal panels. Chalk could hear the walls shifting as she ran deeper and deeper.

Voices screamed, distant and forlorn.

Her heart pounded like a startled horse.

She took random turns, weaving through the panelled walls.

Dappled in simulated moonlight, a Sevante came hurtling towards her. His chest heaved beneath intimidating eyes. They collided with incredible force and tumbled to the ground. On his knees, the Sevante yanked Chalk's hair, slammed his fist into her face. Dazed from the blow, she collapsed against the wall. Tiny lights spiralled in her vision. Pain flowed across her head like flaming brandy over Christmas pudding. But strength found its way to her fingers. She tore a metal pole from her assailant's grip and slammed it against his ribs, knees, head. He stopped moving.

Two more Sevantes sprinted her way in a wild frenzy. In the narrow maze, they could only attack one at a time. Chalk ducked a vicious swipe from the first and cracked the pole across his shins. He fell like a stone, howling in pain. The second came for Chalk. His fingers raked her shoulder, trying to disarm her. But she held fast to the weapon, spun away, bounced off the wall, then cracked the pole against his spine.

She didn't wait to see what they did next.

Chalk ran.

Twisting and turning through the maze.

Back, hopefully, to safety.

Corridors shifted around her. Walls became doorways. Doorways became dead ends. Her legs burned. Eyes streamed. Adrenaline fired through her like a rain of comets. She slowed for a moment to catch her breath, sank forward, hands resting on her knees. Distant cries and wails were dying down. Sounds of fighting quelled to the occasional clang of metal and Sagaroach scream.

Chalk walked steadily, the weapon raised to protect her face. Her eyes scanned the ever-changing maze. When the entrance materialised, Aida was waiting patiently in the clearing on top of five prone Sevantes.

The Tattorian looked unflustered.

"Are you okay?" Chalk asked. "What happened to the—?"

"I vanquished them."

"Oh. Neat. Did you use—?"

"Casting is not permitted outside the citadel," Aida said, "and is impossible without Aether."

"Sure, so how did—?"

Milton burst from the maze to her right, two Sevantes in hot pursuit. He swung a bushel of sticks and leaves amateurishly and connected with fresh air. Chalk shouldered him aside, bashed one Sevante in the chest and swiped the legs of the other. Before they collapsed to the ground, Milton grabbed both and cracked their heads together. That seemed to do the job.

Ripley staggered out of the maze to Obit Venk Tyllimens' grave. He and INFIN-8 dumped three unconscious Sevantes next to the two Milton had dispatched.

"What in the name of—?" Chalk said, gasping for breath.

But Ripley had his hands up in protestation. "I know, I know," he said humbly. "I made a mistake. A big one. Huge."

"You are an untrustworthy, self-centred, lifeforce-decimating, intergalactic—" Aida began.

"—bonehead," Chalk finished.

"Fair."

"What did you do?"

He couldn't look at her. Was it shame? Embarrassment? Anger at the accusations she'd levelled at him on the dorm landing?

"I need to send them back."

"Back?" Aida said.

"The Sevantes," Chalk said, cottoning on. "Through the portal."

"There's a portal here?" Milton spluttered.

"Yes, the engineering portal," Aida said. "But that device was decommissioned seven cycles ago and is not part of the Galactic Institute integrated portal system."

Chalk frowned. "Decommissioned? You told me it was *broken*. That Esme and Spanners needed you to repair it."

"Esme and Spanners?" Milton asked.

"And you *knew* about this?" Aida said, rounding on Chalk.

"Why am I getting attacked?" she said. "This is Ripley's mess." Chalk could feel Aida's stare. "Yes. Fine. Okay," she admitted. "I knew about the portal between the floorboards. We went to … some places."

Aida's big accusatory visor was all she could see.

"Nowhere really," Ripley said. "Gaia 23. Eos Yol."

"Zorik Pol and … Zorik Minor," Chalk added, coming clean. "We saw the Shield of Zorik from the top of an inverted pyramid in Clodvorg."

"That's supposed to be amazing," Milton said, genuinely interested.

"It really was."

"Those are two of the most dangerous places in the SpiralVerse," Aida scolded. "What were you doing there? And why? Actually, I do not want to know. I have wasted enough of my lifeforce running across the Coin and the Flipside and battling Sevantes for one night."

"But—?"

"We need to leave," Aida announced.

Chalk looked at the pile of unconscious bodies. "You two go," she said. "I'm going to help Ripley return the Sevantes to Zorik Pol."

Aida said nothing, simply turned and headed leisurely through the woods. Milton, a yuccagourd in each hand, followed dutifully. "I've no idea what's going on," he said as he departed, "but that was the most fun I've had all cycle!"

Chalk helped Ripley and INFIN-8 haul the Sevantes along the stifling corridors between the floorboards. The Revan fired up a temporal doorway and quickly deposited each limp body through the portal to Zorik Pol.

Chalk could only imagine what this looked like on the other side.

With the last one through, Ripley deactivated the temporal doorway and slumped against the wall. He breathed heavily, hands shaking from exertion. Sure, it was tough work, and Chalk was sweating like a thermoslug, but nothing compared to Ripley. He looked horribly ill, the contours of his skull—

like Sadler Arklan and every Elmori on the Coin—was evident through his skin.

"Come on then," Chalk said, her voice affected by the face mask. "You need to tell me everything. And I mean *everything*."

Ripley slid to the ground. His head in his hands.

Chalk flashed to his side, an arm around his shoulders.

"What is it?" she said. "Ripley? Talk to me. Is this something to do with ... Cressida?"

"No," he snapped. "That's nothing to do with me. How can you—?"

"Then ... what?"

Ripley massaged his fingers. "The Data Drive Relay."

"The ... Data Drive Relay?" Chalk thought of her time on Revus X. "Were you kidnapped? Did they prey on your worst fears, your nightmares, your darkest moments? What happened? Was it—?"

"My Data Drive Relay was an endurance test. Search the catacombs beneath the Temple of Razabelle for Lord Milton Barclay XVII. Sure, there was the odd Sagafly and Sagamoth— and I prayed to Thoden to steer me clear of any Sagarachnids— but halfway through, I was pulled into an empty nesting cloister."

"By what?"

"Not what. Who."

"Who?"

"A man."

"Is that ... unusual?"

"On the Xenothropod colonies? You bet."

"What did he want?"

"He made me an offer," Ripley explained. "A promise of something I could not believe."

"Was it part of the relay?"

"I thought so at the time," Ripley said. "He gave me a second data drive. Told me it contained plans and schematics for the Galactic Institute. Secret doors and codes to the engineering rooms. The integrated portal system. Incredible mathematical theories and equations beyond my wildest dreams."

"Who was he?"

"I don't know," Ripley said. "But he knew about my brother."

"Dante."

Ripley's once purple eyes had turned a solemn grey. "He said there was a way I could … get him back."

Chalk inched away. She'd watched enough *Supernatural* and *Buffy the Vampire Slayer* to know that bringing back the dead always ended in misery.

"He told me about a time portal. A doorway to wherever I wanted, *when*ever I wanted, to my life before Dante was taken. He told me I could save him, that I could have my brother again."

"Is time travel even possible?"

"I'd read hundreds of working theories and Emerging Physics essays on the subject, but nothing actionable," he said. "I looked at the information on the secret drive. It was confusing at first, baffling even. I spent hours deciphering the codes and equations and tried to make sense of putting such a thing together. Of constructing it. Operating it."

"You didn't … You haven't—?"

"It works on a similar principle to any other temporal doorway, but this snagger needs a nuclear fusion reaction—like that of a dying star—to generate a thermal runway while maintaining steady electron regeneration pressure and algorithmic relativity to equalise the spacetime quantum mechanics."

"Great Scott!" Chalk quipped. "Doc Brown was miles off."

"Who's Doc Brown?"

"Doesn't matter."

"Well, basically, it runs on—"

"Polonium," Chalk said, eyes thinning.

Ripley nodded. "Lots."

"I thought you were getting that for—"

"The rubinovium and the dark mercury were for Esme and Spanners," he admitted. "But the polonium … that was for me."

Gingerly, the Revan rolled back his sleeves. Both forearms were covered in dozens of red sores. Some had started to heal. Others were fresh.

Tears bloomed in Chalk's eyes.

URRRH! bleated INFIN-8 despondently.

"Radiation poisoning?"

"No, it's not that. I'm fine, sort of. I've got this pendant, remember?"

"Then what are—?"

"Payment."

"Payment?"

"My blood."

Chalk tightened. "You paid for the polonium with your blood?"

"I'd give anything to have my brother back."

Her mind spun in the insufferable heat. "What do the Sevantes want with it? Are they making that … bloodmetal stuff?"

"I didn't ask. They didn't say. And I hope I *never* find out."

Chalk shook her head. "Have you made it?"

"The time portal?"

"What else?"

He nodded. "I haven't assembled it. I was getting the last of the polonium today but—" He glanced at his punctured skin. "My veins closed up. They couldn't squeeze more than a quart out of me."

"Good," Chalk said. "You've clearly given enough."

"But I needed that last shipment, so—"

"You stole it."

"And ran."

"Thoden help you!"

"They chased me and INFIN-8 along the streets of Zorik Pol, through the portal and onto the Flipside. If you hadn't turned up with Milton and Aida—"

"This has to stop," she said. "For your sake and mine."

"But—"

"Look, risking your own life is one thing, however mine and Aida's and Milton's are not yours to play with. Someone could have been seriously hurt or killed or worse."

"What's worse than being killed?"

"Living with the guilt of another's death," Chalk told him earnestly. "Especially one of your own making. This ... time portal ... is dangerous, Ripley. Properly, fatally dangerous. A polonium-induced nuclear fusion reaction? I'm a relative bonehead at Emerging Physics, but even I know you're attempting to replicate a supernova. One mistake, one tiny mistake, and you'll kill us all. Me, Aida, Milton, the whole student body and faculty, the entire Coin and the Flipside. All of it. Gone! And for what?"

"My brother."

His cracked lips trembled.

Tears sizzled on the treadplate.

Chalk's promised to follow.

"He's gone," she told him.

Ripley winced.

"Dante. Your twin brother. Is dead." The words felt harsh and cruel on her tongue, but they needed to be said. "You can fix all the portals you like, reconfigure a host of automated systems, strip every last piece of tech on the Coin down to its constituent parts and put it back together, but death is not something you *dabble* with."

Chalk pulled him close.

Amber lights throbbed.

Digital drives and coolant fans whirred and hummed.

With arms locked and chests pressed together, their fractious hearts drummed in anxious, syncopated rhythms.

And Chalk wondered just how it had come to this.

GAPSS
KNOWLEDGE
MAINFRAME

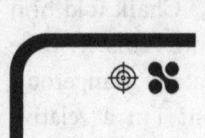 

GRADING SYSTEM
[EDUCATION]

The grading system for research, essays, and examinations
throughout the SpiralVerse is broken into five bands and
named after alumni from the Galactic Institute.

Grade: X [Admiral Xavier 'Rumdog' Xenon] Exemplary

Grade: R [Headmistress Noxious Ranx]
Highly Commendable

Grade: P [Chief Strategist Proxima Proxalto] Merit

Grade: B [Lord Milton Barclay II] Pass

Grade: K [Kommandant Gyar Klimpt] Fail

THE FEELS

Ripley's story kept Chalk awake night after night. She lost focus in Emerging Physics, got tongue-tied in Domestic and Interspecies Languages, short-circuited devices in Empirical Mechanics, and struggled to run a single lap of the flight deck no matter how much Commander Lasco barked encouragement.

Under Constantine's directives, the flight deck had been transformed into a sanctuary for news crews and reporters covering the conflict on Zorik Minor. Tents and canvas sheets were draped between starfighters and battle mechs with rows of folding beds and cots positioned along the concourse. Journalists hunkered on crates and power racks, laughing and jeering as Chalk stumbled by lap after lap, sweating and wheezing, her eczema in overdrive. Qwork News even ran a story the following rotation: *Earthling Struggles To Stay The Pace.*

Chalk caught Marcy-Kate and Dana Dune laughing with Spirit in the living quarters during the dark rotation as they re-watched the clip on an expanded layer screen. The Revan girls shuffled away, but Spirit assassinated Chalk with her eyes and played the clip again at top volume.

Phase fifteen loomed.

Chalk went to visit Ripley.

His hair was a mess. Clothes several rotations old. The smell near Sagaroach levels. Stacks of tech stretched from floor to ceiling like ominous stalagmites. He hadn't touched them since the incident with the Sevantes.

INFIN-8 rocked in the corner.

BRO—KEN, the droid buzzed, his red lights rotating slowly.

"How are you doing?" Chalk asked, not expecting much.

"Same."

His skin had started to darken but remained deathly thin and weak.

"You look good."

"Clawswoggler."

"Ah, you got me," Chalk told him, attempting a playful smile. "You coming to class tomorrow? Dustenberg will need me to complete another ten thousand layer screens if not. And it's about time you did *me* a favour."

Ripley didn't look convinced.

"You're not still—?"

"No," he said. "I promised you. No more portals. No more polonium."

"I feel bad."

"You too?" Ripley half-joked.

"Not like that. The stuff I said by the portal." She rolled her hands into fists. "I want you to be happy, Ripley, but—"

"You were right," he told her. "Attempting to create a time portal was foolish. And dangerous."

"But?" she said nervously.

"But only if I messed up the calculation."

Chalk gave him a sideways look.

"It's frustrating, that's all," he said, gazing through the bio-glass. "I got us off Zorik Major in one piece. I *know* I can do this."

"But you're *not* going to, right?"

"No," he said. Hair fell over his face. "I'll dismantle the tech when I can. Repurpose it for Esme and Spanners or Commander Lasco. Make them some nice air-filtration conductors or something."

"What about the polonium?"

Ripley glanced at INFIN-8.

"It's safe for now," he said. "Unstable, but safe."

URRRH!

"Look, I can't simply throw it through a temporal doorway as it could kill whoever or whatever is on the other side," he said. "And I'm not particularly welcome on Zorik Pol."

Chalk curled her hair behind her ears. "I've been thinking about the man."

Ripley tightened. "The man?"

"The one who gave you the data drive. The one with the plans for the time portal."

Ripley rested his head against the wall. "He was about fifty, with a hard, battle-worn face like Waxler's. A long scar ran diagonally from brow to chin."

"He didn't say his name?"

"Nope."

"And he didn't want anything in return for the data drive?"

The Revan faltered.

"Ripley!"

He tried to hide behind his hair.

"What did you give him? Not more blood?"

"No."

"What then?"

"Access," the Revan admitted.

Chalk's eyes thinned. "To what?"

"The Galactic Institute."

"Wait. Hang on a minute," Chalk said. "He gave you the time portal information in exchange for a way onto the Coin?"

"Yes."

"But anyone can visit—"

"Secret access. Unmonitored. Unchecked."

"And you just … smuggled him in?"

"I wasn't going to. I thought he was full of it. But I went through all the data and concluded that a time portal was impossibly … possible. I performed some experiments and everything checked out. The equation was complex and fraught with variables, but if I could maintain electron regeneration and algorithmic relativity then it could, it would, work."

Ripley's eyes came to life.

"Equalising the spacetime quantum mechanics took some work. I adapted the software I'd written for the temporal doorway—to allow one hundred per cent manufactured materials—so that it manipulated and reconfigured the equation in real-time. Generating enough energy to develop a thermal runway was the final problem. I theorised with radium, uranium, thorium, even plutonium, but none of them had enough punch."

"Oh Ripley—"

"On the Xenothropod colonies, the man said I'd hit a dead end on energy. He said he knew the solution, but he'd only tell once his feet were on the Coin. I thought I could solve the problem … but I failed. That's when I decided to sneak him in at the end of phase one and found out about Zorik Pol."

"What about the pendant? Did he give you that too?"

"Yes," Ripley said. "Protection against radiation."

Chalk's skin rippled. "Let me see it."

"Why?"

"Just do it."

Ripley pulled the necklace from beneath his shirt. On the end hung a slim silver pendant that tapered to a sharp point. Flecks of purple and green vapour danced along its edge.

"What's inside?"

"He told me not to open it. A reaction to chemicals in the GI atmosphere would render it useless."

Chalk reached for the pendant.

Ripley pulled away.

"Seems … weird."

"What does?"

"Nothing." Chalk sighed. "Get some sleep."

Ripley obliged.

Ripley Flinch was a no-show in Metaphysical Mathematics or Biodiverse Medical Science. Chalk hoped he'd appear for Empirical Mechanics, even though he wasn't officially supposed to be there, but no. If the chance of a mechanical dabble with Commander Lasco couldn't stir Ripley from his bed, what could?

Phase fifteen passed slowly.

Phase sixteen a laborious drag.

Milton joined Chalk in Ripley's room from time to time, but Aida shunned the Revan wholesale. Whenever she tried to coax the Tattorian from her layer screens to spend time with him, she received a curt missive about betrayal and endangerment and lifeforce abuse.

She read to Ripley from *The Hunger Games* in the hope that a tale of survival over adversity would distract him from his own worries. But Katniss and Peeta's plight only seemed to exacerbate his misery. She carried on, visiting her friend, reading her stories, slowly bringing him back to life.

Attendance warnings arrived on Ripley's GI-VR. He swiped them away nonchalantly, insisting his journey at the Galactic Institute was all but over.

"What kind of talk is that?"

"I'm too far behind," he moaned, now out of bed and shuffling across his room like an old man. "If anything, I'd have to start the first cycle again. You and Milton and everyone would move to the second cycle dorms, and I'd be left here with all the newbies."

"Would that be so bad?" Chalk said. "Considering the alternative."

"What alternative?"

"Well, not being here. Going back to Revus X," she said. "I thought you were happy to leave that behind."

"I was. I am," he began. "It's a dead planet. Nothing exciting happens and no one goes anywhere. But everything I love and care for is there. My foster parents, my foster siblings—and every memory of Dante."

"Memories can go with you."

"And some are rooted in the ground," he said, sitting on a large block of complicated-looking tech. "Buried deep in the soil."

"I miss my family too," Chalk admitted. "Mum and Grandpa Milo, my school friends, and … Dad."

Ripley's eyes softened. "You never talk about your father."

"It's … I just—"

She hadn't spoken of the events with her father since her MI5 debrief in the SIS bunkers beneath Whitechapel. Chalk and her mother had both signed non-disclosure agreements that came with severe infringement repercussions.

Ripley had shared every ounce of sadness in his heart.

What jurisdiction did MI5 have on the other side of the SpiralVerse anyway?

"The Hundred Hours War started as a cyber-attack. Every financial, intelligence, and power network was hacked simultaneously. We were taken—me and my father—and held in darkness. In silence. There were threats and demands but, despite the government's policy of non-negotiation with terrorists, I went home. Alone."

"What about your father? Is he—?"

"Dead?" she said, the word numb on her lips. "We don't know. Two cycles have passed and we still don't know."

He pulled her close. "Why didn't you say anything?"

"You have your own problems."

"Hale …"

"My point is, I understand the desire to retreat to a safe place—like a wounded animal—when your world comes crashing down. I spent two years like that, cocooned in my bedroom, taking classes online, losing myself in books and games. But since coming here I've realised I can fight, and survive, and live my life without someone I loved with all my heart." She pulled back and looked at Ripley. "Some days are hard and painful. Others seem impossible. But if I can do it, I know you can too."

Only two phases of lessons and one of revision remained in the first cycle. Phase seventeen began with the excitement and abject horror of the exam schedule. Chalk wondered how complex the exams were going to be, whether they truly meant anything more than a chance for the professors to gauge her progression, or was her commencement into the second cycle utterly dependent on impressive grades?

Aida, of course, had surged ahead and began studying topics from the second and third cycles. Just to be sure. Milton looked at his exam timetable, let out a terrified whimper, and vanished into his room to pore over notes and essays from all sixteen phases in the hope that something stuck.

Unrest between the Veroselli and the Garrangulars festered like an open wound.

Kiln and Kroket loitered in doorways snarling venomously whenever Clementine and Claridge dared to leave their rooms. The monitors in the living quarters played nothing but rolling news of the vicious conflict on Zorik Minor. Orbital footage of air attacks and ground skirmishes covered every inch of the planet. Information packets leaked from the surface. The propaganda and spin war was almost as brutal as the fighting itself.

The news crews on the flight deck grew desperate for a scoop. For a story to steal the viewing figures of the SpiralVerse. They even pestered passing students for opinions, soundbites, rumours, anything they could turn to their advantage. They spliced a fumbled interview with a fourth cycle Garrangular into a vitriolic spew of hate-speech, portrayed Spirit as an advocate for Veroselli extermination—which Chalk watched gleefully on repeat—and made Lord Milton Barclay XVII look like a witless fool bereft of opinion and spine.

In light of increased hostilities, Counsellor Van Wyrm issued a campus-wide curfew. Students were permitted to attend classes but must return to their dormitories immediately afterwards. The Flipside, the observation hall, the arcade, and *Orbit Strike!* arena were off limits. He'd even cancelled the last three matches of the season.

Frustrated and outraged, everyone lived and ate and worked from their rooms.

The Tattorian maintained her Revan embargo so Chalk flitted between study groups with Milton and Aida, then Milton and Ripley. It made their small, closed-in world a lot more complicated, but Chalk could do nothing to change Aida's mind.

History of the Galaxy, now officially under the instruction of Professor Snider, led them through more mind-crushing layer screens about the construction and maintenance of sanitation and hygiene systems during the Ancient Montizoan Empire. Professor Mirage exposed them to the SpiralVerse super texts in Narrative of Story while continuing to infect the class with her political stratagems, dogmas, and anxieties over the Zorik Civil War. Chemical Cosmology and Domestic and Interspecies Languages finished the rotation perfectly, giving Chalk a burning migraine and a desire to eat her body weight in pungent cheddar.

Information from Zorik Minor, no matter how small or inconsequential, was broadcast by the news networks as breaking headlines.

Veroselli Admiral Seen Boarding His Ship!

Garrangulan Army Sit Down To Nine Course Meal!

Tattorian Seer Tells Of A Coming Storm!

Rumours about the Zorik Civil War and the future for the SpiralVerse soared around the dormitories. Most were laughable, some concerning, and others that just might come to pass. Chalk and Ripley were reading from *Harriet Starlight and the Rings of Spacetime* when Milton appeared.

"There's going to be a Reckoning!" he blurted excitedly.

"Like in the Bible?"

"What's a Bible?"

"Doesn't matter."

"It's a fight," Milton explained.

"A showdown," Ripley added. "Winner takes all."

"For what purpose?"

"For the Zorik Civil War," Milton said, shuffling in circles. "Well, perhaps not the *actual* war, but definitely bragging rights here on the Coin."

"Where? When?"

"I don't know," Milton said. "It's a secret."

"Can't be that secretive if *you* know about it."

"I overheard Sadler and Olivia whispering at the drinks dispenser."

"Speculation and rumours," Chalk said. "And from the Vyshan Order, no less."

"I don't think so," Milton said. "The Vyshans do not deal in idle chatter."

"Okay," Ripley said. "Who'd be fighting?"

"Sixth cyclers most likely," Milton said. "Krump and Korg and Klang probably."

"And for the Veroselli?"

"Clandestra. Cystan, maybe. Crinella for sure."

"Brute force versus disciplined finesse."

"I've no idea who would win."

"I guess we'll see soon enough," Ripley said, seeming to enjoy the idea of a pre-arranged scuffle somewhere on the Coin.

"Hasn't there been enough suffering?" Chalk said, snapping *Harriet Starlight* shut and sweeping towards the door. "Cressida gone. Krieg gone. Hundreds, thousands dead on Zorik Minor, and yet some ghastly interspecies brawl has you two more excited than if you'd won tickets to the *Orbit Strike!* tournament finals."

Ripley and Milton bowed their heads.

Their smiles remained.

Chalk huffed irritably and stormed off to her room.

GAPSS
KNOWLEDGE
MAINFRAME

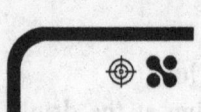 

RECKONING
[CULTURE]

A traditional—and, under GAPSS law, governmentally approved—gladiatorial duel between two or more species, races, or civilisations resulting in victory via contrition or death. Reckonings can involve a single warrior or multiple combatants. Unlike open war, Reckonings are limited to a designated battleground or arena which exacerbates the encounter and brings a swift finality to proceedings.

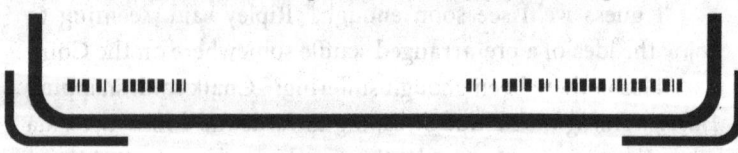

THE DARK ROTATION

Rumours of the Reckoning found Chalk time and again. Milton was convinced he'd overheard Kiln mention the fight while typing an aggressive message to Kroket. Despite her early protestations, Aida admitted that she'd caught whispers of the Reckoning from Veroselli students in line for the food dispenser. Even Lachrymosa teased a watery-eyed grin as she recounted the moment Necrotta boasted about the Reckoning being less than a handful of rotations away.

But phase seventeen came and went and nothing transpired.

Not one fist, claw, or pincer raised in anger.

Chalk settled into phase eighteen and another rotation of Metaphysical Mathematics, Biodiverse Medical Science, and Empirical Mechanics. Opening her notes on a layer screen, Ripley slipped into the seat beside her.

Seeing him out of his room, fully dressed, his face full and healthy, was too much.

"What the hell are you—?" she started. "What I mean is, welcome to class. It's about time you started using that big brain of yours."

"I'll take that as a compliment."

Professor Dustenberg shambled into the room. "Quiet please."

"Listen," Ripley whispered. "I need to apologise—"

"Is that so?"

"—and say a huge thank you for all you've done. Seriously

Hale, I don't know what I would have done without you."

"Been expelled. Or killed. Or annihilated everyone on the Coin," she told him, opening *Calculating Chaos and Decimalising Dimensions* at Dustenberg's request.

"True," he nodded. "I wanted you to know I appreciate everything. Looking after me when I had less blood in me than a starving Sagaflea, reading me those amazing stories—*Armada Cadavar!*—and handling all the administration stuff."

He smiled as he spoke. Purple eyes sparkled.

"Thank you," she said, blushing. "And if you're planning on using the killing curse properly—which I strongly advise against—it's pronounced *Avada Kedavra!*"

"You had no reason to do any of that after all the trouble I caused."

Chalk let it sink in. He was right. It was a lot.

"It's way more than most people have ever done for me."

"Well," she said. "I suppose I like you more than most people."

Ripley grinned. For a flicker, he looked like his old self.

"It's good to have you back."

"It's good to be back," he replied. "I'm ready."

"For what?"

"Anything."

Phase eighteen evaporated in a whirl of late-night study sessions, eye-straining essay writing, and monolithic stacks of triple cheese pizza. Returning from her last Conflict Engagement class in rotation ten, where Chalk and Ripley had come second in a Garrangulan hellrazor disc-throwing competition behind Kroket and Kiln, she treated herself to a long, hot shower—eczema be damned—happy in the knowledge that first cycle classes were finally done.

Just one phase of revision to go.

Then exams.

Chalk daydreamed of the moment the entire cycle would be done—classes, revision, exams, the lot. She hoped the portal embargo would be lifted and she could return to Earth. There was so much to tell her mother, plenty more to share with Kit, and Bloue, and Zara, and an entire cycle of hugs to give Grandpa Milo.

And, who knows, perhaps news of her father would be waiting on her return.

Her mind switched from revision to the disappearance of Cressida and Krieg. Ripley had derailed the investigation into her missing classmates. But no matter what way she sliced it, she couldn't formulate a plausible solution—or even a wild, untethered theory—that added up.

Growing restless, she did a quick lap of the landing. She peered into Milton's room but the Sagaroach wasn't home. Chancellor Van Wyrm's curfew remained in effect so he couldn't have gone far. She found him alone in Ripley's room, loading his St4rCr4ft™ 85R with the last of the Revan's bulky tech.

"Hey," she said. "What's going on?"

"Just helping Ripley transport all this stuff to the flight deck."

"Out of sight, out of mind," Chalk said, nodding. "Do you think this is the—?"

Milton looked around. "Time travel tech?" he said. "Probably. Although, this isn't my speciality."

"No," she said. "Perplexingly, crystals are your thing."

"That's right," he said. "Always been fascinated by them."

Chalk drummed her bottom lip. "Zorikanthium, right?"

"Well, sure," Milton said. "That is a crystal."

"But it's the one that gets the Roses' and Grangs' blood boiling."

"In theory," he said. "Never been proven."

"And you don't have any zorikanthium on you?"

Milton stopped loading his eduhelper. "What are you implying?"

Chalk shook herself. "Sorry, Milton. Forgive me. The mystery of our missing classmates is still driving me nuts."

"Not this again," the Sagaroach grumbled, returning to his task. "Aida and I had hoped you'd let it go."

"With Ripley back to full operating status," she said, half-seriously, "I need something else to obsess over."

"Obsess over your grades or *Orbit Strike!* match statistics or Harriet Starlight," Milton said impatiently. "Just leave the Roses and Grangs alone."

Chalk buried herself in a late-night session of particularly mind-bending layer screens on kinetic kaleidoscopathy. Exhausted, she wrapped herself in the duvet and dimmed the window. But the harder she tried to sleep, the quicker she returned to the abductions.

She couldn't shake it.

It was too close to home.

Somebody has brought zorikanthium onto the Coin—

She rolled her mother's fountain pen on her palm.

—removed Cressida and Krieg—

Light from the Waterfall Nebula flickered off the green pen.

—with the purpose of reigniting the Zorik Wars—

Chalk tapped the lid against her lip.

—and laid the blame at Waxler's door.

Her skin crawled. Dark memories circled.

Was it GAPSS? Another professor? A corrupted droid? One of her classmates? Even Constantine Van Wyrm himself?

The pen fell onto the bed.

The man.

Chalk's hand went to her throat.

The pendant.

Whispered words and urgent feet spilled from the landing. Half-dressed, Chalk swooshed her door open. Despite being the middle of the night, everyone swarmed for the living quarters. Chalk pulled her trousers on and followed, peppering Marcy-Kate and Rani Romesh with questions.

"Not sure," Rani replied. "Something to do with the Veroselli."

"And the Garrangulars," Marcy-Kate added.

"I heard it was the Reckoning," said Spirit, storming past to catch up with Clementine and Claridge. The Vyshan Order were first into the AGT—their thick, red robes billowed menacingly—Necrotta and Ironlung 8-47 close on their heels.

"What is happening?"

"It's the fight, isn't it?" said Milton, pulling up beside the embarkation pod. "The Reckoning!"

"The Coin is at its quietest," Aida said.

"The whole place shut down," Milton added.

"The dark rotation."

"Perfect time to sneak about unnoticed," Spirit said spitefully, directing her words in Chalk's direction.

"What about the curfew?" Dana Dune said, stepping onto the embarkation pod. "Enforcers will be on us in no time."

"Up to you," snarled Necrotta. "With every *Orbit Strike!* match cancelled, I'm not about to miss the chance to see some action!"

Pressurised wind ruffled Chalk's hair. Everyone else had made their choice and now, only she, Aida and Milton remained.

"Where's Ripley?"

"I buzzed for him," Milton said. "No answer."

"I need to speak to him."

"You could message him."

Chalk grumbled. "Gods below, I'm such a bonehead."

CHALK: Where are you?

CHALK: I think I know who took them.

CHALK: Ripley? Please.

"If we're going, we need to go now or we'll lose them," Milton urged. "I'm sure Ripley will find his way there."

A trail of Aktari students from all six cycles swooshed around the hyperloop. Chalk wondered where the eldest Veroselli and Garrangulars would lead them. The observation hall, the Flipside, or the Casting citadel itself? But half a dozen sixth cycle students suddenly twisted, robes billowing in the pressurised air, making for the flight deck.

Chalk zoomed behind.

Gossip and rumour and speculation tumbled against the sides of the AGT.

Dozens of students spilled out onto the dimly lit flight deck. Shadows of battle mechs and starfighters ribboned the treadplate. Slowly blinking amber landing lights stretched end to end. Students ran for the launch bay and the propellosphere beyond.

Veroselli formed up on the left.

Garrangulars on the right.

A melee of Aktari students from every cycle swarmed between them, creating a crescent of waving arms and raucous barks that echoed through the vaulted space. Chalk wondered why they'd chosen to hold the Reckoning here, in this enormous, cacophonous room. It wouldn't take long for someone to hear the noise and raise the alarm.

And then, as Pristina tore past, wheezing into her poisoned-breath regulator, and Vitarus trundled by in his watery orb, it dawned on her.

Ahead, fighting their way through the growing crowds, were news crews and reporters from every system in the SpiralVerse. Shaken from their beds, they pushed cameras and microphones to the front of the sprawling mass.

Chalk, Aida, and Milton scurried down the flight deck. The noise of the imminent battle grew with every footstep. Necrotta and Ironlung 8-47 were knitted between rows of angry-looking Garrangulars. War cries and tribal songs blared. The Revans and the Genks and the Vyshan Order stood with the Veroselli. A sense of inner calm radiated from each of the tall, elegant creatures.

Chalk found herself shoulder to shoulder with a tentacled octopod operating three cameras and pointing halofire lamps at a pretty Genkanese reporter.

"You join us here," the woman began, her eyes zeroed towards the cameras, "on the flight deck of Centurion H, the Galactic Institute, where students have taken it upon themselves to decide the Zorik Civil War once and for all!" The octopod raised one of the cameras, spanning the flight deck. "From what we can tell, Veroselli and Garrangulars will choose three champions to represent them in this Zorikian tradition—a Reckoning! A battle to the death!"

Other news crews seemed to be relaying similar information.

Were the Veroselli and the Garrangulars really going to fight and kill one another here, on the flight deck, in front of the news cameras of the SpiralVerse? It seemed impossibly barbaric that such a thing could be broadcast to the entire galaxy.

She certainly wouldn't expect to see anything like that on the BBC.

Even Netflix would have reason for pause.

Chalk stumbled away from the angry, feverous crowd. Where were the Enforcers? Where was Counsellor Van Wyrm? And Commander Lasco and Cozy for that matter? There was no way they couldn't hear this racket from the workshop.

But no one came.

Chalk found it impossible to think the violence sensors that had been so ruthlessly effective over the last eighteen phases had failed to detect this disturbance. And what about the counsellor's additional cameras and sensors and biometric readouts? It was laughable that they could miss an outbreak of these proportions.

Unless—

No. She couldn't think it. Wouldn't think it.

But the idea kept hammering on the door until she flipped the bolts and let it in.

—someone had turned them off!

She spun in circles, scanning every face in the crowd.

CHALK: *Ripley Flinch. Where ARE you?*

GAPSS
KNOWLEDGE
MAINFRAME

PROPELLOSPHERE
[TECHNOLOGY]

Constructed using iridian stones, propellospheres are
positioned at the mouth of all GAPSS flight decks and
landing ports to repel unauthorised spacecraft, galactic
detritus, and anomalies. Iridian stones, found in the oceanic
trenches of Predoria, generate a matrix of powerful energy
when positioned in close proximity. Anything entering
the matrix—that does not resonate with an iridian
spectographic signature—is crushed and ejected. The first
propellosphere was conceptualised, built, and tested by
Horax Lemaître [deceased].

DOUBLE EXPOSURE

Chalk stomped along the edge of the baying mob that swelled and shook like a monstrous beast. She searched desperately for Ripley's face, but interlocked arms of Veroselli and Genks, Garrangulars and Zillamoths, Montizoans, Pyramists, Karmethians and Revans blocked her view.

She whirled away, running towards Lasco's workshop. The commander was asleep on his rack, dead to the world, two bottles of *Wimbam's Finest Retrograde* discarded on the floor.

"Cozy," Chalk whispered. Then more loudly, "COZY! Where are you?" The nervous Qwork's trunk emerged from a wardrobe. Her huge ears lay flat to her head, eyes filled with fright. "What happened?"

"M-man came," Cozy replied. "Left h-h-hooch."

"A man?" Chalk's mind whirred. "What man? Counsellor Van Wyrm? Professor Snider? Master ... Flinch?"

"No, no, no," the frightened Qwork said. "Mechanical m-man."

"An eduhelper?" Chalk said. "One of the Garrangulars?"

"No." Cozy's head shook. Her trunk coiled in knots.

"Not ... INFIN-8?"

"M-mechanical man. B-big and mean."

Chalk couldn't believe what she was about to say.

"The C1000? Cressida's eduhelper?"

"Yes, yes, yes," the Qwork squeaked. "Mechan-n-nical man poisons H-hank. Get help. Get help n-n-now!" Cozy's whiskers quivered like a Sagamoth's wing as she retreated into the safety of the wardrobe.

"It's okay," Chalk said gently. "I'll find someone. Don't worry. The commander will be okay."

"Thank y-y-you, Miss Hale," Cozy quivered. "H-h-hurry."

Chalk burst onto the flight deck. The colossal room rang with the clamour of fists and feet pounding in ominous, tribal rhythms.

And still no one came.

The sensors dead.

Chalk had to find someone, warn someone, do something before the Reckoning got dangerously out of control. She couldn't imagine the leaders of Earth sending their best boxers or MMA fighters to settle border disputes, and trade deals, and holy wars.

She darted through a maze of battle mechs and retired starfighters. Once in the open, Aida and Milton came flying towards her, their faces stricken with panic.

"Seriously, what is happening?"

Amber lights pulsed beneath Chalk's feet.

Her head swam.

"It's the Reckoning."

"Thank you for your keen observation," Aida chided.

"There's … something else."

The Tattorian's visor tilted slowly. "I worry to ask."

Chalk took a breath. "Ripley—"

"And there it is."

"—smuggled someone onto the Coin."

"Smuggled?"

"Someone?"

"Who?"

"I don't know. He doesn't know."

"Loras' Whisper! Why would he do such a thing?"

"It was a trade," Chalk withered. "Secret passage onto the Coin in exchange for—"

"I have a bad feeling about this."

"—the power solution to his time travel device."

"Time travel is impossible," snorted Aida. "Laughable, in fact."

"What kind of person is brought onto the Coin in secret?" Milton asked. "They could have come as a day visitor."

"The kind of person who wants to hide in the shadows, kidnap students, evict a headmistress, and start a civil war!"

INAPPROPRIATE LANGUAGE DETECTED . . .

"How did you not connect this sooner?" Aida asked, foot tapping.

Chalk's mouth hung open. "Well, excuse me. My head was—"

"Yes, we know exactly where your head was!"

Milton choked on his yuccagourd.

"Not *there*, Milton!" both girls wailed.

Chalk wrung her hands. "This is *not* my fault!"

"Where is that Revan?"

Chalk checked her GI-VR.

Nothing.

Roars and screams detonated inside the Reckoning.

"Erm … Chalk?"

"What is it, Milton?"

"You know St4rCr4ft™ 85R and I transported all Ripley's tech to the flight deck—"

"Yes."

"—so Commander Lasco could decommission it—"

"Uh-huh."

"—so Ripley wouldn't have a constant reminder of—"

"Get on with it!"

The Sagaroach pointed away from the Reckoning and straight at the SpiralVerse military museum. "Well … most of it is missing."

Chalk spun. A handful of dark shapes loomed in the mouth of the portal chamber.

"Where's the rest?"

"I dunno."

"And where in Thoden's name is—?"

Beyond the massive arch that linked the flight deck to the museum, a flurry of white-gold sparks rained onto the smooth floor. Terror filled Chalk from head to toe.

No. It can't be. He wouldn't.

She erupted, running pell-mell, legs buckling as emotions spiralled out of control.

Love is like a gas giant, Harriet Starlight began.

"Now is not the time," Chalk snapped.

The thud of her Converse on the treadplate reverberated through her bones.

Cube bounced awkwardly on her shoulders.

The sensors haven't been turned off for the Reckoning.

Aida and Milton charged after her.

They've been turned off for something else entirely.

She passed the outskirts of the news camp, tore between Gamma Ray's Grill and the portal chamber where scuffed tracks and dents led away from the remnants of Ripley's tech.

The Reckoning was a distraction!

Inside the museum, golden rain illuminated shadowy halls.

Chalk knew what she was about to see, but hoped with all her heart to be mistaken, and wrong, and false. But there, suspended at the base of the giant mobile of starfighters and interstellar spacecraft, hung the worldgate. And upon it, his face concealed by a welding visor, spun Ripley Flinch.

Chalk slowed to a walk.

Sparks danced.

"You promised me!" she screamed.

Ripley glanced down, the visor alive with golden fire. His hair shimmered as the worldgate rotated in slow, purposeful arcs. Positioned at two o'clock, where several pieces of the device had been missing, were blocks of Ripley's repurposed tech. He clambered higher and slotted two cables into empty ports, running a third to fibre-optic elements housed in the worldgate's massive superstructure. As the filaments connected, the worldgate bloomed with glorious amber light, creating gigantic shifting shadows.

Ripley launched himself off the worldgate and landed on the museum walkway, knees bent to the ground like a superhero.

Heat flooded Chalk's face.

Thunderous anger pricked her tongue.

"You promised," she said again, now a whisper, venom and rage restrained with everything she had.

"I know. And I'm sorry," Ripley told her, stopping just out of punching distance. "It's ... unfortunate."

"Unfortunate?"

"I tried to protect you from this. Tried to keep you away. But you kept coming. Undeterred, unrelenting."

"I prefer *determined*," Chalk told him. "You should have said something."

"And what would I have said?" he replied. "I care for you, Hale, more than you know, more than I could ever truly express ... but I *love* my brother more."

Chalk wanted the universe to eradicate her from existence.

"Never trust a Revan," spat Aida, arriving at Chalk's side. "Nothing but crooks and thieves, descendants of the damned!"

"Ripley?" came Milton's voice, small and hollow. "What have you done?"

The Revan moved closer. His plasma-oil-coated fingers gripped Chalk's shoulders. The familiar smell of him bloomed in her nostrils. "When we arrived at the Galactic Institute, I was in free fall and you were finding your feet," he told her. "There was a moment in the middle. A glorious, perfect moment when our lives were aligned. You going up. Me coming down."

"The Shield of Zorik."

"No matter what happens next, we'll always have that."

He opened a layer screen and entered a code. Frowning, he tapped again. "What in Thoden's name—?"

A haunting cry erupted from the other end of the flight deck.

"What is happening?"

"Something's wrong," Ripley bleated.

"Too right something's wrong," Chalk told him.

Ripley opened a dozen layer screens, each filled with hundreds of lines of complex code. "No. No! NO!"

"Ripley? You're scaring me."

"I was meticulous. I was perfect. I checked and checked. Dozens of times. Hundreds of times! This *must* be right. This *is* right. I cannot be wrong! That's impossible."

Veroselli screamed and Garrangulars roared as the Reckoning looked set to explode.

"What are you talking about?" Chalk bellowed.

"The worldgate."

"But it's a fake, a replica. Nothing more."

"No," Ripley said, his eyes flickering with golden light. "It's real."

The huge device spun above their heads.

"Who told you that?" Chalk said. "The man you smuggled onto the Coin?"

"Yes."

"And what exactly happened to him once he arrived and fed you all his secrets?"

"I don't know. He disappeared. Never saw him again."

"Ripley. I think he's responsible for everything that's been happening. Cressida and Krieg, General Waxler, and the Zorik Civil War!"

Ripley stared disbelievingly at his layer screens.

"Who is he?"

"Who?"

"The man!"

A new voice rumbled through the shadows. "He ... is me!"

Through glowing amber light strode a humanoid figure. Dark blue panels covered its entire body. Orange light shone through joints and angular facial features. It approached one of Ripley's control desks where thick cables and tubing looped from the walkway to the base of the worldgate like the stems of a flower.

"Hey," Ripley cried. "Get away from there!"

INFIN-8 loitered behind the Revan, red lights spinning.

But the figure flicked several buttons. Twisted a handful of dials. Steam hissed from each segment of the worldgate as its amber light grew full and strong.

"You?" Chalk said, her fingers reaching through the smoke. "But you're a—?"

"A what?" the figure said, turning to look at her. "A droid? An eduhelper?"

"A machine."

"Careful. Those sorts of words could hurt my feelings," it said. "How did you feel when they called you Mudder, or Human Garbage, or Earthling?"

"Get away from my equipment," Ripley yelled. "It's delicate."

"More lies," Chalk said, pushing Ripley. "You said it was a man, not a machine!"

"It was a man," Ripley insisted. "I don't know who or what *this* is."

"It's Cressida's eduhelper!"

"It cannot be," Aida said. "Positronic directives negate all eduhelpers from hurting or betraying any living thing. If anything, they'll sacrifice themselves to circumvent a life-threatening occurrence."

"Then what in the blazes is it?"

The C1000 entered a passcode on its chest. Chalk looked at the worldgate, half expecting a temporal doorway to develop and the C1000 to launch itself through in a bid for freedom. But the droid remained rooted to the spot. Panels on its head retracted, folded into one another, and disappeared into the shoulder mountings.

Chalk's breath caught in her throat.

URRRH! URRRH! URRRH!

"You see," it said. "I'm not an eduhelper, not the spiteful princess's C1000 at all. Although this battle suit is virtually identical."

Behind the droid's endoskeletal panels was a face. A man's face. Battle-worn and greying at the temples. A long scar ran diagonally from brow to chin.

"See?" Ripley said.

"Cressida's *machine* is safely stowed. Just like the Veroselli princess and that surly Garrangular."

"I know you," Chalk said.

"Impossible."

Her mind reeled. Memories danced into view. She swivelled to the displays and holograms around the museum and took three purposeful steps towards the Battle of Lost Shadows. A hologram appeared in a grey, fitted suit and beige padded tunic, a sky-blue helmet with a yellow visor in his hands.

"For death and glory and the SpiralVerse! That was the last thing I ever said," the hologram told her. "Hello. I'm Captain Dak Einhorn. Stingray Squadron second in command, *Yazanti* champion three years running, and—"

Chalk turned to look at the older man in the shiny battle suit.

"It *is* you!"

Amazement and confusion boiled inside.

"You sound surprised," said Captain Einhorn, inspecting his hologram.

Chalk looked at Ripley. "But he's dead!" She turned to the captain. "You're dead. Your hologram just told us that 'For death and glory and the SpiralVerse!' were the *last* words you ever spoke."

"GAPSS propaganda."

"Did you really fight under General Waxler?" she asked.

"Yes," Einhorn said, smiling grimly.

"And this was all about her, wasn't it?"

"Not in the way you think."

A growl rose in Chalk's throat. Her hands balled into fists. Einhorn laughed wickedly. "You're no match for me, Earthling. Even without this battle suit, I could break every one of your fragile bones as if they were twigs."

Chalk launched herself at him, but Ripley grabbed Cube's straps.

Around the worldgate, amber lights morphed into glorious white. "You've done a fantastic job," Einhorn said, nodding at the huge device. "I doubt there's another soul on the Coin—nay, the SpiralVerse—who would have retrieved all the missing tech, repurposed it, and traded their own blood for the polonium needed to power the Gods-damn thing." His thick grey eyebrows rose in wonder. "You're quite the mark, Master Flinch."

"You traded your blood?" Aida exploded. "That is exceptionally irresponsible!"

"And you think *I'm* the disgusting one," Milton hissed.

"Mark?" Ripley said, brow furrowed.

Einhorn laughed, deep and malicious. "Mark, target, stooge. Call it what you will."

"What did you do?"

"I needed access to the Coin, to that vile princess and her Garrangulan counterpart. Once they were out of the picture it was only a matter of time before Zorik Minor fell into chaos and GAPSS levelled the blame at Gertrude's door."

"Gertrude?" said Milton.

"General Waxler!"

"Of course," Einhorn said. "You're all fans. You're all Team Waxler. I don't blame you. I was smitten myself."

"Something happened at the Battle of Lost Shadows," Chalk said. "Something Commander Lasco wouldn't discuss."

"Hank Lasco is a coward and a deserter," Einhorn spat. "He turned tail and ran the moment things got hairy. We'd lost half the squadron before the worldgate even appeared on our scanners." Captain Einhorn looked lost in the memory. "She ordered us through," he said, pointing at the worldgate. "But your beloved Waxler didn't fly with us," he said, his eyes filled with a dark sadness. "I looked for her as I barrel-rolled through. Into the hell waiting beyond. The rest of the squadron fell, consumed and vaporised in a heartbeat, but I managed to drag the eye of Miasma deep into that chaos dimension. I looped around. Almost out. Almost clear of the monster. Of her diabolical words. Almost free. And then, I saw her. *Waxler*. She opened fire. Destroyed the worldgate. Trapped me inside!"

Sparks erupted from the worldgate.

"But you're alive," Milton said, shielding his eyes.

"Clearly top of the class," Dak scoffed. "I was trained to survive. Whatever it took. You have no idea the despair and turmoil I have endured." His nose wrinkled with defiance. "Waxler is in StasisStation10, where she belongs, and I'm here … at the end of all things!"

He opened the panel on his chest and punched in another code.

Amber lights turned blue.

A temporal doorway attempted to form. But this doorway was not created of serene black ripples. A chaotic wave of iridescent light formed and reformed in erratic bursts across the expanse, while bolts of charged energy spiked the museum walls.

"What are you doing?" Ripley said, striding forward. "That's set for my brother!"

"Your brother?" Einhorn said. "You think the worldgate is going to send you back to that cafeteria on Revus X and stop the bombs from going off?"

Ripley froze.

"What was it he was having … poached kritten tail, right?"

"How do you—?"

Captain Dak Einhorn smiled wickedly.

"No," Ripley seethed. "It was you? YOU?"

Ripley hammered his fists against Einhorn but they bounced

off the battle suit without leaving a scratch. The captain tossed the Revan aside. INFIN-8's red lights flashed angrily.

"I needed you motivated," Einhorn said, placing a mechanical boot on the Revan's chest. Ripley's lips quivered, searching for words that never came. "Nothing drives ambition harder than the chance to save a loved one … or avenge a betrayal."

"Does the worldgate even—?"

"Time travel?" Einhorn grunted. "Impossible."

"I told you." Aida snorted, folding her arms. "But did you listen?"

The fight seemed to leave the Revan. "I'm sorry," he whispered. "Ripley … I've failed you."

"What?" Chalk said, dropping beside him.

"He is in shock," added Aida. "Delirium will follow."

"Ripley," the Revan muttered. "I'm so sorry."

"You mean … Dante?" Chalk urged. "You're Ripley … aren't you?"

He looked her dead in the eyes.

And shook his head.

GAPSS
KNOWLEDGE
MAINFRAME

ZILLAMOTHS
[SPECIES]
Homeworld: Tyros, Lang. Krackeragnian

Descendants of prehistoric birds and lizards, Zillamoths inhabit a fractured, dystopian society where the powerful dominate and the weak perish. However, a small percentage of their number live and worship under a secret religion where benevolence and passion for academia and the arts are held in high regard. Despite this group standing apart from their deadly cousins, Zillamoths must never be underestimated, for they are a species designed, built, and bred for violence.

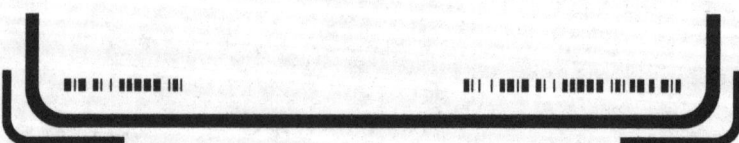

ARRIVAL

Sub-space soundwaves shook the museum. Monitors and panels tumbled from the walls. Amber sparks fell from the worldgate onto the walkway a dozen metres below.

Captain Dan Einhorn strode away.

Chalk's head pounded. Her senses choked. The Coin seemed to shift under her feet. She stared at the Revan, who was crying uncontrollably, his head in her lap.

"He killed my brother. He killed Ripley Flinch."

"What in all that is holy is happening?"

Milton pushed two yuccagourds into his mouth, presumably to stop himself saying something impossibly insensitive, and grabbed the rail for support.

"I didn't land a seat at the Galactic Institute," the Revan told her. "My brother did."

"Your brother—?"

"Ripley Flinch."

The words found Chalk's brain but their meaning floated out of reach.

"So … that makes you—?"

"Dante Flinch."

Everyone took a moment.

The threads of Chalk's universe began to unravel.

"We both applied to the Galactic Institute," he explained. "But I didn't get in. Attitude and mental instability apparently."

"Seems they were onto something."

"Now is not the time, Aidriendretta!"

"So, I pretended to be my brother, enrolling at the Galactic Institute and taking all the classes he loved, hoping to live his dream for both of us."

Einhorn snickered darkly, adjusting levers on the control panel.

Ripley wiped his eyes and pulled the pendant from beneath his shirt. "And what's this? Another lie?"

Dak Einhorn didn't answer.

"What are you doing with that?" Milton asked in alarm.

Chunks of museum wall careened past them and shattered on the ground.

"It's a protection amulet," he replied. "Isn't it?"

Milton swallowed a mouthful of putrefied sludge. "Well, there's purple and green vapour coming off it—"

"So?"

"—because it's filled with zorikanthium," Chalk finished.

"Zorikanthi-what?"

"The Crystal of Shadows!"

INAPPROPRIATE LANGUAGE DETECTED . . .

The Sagaroach studied the flight deck. "You have to get rid of it!"

"Do as you will," Einhorn yelled. "The Crystal of Shadows has done its work!"

A blue square appeared on the captain's digital readout. He slammed a thumb against it. Darkness swallowed the museum. The worldgate fizzed with spikes of brilliant light before a formidable aftershock bowled everyone over. Chalk curled into a ball, slid across the smooth floor, and clattered against broken display cabinets.

Ripley struggled to his feet. He ripped the pendant from his neck and stamped on it furiously. The silver case fractured and snapped but the crystal remained whole. The black vapour inside the Crystal of Shadows swarmed in undulating curls, hypnotic and menacing.

"You cannot destroy it like that," Milton yelled. "It's zorikanthium!"

"I don't know what that means!"

"Didn't you take Chemical Cosmology?"

"Yes ... but—"

"If rumours are to be believed, you need to get it away from the Veroselli and the Garrangulars."

"How far away?"

"Far, far away!"

"The other side of the Coin? The Flipside? Where?"

"Well, yes," Milton said. "But, ideally, take it back to Zorik Major or fire it out an airlock or hurl it into a black hole."

Chalk gazed towards the Reckoning. "The launch bay!"

"What about it?"

"The propellosphere," she said, scrambling to her feet. "The iridian stones."

The worldgate groaned.

Einhorn's temporal doorway expanded like an elongated water balloon, precarious and unstable. Violently, it snapped back into place. The museum shuddered. Chalk dragged Ripley to his feet and stifled a scream as an enormous black tentacle breached the temporal doorway and swept around the room. It swished viciously through the air, then faded, flickering in and out of existence like a ghost. The tentacle became a slender arm with clawing fingernails, a thunderous vine with razor-sharp thorns, a tumbling column of thick, poisonous vapour. Returning to its original form and oozing with purple slime, it slammed left and right, destroying museum displays and tumbling starfighters end over end.

Commander Xander Xenon's Red Thorn landed beside the Revan. The tip of its wing clattered against the Revan's head, sending him to the ground.

INFIN-8 let out a sorrowful *URRRH!*

The tentacle came hurtling round the room, spinning inside the worldgate like a fairground ride. Chalk glimpsed Aida and

Milton strewn along the walkway, their bodies motionless, half buried in rubble and dust.

"At last! My Queen has arrived," Einhorn bellowed, firing up his Zenith PowerDread TX shoulder-mounted jetpack. He rocketed into the air, buzzing like a hungry Sagafly. "Finally, Miasma is here!"

Ripley lay unconscious, the Crystal of Shadows in his outstretched hand. Chalk grabbed it, heaved the Revan onto her shoulder and moved as best she could down the walkway. She glanced back. Searching for Captain Einhorn. He buzzed from one control panel to the next, adjusting the settings, while deftly avoiding Miasma's monstrous attacks.

Chalk's boots crunched on shattered glass. She zigzagged through fallen starfighters and out of the museum. Adrenaline carried her towards the launch bay, the blood-crazed ensemble, and the propellosphere beyond.

She staggered under Ripley's weight as students from Osmotrino, Zalazor, and Qantoculus poured from the AGT and sprinted, lumbered, floated, and slithered across the flight deck. Her legs pumped like pistons. Her fingers coiled tightly around the Revan and the Crystal of Shadows.

"This is all your clawswoggling boneheaded fault!"

Ripley grumbled something incomprehensible.

INFIN-8 ran beside them.

TEAR—REE—FIED!

Sure, Ripley had been sold on a lie, his life destroyed, his emotions manipulated beyond their limits, but he'd broken every Galactic Institute rule and regulation, risked his own life on numerous occasions, and lied to the people he professed to value the most. And all for his brother, for Dante—no, for Ripley!

Chalk roared with anger, shaking her head as she ran and ran and ran.

The Reckoning had escalated, spreading like a virus. There were twenty or more deep at every point. Chalk tried to peek through, but students were knitted tightly, disinterested in relinquishing their vantage point to anyone, much less an Earthling.

She estimated that the yellow warning lines of the propellosphere were more than fifty metres away. Could she hurl the Crystal of Shadows that far? Maybe, but if she failed, she'd leave it right under the noses of the Veroselli and Garrangulars.

"Now what?"

"You need a way through," Cube said, which made Chalk jump as she'd almost forgotten she had the eduhelper strapped to her back, "or a means of launching the zorikanthium into the propellosphere."

Nervous energy overwhelmed her. Terror burned in her chest. She was revved up to one hundred with deadlock brakes securely fastened. "Any ideas?"

CALCULATING . . .

There must be something she could use. There had to be a way to break the lines and forge a path to the propellosphere. "There," she said, hauling Ripley between two rows of retired ships. She slid to a halt at the foot of a battle mech, cradled the Revan's head, and looked into his swimming eyes.

"I need your help," she pleaded. "Ripley. Please."

Nothing.

"DANTE FLINCH!" she barked and struck him hard across the face.

Ripley straightened, hands raised to defend himself.

"What the hell was that for?"

"A million things ... but right now I need *this*." Chalk kicked the enormous foot beside them. It chimed with a hollow *clang!*

"A Gigantor battle mech?"

"We need to break through the Reckoning and hurl the Crystal of Shadows into the propellosphere!"

"Is that all?"

"This'll do it, right?"

"All the battle mechs are broken, Hale," he hissed, dabbing his head wound. "Redundant. Dead."

"Well … fix them!"

"How?"

"I don't know," she said. "You're the Empirical Mechanics wizard!"

Ripley looked beaten.

"Look, the Roses and Grangs are going to murder one another any moment and I can only presume that Miasma has a mind to consume the rest of us!"

"Miasma—?"

"The fluctuating monstrosity that's trying to burst through your worldgate!"

Ripley winced. Panic swirled in his eyes. "Okay, I'll try!"

"Do or do not. There is no try!"

He ripped panels open on the legs of the battle mech and stared into the mass of dirt-encrusted circuit boards, propellent pistons, and cables. "This'll never work in time—"

"Yes, it will," Chalk told him. "It has to. For all our sakes!"

"Who's going to drive it? You?"

"You bet I could!" she paused. "But … no."

"Then who?"

"Keep working!"

"Where are you going?"

"To fetch a war hero!"

Chalk rocketed into Hank K. Lasco's personal quarters for the second time that night. Cozy hopped from one foot to the other at the end of the commander's rack.

His eyes cracked open, pallid and bloodshot. "What in the blazing solar winds is going on out there?"

"The Veroselli and the Garrangulars have incited a Reckoning—"

"A death fight?"

"—and Captain Einhorn has tricked Ripley—possibly Dante—into building a worldgate to bring Miasma back from—"

"Hang on," he said, cradling his head with both hands. "Dak Einhorn is alive?"

"It would appear so."

"But he was lost in a chaos dimension with the rest of the squadron."

"You *were* there."

"Not at the end," the commander admitted sorrowfully.

"Einhorn said you ran."

"Wouldn't you?"

"Then it's time for redemption!" she said, dangling the Crystal of Shadows before him.

"Zorikanthium!" Lasco said, squirming away. "What in the nine rings of Zantia are you doing with that?"

"No time to explain," she bleated. "We need to get rid of it."

"Too right you do," Lasco said. "That stuff'll have the Veroselli and the Garrangulars ripping each other ... oh, I see."

"Ripley is jump-starting a battle mech, but I need you to pilot it through the masses and jettison the crystal through the propellosphere while I go and deal with Miasma."

"Okay, fine," he said, then stopped. "Sorry? Miasma? That cannot be right. You *have* to be mistaken."

"No mistake. Although she keeps changing, fading in and out."

"Sounds like an unstable worldgate," Lasco said. "She's struggling to materialise on this side. You must deactivate it immediately!"

"No kidding. But what about the Reckoning?"

"I'd be more concerned about one of the Dark Trinity returning to this dimension than a flight deck scuffle between a handful of students!"

"What are you suggesting?" Chalk wailed. "We're going to save them all." She kicked both bottles of *Wimbam's Finest*

Retrograde under the bed and threw a high-collared jacket at him. "I hope you're fit for duty, Commander."

Outside, Ripley hung from the spine of the battle mech, tearing out defunct cables and rewiring the central cortex system.

"How's it looking?" Chalk asked.

"She'll walk," he said, pulling himself into the cockpit and punching a dozen buttons. "But she needs power. Can you bring my surplus power cells from the portal chamber?"

"But aren't they charged with … polonium?"

"Yes, yes," he barked. "It's all we've got."

"Are they compatible?"

INFIN-8 emerged from the tech stacks holding a coil of wires.

"Take INFIN-8," he said. "And hurry up."

URRRH! he buzzed, dropping the wires.

"Come on," Chalk said. "Looks like you'll be saving my life … again."

BING! Green lights flashed. *BING! BING!*

Only two power cells remained among Ripley's tech. She placed them inside INFIN-8 and glanced at the massive archway to the museum. A dozen arms with curved, blackened fingernails pushed through the worldgate, carving deep trenches in the plaster.

Sparks of electricity cut through the threatening dark.

Aida and Milton were in there somewhere, cloaked in the shadows, hidden, buried.

Was Commander Lasco right? Should she risk the lives of the Veroselli and the Garrangulars and turn the battle mech on Captain Einhorn and Miasma?

We need help. We need warriors. Casters.

URRRH! INFIN-8 bleated. *URRRH! URRRH!*

"Yes, yes, yes," she said, pushing his lid shut and hammering her feet into the treadplate. "Let's get the snag out of here."

At the battle mech, Ripley connected the last of the cables

while bypassing the weapons and security systems.

INFIN-8 skidded into Commander Lasco who slotted the power cells into the heel of the battle mech. Chalk snapped the panel shut. "She's good to go!"

The commander gave Ripley a nervy salute and slid on a white battle-damaged helmet splashed with chevrons in red and gold.

Lasco swallowed hard. His hand circled his belly. "I feel terrible."

"Well, none of us are going to feel anything for all eternity if you don't get a move on!"

Lasco's eyes rolled into his head. He stumbled and collapsed over a pile of empty crates. Chalk grabbed the commander and pulled him by the arms. "On your feet, soldier!" she bellowed. "On … your … feet!"

But Lasco crawled onto all fours and threw up over a pile of broken Touch3s.

DIS—GUST—ING!

"I'm sorry," Lasco grumbled, removing his helmet and handing Chalk. "I'm totally out of commission."

GAPSS
KNOWLEDGE
MAINFRAME

BATTLE MECHS
[TECHNOLOGY]

First constructed during the Thousand Moons War, battle
mechs became a staple feature of the SpiralVerse conflicts.
Taking humanoid and quadrupedal form, battle mechs
are predominantly designed for single pilot use. Original
battle mechs stood twenty feet but later models dwarfed
the originals, rising to one hundred feet or more. Core
construction utilises triangulated testostrophene with
fortified ionised membranes, powered by digital, biological,
and hybrid technologies, and armed with an abundance of
lethal weapons and countermeasures.

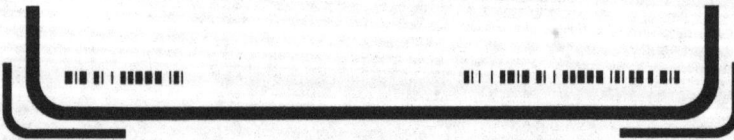

THE CRYSTAL OF SHADOWS

Chalk stuffed her head into the helmet and grabbed the ladder.

"What are you doing?" Cube asked. "You cannot operate one of these?"

"I watched the instruction video in phase two. How hard can it be?"

"Very," Cube told her. "You do remember your catastrophic failure on the commander's flight simulator?"

"That's very kind of you to remind me."

"The AstroTech Gigantor battle mech is not a child's toy. It was built for—"

"I don't need a history lesson right now," she said. "And I'm no child."

Below, Lasco rolled onto his back and gave her a thumbs-up.

Steam and sparks erupted from the battle mech.

"What's going on?" she yelled, levering herself into the cockpit.

"She's overloading!"

"How come?"

"Could be a thousand things … but best guess would be polonium!"

"Ripley!"

"Polonium-based power cells burn hot and fast," he said. "Overheating the coaxial distribution system and causing the central neural-network to red-line is ill-advised, but it's the only solution I have within this limited timeframe."

"In English?"

"Is your GI-VR translation software corrupted?"

"No, I mean explain it in words I can understand!"

Ripley wiped his forehead. "Just whatever you're going to do … do it fast!"

Chalk bounced into a worn leather seat. Monitors and digital dials, panels of coloured levers and switches surrounded her. Two control yokes sprouted in the centre, festooned with yet more switches and triggers. By her feet lay five identical pedals.

"The control yokes operate the arms and torso," yelled Lasco. "The pedals rotate the feet."

"Yes, I remember. But there's five of them. FIVE!"

"The outside ones operate the walking mechanism," Cube said calmly.

Chalk adjusted the helmet and gripped the control yokes.

Ahead, the Reckoning raged.

Away to her right, Professor Snider and every Enforcer at the Galactic Institute raced towards the fight. Counsellor Van Wyrm and his advisors stormed down the centre of the flight deck, trailed by Balefire, de Rema, Mirage, Krazkow, Asimov, and the rest of the faculty. Word of the Reckoning must have finally got out.

They probably saw it on the Gods-damn news!

Chalk surveyed the Reckoning. All six warriors were out on their feet, breathing heavily, clothes ripped, skin ripe with cuts and burns. Krump launched himself at Clandestra who ducked his blow and countered with a swift strike to the ribs. Krump collapsed in pain. Korg and Klang hurdled him, landing deft blows to Clandestra's face. She toppled into the crowd, who held her up like boxing ring ropes, before launching her back into the fight. Cystan and Crinella stalked the edge of the arena, generating a pulsating white light. Bolts of electricity launched across the arena. One hit Korg, sending him spinning. Klang generated a shield of red light to deflect the attack. Scorch marks branded the treadplate.

"Casting," Chalk whispered to herself.

The Veroselli shot plasma bolts again. Klang expanded his shield to protect the other Garrangulars who levitated a dozen damaged crates and launched them towards their opponents. Clandestra and Crinella evaded the attack, but Cystan caught one in the face and clattered towards the yellow warning lines. Krump rushed him, grabbed the Veroselli, and forced his shoulders past the lines, towards the propellosphere, and the crushing vacuum beyond.

Chalk secured the Crystal of Shadows around a control lever above and activated the manual override. Warning lights and sensors flashed on every panel.

Those who sit and gaze at the stars, said Harriet Starlight, *can only dream of the adventures within.*

"Join me now," Chalk finished the quote aloud, "as we dream no more!"

She stamped on the pedals, ground the gears. Steam and plasma oil exploded from the battle mech's arms and legs.

"Hang on, hang on!" bellowed Ripley, but Chalk could barely hear him.

She shifted her feet and pressed the other pedals. The right foot lurched forward, bashing a Starfighter out the way. She grimaced at the huge dent in the antique spacecraft's flank.

"I thought you said—" she accused Cube.

"It would appear the last person to operate this device preferred the controls to be inverted."

"How inconvenient!" Chalk pulsed her feet from one pedal to the other, like riding a bike, and the battle mech advanced. Starfighters and personnel carriers got dinked and cuffed as she forced her way towards the propellosphere.

"What are you doing, Miss Hale?" cried Asimov, swamped by the shadow of the approaching mech.

Counsellor Van Wyrm turned and stared. "Get down from there at once!"

"Do you even qualify for a battle mech licence?" added

Dustenberg, firing up her layer screens.

But the deafening crowd, the grind and hiss of the battle mech, and the snugness of the helmet disguised their words. It was the frowns, wagging fingers, and eyes filled with fury and fright that needed no translation.

Her battle mech lunged onward.

The zorikanthium swung back and forth.

Students disbanded, stumbling under the vibrations from her approach, creating a space between her and the propellosphere.

In the confusion, Cystan elbowed Klump in the face and squirmed from under his weight. The Garrangular snorted and wrestled the Veroselli to the ground. The other four piled on top, grappling and pulling, punching and kicking in a vicious scrum of limbs and verbal abuse.

Chalk wrapped her hand around the Crystal of Shadows and ripped it from the lever. The battle mech's enormous feet crunched against the ground, sending shockwaves through the launch bay. The propellosphere approached fast. Yellow lines less than a dozen metres away. Surely, she'd got close enough. One perfect throw and the zorikanthium would break the plane, get crushed to dust, and be sent spiralling, harmlessly, into space.

Chalk stopped pedalling but the battle mech's momentum pushed on.

Each stride fell short of the last, but gained ground all the time.

Panic lodged in her throat.

"Stop! Stop!" she cried. "We're not done. I need you for Einhorn and Miasma."

Chalk wrenched the control yokes.

Nothing.

The brakes.

Same.

She stamped on the other pedals.

Steam and scalding plasma oil ejected in every direction.

The battle mech marched on, dangerously out of control.

She couldn't stop it.

There wasn't time.

Chalk stared into the fathomless dark beyond the launch bay. Fear and wonder gripped her. She unbuckled her harness, clambered through the side of the cockpit and balanced precariously on the battle mech's gyrating shoulder.

Asimov and Van Wyrm, the entire faculty, and over half the student body watched. What must they be thinking? What sort of punishment was due if she survived this ordeal?

The Crystal of Shadows glimmered under the warning lights.

The battle mech's right foot towered over the Veroselli and Garrangular warriors then crashed down on the double yellow lines.

WARNING ... WARNING ... WARNING ...

Both sets of students abandoned their differences and scattered for their lives.

Faint cracks of green light etched the plain of the propellosphere, pulling at the battle mech like quicksand.

Time was up.

Chalk braced herself and jumped, cocked her arm and launched the zorikanthium with all her might. It twisted through the air, chimed against the battle mech's buckling cockpit, changed trajectory, and skidded to a halt beyond the yellow warning lines.

The battle mech juddered horribly. The power of the iridian stones consumed its metal frame, its pistons, the polonium power cells inside. The pressure intensified. The mech folded in on itself, becoming a dense ball of hot metal that blasted into space at an incredible velocity. The escaping polonium ignited in a blinding explosion. The aftershock rattled the Galactic Institute. Staff and students staggered and collapsed on top of one another.

Chalk clattered painfully to the ground.

"What is the meaning of this?" Counsellor Constantine Van Wyrm roared, his face like thunder.

New fights kicked off across the flight deck. They converged into larger brawls between Genks and Zillamoths and Revans and Pyramists and Montizoans who raised their fists to protect their friends and classmates. Bolts of coloured lights scorched and ricocheted off disabled spacecraft and knocked students to the ground. Huge gulps of smoke belched into the air, smothering and confusing everything.

Chalk scrambled to her feet, zigzagging through the confusion.

"Stop! Miss Hale!" cried the counsellor. "Stop this instant!"

WARNING . . . WARNING . . . WARNING . . .

"Harper Hale! What do you think you're doing?" cried Headmaster Asimov, stumbling down the lopsided flight deck.

But Chalk kept moving, staggered and dizzy. Pain burned like liquid magma through her shoulders, down her back. She scanned the treadplate knowing the zorikanthium was still onboard.

She approached the yellow lines.

Spied it.

Somehow, the Crystal of Shadows had slid *beneath* the propellosphere.

Shaking Cube off, Chalk slithered on her stomach, crawling, stretching for the crystal.

WARNING . . . IMMINENT DANGER . . . WARNING . . .

So close now. Just a few more inches.

Her fingertips almost brushed it when someone grabbed her foot and started dragging her back to the flight deck.

"What are you doing?" Chalk screamed. "Get off me!"

"Are you trying to kill yourself?" Asimov croaked, lying prone, a hand around her ankle. "Miss Hale, stop this madness!"

"Zorikanthium," Chalk said, rolling onto her back and wriggling wildly. "I have to get it. I have to destroy it."

"Zorikanthium?" Asimov said, his face creased in fright. "What is *that* doing on the Coin, hmm?"

Chalk broke free.

"Come back," Asimov begged. "The propellosphere is not to be trifled with."

But Chalk's eyes were locked on the crystal. She dragged herself towards it. With each movement she expected the propellosphere to tear her from the ground, crush her into a ball of bones and ooze, and spit her out into space—but she clung on, the battered treadplate reassuring under her grip.

Closer and closer.

The Crystal of Shadows was almost in range.

Stay on target.

Stretching every sinew, Chalk's trembling fingers coiled through the silver necklace and whipped it towards her. Bouncing, the tip of the crystal broke the underside of the propellosphere. Trails of green light tore across the surface. An immense pressure coiled through the necklace, into Chalk's finger, up her arm.

Suddenly, she was airborne, thundering into the centre of the propellosphere where she stopped, paralysed in the grip of the iridian stones.

WARNING . . .

PROPELLOSPHERE BREACH . . .

DANGER OF DEATH . . .

Pressure seized her in every direction. It felt like the AGT and the AGE and the gyrosphere all at once, but a thousand times more powerful, more painful. Her skull and ribs felt like they were going to implode *and* explode at the same time. She shook horribly. The crystal danced excitedly. The necklace wrapped around her outstretched finger.

"Let go!" yelled Asimov, his hands raised towards her. "You have to let it go. I cannot hold on much longer."

Counsellor Van Wyrm stood beside him, hands raised too. Professor de Rema quickly joined them. The pressure increased. Was this it? Was this the end? Was this what Waxler had sensed in her? That she was destined to sacrifice herself and save the Galactic Institute?

Chalk eased towards the flight deck.

The crushing vacuum of space inched away.

She looked at her trailing hand, at the Crystal of Shadows, and forced her finger to straighten. It took all the strength she had, every last drop of energy in her battered body, but slowly, surely, the necklace inched down her finger—and slipped off the end.

It zoomed to the centre of the propellosphere, spinning end over end. Pressure from the iridian stones crushed it into dust and ejected it into space.

Chalk burst from the clutches of the propellosphere, flew over the yellow warning lines, and clattered into Asimov and Snider.

And then, as if flicking a switch, every skirmish eased.

Students gazed around in wonder and disbelief.

"Miss Hale!" Counsellor Van Wyrm erupted, rising over her. "I don't have to tell you the level of trouble you are in, do I? In all my cycles I have never seen such a flagrant disregard and wonton, irresponsible—"

But his vitriolic accusations were silenced by an enormous howl from the SpiralVerse military museum.

"What in Kellzion's Nine Eyes—?"

"This isn't over," she said. "Not by a long … um … chalk."

The counsellor looked bewildered.

Asimov and the rest of the faculty stared in horror.

"What *is* that?"

Chalk straightened her jacket and flattened her hair. "A most unwanted guest!"

GAPSS
KNOWLEDGE
MAINFRAME

CASTING
[ANOMOLY]

An anomaly as old as the SpiralVerse itself. Casting abilities develop during the adolescent cycles of most lifeforms. Casting is incredibly dangerous, and many choose to ignore the signs when they present. Those who embrace their power will show an exclusive aptitude for one of three Casting classifications. On extremely rare occasions, individuals have shown an aptitude for two classifications. Individuals with no Casting ability are classified: VOID.

Casting Classifications

Physical: the governance and manipulation of physical objects
Cerebral: the governance and manipulation of thought and ideas
Elemental: the governance and manipulation of the natural world

THE BIG BAD

"Miasma? The Dark Trinity? Here on the Coin? Impossible," Van Wyrm scoffed. "The Earthling's ordeal inside the propellosphere has clearly scrambled her brain."

"The Dark Trinity were exiled to chaos dimensions more than a decade ago," Asimov added. "The possibility of their return is almost zero."

"Well," Chalk bit, frustrated with everyone's lack of urgency, "*almost* is upon us!"

She slipped Cube's straps over her shoulders and dashed for the museum.

The headmaster ran beside her. "Are you sure, Miss Hale?" he said cautiously. "The presence of one of the Dark Trinity here on the Coin is impossibly dangerous."

"I know," Chalk said, quickening her step. "But somehow Captain Dak Einhorn has returned from one of those chaos dimensions and got the worldgate working again and—"

"Lies and propaganda!" bleated Van Wyrm, charging along. "The Earthling is a fool like the rest of her civilisation. I shall have her species expunged from the *Declaration of Interplanetary Inclusivity* before this rotation is done!"

"Captain Einhorn died in the Battle of Lost Shadows," Asimov told her. "I've taught it hundreds of times."

"So the story goes," Chalk said. "But you know what, I guess that's a bunch of clawswoggle too. He survived—somehow— and he's back and he's trying to open the worldgate and bring

Miasma through. Called her ... his Queen!"

They passed beneath the museum arch. Ahead, the worldgate spun chaotically. A temporal doorway bulged and squirmed, expanding out one side, then the other, struggling to form. Tentacles forced through, spiked left and right, and scraped the museum walls before dematerialising as the temporal doorway collapsed. Above them, Captain Einhorn zipped from one control station to the next, frantically trying to balance the worldgate.

Chalk's heart leapt to see Milton on his feet, throwing chunks of masonry and broken monitors to slow the captain's progress. One ricocheted off the bannister and clattered to the ground by her feet. The words *Danger Level:* CRITICAL blinked on the cracked screen and died.

"Gods below," Asimov whispered. "So, it is true?" They stood in terrified silence for a moment. "Sigma, Gabriella, Hypocrates, Hexlag—combine your Aether, hold the ground floor, repel anything that comes your way. Calignious, Constantine, and I will ascend and confront the very much alive Captain Einhorn."

"And get Aida and Milton out of there."

"With haste!"

The professors assembled.

Those students who hadn't fled to safety filtered into the museum.

Veroselli and Garrangular warriors pushed to the front.

"What's going on?" ordered Clandestra, her clothes shredded, face cut and bleeding.

But Chalk didn't need to answer. The temporal doorway developed again and a monstrous tentacle squeezed through. It slammed against the floor, bowling professors onto their backs. The tentacle flapped chaotically, like a fish out of water. Purple slime and ooze splattered the walls. Then, as Chalk thought Miasma couldn't get any more terrifying, hundreds of bloodshot eyes opened along the tentacle and gazed at the world.

Dozens of students screamed in terror.

Many froze in fear.

A handful inched forward, ready for battle.

Chalk pin-balled to and fro as students forced themselves in all directions, making bids for freedom or glory. Asimov, Van Wyrm, and Snider sprinted up the walkway. Bolts of orange and green light burst from Asimov's hands. Explosions shook the worldgate's superstructure. Snider and Van Wyrm stood either side, their hands on the headmaster's shoulders. Spirals of strange vapour encircled the three.

Einhorn barked threats as he swept a long blade through the air. The professors and the high judge ducked and jumped his attacks, returning fire before disappearing into a melee of choking flames and smoke.

Clandestra grabbed the Veroselli and Garrangulars closest to her. "We've stood apart for centuries. Through war and peace. Through light and dark. We've been on the brink of doom this entire cycle," she told them, her bloodied chin raised and triumphant. "But that time is over. We've stood apart too long. Today we stand together … and FIGHT!"

Chalk's heart shuddered.

"For death and glory and the SpiralVerse!" roared two dozen throats.

Chalk swarmed into battle with teeth clenched and fists raised. She didn't know what she could do, how she could fight, what use she'd be against Miasma or Captain Einhorn. She didn't have advanced Casting abilities like the sixth cycle students and her battle mech was crumpled space junk.

She had nothing at all.

She was human.

An Earthling.

VOID.

But Chalk ran with them all the same.

A cry of anger tore up her throat as Miasma's tentacle dealt a devastating blow. Revans and Montizoans went flying. Garrangulars rolled beneath. Veroselli vaulted with majestic somersaults and backflips. Research eduhelpers became spare parts while battle droids and Enforcers opened fire in a flurry of deafening laser blasts.

Chalk dropped and skidded, her clothes drenched in sizzling purple slime. Scrambling to her feet, she pushed on, up the walkway with the others, circling round and round. Ahead, Aida hunkered behind the crumbling walkway. Milton quivered beside her. Masonry and glass crashed against his hardened wings. The air fizzed with energy. Casters fired elemental bolts and manipulated power surges towards the worldgate. The colossal device spun faster and faster as Miasma ripped holes in the museum walls.

Chalk collapsed beside her friends.

"This is intolerable," yelled the Sagaroach.

"Is Aida okay?"

"I don't know. Been limp ever since Einhorn forced us to the ground."

Chalk peered over the barrier.

Pandemonium and chaos reigned.

Smoke and fire and elemental blasts consumed the museum.

Asimov, Van Wyrm, and Snider had regained their feet and were ordering the professors below to concentrate their firepower on the base of the worldgate. Cystan and Crinella had found their way to the top of the device and were attempting to rip the power cables loose. To Chalk's right, Captain Einhorn smashed Genks and Pyramists aside with ease.

"This is hopeless," Milton yelled.

"Any thoughts, Cube?"

"I have a bountiful selection."

"To do with our situation!"

"The chances of any known species surviving an encounter with one of the Dark Trinity are almost zero."

"Again with the *almost*."

"Current situation survival percentage stands at 0.000154."

"Strong odds," said Milton.

"But you'll need a fast ship," Cube added.

"Thanks," Chalk snapped. "That was next to useless."

"According to my calculations, you are likely to survive for another six point three minutes. Should Captain Einhorn stabilise the worldgate and fully release Miasma into this dimension then you will have … considerably less."

"Again, solid stats."

"Einhorn is the key," Milton said.

"True," Cube confirmed. "Disable the captain and the worldgate will fail."

Shards of glass, mangled monitors, and chunks of masonry surrounded them. Scattered amongst the detritus were the historic weapons that had once lined the museum walls. Chalk crawled into the open. She grabbed one for herself and slung another at Milton.

"What are these?" he said, holding it backwards.

"That is an Equinox bio-blaster," Cube informed him. Milton fiddled with the device for a moment. "A plasma-based arm-cannon." Milton continued to inspect it. "It goes over your arm, Lord Barclay."

"Oh, right," the Sagaroach replied, sliding his right-middle limb into the weapon.

Fifth and sixth cycle students ran past, scavenging for weapons. Captain Einhorn blocked access to the modern firearms at the top of the museum, sending students skidding through glass and rubble like discarded holoballs.

Milton hoisted the bio-blaster onto the crumbling walkway and aimed it towards Einhorn. The captain cleared the latest advance of plucky students and zipped through the air to the next control panel. Sparks and smoke swirled around him.

"How do I even—?" Milton began, as an orb of glowing red matter rocketed across the museum.

The captain staggered as the projectile deflected off his bodysuit.

"Good shot," Chalk encouraged. "Fire at will!"

Milton frowned. "I ... can't," he said, shaking his arm. "It doesn't want to work."

"The Equinox bio-blaster requires a minimum of three point seven minutes to recharge," Cube said calmly.

"What use is that?" Chalk exclaimed. "We'll be dead in two!"

Headmaster Asimov, Constantine, and Snider blasted Miasma's tentacle with bolts of conjured light. The chemical heat made Chalk's skin prickle. She'd never seen such a thing. No human ever had. It was everything she and Grandpa Milo had dreamt about. But here she was, stuck in the middle of it all, surrounded by chaos, and fear, and the dark grin of death.

Swiping two more bio-blasters, Chalk slipped one on each arm and levelled them at the worldgate. "Stop," Cube said. "A polonium-fuelled explosion will parallel that of a supernova. I am the only one who would survive a detonation of that magnitude."

Miasma's repulsive tentacle retracted through the temporal doorway.

Everyone held their breath.

Chalk fired two coloured energy balls at Einhorn. One orange, the other blue. They glanced off the captain's chest and buried themselves in the wall. He smiled magnificently, like a prize fighter collecting every belt in the game.

Aida sat up. "Something is happening."

She wasn't wrong.

Something new came through the worldgate. It wasn't a slime-laced tentacle, hideous arms, or massive vines sprouting lethal thorns.

It was a voice.

A laugh.

Chalk stiffened. Her spine pressed to the bannister.

The sickening laugh boomed around the museum, shaking the crumbling walkway. Captain Einhorn abandoned the control desks and rocketed towards the museum turnstiles.

"He's getting away," Milton bleated. "Einhorn was our only hope."

But it was the worldgate that stole Chalk's attention.

The chaotic temporal doorway morphed into a massive twitching eye.

It gazed at Chalk, opalescent, bloodshot, crawling with parasites behind sheens of thick, repulsive slime. The horrific pupil protruded, pushing the hardened cornea forward, shaking like it was about to burst.

Asimov, Van Wyrm, and Snider landed on the bannister above Chalk.

Miasma considered them for an instant then erupted in a baleful laugh.

Below, professors stood among bricks and rubble, their hands directed towards the worldgate.

"*IS . . . THIS . . . IT?*" boomed the voice, low and menacing.

"Miasma," Asimov yelled. "Dark Goddess of the Unknown Realms. You were banished from the SpiralVerse. Your return is not welcome."

She laughed again, slow and dreadful.

"*BANISHED?*" Miasma said. "*LURED . . . ELSEWHERE . . .*"

Asimov's feet trembled on the edge of the walkway.

"*NOW . . . RETURNED!*"

"We will fight you," the headmaster went on. "As we did before. Victory will be ours once more."

"*VICTORY?*" the Dark Goddess sneered. "*TRICKS . . . NOTHING . . . MORE.*"

Professor Snider took his hands off Asimov's shoulders.

He spread his arms wide and fanned his fingers.

"No," Constantine barked. "Don't be a fool!"

Snider's body shook uncontrollably. His watery eyes became wide and wild.

Chalk stared, aghast. Was Snider really trying to use his Shadow Seeing abilities on one of the Dark Trinity?

"Calignious!" cried Asimov, but it was too late.

Snider levitated above the walkway, above Chalk and Milton. A horrifying scream tore past his lips. He hung there for an instant, shaking, then flew over their heads, slammed into the wall and crumpled to the ground.

Constantine faced Miasma.

His hands whipped into the air but quickly found himself lying next to Snider.

Miasma laughed darkly.

Alone on the bannister, Asimov's confidence wilted.

His feet shuffled from side to side.

His knees trembled.

Chalk looked up at the headmaster. He wasn't cut out for this. Snider had been a master at two of the three Casting classifications and Counsellor Van Wyrm was a revered cerebral Caster. Both now lay in a battered heap.

"*I . . . AM . . . EVERYTHING . . . YOU . . . HAVE . . . KNOWN,*" Miasma roared defiantly. "*EVERYTHING . . . YOU . . . HAVE . . . DISCOVERED!*"

The eye widened. Slime and ooze dripped in ectoplasmic tendrils. Asimov grabbed the side of his head with all four hands, his face wracked in pain. Chalk reached for the headmaster, but he sank to his knees, head bowed, and toppled end over end to the ground far below.

"*THERE . . . IS . . . NOTHING . . . I . . . CANNOT . . . OVERCOME.*"

The museum reverberated with the sound of her voice.

"*IS . . . THIS . . . IT?*"

The great eye roved menacingly.

Something stirred in Chalk.

"*IS . . . THIS . . . ALL?*"

The battle cry of the Veroselli and the Garrangulars, the heroism and courage of all her favourite characters, the faces of her friends—Aida, Milton, and Ripley—melded together, filling her with a powerful, overwhelming sensation. A resolute conviction.

Courage is like a supernova, said Harriet Starlight. *Powerful and luminous!*

Was this the end? There had to be more. There had to be a way. She replayed Miasma's words in her head.

I am everything you have known. Everything you have discovered. There is nothing I cannot overcome.

Chalk put her hands on the bannister.

"Your chances of defeating this foe are almost zero," Cube reiterated.

"Never tell me the odds!"

"What are you doing?" Milton wailed. "Chalk. Stop."

But she stood, planted her lime-green Converse on the crumbling museum wall, and stared Miasma dead in the eye.

"Miss Hale," came Asimov's pain-ravaged voice from far below. "Get away from her!"

"WHO . . . IS . . . THIS?"

Chalk's entire body shook, her heart galloped, a tsunami of fear reared inside. But still she stood, eye to eye with the monster.

Stubborn.

Defiant.

Determined.

"A . . . GENK? A . . . PYRAMIST?" Miasma said. *"NOT . . . A . . . REVAN?"*

"I'm a Mudder," she whispered, lips trembling.

"WHAT?"

"A Mudder," she said, louder.

Proud.

The eye flickered.

"Human Garbage."

Miasma snorted.

"You do not know me."

Miasma laughed again. *"I . . . KNOW . . . ALL."* Lights from the worldgate pulsed and strobed against the broken walls. *"AND . . . I . . . WILL . . . CONSUME . . . ALL!"*

The eye closed, retracted into the temporal doorway. In its place, a colossal tentacle reared overhead like the tail of a maddened serpent.

"Chalk!" wailed Milton.

"Get down!" Asimov cried.

But she held her ground.

This was either the bravest thing she'd ever do—or the last.

There seemed no other choice.

Miasma towered above her. Ready to strike. Slime and filth peppered the ground. Along the length of the tentacle, hundreds of repulsive eyes glared.

"*AND . . . NOW . . . YOU . . . DIE!*"

The tentacle descended.

Milton screamed.

Chalk raised one hand to cover her face, the other outstretched to meet the attack.

The force drove her to her knees.

One hand pressed against the bannister.

The other against the tentacle.

Against Miasma.

Purple slime oozed over her hand and down her arm, sizzling and burning, bubbling like a witch's broth.

INAPPROPRIATE LANGUAGE DETECTED . . .

Miasma pressed down again and again. Despite the crippling pain and the horrifying sight of her own burning flesh, Chalk found the strength to resist, unbroken beneath the weight of the grotesque mass.

Miasma's laugh turned to a desperate wail.

They froze, locked together, reverberating with incredible power.

"*WHAT . . . IS . . . THIS?*" she hissed. "*WHAT . . . ARE . . . YOU?*"

Chalk gritted her teeth.

Miasma's slime flecked her face.

"I'm Harper Hale," she cried. "And I'm an Earthling!"

Cube erupted from the mystery ball in a blinding wave of orange light. The gelatinous eduhelper encased Chalk like Vitarus in his watery orb. Thrusting skyward, she threw her entire weight behind her slime-covered hand and forced Miasma up, up, up.

The Dark Goddess wailed as each row of revolting eyes shook and flickered, clouded over and popped. Vile acidic pus jettisoned on students and professors below. Miasma's slime hardened. Crisped. Fell away in revolting purple flakes. The massive tentacle deflated, shrivelling like a balloon. Retreating through the temporal doorway, Miasma wailed and screamed vitriol and vengeance.

The temporal doorway rippled, evanesced.

The worldgate fizzed and shook.

Lights faded to amber and blinked out.

Silence swept the museum.

A long hollow ache.

Chalk pulled her arm to her chest and collapsed against the inner edge of Cube. Hanging there, suspended inside her eduhelper, Chalk's world became edged with shadows.

Every muscle burned.

Every hair …

and molecule …

and atom stung.

Darkness pressed in.

Chalk let it take her.

GAPSS
KNOWLEDGE
MAINFRAME

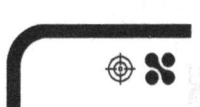 

KRAKEN-WEEVIL
[SUBSPECIES]

Orthopterous insects of the weevil family characterised by oversized, flattened bodies, sharp pincers, antennae, and foul-smelling mucus discharge. They can be found in dark, damp recesses, feeding on power lines and communal waste.

BACK IN BLACK

Chalk woke in a sterile room. Ocean-blue walls and smooth floors reflected soft light across her bed. Large circular windows framed the observation hall and the first cycle dorms. Thin columns of smoke twisted towards the environsphere above the SpiralVerse military museum where vast chunks of outer wall were missing. Repair droids circled industriously.

She glanced at her left arm. A strange white fabric ran from her elbow to her fingertips. It still hurt, but nothing like the pain she'd experienced touching Miasma. To be honest, she struggled to correctly remember. The memory lingered as a concoction of dazzling light, burning electricity, pain and horror and stubborn resolve.

Miasma's laugh echoed in her thoughts. Thick and vile and divorced of empathy. Cruelty of the strictest kind. And then she thought of Cube. Of INCUBE-8. How the eduhelper had wrapped itself around her, cradled her, saved her from certain death.

Doctor Silas' appearance at the end of the bed pulled her from the daydream.

"Miss Hale," he said, blinking erratically with his lone eye. "You're awake."

"You sound surprised," she replied.

"Well," he said, raising a single eyebrow. "You *did* die."

"What?" Chalk sat up and regretted it.

"Just for a minute," he said, easing her against the soft pillows. "Perhaps a little longer."

Chalk's mouth hung open.

"It's a good job the Sagaroach was there."

"The Sagaroach?"

"Lord Milton Barclay XVII."

"He ... saved me?"

"On Earth you call it ... mouth-to-mouth resuscitation."

The idea of Milton's yuccagourd smeared pincers clamping over her mouth made Chalk feel woozy.

"He's here," Doctor Silas said. "The belligerent Tattorian, too."

"Aida survived!"

"Yes," the doctor said. "Despite all probability, there were no fatalities. None. We've had concussions, breaks, internal bleeding, one amputee, and a multitude of burns and scrapes." He looked at Chalk's arm. "Although, I'm afraid your injury is by far the most troubling."

"Oh," Chalk said, lifting her arm. "Will I ... lose it?"

"Perhaps," he told her honestly. "Human biology is a complete mystery to me. Learning as we go, I'm afraid. But I'm confident if you heal well and remain positive, your arm could mend itself in time."

"How long?"

"How long is a Qwork's patience?"

"Um—"

The doctor smiled politely and left.

Chalk studied the white bandage. It appeared to be moving, binding and stitching itself over and over, as if alive. When she glanced up, Milton and Aida were standing beside the bed beaming insanely.

"Chalk!" Milton said. "I'm so happy you're not dead."

"Me too," she said. "And Aida, what happened? We thought you were a goner for sure—like your lifeforce had expired or something."

"We Tattorians have a self-preservation instinct that kicks in during life-threatening scenarios. Anxiety and stress and panic can put a serious dent in your life expectancy."

"Tell me about it," said Chalk. "My heart was beating like a quantum piston towards the end."

"But you are okay now," Aida said, her visor tilted towards Chalk. "Your energy feels good. Changed … but good."

"Changed?"

"Stronger," Aida said. "Perhaps contact with Miasma has something to do with it."

"I'd be surprised if it didn't."

"How is your arm?" Milton asked, peering over.

"Still attached," she said, waving it for him. "And hurts like hell, so …" Chalk looked beyond her friends. "Where's Ripley? The doctor said there were no fatalities, so …"

"No one knows," Milton said. "Last time I saw him, you were hauling him out of the museum on your shoulder, heading for the propellosphere."

"Counsellor Van Wyrm is conducting a thorough search," Aida added. "They want to charge him for breaking school rules and ethical codes of conduct, for ignoring the Terrazuma Treaty, numerous cases of criminal activity including unauthorised portal travel and trading outlawed and radioactive materials. Oh, and endangering the Galactic Institute and every soul on board."

"Gulp," Chalk said. "But how—?"

"They have Captain Einhorn," Aida explained. "Apparently it did not take Van Wyrm long to extract every last detail from him. I guess he snitched on the Revan after spinning him all those lies about time travel and saving his brother."

"Poor Ripley."

Aida looked annoyed. "The inconsiderate Revan broke a dozen laws and every rule and code of conduct on the Coin. His actions could have killed us all."

"Those aren't the kind of charges you come back from," Milton added.

"Once they catch him, Ripley will be in StasisStation10 for aeons."

"I guess he ran," Chalk said glumly.

"Wouldn't you?"

"Yeah." Her gaze rose from the smoking museum and found the glorious Waterfall Nebula spread above the Coin once again. "I'd run far, far away."

Chalk remained in the infirmary for three rotations. Aida and Milton brought their revision notes and formed a study group around her bed. They retrieved Chalk's paperbacks and Milton read from *Harriet Starlight and the Neutron War*.

Doctor Silas came to her on the tenth rotation of phase nineteen accompanied by Headmaster Asimov and Professor Snider. They looked far better than she had expected after their confrontation with Miasma. Cuts and inflammation had faded, yet the horror of the ordeal still burned in their eyes.

"And to what do I owe the pleasure?"

Silas looked at her arm. "Time for that to come off."

"Amputation after all?" Chalk half-joked.

"Always cracking-wise, this one," the doctor said to Snider. "The bandage, Miss Hale."

"Really?" Chalk said. "Are you sure it's all … mended?"

The doctor rubbed his thin face. His eye spun in its socket. "As sure as I can be," he said confidently. "As I've said on numerous occasions, never had a human in my care and certainly not one who's been in direct contact with one of the Dark Trinity." He produced a slim, pen-like device. "Let's have a look, shall we?"

The device emitted a thin blue laser which the doctor ran down the bandage, then he spread the dressing, like opening a chest cavity.

Asimov and Snider inched closer.

Chalk couldn't look.

The smell registered first. It reminded her of stale sweat and fungal infection—like gym lockers and sweaty shin pads—and of the moment her skin bubbled under Miasma's repulsive ooze.

"Come on then," she said, trying to keep positive. "What's the damage?"

No one spoke.

Chalk flicked her gaze from Silas to Asimov to Snider. They all looked thoroughly puzzled. Not shocked or appalled. *Puzzled.*

Chalk swallowed hard and risked a glance.

Where her skin had once been—light olive, flecked with the odd seasonal freckle and outbreaks of eczema—it now resembled the colour and consistency of charcoal. The strange lumpy substance covered her entire hand and ran to the elbow where it ebbed like a gossamer glove. Chalk lifted her arm out of the bandage, turned and twisted it, coiled and fanned her fingers. Dark flecks cascaded onto the bed, like ash drifting from a bonfire.

Silas and Asimov's faces turned from puzzlement to genuine interest.

"Does it hurt?" asked the doctor, prodding her with his deactivated laser pen.

"Feels like I shut it in a door."

"Sounds like you're fine," Silas told her, clapping his hands together.

Chalk laughed nervously. "Fine?" she said. "I've got a briquette for an arm."

"But it seems to function in all the usual ways," the doctor said matter-of-factly, prodding her again. "I can run some blood tests to detect any changes in your genetic make-up."

"But what about the dusty, flaky black dandruff?" Chalk said. "Looks like I dipped my arm in a volcano."

"Very few have touched one of the Dark Trinity and lived to tell," Asimov told her.

"Indeed," Silas added, wagging his pen. "Could shed away and return to normal. Could be like this forever. Could drop off. Could—"

"That is not very reassuring."

"We'll keep a close eye on you," Professor Snider said. They all turned to the Casting Professor. "I'm sure we can learn a lot about Miasma and the Dark Trinity from Miss Hale, do you not agree?"

"Yes, yes," Asimov said quickly. "But for now, I think Miss Hale—Chalk—would benefit from returning to her dorm and spending some time with her friends before examinations begin."

"Thank you, prof ... headmaster."

"Oh, it *is* professor again, Miss Hale."

Chalk's eyebrows rose. "Really? Does that mean—?"

Asimov nodded. A huge grin of relief on his face.

GAPSS
KNOWLEDGE
MAINFRAME

HYDRALUNAS SYNDROME
[MOON STARING] [ILLNESS]

A severe state of dehydration caused by staring at a moon
or moon(s). Prolonged exposure to hydralunas syndrome—or
moon staring as it is more commonly known—has many
documented side effects ranging from apathetic social
disconnection to nocturnal blood rages. Symptoms differ
greatly between species.

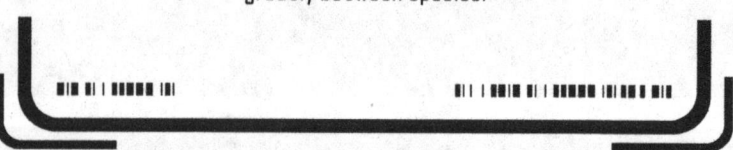

THE BOY WITH TWO FACES

Chalk landed on the disembarkation pod and took several nervous steps into the rec room. Every eye zeroed in on her. She tried to remain cool, wave, nod, and be as inconspicuous as humanly possible.

But Chalk was dead centre of everyone's attention.

Her name on everyone's lips.

Spirit looked like she was going to burst.

On the dorm room landing, she found Kiln embracing another of his kin. Chalk presumed it to be Kroket, but as they released one another, she saw the unmistakable grimace of his missing friend, Krieg.

Here. In the dorm. On the Coin.

Alive.

As Chalk looked beyond the Garrangulars, Princess Cressida Van Wyrm drifted majestically up the stairs and gave her friends a shallow bow.

Students appeared in every doorway looking amazed as the missing students returned home. A wave of cheers swelled across the landing. Questions fired at Cressida and Krieg about their ordeal. Others muttered to themselves.

But neither had time for anecdotes or to bask in the platitudes of their classmates. Krieg shouldered through the crowd, approaching Chalk with heavy footfalls, his eyes thin, massive fingers flexing. "Earthling!"

Chalk wondered if he had any other volume. "Um … yep?"

He looked awkward. "I need to … apologise."

Spirit gasped.

"Sorry," he said gruffly, "for everything."

Chalk wasn't sure how to respond.

"I heard what you did," he said, looking at her blackened arm which was mostly concealed beneath her jacket. "You saved me. And Cressida. You saved us all."

The Veroselli princess approached.

"He is … correct," she said, and it clearly hurt her to say so. "Einhorn corrupted our GI-VRs, off-set our location, and kept us bound in some rancid, sweltering, data-mining server room. I suppose we both owe you a great debt, Earthling."

"I'd settle for a favour."

Krieg grunted.

Cressida raised an eyebrow.

"How about you call me Chalk from now on."

A second wave of commotion flooded the landing. Silent and wide-eyed, First Cycle Atari students shifted aside as General Waxler came to a dramatic halt above Chalk.

"Shall we go for a walk?" the headmistress asked.

Chalk glanced longingly into her dorm room.

At her books and clothes and toys.

And her eduhelper.

Cube.

"Miss Hale?"

"Yes, of course," she said. "A walk would be lovely."

Harper Hale and General Waxler took the AGT, circled the hyperloop, and rode the off-tube towards the lobby and administration offices. Disembarking, Waxler strolled onto the surface of the Coin. Chalk walked at her side, clueless about where they were headed. Students she did not know—and species she could not name—made strange noises and gestures at her.

The headmistress considered Chalk's damaged arm. "How is it?"

"Doesn't really hurt anymore," Chalk lied. "Silas did a bang-up job."

"*Doctor* Silas," General Waxler corrected.

Chalk flexed her fingers as if to demonstrate. "All in tip-top working order."

"No unusual side effects? Nothing out of the ordinary?"

"Nope." Chalk sighed. "Magical power transference from a monstrous, intergalactic evil: negative."

General Waxler nodded happily. "That is both good and bad news, I suppose," she said. "I understand being VOID was quite the disappointment."

"Yeah," Chalk murmured. "But I'm thankful to have all my limbs right now—and still be alive to use them."

"Having one less biological limb is not so bad," said the general, raising her robotic hand.

"How did you lose that?" Chalk asked. "You promised to tell."

"One rotation," General Waxler said. "But for now, Miss Hale, I need to extend the thanks of GAPSS and the entire Galactic Institute—every student, professor, administrator, chef, Enforcer, Qwork, and eduhelper on the Coin. And my own personal thanks too."

Chalk blushed.

"As you may have heard, Captain Einhorn has taken my place on StasisStation10 where he shall remain indefinitely. Interplanetary law sadly negates me from telling you more."

"You mean about the Battle of Lost Shadows?"

"It appears you know more than you should already. The decisions I made that rotation were some of the hardest of my life." The general softened a little. "The Spiral Wars have left their mark on us all," she said wistfully. "It would appear they have left something on you too."

"Will it go away?"

"I do not know."

"What is it?"

"Another mystery of the SpiralVerse."

Chalk drummed her lip. "Doctor Silas said I died."

"Only for a few minutes. You are incredibly resilient."

"Is this what your seventh sense saw in me?"

"Saving the galaxy?" the headmistress said plainly. "Perhaps. But I believe your story is only just beginning."

They approached a circular tower that bloomed from the surface of the Coin like a giant mushroom. General Waxler pressed her biological hand to a wall sensor and scanned her retina.

Double doors fizzed open.

The room beyond was impossibly high, and eerily empty. Chalk stared up at the ceiling, some eight or nine stories above, that formed the base of the mushroom cap.

"My private quarters," the headmistress explained.

"Neat." Chalk glanced around. "But how do you—?"

Treadplate shifted in beautiful spirographic patterns to reveal a hole in the middle of the floor. Chalk gasped as an elevator silently emerged. It spun like a top, gently slowing.

General Waxler stepped inside. "Are you coming?"

"Where does this go?"

"Everywhere."

The device was incredibly sparse with no visible levers or buttons or dials. Chalk ran her hands over an ornate frame of gleaming metal that surrounded teardrop panels where bio-glass ought to be. It reminded her of a giant golden seed, something stolen from the elven architects of Middle-earth.

The headmistress tapped her GI-VR and they began to spin. Chalk looked up but instead of scaling the tower, they dropped into the darkness below. She instinctively grabbed Waxler as the elevator swept back and forth, pivoting and plummeting through the dark.

A moment later, they swept between parting walls and

stopped. Light flooded Chalk's eyes. Familiar smells filled her nostrils. Stacks of tech throbbed and whirred and beeped. Tiny diodes flickered like distant stars.

"We're ... between the floorboards," she said. "How did we—?"

General Waxler ignored her question and led them out of the server room, through a complex web of tunnels, and into a familiar corridor. Her long white cape whipped in step with her purposeful march. Chalk was halfway along the corridor when she realised she could breathe without a face mask. Something had changed.

Esme and Spanners spun as Waxler entered the workshop.

"Gertrude." They beamed in unison.

"Afternoon," she replied, leaning against the long workbench. "I've brought Miss Hale to see you."

"Hey," said Chalk, waving.

Esme and Spanners waved back.

"Hey yourself," said another voice, one she knew instantly, one she had not expected to ever hear again. Her eyes scanned the shadows and sure enough, there he was.

Ripley Flinch.

He wore an orange boilersuit like Spanners with a huge belt of gadgets and tools. Grease and dirt covered his face and hands.

"You're ... here! On the Coin? Why didn't you escape through a portal to some sleepy backwater planet on the other side of the galaxy?" Chalk looked at General Waxler. "I mean, why haven't you arrested him and thrown him in StasisStation10?"

"Don't encourage her!" Ripley said with a half-smile.

General Waxler brushed a lock of white-gold hair from her face. "I was conflicted," she said. "For all he has done, and by the laws of the SpiralVerse and the rules of the Galactic Institute, Master Flinch should be suspended for all time in a stasis cell alongside Dak Einhorn." She fidgeted with her mechanical hand. "And, if Constantine Van Wyrm and his band of ruthless zealots got their way, he would have done. But I have to thank the counsellor. My time in StasisStation10 taught me a great deal. While stasis is preferable to cold, hard prison, it is still a hopeless waste."

Chalk looked at the Revan.

His purple eyes shone mesmerisingly.

"To lock away a brilliant engineering mind such as Master Flinch," Waxler went on, "would be the definition of wasteful."

"So," Chalk started. "He'll be taking his exams with us next phase?"

Ripley's head dropped.

"Master Flinch has been expelled from the Galactic Institute."

"What? No! You cannot … that's not—"

"Fair?" said the general, rounding on Chalk. "It is more than fair. But, while Master Flinch is no longer a student, he now works for the Galactic Institute, here, between the floorboards, where he can make a difference and put his exceptional skills to better use than floating in eco-hydrated bio-plasma."

It made total sense, but Chalk still hated it.

She wanted Ripley in the dorm next to hers. She wanted him with her in class, at school dances and banquets and *Orbit Strike!* matches, messing around in Lasco's workshop building strange devices and honing their skills on the flight simulator. Instead, he would be here in the dark with Esme and Spanners and the Gods-damn krittens, repairing atmospheric pressure simulators and anti-gravity power couplings and other things she would never fully understand.

An almighty *clang!* erupted as INFIN-8 bustled through the workshop doorway and deposited a load of bent piping on the floor.

BING! he chimed merrily, waddling towards Chalk. *BING! BING!*

"You made it too," she said, patting the droid on the head.

"He's been incredibly useful," said Spanners. "Being an infinite storage droid."

"That's a real thing?" Chalk asked, amazed.

"I've allowed Master Flinch to keep his eduhelper," Waxler said. "The droid still belongs to the Galactic Institute, but while he continues to help down here, INFIN-8 can remain by his side."

OH—VER—JOYED!

Green lights flashed on his lid. His torso spun gleefully.

"Chalk?" the Revan said, leading her away from the others. "Can we …? Are we …? You know … still … friends?"

Chalk mussed her hair. "You brought Dak Einhorn onto the Coin. You've inadvertently been part of General Waxler's incarceration. You endangered the lives of every soul on the Galactic Institute, not to mention the horrors of the Zorik Civil War."

"I know."

"But there's one thing that bothers me more than all that."

"What?"

"The lie about your name."

"My name?"

"I met a boy called Ripley Flinch. I made friends with him, grew close to him, cared for him … kissed him. But you were never Ripley Flinch. He's someone else. Someone I'll never know."

"Hale—?"

"I should hate you."

"But—?"

"I don't," she said sadly, taking a long, calming breath. "Believe me, I understand that living with incredible loss can make you do unimaginable things."

The Revan nodded.

"I'm going to miss the future we could have had," she told him. "But I'll settle for the one we've been given. It's not perfect, but at least it'll be real."

"I could have run," he told her. "I could have got away."

Chalk kicked a rusty screw across the floor. "Why didn't you?"

Ripley's eyes sparkled again.

She felt transported to that winter's day on the Flipside.

"Oh," she said, trying to hide a bashful smile.

"I'll be here," he said, "making the Galactic Institute better, making your time on the Coin the absolute best it can be."

"Okay."

"And come visit me whenever you can."

Chalk nodded, unsure. "But … what do I call you? You're not Ripley. You're Dante."

"True," he said, rubbing his chin. "But I'm still a Flinch."

"I guess that will have to do," she said. "Flinch."

"Hale."

"It's Chalk."

"Why is that?"

"I'll never tell."

"Well," he said, rolling his eyes as if to search for something in the back of his mind. "May the Force be ever in your favour!"

Chalk shook her head.

"Snagger."

"Bonehead."

GAPSS
KNOWLEDGE MAINFRAME

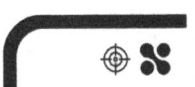 

GRIMAGOURDS
[FRUIT]

A soft subterranean cylindrical fruit with a porous rind
cultivated on the Xenothropod colonies. The grimagourd
is the only source of nutrition for Sagamoths and
Sagaflies, many of whom suffer fatal reactions to all other
foodstuffs. See also, yuccagourds.

HOME

Chalk's dorm room was just as she'd left it: the bed unmade, clothes strewn haphazardly in all directions, an army of lipsticks and other vanities occupying all available workspace. She slid onto the bed and let the Waterfall Nebula consume her. She'd missed its colourful blooms of dust, its mesmerising hydrogen and ionised gases.

Her mind wandered to the blue sky and white fluffy clouds of Earth. For some reason they did not compare. Space finally felt like home.

Chalk opened the bedside drawer and retrieved her mother's fountain pen. Twirling it between her charcoaled fingers, memories of the past cycle cascaded through her mind. Most of it came as a blur, a chaotic collage of snapshots, emotional highs and lows, excitement and pain.

Cube mirrored Chalk, sitting cross-legged on the side of the bed.

She smiled at the eduhelper.

"Your Galactic Institute medical record states you are currently alive," Cube said. "But it is reassuring to see you in the flesh."

"You too," Chalk said. "You saved my life."

"The results of our interaction with Miasma are incalculable."

"Milton gave me mouth-to-mouth."

"I imagine that gave you the wiggins."

"Yeah," she said, laughing. "It's reassuring to have friends like Milton and Aida. And you. Friends that will always be there for me, no matter what."

She tried to process her thoughts and emotions by writing in her journal. She sketched out the details of the past few days with flashpoints that covered the fury of the Reckoning, piloting the battle mech, the grip of the propellosphere, Captain Einhorn, and her confrontation with Miasma, in the form of a letter to her mother. She kept all word of Flinch from the page. She needed more time to process that. Much more time. Chalk wondered if she'd ever fully come to terms with everything he'd done.

On the landing, a Garrangular roared. Chalk jumped. Her mother's fountain pen slipped from her grasp. She moved to catch it but the pen stopped mid-air, hovering inches from her outstretched, blackened fingers.

Heart racing, Chalk stared.

The pen turned in slow, measured circles.

She glanced at Cube.

The eduhelper mimicked her. A translucent orange pen floated above its outstretched gelatinous hand.

"What in the Ungodly Realms of—?"

"Congratulations."

"Am I"—Chalk stared at the pen—"doing this?"

"It would appear so."

"Is this … *Casting?*"

"Affirmative."

"But I'm not *doing* anything?" Chalk said. "I tried to catch the pen and then—"

"Perhaps your subconscious mind is controlling the pen."

"What? Really?" Chalk said. "But what about Aether? Isn't that needed to Cast?"

"You know I am not permitted to discuss that."

"Because I'm VOID?" She glared at the levitating pen. "Am I still … VOID?"

CALCULATING …

"Pause for dramatic effect much."

CASTING STATUS . . .

"What's the delay?"

UNKNOWN . . .

"Unknown?" Chalk wailed. "What does *that* mean?"

"Unknown: undecided, uncertain, unexplored—"

"Yes, thank you. Helpful as always."

"Well," Cube said, morphing into a perfect sphere and gently descending into its outer casing. "At least you are not VOID anymore."

"Finally," Chalk said, snatching the emerald fountain pen and squeezing it tightly in her blackened hand. "Progress."

Harper Hale will return!

Check out your local Qwork News affiliate
or visit **www.neiljhart.com** for more info!

ACKNOWLEDGEMENTS

As one of eight billion humans, orbiting one of four hundred billion stars, in a galaxy among a hundred billion more, I'm eternally awed by the unfathomable and bewildering scale of our ever-expanding universe, but also by the power each of us hold to create, inspire, and dream.

Great stories are a true magic, transportative and spellbinding. From a young age, I've loved nothing better than following great characters on thrilling adventures, defying the odds, overcoming the darkness, and risking it all in a galaxy far, far away. I hope a little of that has found its way into this story.

Orbit Strike! airhorns blasts to my early readers Josh Morton, Jen Moss, John Repplinger, J. Brandon Lowry, Evelyn Hail, and Scarlet Frost for their invaluable feedback and commentary on the 'Chalkiverse'. Delicious quarts of GanyMead for my awesome extended family and friends: the most incredible gang of magical aliens and misfits the galaxy has ever known!

Bows, nods, and finger wiggles to my editor Manda Waller for her critical eye and genuine enjoyment working on this book, Shane Melisse for his wonderful illustration of Chalk in action, and my new book buddy Wayne Kelly for his kindness and friendship at numerous book fairs across the UK!

And to every one of you for taking a chance on this book and reading all the way to the bottom of the acknowledgements! Defy the normal. Embrace the weird, the strange, and the odd. Be the alien. And may the Force be with you. Always.

THANK YOU

Thank you so much for reading *Harper Hale and the Crystal of Shadows*. I hope you enjoyed it!

If you have the time to write a brief and honest review on Amazon, GoodReads etc, that would help me enormously to reach new readers.

I have a growing mailing list with exclusive news, writing tips, and giveaways. Scan the QR code above or visit **www.neiljhart.com/sign-up/** to get **FREE** downloads including the *GAPSS Knowledge Mainframe*, *Orbit Strike! Rules*, and *Gamma Ray's Grill Menu*. You can unsubscribe at *any* time.

I'm active on Facebook, Twitter, Instagram, and TikTok. If you have a question about this book, or my writing, you can get in touch with me there or follow for updates and news about future books and promotions.

Once again, thank you for reading
Harper Hale and the Crystal of Shadows.

Best wishes, NjH

OUT NOW!

WATTY'S 2021 WINNER FOR HORROR

THE LAST SCARECROW

MULTI *AWARD-WINNING* AUTHOR

NEIL J HART

Return to Oz meets *The Nightmare Before Christmas* in Neil J Hart's award-winning adorably terrifying fantasy adventure where climate change has flooded the earth, destroyed humanity, and ushered in a grave new world!

Unlock the power of music, magic, and memory in Neil J Hart's award-winning haunting fantasy adventure—*His Dark Materials* meets *The Mortal Engines*—where dark secrets and an ancient melody, spark the flame of belief.

ABOUT THE AUTHOR

Neil J Hart has won awards for his haunting fantasy novels *The Last Scarecrow* and *Sadie Madison and the Boy in the Crimson Scarf*.

Neil also works as a graphic designer.
He fosters for Cats Protection. Relies on coffee.
Adores cheese and cucumber sandwiches.
And collects Tomb Raider memorabilia.

More info and links to Neil's social media at
www.neiljhart.com